Pat
The Right of Way

Other Fiction in Rupa Paperback

Translation © Prasenjit Mukherjee 1993

An Original Rupa Paperback

First published 1993
Second impression 2001

Published by
Rupa & Co.
7/16, Ansari Road, Daryaganj,
New Delhi 110 002

Offices at:
15 Bankim Chatterjee Street, Calcutta 700 073
135 South Malaka, Allahabad 211 001
PG Solanki Path, Lamington Road, Mumbai 400 007
36, Kutty Street, Nungambakkam, Chennai 600 034
Surya Shree, B-6, New 66, Shankara Park,
Basavangudi, Bangalore 560 004
3-5-612, Himayat Nagar, Hyderabad 500 029

ISBN 81-7167-124-1

Typeset in 11/12 Baskerville by
Megatechnics
19 A Ansari Road
New Delhi 110 002

Printed in India by
Gopsons Papers Ltd.
A-14 Sector 60
Noida 201 301

SARAT CHANDRA CHATTERJEE

PATHER DABI
The Right of Way

Translated from original Bengali by
Prasenjit Mukherjee

Rupa & Co

that. You should write if you feel that it is your duty to do so, but you should be fully prepared for the punishment. Wherever there has been a conflict between any government and its subjects, the rebellious subjects rose against their government knowing fully well that it would not leave them in peace.

'Had you written seditious things in newspapers, it would not have had any lasting effect. But when a writer of your standing writes against the government even in a novel, it will have enormous effect on the people for all times to come. Every reader, from boys and girls in their teens to old men and women, will be greatly influenced by your writing. In the circumstances, had the British government not proscribed your book, it would have proved that they were either unaware of your power as a writer and your high position in Bengali literature, or were contemptuous of your influence. When you attack a powerful government, you must be prepared for a counter-attack. Only then will your attack be meaningful. If, however, you start bemoaning the government's counter-attack, your own attack will lose all its significance.' (27th *Magh* 1933.)

This letter of Rabindranath aggrieved Saratchandra who felt it contained a veiled insinuation that he wanted to protest against the action of the government merely to save his own skin. He wrote the following reply but, on second thoughts, did not despatch it.

'I am in receipt of your letter. Very well, let it be as you say.

'As I am the author of this book, its proscription by the government might have made me unhappy, but that need not be taken into consideration. I have nothing to say about your decision and about your views. But I would like to say something on one or two points raised by you in your letter. If it appears as an explanation of my conduct, well, I can offer that to you alone.

'You say that a perusal of this book causes disaffection in the reader's mind towards the British government. That indeed was the intention. But had I done so by writing something false or untrue, certainly I would have had reason to feel ashamed or guilty. But to the best of my knowledge and belief, I have not written anything that might be regarded as untrue. Had I done so, the book would have become a piece of political propaganda, and not a work of art. For various reasons no writer in Bengal has written such a book before. When I wrote it and published it, I did so knowing fully well what might be the consequences.

'When, throughout India, large numbers of people are being imprisoned or externed by the government on flimsy grounds without trial or in flagrant miscarriage of justice, I did not entertain any hope that I would escape scot-free; nor do I have any such hope even today. The government will choose its own time to take action against me sooner or later. I have reason to believe that the delay in taking action does not mean that they have given up the idea of prosecuting me. However, that's entirely my personal affair. If, as a writer of Bengal, I have to suffer punishment even though I have not written anything untrue in my book, I am prepared to face it, whether I do so quietly or by shedding tears. But does that mean that there is no necessity for protesting against the government action in proscribing the book? The protest may bring in further punishment, but I feel that there should be further protest against that. Otherwise our silence may be interpreted as acceptance of the government's physical force as justifiable. That is why I wanted that there should be a formal protest against the government's action. Otherwise I had not the faintest hope that as a result of our protest, the government would lift the ban and the book would be printed again.

'If one is imprisoned on a charge of theft or dacoity, one can file an appeal in the High Court. If the appeal is dismissed, one should not bewail his lot because he was given three years' rigorous imprisonment instead of two years'! A prisoner is not given milk or butter in the jail. I feel it is shameful to start an agitation over this. But if the jail authorities supply them grass to eat instead of coarse rice and force them to eat it by belabouring them with sticks, the prisoners have, I feel, a right to call such action oppressive and to protest against it.

'As I have written the book myself, I alone am responsible for it. The important point is whether I have said all that was considered necessary. I did not bank on the British government's sense of justice or forgiveness. I wrote whatever I considered necessary for the good of my country. All my literary work is based on this basic conception.

'You say that no other government in the east or the west, including Indian rulers, has as much patience as the British government. I do not have the necessary experience to deny this. But that was not my point at all. What I wanted to emphasise is this: if the British government has any justification for proscribing this book, the people of subjugated India have an equal justification in protesting against the government action.

'I feel that an injustice has been done to me when it is hinted in your letter that I wanted to protest against the government action simply to escape punishment and to save my own skin. That was not my intention. If my countrymen do not wish to protest, I will have to do it myself. I propose to do so not by starting an agitation, but by writing another such book.

'You have been engaged for a long time in the service of the country. You have vast experience of the state of affairs in other countries. Had you told me that the publication of this book would be harmful for the country, I would not have minded it. To err is human. I would have thought that I had made a mistake.

'I am not writing this letter as a complaint. I have expressed freely what was in my mind. Had I any sense of grievance against you, I would have kept quiet. I am in quest of truth. That is why I have exiled myself to this obscure place. I feel my days are numbered. So I wanted to do something really good for the country.

'If due to my ignorance or excitement, this letter appears to be impolite at any place, kindly forgive me. I am one of your many admirers. I cannot think of giving you offence in any way, by my speech or writing.' (2nd *Phalgun* 1333.)

Saratchandra had originally planned to write a sequel to *Pather Dabi*, but he gave up the idea due to ill health.

Saratchandra died on 16 January 1938. On 16 January 1939, a public meeting was organised at the Albert Hall in Calcutta, on the occasion of his first death anniversary. A resolution was passed in this meeting requesting the government to lift the ban on *Pather Dabi*. After two months, the Fazlul Haque ministry, which was then in power in Bengal, lifted the ban.

In *Baishakh* 1346 (April-May 1939), a second edition of *Pather Dabi* was published.

CHAPTER 1

Apurba's orthodoxy got him into frequent arguments with his friends. 'While your brothers observe no rituals,' they would say, 'there's nothing that you don't follow.'

'Not at all,' Apurba would reply. 'I don't follow my brothers' example, nor your advice.'

His friends would repeat their old joke. 'You've studied in a college, hold a Master's degree in Science, and still sport the holy tuft of hair on your head. Does it serve as a conductor for electricity to your brain?'

'There's nothing in the science books against sporting the tuft of hair,' Apurba would reply. 'Hence I'm not convinced that it's wrong to sport one. As for electricity, its full facts haven't yet been ascertained. If you don't believe me, ask the teachers.'

Disgusted, they would grumble, 'It's no use arguing with you.'

At this Apurba would burst into laughter. 'That undoubtedly is a truism, yet you people don't realise it.'

Encouraged by the example and conduct of their Deputy Magistrate father, when Apurba's elder brothers began to eat chicken curry and bread openly, and hung their sacred thread on a nail before taking their bath and often forgot to retrieve it afterwards, and also joked about the desirability of getting it washed and ironed by the washerman, Apurba had not yet been invested with the sacred thread. Yet, though a child, he noticed his mother's silent tears and deep anguish. She did not say anything. Her sons would not have listened to her even if she had; it would have merely resulted in needless quarrels with her husband. Hinting sarcastically at the priestly profession of his father-in-law, he would say, 'If the boys follow the example of their father rather than their maternal

15

uncles, what can be done? If they prefer to wear hats instead of sporting the holy tuft of hair on their head, I don't think they deserve to be beheaded!'

Since then Karunamayee had refrained from saying anything about the behaviour of her two sons. Silently, she followed her own orthodox code of conduct. After the death of her husband when she became a widow, though she continued to live in the same house, she had in a way dissociated herself from the household. Adjacent to the room on the first floor where she lived was a verandah. She got a part of it enclosed, and used it as her kitchen and store-room. She refused to eat food cooked by her daughters-in-law. And so the days rolled by.

Apurba, on the other hand, started sporting the holy tuft of hair on his head. While excelling in studies and winning merit scholarships and medals in the college, he did not forget to observe the various rites and rituals, the daily prayers and the prescribed fasts. While exhibiting great enthusiasm for the various games and sports, he always had the time to accompany his mother for her daily bath in the river Ganga every morning.

Feeling that Apurba was making too much of a fuss over the whole thing, his sisters-in-law would sometimes make fun of him. 'Now that you've finished your studies, why don't you put on a loin-cloth and become a regular mendicant? After all, you seem to excel even a Brahmin widow in your observance of austerities!'

Apurba would laugh. 'It's not for fun that I do all this. You see, mother has no daughter. She has also grown old. If suddenly she were to become an invalid, at least I would be able to cook something for her . . . . As for the loin-cloth, who knows, I may have to resort to it some day staying with you people.'

His sisters-in-law would reply, 'That indeed is our bad luck.'

'Yes, indeed.' But to his mother, Apurba would say, 'It's wrong on your part to refuse food cooked by your

16

daughters-in-law. Whatever my brothers might be doing, their wives neither eat hotel food, nor touch chicken . . . . D'you intend to cook your own food all your life?'

'Boiling a small quantity of rice is no problem for me, my boy. By the time I'm unable to do even that, your wife will be there to do it.'

'Then why don't you get a good Brahmin girl? I know I'm unable to maintain a wife, but when I see your hardship I feel I'd rather be a parasite on my brothers than let you suffer thus.'

'Don't ever say that, Apu! Can't feed a wife, eh? You're capable of feeding the whole family!'

'What nonsense! You seem to think there's none like your son in the whole world.' So saying, Apurba would quickly push off.

Whatever Apurba might say about his inability to maintain a family, fathers of marriageable daughters were not idle. They began to besiege Apurba's eldest brother, Binode Babu, every now and then, at all sorts of places, making his life miserable. He told his mother, 'Catch hold of some religious-minded Brahmin girl and get over the problem of Apurba's marriage or else I'll be forced to leave this house and run away! Being the eldest son, outsiders think I'm the head of the family.'

Binode's harsh words pained Karunamayee. But she controlled herself. In a mild but firm tone, she said, 'They're not wrong, my boy. In the absence of your father, you are indeed the head of the family. However, don't commit yourself to anyone regarding Apu's marriage. I don't want beauty or dowry . . . . Binu, just leave this to me?'

'All right, but do so quickly. Don't keep the people in suspense much longer!' Binode left in a huff.

Karunamayee had a plan in her mind. For some time past she had been noticing a girl at the river bank. The girl often used to come with her mother for bathing in the Ganga. Karunamayee had made con-

17

fidential enquiries and learnt that marriage between the two families was permissible. After her bath, the girl would offer prayers to Lord Shiva. Karunamayee used to observe whether she made any aberration in the ritual of worship. Some more information remained to be collected and Karunamayee set about it. She had tentatively decided that if everything proved favourable, Apurba's marriage would be performed in the coming summer.

At this juncture, Apurba came one day and told his mother unexpectedly, 'I've got a good job!'

Karunamayee was delighted. 'That's wonderful, Apu! But you passed your final exams just the other day. Who offered you a job so soon?'

'One who needs my services,' said Apurba, with a smile.

He then narrated to his mother the whole story.

The Principal of his college had arranged the job for him. Messrs Botha & Co had opened a new branch at Rangoon in Burma. They were in need of an educated, intelligent and honest Bengali youth to run the office. The starting salary would be four hundred rupees per month, besides house rent, followed by an increment of two hundred rupees after six months if the company did not go into liquidation.

But the mere mention of Burma dampened his mother's enthusiasm. 'Have you gone mad, Apu?' she said. 'Is that a place to go to? I'm told it's an absolutely irreligious country. How could you think I'd agree to send you there? I've no need for such money!'

Apurba was alarmed at his mother's opposition. 'You may not need any money,' he said, 'but I do. I'm prepared to live like a beggar should you order me so, but shall I get another chance like this in all my life? There's no dearth of qualified persons in the city, so it won't make any difference to Botha & Co. But consider the embarrassment to our Principal, who has given his word on my behalf. Besides, the actual financial condition of our house is not unknown to you.'

18

'But I'm told that's a country inhabited only by barbarians!'

'Oh! Someone must've exaggerated. Ours is not a savage country. Any yet, if someone wants to behave like one, no one can stop him.'

After keeping quiet for a while, Karunamayee said, 'But I've already decided to get you married this summer?'

'Have you already finalised the matter? Otherwise, please postpone it for a couple of months . . . . I shall come back whenever you send for me.'

Though outwardly old-fashioned, Karunamayee was in fact quite intelligent. She pondered over the matter for some time, and then said calmly, 'If you have to go, that can't be helped. Still, consult your elder brothers and obtain their permission.'

The mere reference to her two elder sons overwhelmed Karunamayee. It seemed as if all her bottled up mental anguish, both past and present, had been stirred. But she did not show it. She was the daughter of the well-known Bandopadhyays of Gokuldighi. Traditionally, they were a pious and orthodox Hindu family. Her notion of good Hindu behaviour that had been firmly rooted in her mind since childhood had been rudely shocked later by the conduct of her husband and two elder sons. She had tolerated all those indignities in the hope that Apurba would not disappoint her. But even this son of hers was talking of going away to a distant unknown land. This filled her mind with fear and anxiety. But she simply said, 'As long as I live, Apu, don't do anything that might hurt me.' Saying this, she wiped her tears with the border of her *sari*.

Apurba's eyes filled with tears. He could only blurt out, 'You're still amongst us, mother. But a day will come when you may have to leave this son of yours and depart. If I've known you correctly, I can assure you that you'll never have to repent for me even then.' So saying, he hastily left.

That evening, Karunamayee could not concentrate on her prayers. Anxiety and anguish filled her mind. Disturbed and confused, she went and stood silently in front of her eldest son's room.

Binode Babu had returned from his chamber. He had changed into evening clothes and was about to leave for the club. He was startled to see his mother. In fact it was so unexpected that it rendered him speechless.

Karunamayee said, 'I've come to consult you regarding a particular matter.'

'What's it, mother?'

Though Karunamayee had carefully wiped her tears before coming, her voice betrayed her feelings. She narrated the whole episode and finally, coming to the matter of Apurba's prospective salary, said in a sorrowful tone, 'I wonder if I should send him to that place for the sake of a few extra rupees.'

At this, Binode lost his temper. He said rudely, 'We all agree that there's none in the whole world like your Apurba. But at the same time, being practical people, we can't forget that a starting salary of four hundred rupees and an increment of two hundred after six months is too good even for him!'

Aggrieved, Karunamayee replied, 'But I'm told it's an absolutely primitive place?'

'Whatever you have heard or learnt may not be absolutely true.'

These words of her eldest son deeply hurt Karunamayee. 'If I haven't learnt a thing in all these years,' she said, 'don't try to teach me now. I didn't come here to ascertain the real worth of Apurba, in terms of money. I came simply to consult you whether to send him to such a faraway place or not.'

Binode bowed down and took the dust from his mother's feet. 'I didn't mean to hurt you,' he said. 'It's true that we had more in common with father. From him we learnt that money is valuable and necessary in day-to-day life. But in this case, it's not greed that

20

prompts me. Believe me, despite my English clothes, I haven't become so much Anglicised as to send my younger brother away simply to be relieved of the burden of maintaining him. Yet, I· say, he should go. The atmosphere here has become so vicious these days that if he leaves the country and takes up a job elsewhere, even for a while, it'll not only be good for him but also for all of us. You remember, during the *swadeshi* movement, though he was a child, his activities had put father's job into jeopardy.'

Alarmed, Karunamayee said, 'No, no, Apu doesn't indulge in such activities any more. Even at that time . . . seven, eight years back . . . how old was he? It was simply at the instigation of others that . . . .'

Binode shook his head. 'Perhaps you're right,' he said, 'Apurba may have given up those activities these days. But in every country there's a group of people who're different from the others . . . . Your youngest son belongs to that group. To them the soil of their native land is dearer than their own flesh, the water of its rivers like the blood flowing through their veins! Not only its air and light, but its hills and mountains, forests and jungles, sun and moon, rivers and rivulets . . . they try to absorb the entire nation within themselves! Perhaps it was one such person who in the past described his motherland as his mother! Where their motherland is involved, never trust them . . . you'll be let down.'

Pointing to the tip of his forefinger, he added, 'To them the difference between life and death is as negligible as this . . . . I'd rather say that this unorthodox son of yours is far more dependable than your god-fearing, orthodox, M. Sc. degree-holder, youngest son!'

Not that Karunamayee was totally convinced by what her eldest son said. At the same time, she had suffered a lot of anxiety on account of Apurba's activities on the earlier occasions. Also, she was not totally ignorant that something like a dark cloud had appeared on the country's western horizon. Her first thought went out

21

for Apurba's father, then alive; now he was no more.

Binode could sense from his mother's face what was passing through her mind. But as he was in a hurry to go out, he said, 'Well, what's the hurry? Apurba isn't leaving tomorrow! We can all sit down later and come to a conclusion.'

So saying, he hurried off.

CHAPTER 2

On the steamer, Apurba ate only rice and *sandesh*, and drank the milk of tender coconuts. Thus, while he managed to keep his Brahminhood intact, he was weak and half dead by the time he reached Rangoon. He was received at the jetty by two watchmen and a south Indian official of Botha & Co. who accorded him a hearty welcome. The official did not delay in imparting the information that he had already rented a house for the new manager at a monthly rental of thirty rupees, and had furnished it as best as possible at the Company's expense.

Summer was approaching. It was already pretty warm. The prospect of a quiet nap at the end of a tiring sea voyage seemed rather attractive to Apurba. Karunamayee had sent with him the old Brahmin cook of the family. Though it would mean considerable inconvenience to the family, she would at least be assured of the purity of his meals. Not only the cook, but groceries like rice, lentils, *ghee*, oil, spices, even potatoes and other vegetables had been sent by her. So the prospect of having a freshly cooked hot meal in place of the dry pressed rice excited Apurba.

A hackney carriage was hired. While the south Indian official took leave of him, the two watchmen stayed behind. They took charge of his heavy luggage and went ahead, leading the way. After the long sea voyage, to be on firm earth again and to ride in a hackney carriage seemed most comfortable.

About ten minutes later, the carriage stopped in front of his new quarters. While the watchmen arranged to take the luggage upstairs with the help of about a dozen coolies, Apurba looked at the house and was sorely disappointed. It was a dull and drab structure, unattractive in appearance, having no inner or outer apartment and no courtyard except the

23

thoroughfare on which the building stood. A narrow wooden flight of stairs rose to the second floor straight from the main road. They were steep and dark. It was a common staircase for all the six tenants. If one managed to lose his balance and fall, it would be straight onto the road, then to a hospital; the third possibility was better left unsaid. It would need long practice to be able to negotiate such a difficult stairway. Apurba was new to the job, so he followed the watchman very carefully, watching each step he took. After some time, the watchman turned right and stopped in front of a room on the first floor. Opening the door he announced, 'These, sir, are your rooms!'

Pointing to a closed door across the passage, Apurba enquired, 'Who lives there?'

'A Chinese gentleman, I'm told.'

'And who stays on the second floor?'

'I saw a dark-complexioned man once. Possibly a south Indian.'

Apurba kept quiet. The information about the two nearest neighbours, who would be sharing the same stairway, evoked a sigh of disappointment. His disappointment increased further on entering the rooms. There were three adjacent rooms of different shapes and sizes, separated from each other by wooden partitions. One of the rooms had a water tap, a place to take bath, and a small kitchen with all other necessary paraphernalia. The room in the centre was opening out to the dark staircase — one could euphemistically call it the sitting room. The room at the extreme end, facing the road, was relatively cleaner and well lighted. This was the bedroom. This had been furnished with a bed, one table and a few chairs, on the Company's account. A narrow balcony overlooked the road. When time hung heavy, one could stand there and watch the traffic.

The rooms were stuffy, dark, one opening out into the other. The whole structure was made of wood — the walls, the floor, the ceiling, the staircase, everything

24

was wooden. When one considered the fire hazard, it appeared as if even the evil prince Duryodhan in the epic *Mahabharata* could not have conceived of a better house in which to burn his Pandava cousins. The thought of having to pass his days in such an apartment, in this distant land, far away from home, from friends and relatives, from his family, specially his mother, made Apurba sad. But he controlled himself and set about examining the rooms. One thing that gave him some satisfaction was that the tap had regular flow of water, for bathing as well as for cooking.

The watchman remarked, 'Unless one is wasteful, there's no dearth of water in this town. One large overhead tank has been provided for each pair of tenants in this building, and water is available day and night.'

Reassured, Apurba said to his cook, 'Mother has sent with you everything that may be necessary for cooking a meal. Take a bath and then get about it, while I arrange my things with the help of the watchman.'

There was a stock of coke in the kitchen, besides a concrete oven. But this was rather untidy and had marks of soot. Evidently someone had used it before him. Who knows what was his caste and what all he had cooked on it? Apurba felt a revulsion and said to his cook, 'It's not possible to use this stove, Tewari. You've to make some other arrangement. If you could arrange for a portable stove, you could set it up in the other room. But is it possible to get one in this god-forsaken place?'

The watchman remarked that portable stoves were easily available. Given the money, he would produce one within ten minutes. He was despatched, with the money. While Tewari began preparations for cooking, Apurba dragged the trunks and suitcases to his bedroom and attempted to arrange his things. He first took out his clothes from his trunk and arranged them on the clothes horse. He then opened the bedding and made his bed. Taking out a new table cloth from the trunk, he laid it on the table. On it he placed his books and some writing material. Finally, he flung the window shutters wide open and plugged them with bits of paper. Observing that this made the room somewhat brighter and attractive, he lay down on the newly made bed with an air of contentment.

Soon the watchman returned with an iron stove. Apurba told Tewari to quickly cook some *khichri* and fry-ups and was about to lie down on the bed again when he remembered his mother's earnest request to send her a telegram immediately on arrival. So he put on his coat and accompanied by his guide, the watchman, left in search of the telegraph office. As assured by the watchman, he told Tewari that he would be back in less than an hour, and that the food should be ready by then.

It was a holiday on account of some Christian festival. As he walked down the road he could make out that this was a predominantly Christian locality. Signs of festivity were visible in each house. He turned to the watchman, 'I had heard that there's a sizeable Bengali population here. In which locality do they stay?'

The watchman clarified that there were no separate localities for different communities. People lived wherever they liked. However, officers generally preferred this part of the town. Apurba was an officer himself, as he had come to occupy a high post, and though he was a staunch Hindu, he had no prejudice against any religion. Nevertheless, he did not quite like the idea of being surrounded by Christians on all sides. 'Isn't it possible to hire a house somewhere else?' he asked the watchman.

The watchman was not well-informed in this matter. He pondered over the question for some time and then volunteered what he thought was a reasonable answer. 'It might be possible to get one if a search is made, though it may be difficult to get a better house at this rent.'

Apurba did not offer any comment. When, following the watchman's directions, he finally reached the branch Telegraph Office, he found that the south Indian official there had already left for his lunch. Apurba waited for an hour or so. But when the official returned, he said, pointing at the clock, 'Today is a public holiday. The telegraph office closes at two and it is already quarter past two.'

Greatly annoyed, Apurba said, 'That's your fault, not mine. I've been waiting here for the past one hour.'

The man looked at Apurba and, without the least hesitation, said, 'I had been absent for not more than ten minutes.'

Apurba shouted at him, called him a liar and threatened to report against him, but none of this produced any effect. Totally unconcerned, the man began to close his books; he did not even bother to give a reply. Realising that no useful purpose would be served by further arguments with this man, Apurba left. Exhausted by hunger and thirst, fuming and fretting with anger, he jostled through the crowds to the main Telegraph Office and despatched the telegram. It was nearly evening.

The watchman turned to him and said, 'Sir, I've to go a long distance.'

Apurba was extremely tired and lost in thought; so he raised no objection. He was hopeful that as the streets were straight and parallel and serially numbered, it would not be very difficult for him to find his way back. The watchman departed and Apurba started negotiating the different streets till at last he reached the house.

As he started to climb the stairs, he noticed Tewari, with a thick stave in his hand, standing in front of his apartment, shouting at someone. His adversary, bare-bodied and clad only in a pair of trousers, stood in front of the open door on the second floor, shouting in a mix of Hindi and English, and brandishing a whip

27

with which he periodically slashed the air. Tewari was challenging him to come down, while he was suggesting that Tewari come up instead. The language they were using was quite unprintable!

Apurba, transfixed at the foot of the stairs, was unable to comprehend the situation. What could have transpired during such a short while so as to inspire Tewari to forge such an intimacy with his neighbour? Suddenly he attracted the notice of the two adversaries. Emboldened by the presence of his master, Tewari banged the floor with his stave and hurled another intimate address. His adversary replied with a loud crack of the whip. But before they could declare renewal of their fight, Apurba hastily climbed up the stairs and, catching hold of Tewari's hands along with the stave, said, 'Have you lost your senses, Tewari?'

Without giving Tewari any opportunity for protest, Apurba forced him indoors. Choked with anger, sorrow and excitement, Tewari cried, 'Come and see what that rascal has done!'

The damage was so devastating that Apurba's fatigue and drowsiness, hunger and thirst, all disappeared in a moment. The pot of *khichri* was still invitingly warm and let off a tasty aroma of spices, but there was water everywhere — on the top of the pot, around it, and on the floor. In the bedroom, his milk-white new bedsheet was soaked in murky water. Water splashed on the chairs, on the table, on his books, on the trunks and suitcases. Even the clothes horse standing in one corner of the room had not been spared; his expensive new suit had black stains all over it.

Controlling himself, Apurba enquired, 'How did this happen?'

Tewari pointed to the ceiling and said, 'This is the work of that rascal. See there . . . .' Dirty water was still dripping through the chinks in the wooden ceiling. The story narrated by Tewari was briefly as follows:

The gentleman returned home soon after Apurba had left. It was a day of festivity. He had apparently

28

had a bit too much of fun and returned home quite drunk. He first started singing and then dancing. Soon the music became so boisterous that Tewari was afraid the ceiling would collapse on his head. Even this could be tolerated, but when water began to drip through the ceiling over the cooking pot, Tewari came out to protest fearing that it would spoil the food. This insolence on the part of a native was too much to tolerate, and the Sahib became no infuriated that he began to pour down bucketfuls of water through his wooden floor. It was needless to describe the rest of the happening. Apurba had himself winessed the final drama.

Apurba kept quiet for some time and then asked, 'Was there none else in his house?'

'Possibly there was,' replied Tewari. 'It seemed as if someone was struggling with that drunkard.'

Tewari looked piteously at the pot of food. The meaning was quite clear. Someone had tried hard to stop the drunkard's fury, but had failed.

Apurba remained silent. It was a *fait accompli*. However there were no fresh attacks from the other side. The Sahib's enthusiasm appeared to have abated; apparently he had passed out. But from his occasional indistinct mumblings, it was clear he had not forgiven the nigger Tewari.

Apurba made an effort to smile. 'If the gods are against you, what can be done? Come, let's still think we're on the high seas. We still have some dried foodstuff left. That should suffice for tonight. What d'you say?'

Tewari nodded his assent. Casting a last wistful look at the pot of food, he searched for pressed rice. Luckily the box in which this was kept had not been shifted from the corner of the kitchen where it had first been placed — it had thus escaped defilement.

While preparing the snack, Tewari called out from the kitchen, 'Sir, I don't think we can stay here.'

Apurba replied casually, 'Perhaps not.'

Tewari was an old servant of the Haldar family. He remembered all that Apurba's mother had told him at the time of departure, and said in an anxious tone, 'No, sir, not a day more in this house! In my anger I've done a wrong thing — I've called the Sahib names!'

'You should've thrashed him instead,' said Apurba.

Tewari's anger had by now cooled down. He immediately disagreed and said, 'No, no! Everything said and done, he's a Sahib and we're but Bengalis.'

Apurba kept quiet. Encouraged by his silence, Tewari ventured, 'Can't we call the watchman and shift tomorrow morning itself? I think it'd be best for us to shift as soon as possible.'

'All right. Call him.' It was clear to Apurba that Tewari had suddenly become conscious about a native's duty towards a Sahib. He no more had any complaint against the villain. Instead, he thought it prudent to leave the place as quickly as possible.

'Okay, we'll shift,' repeated Apurba. 'But first, give me something to eat.'

'In a minute,' said Tewari and, somewhat relieved of his anxiety, set about it.

But Apurba kept ruminating over the incident. Recalling the insolent behaviour of the Anglo-Indian, he became furious. He thought, 'It's not just between that drunkard and myself. It's because we as a race have tolerated such insults meekly that they've become bold enough to treat us so brutally. Because we've submitted ourselves to such insults silently, without protest, that they have assumed it to be their right to display such arrogance. That's why even my servant today has the cheek to suggest that I run away to save my skin; it didn't occur to him what a shameful retreat that would be!'

Tewari was blissfully engaged in preparing his master's meal in the kitchen. He was unaware that Apurba had in the meantime picked up the thick bamboo stave and, slipping out of his room, ascended the stairs.

The door was closed. Apurba began to hammer upon it with his stave. After a few moments he heard a frightened female voice call out in English, 'Who's there?'

Apurba replied, 'I live on the first floor. I want that man.'

'Why?'

'To show him the extent of damage he has caused. He's lucky I wasn't at home!'

'He's sleeping.'

Apurba thundered, 'Wake him up! This is no time for sleeping! I won't come at night to disturb him. But right now, I won't move an inch until I've spoken to him.' Without meaning to, Apurba hit the floor loudly with his stave.

Neither the door opened, nor any further reply came from behind it. After a couple of minutes, Apurba again shouted, 'I won't move from here. Tell him to come out!'

The person on the other side now came close to the door and said gently, 'I'm his daughter. On behalf of my father, I ask your forgiveness. He was not in his senses at that time. But we'll try to make good all your losses tomorrow morning.'

Her gentle tone softened Apurba, but did not mollify him completely. 'He has behaved like a brute,' he added, 'and not only caused considerable damage but also kicked up a rumpus. I'm a newcomer here, but I hope he'll meet me tomorrow and settle the matter.'

'Okay,' said the girl. She added after a few moments, 'Like you, we're also new here. We arrived only yesterday afternoon.'

Without saying anything further, Apurba returned to his room. Tewari was still busy in the kitchen; he was unaware of what had transpired in the meantime.

After dinner, Apurba went to his bedroom, threw away the wet bedsheets and mattresses and somehow improvised a bed for the night and lay down. He

31

remembered all the harassment and damage he had suffered since his arrival in this new place and wondered how things would go on and when all this trouble would end. Along with these uneasy thoughts, another matter also engaged his mind — the unknown Christian girl. She had not appeared before him, so he had no idea about her appearance, age or temperament. All he had heard was her voice and it was apparent from it that her accent was un-English. Possibly she was a south Indian or a Goan or from some other community. But whosoever she may be, it was clear that unlike her father, she was not proud or puffed up with the knowledge of belonging to the same religious fraternity as the rulers of India. She had instead been ashamed for his uncivilized behaviour. Apurba remembered her plaintive request for forgiveness; his own behaviour appeared in contrast boorish. He was, by nature, a person of gentle manners; he did not like being rude to anyone. When it struck him, from what Tewari had earlier told him, that possibly this girl had tried her best to stop her drunken, rowdy father from doing the mischief, he felt sorry for his own conduct. Whatever had happened, had happened; it would have been better if he had not later gone upstairs and shouted at them.

From the other room he could hear the rattling sound of Tewari cleaning the utensils. Suddenly the sound stopped. Tewari called out, 'Who's there?'

Apurba was startled. He could not hear the reply, but Tewari's voice was loud and clear. He was saying in Hindi, 'No, no, Memsahib. Please take these away. Babu has already had his dinner. Besides, we don't touch these things.'

Apurba sat up in bed and pricked up his ears. He could recognise the voice of that Christian girl, but could not make out what she said. Tewari's reply made the matter clear. 'Who said we've not had dinner? We've just finished. So, please take these things back. If Babu comes to know of it, he'll be very angry.'

Apurba came out of his room. 'What's the matter, Tewari?' he enquired.

The girl, who was standing on the threshold, immediately moved away. The evening had set in, but the lamps had not yet been lighted. A dark shadow fell across the room from the landing. Though the girl was not clearly visible, yet one could make out her general appearance. Though not as fair as an English girl, she was still remarkably fair. Possibly she would be nineteen or twenty, or maybe slightly more. She looked thin, possibly because she was tall for her age. But for her slightly prominent front teeth, she was quite pretty. She was wearing slippers and a beautiful south Indian sari, maybe because of the festival, though she had draped it as a Bengali or Parsee lady would do. A Japanese basket containing some fruits — apples, pears, pomegranates and grapes — lay on the floor.

Apurba asked, 'What's all this?'

The girl replied softly in English from the other side of the door, 'It's our festival today, so mother sent these fruits. Besides, you couldn't have possibly had your food today.'

'Please convey my thanks to your mother, but I've already had my dinner.'

The girl kept quiet.

'Who told her that we didn't have our food?' asked Apurba.

The girl replied bashfully, 'That's what first started the row. Besides, we know it for certain.'

Apurba shook his head and said, 'Thank you very much. But believe me, we've already had our dinner.'

The girl remained silent for a moment, and then said, 'Even so, it couldn't have been very satisfactory. Besides, these have been purchased from the market. There can't be anything wrong in accepting them.'

It was clear to Apurba that the two ladies were trying to placate him. His thick stave and shouts had created such an impression of his ill temper that they were

33

apprehensive as to what would happen the next morning. Hence these gifts.

He said gently, 'That's all right.'

Turning to Tewari, he said, 'There can't be any objection in accepting these fruits, can there?'

Tewari was not pleased. 'If you need fruits, they can easily be purchased from the market,' he said. 'Besides, we don't need them tonight. Also, your mother had repeatedly asked me not to touch such things. No, Memsahib, we don't need these. Please take them away.'

It was quite possible that his mother had given such instructions. It was also quite possible that she might have entrusted her old and trusted servant with the responsibility of acting as his guardian in this foreign country. He remembered the promises he had made to her before setting out. 'It's not just mother's orders,' he told himself. 'I've also to remember the promises I made to her.' And yet he was not entirely convinced that it was proper to refuse these fruits, which this girl had brought as a present for him, as something unclean and untouchable. But he could not bring himself to say anything.

Tewari said again, 'Memsahib, we won't touch these things. Please take them away. I've to clean the place.'

The girl waited for a little while. Then, picking up the basket, she quietly left.

Apurba turned towards Tewari. 'You didn't have to eat them. We could've thrown them out later,' he said in a low voice.

'Throw them!' said Tewari, surprised. 'But what do we gain thereby?'

'Gain thereby? Stupid fool!' Apurba stalked out of the room.

Later, lying on his bed, as he thought over Tewari's action, he felt furious. But gradually, as he analysed the matter threadbare, his anger subsided. 'I couldn't have done it,' he thought. 'But perhaps it was good that he returned the fruits.'

Suddenly he remembered an incident concerning his eldest uncle, his mother's brother. One day that orthodox virtuous Brahmin had refused to eat in their house. Karunamayee knew the reason, but she tried to adopt a stratagem to save the situation. But his uncle had said, 'No, sister, that's not possible. I know your husband is a short-tempered person, he won't forget this affront. Perhaps you'll also have to suffer because of that. But as my late preceptor used to say, to attain truth one has to suffer a lot. One can attain truth through suffering, but never through a compromise with deception. Perhaps it's best, my sister, that I go away from your house without eating anything.'

This had made Karunamayee very unhappy, but she had never blamed her brother. Remembering this, Apurba convinced himself, 'It's good that Tewari has done this. He has done the right thing!'

CHAPTER 3

Apurba had decided to visit the market the next morning. The amoral ways of this place were known to him even when he was in India. There was no point in wishing them away; it had to be accepted as a fact of life. But surely he was not the first orthodox Hindu to have come here! There must be others who had succeeded in striking a balance between the necessity for earning a livelihood and following the injunctions of Hindu religion and were living in peace and happiness. To discover this middle path it was necessary to be acquainted with these people, and what better place offers such an opportunity than the local market? He wanted to ascertain for himself whether it was possible to live here within the confines laid down by his mother or not. But he could not go out, as he had to wait for the Sahib upstairs to come down and ask for his forgiveness. There was no doubt that he would come. For one thing, he had committed the offence under the influence of liquor. When he would come back to his senses in the morning, his wife and daughter would give him no respite till he apologised — Apurba had obtained such an assurance, though not overtly, the previous night itself.

His thoughts turned towards that Christian girl several times since the morning. Even during his sleep, her courteous, gentle manner and soft voice seemed to have wafted through his consciousness like a familiar sweet melody. Just as that girl had been ashamed for her drunken father's misconduct, Apurba could not help feeling embarrassed on account of Tewari's rudeness. This feeling of guilt for the faults of others seemed to have forged a delicate bond of sympathy in the mind of these two young strangers, a bond which, though imperceptible, could not be denied.

Suddenly, Apurba's thoughts were disturbed by the noise of his neighbour upstairs, who appeared to have woken up. At the sound of each footstep, he expected the Sahib to come down. That he would forgive him was certain; the only thing worrying him was how to wipe clean all signs of the previous day's unpleasantness and establish normalcy. But time was running out.

Along with the sound of light footsteps could be heard the heavy tread of the Sahib's boots. Gradually the pace increased and grew louder — this indicated unmistakably his girth and weight, but not his penitence. After waiting for a long while in hope and expectation, when it was time for Apurba to at last leave for his new office, he finally heard the Sahib coming down the stairs. Apurba could hear a pair of gentler footsteps behind him. This was followed by a loud clanging of the knocker on the door. Tewari came running from the kitchen. 'That Sahib has come. He's knocking at the door!' His excitement was apparent from his tone.

Apurba said, 'Open the door and show him in.'

As soon as Tewari opened the door, Apurba heard a deep voice demand in Hindi, 'Where's your master?'

Tewari's reply was not clearly audible — possibly he had extended a respectful welcome — but the next moment the thunderous shout of the Sahib echoed through the house. 'Call him!'

Apurba was startled. What kind of repentance was this? For a moment he thought maybe the Sahib had again got drunk in the morning. But before he could decide whether it would be prudent to go or not, there came a peremptory command, 'Call him immediately!'

Apurba slowly came out and stood in front of the doorway. The man eyed him from top to bottom, and then enquired, 'Do you speak English?'

'Yes.'

'You had come over to our place last night after I'd fallen asleep?'

'Yes.'

'Right! You had banged the stave, eh? You also tried to break open the door, didn't you?'

Apurba was dumbfounded. The man went on, 'If the door had been open, you'd have entered and attacked my wife or daughter! That's why you didn't come up as long as I was awake, eh?'

Apurba said slowly, 'You were asleep, then how could you know all this?'

'I've heard everything from my daughter! You had the cheek even to abûse her?' He pointed to his daughter standing behind him.

She was the same girl, but as on the previous evening, Apurba could not see her clearly even now. Shielded behind the immense figure of her father, nothing excepting the border of her *sari* was visible. It was also not clear whether she nodded her assent or not; the only thing that was certain was that they were not simple people. They were deliberately trying to twist and misrepresent the whole affair. This called for extreme caution.

The Sahib added, 'Had I been awake, I'd have kicked you out and knocked out all your teeth! Since I've lost that opportunity, I've to be satisfied by whatever justice I can get from the police . . . . We're leaving. Be prepared for the consequences!'

Apurba could only shake his head. His face had turned ashen.

Catching hold of his daughter's hand, the Sahib said, 'Come, let's go.' As he descended the stairs, he turned to Apurba. 'Coward! You attempted to assault unprotected, helpless women? I'll teach you such a lesson you'll never forget in your life!'

Tewari had been standing nearby. He had heard everything. As soon as the Sahib and his daughter disappeared, he came and tearfully enquired, 'What'll happen to us now?'

Apurba tried to sound carefree. 'What'll happen? Nothing!' But his face told a different story. Tewari could read it. He said, 'I'd already told you. Whatever has happened, has happened. No point in irritating them further. After all, they're sahibs!'

'What if they're sahibs?' replied Apurba.

'But they've gone to the police,' cried Tewari.

'Let them.'

'Why not send a wire to your eldest brother and ask him to come over immediately?' suggested Tewari frantically.

'Have you gone crazy, Tewari? Go and do your cooking. It must've all got burnt by now! I've to leave at 10.30 sharp.' Apurba went to his bedroom.

Tewari entered the kitchen. His cooking, Apurba's going to office — everything suddenly seemed immaterial to him. The more he considered himself to be responsible for all the trouble, the more his bewildered mind sought to grab at straws — the savage behaviour of the locals, evil influence of planets, wrong calculations by astrologers and most of all, Karunamayee's greed for money — to shift the blame on them and absolve himself.

It was with such a distraught mind that Tewari finished his cooking. He had received his training from Karunamayee, so however tense he may have been, he made no mistakes in his cooking. When Apurba sat down to eat, he heaped praises on Tewari to boost his morale. First he praised the appearance of the food and then, after taking a mouthful or two, said, 'You've cooked wonderfully well today, Tewari. Hadn't had a proper meal in days . . . . I was afraid you'd have burned everything. You're such a timid fellow! Mother couldn't have chosen someone worse to come with me.'

Tewari simply grunted.

Apurba laughed. 'Why such a long face?' he asked good-humouredly to lift the gloom of their minds. 'Did you hear the threat made by that rascal of an Anglo-Indian — will go to the police! Go, by all means! But to what avail? Who'll bear witness?'

'They don't need witnesses,' said Tewari. 'It's enough if they themselves say so.'

'How can that be? Is there no law in this country? Besides, what type of a sahib is he? His complexion is as black as my shoes! The fellow thought I was a kid . . . thought he'd frighten me! Rascal! Scoundrel! Bastard!'

Tewari kept quiet. He did not have the courage to abuse the Sahib even in his absence any longer.

Apurba ate silently for a while. He then suddenly burst out, 'How wicked that girl is! Yesterday she acted so naive and sweet . . . and has then told all sorts of lies against us! Really, it's difficult to understand people!'

'After all, Christians!' commented Tewari.

'Yes, indeed.' It suddenly struck Apurba that these people had no idea of good or bad, had no scruples, no sense of social propriety. He said, 'You know, Tewari, how much the British hate these people? They don't mix with them, no matter how much they may put on European appearance or go to churches! Those who've renounced their ancestral faith, how can they ever be good people?'

Tewari had no doubts about it. However, faced with imminent danger, he just had no desire to enter into a discussion for or against the issue. Apurba would soon leave for his office. He would be left alone at home. He wondered what was in store for him. The Sahib had gone to the police station. He would return. Possibly he would break open the door. Possibly he would come with a posse of policemen to arrest him. Whatever may happen — it was all so uncertain. In these circumstances, he had not the least curiosity to discover the actual difference between genuine and fake sahibs, whether they mixed with each other, and if not, how much remorse and anguish it caused to the latter.

Apurba had taken his food, and was dressing up. Tewari peeped in from behind the door and said, 'Wouldn't it have been better to wait for a little while?'

'What for?'

'Till they return.'

'How's that possible?' said Apurba. 'Today is my first day in office. What'll they think if I'm late?'

Tewari remained silent. Apurba continued, 'Shut the door and sit tight! I'll try to come back as soon as I can. What can that fellow do? After all, he daren't break the door!'

'All right.' But it was clear to Apurba that Tewari was not convinced. Before closing the door, Tewari advised in a low voice, 'Don't walk down today; better take a carriage.'

'All right, I'll see,' replied Apurba, as he went down the stairs. Looking at him, it appeared as if his enthusiasm for his new job had disappeared.

Mr. Rozen, partner in the firm of Botha & Co. and manager in charge of their eastern region, was in town those days. It was he who had opened the office at Rangoon. He received Apurba most cordially and expressed satisfaction at his appearance, behaviour and university degrees. He introduced Apurba to the members of his staff and assured him that he would teach him the trade secrets during his stay of two-three months at Rangoon. On meeting new people and talking to them Apurba felt enthusiastic and cheerful once again.

Among the staff one man specially attracted his attention. He was the accountant, a Marathi Brahmin called Ramdas Talwarkar. He was about the same age as Apurba, or maybe slightly older. Tall, well-built and fair-complexioned, it would be no exaggeration to describe him as handsome. He was dressed in trousers and a long coat. He had a turban round his head and wore red sandal-paste marks on his forehead. He spoke English fluently, but from the very beginning insisted on conversing with Apurba in Hindi. Apurba was not fluent in Hindi, but when he found that Ramdas spoke only in that language, he had also to switch over to Hindi.

'I can't speak Hindi correctly,' said Apurba. 'I'm

41

afraid I'll make many mistakes.'

'I also make mistakes. It isn't my mother-tongue either.'

'Then what harm has English done?' enquired Apurba.

'I'll make more mistakes in English,' Ramdas replied with a smile. 'You may speak in English if you like. But kindly excuse me if I reply in Hindi.'

In the midst of this conversation, Mr. Rozen entered the room. He was Dutch, about fifty years old, and not very particular about his dress. He sported a bushy beard and moustache. He spoke broken English, but was an experienced businessman. He had already visited different parts of Burma, collected information from a number of people and drawn up a programme. for expansion of their business. He now placed a copy of the programme before Apurba and said, 'I'd like to have your views on this.'

Turning to Talwarker, he said, 'I've sent a copy to you as well . . . . No, no, let it be for today. We'll have the afternoon off in honour of our new Manager. I'll be leaving shortly. After that the fate of this firm will depend on you two. I'm not an Englishman . . . though this could well have been a Dutch colony . . . . Unlike them, we don't look down upon Indians. We treat them as equals . . . . Not only the firm's future, but your own promotions will depend on your sense of duty . . . . Anyway, good-day . . . the office must close at 2 p.m. sharp!'

He left as hurriedly as he had entered. Soon the sound of his car could be heard, as it swung out of the main gate.

At 2 p.m., Apurba and Ramdas left together. Talwarkar lived with his wife and daughter in the countryside, at a place called Insein, about ten miles west of Rangoon. There was a vacant plot of land next to his home, which he had converted into a kitchen garden. It was open country, away from the din and bustle of the city. Transport was no problem; there were a number of trains.

'Mr. Haldar, you must come and have tea with us tomorrow evening,' invited Talwarkar.

'But I don't take tea,' replied Apurba.

'You don't? Well, previously I didn't use to take too. My wife still chides me for that. Doesn't matter, something else then . . . fruits, sherbet . . . or, well, we're also Brahmins like you . . . .'

'Undoubtedly. I've no hesitation in eating in your house, but only if you've no hesitation in reciprocating.'

Ramdas said, 'I've no objection whatsoever. As for my wife . . . well, I'll have to ask her. Women can sometimes be rather . . . . Your house is quite near. Come, I'll see you to your place. My train is only in the evening.'

The suggestion upset Apurba. Till then, he had forgotten everything. Suddenly, he was reminded of all that unpleasantness. His cheerfulness vanished. He felt ashamed to disclose that he had got himself involved in such an unpleasant affair immediately on his arrival. He did not know what further developments might have taken place in the meantime that he would now have to face. The presence of a colleague would certainly have proved helpful and given him courage. But he was unsure of what his new acquaintance would think of him. He said, hesitantly, 'You see, the whole place's in a mess . . . .' But he could not finish his sentence.

Understanding his hesitation, Ramdas said with a smile, 'Well, I didn't expect you'd have settled down properly within one night. I too had set up house one day. At least my wife was there to help me. You've no one. You're feeling shy, but I tell you, unless you bring her over, things won't be all right even after a year. Anyway, come, let's see what I can do for you. It's only in times like these that you need a friend.'

Apurba kept quiet. By nature, he was a jovial fellow. Had it been some other time, possibly he would have joked about his not having a wife. But such light-hear-

43

tedness did not occur to him now. He was in dire need of a friend in this unfriendly, foreign country. But at the same time he felt embarrassed to open up before his new friend. Though he did not openly express his consent, by the time they reached his house he was left with no other alternative but to invite Talwarkar in. As they climbed the stairs, Apurba noticed the Christian girl coming down. Her father was not with her; she was alone. Both stepped aside. The girl did not glance at them but slowly went her way. When she had gone, Ramdas asked, 'They stay on the second floor, no?'

'Yes.'

'Bengalis like you?'

Apurba shook his head. 'No. They're native Christians — most probably south Indians, or Goans, or some such — but not Bengalis.'

'But she had worn her *sari* just like a Bengali.'

Apurba was a bit surprised. 'How did you know?'

'Well, I've seen many Bengalis in places like Bombay, Poona and Simla. No other community in India has such a decent way of putting on *saris*.'

'Maybe,' said Apurba rather unmindfully. Then, standing in front of his flat, he began to knock at the door. After some time a cautious voice came from inside, 'Who's there?'

'Me. Open the door. You don't have to fear,' said Apurba, laughing. It was clear that nothing serious had happened during his absence and that Tewari was quite safe. This removed a load off his mind.

Ramdas went through the rooms. 'Things aren't as bad as I had feared,' he said. 'You've got a good servant. He has already arranged everything. I had selected the furniture myself. If you need anything else, please tell me. I'll arrange to have it sent across. These are Mr. Rozen's orders.'

Tewari spoke in an undertone, 'No need for more furniture. Let's get out of here while we can.'

Only Apurba could hear what Tewari said. After

44

some time he took him aside and asked, 'Has anything else happened?'

'No.'

'Then why did you say that?'

'Not just like that. The whole afternoon the Sahib pounded about like a race-horse. Impossible to tolerate such disturbance!'

Apurba decided it was not really such a serious matter. In any case, there was no point in joining issue with Tewari or in complaining about every little inconvenience. So he tried to make light the whole thing and said, 'Do you mean to say he won't move about in his house? The wooden flooring just makes the sound louder.'

Tewari replied angrily, 'Is pounding on the floor like a horse called moving about?'

'Then he must be drunk again!'

'Maybe. I didn't go and smell his breath. In any case, we can't stay here.' Tewari marched off angrily to his kitchen.

Tewari's complaint was neither unfounded nor improper. Apurba had also not expected the harassment to end within one day, and yet the uncertainty and apprehension of further trouble made him morose and unhappy. His first morning in this foreign land had begun with a cloud. Only a few hours in the office had been sunny and bright; now the evening sky appeared to him again dark and overcast with clouds.

It was time for Ramdas to take leave. It was not clear whether he had guessed something from Tewari's complaints or from Apurba's anxious looks, for he suddenly asked, 'Aren't you comfortable here?'

'No,' said Apurba, with a wan smile. Noticing that Ramdas continued to look at him expectantly, he added, 'Actually, our second floor neighbours haven't been too pleasant.'

Ramdas was surprised. 'You mean that girl?'

'Yes, particularly her father.' Apurba went on to narrate the events of the previous evening and the following morning.

Ramdas kept quiet for some time and then said, 'Had I been in your place, the story would've been different. I wouldn't have allowed him to move till he had apologised!'

'What'd you've done if he had refused to?'

'As I said just now, I wouldn't have allowed him to go!'

Apurba was not fully convinced. Nevertheless Ramdas's words gave him some courage. He said, smilingly, 'Anyway, let's make a move now. It's time for your train.' So saying, he held Talwarkar's arm and started descending the stairs. Surprisingly, they encountered the Christian girl this time also. She had a small packet in her hand; possibly she had gone out to buy something. Apurba stepped aside to let her pass, but was perplexed to see that Ramdas stood there, completely blocking her way. He said in English, 'I'd like to talk to you for a minute. I'm the friend of this young gentleman here. I feel you people ought to express regret for your unpleasant behaviour towards him.'

The girl said roughly, 'Why not say so to my father?'

'Is he at home?'

'No.'

'I haven't time to wait. Tell him, on my behalf, that his rude behaviour is making my friend's stay here rather disagreeable.'

The girl continued in the same bitter tone. 'And I say, on his behalf, that it's open to him to leave this place if he so likes.'

Ramdas said with a little smile, 'I know the native Christian bullies very well. I didn't expect anything better from you. But let me tell you, that's not going to make things any better. Because, if he goes away, then I'll come to stay here in his place. My name is Ramdas Talwarkar . . . . I'm a Marathi Brahmin. The word *talwar* has a particular meaning. Tell your father to find out what that is! Good day! . . . . Come, let's

46

go.' He caught hold of Apurba's hand and climbed down the stairs.

From the corners of his eyes, Apurba had observed how the girl's face had turned stern towards the end. He could not regain his voice for some time. Then, slowly, he said, 'What was all this, Talwarkar?'

'Simply that, should you happen to move out, I'll have to come over in your place. Just let me know well in time.'

'And your wife will be all alone when you go to office?'

'Not totally alone. I've a two-year-old daughter also.'

'You're joking,' said Apurba.

'I'm not. I'm serious.'

Apurba cast a glance at his companion's face, and then said deliberately, 'In that case, I'm not going to vacate this flat.'

Before he could finish, Ramdas clasped both his hands and violently shaking them, exclaimed, 'That's how it should be, just what is needed! For long we've retreated out of fear of oppression, but no more!'

He continued to hold on to Apurba's hand till the train was about to leave. Then, giving it one last vigorous shake, he folded his palms in obeisance and bade goodbye.

It had not yet become dark. No train was due for another hour or so; hence the platform was deserted. Apurba started walking from one end of the platform to the other. Suddenly it struck him that he had aged considerably within the space of the last twenty-four hours. He seemed to have fallen asleep somewhere in the midst of his youthful sports and games and other frivolous activities, but when he woke up he found himself in the midst of unceasing activity. There was no rest, no recreation, no joy, no leisure, only a constant conflict between man and man. Each wanted to capture the sun within his palms, and to burn the other if need be. His mother, brothers, sisters-in-law, love and affection, had no place here. The wheels of human activity continued to grind around him, on all sides, unceasingly, threatening to crush him at the slightest carelessness. There was no escape; all routes appeared inexorably closed.

Tears welled up in his eyes. There was a wooden bench nearby. Apurba sat down on it and began to wipe away his tears. Suddenly there was a violent push from behind and he found himself on the ground. When he managed to get up he found five or six Anglo-Indian boys, some with cigarettes and some with pipes dangling from their lips, grinning at him. One of them who had possibly knocked him down now pointed to something written on the bench and said in broken Hindi, 'Bastard, this bench is meant for sahibs; not for you!'

Shame, insult and indignation made Apurba miserable. His eyes turned moist and red, his lips began to quiver. He was unable to say anything. His plight caused great amusement among the Anglo-Indian boys. One of them said, 'You native milkman, you've the cheek to glare at us! Wish to go to jail, eh?' All burst into loud laughter. One of them let out a whistle and made an obscene gesture.

Apurba's sanity deserted him. In a moment he would have pounced on the boys. But some north Indian workmen, who had been sitting nearby cleaning the lamps, intervened and pushed him out of the platform. One Anglo-Indian boy pushed his way in and kicked Apurba from behind, leaving the imprint of his boot on Apurba's white shirt. Apurba was trying to free himself from the clutches of the workmen when one of them gave him a push, and said mockingly, 'Bengali Babu, if you even so much as touch a sahib, you'll be put behind bars for one year. Go . . . . run away!'

Another said, 'Can't you see he's a Babu? Don't push him like this!' Saying this, he closed the platform gate.

Soon a crowd gathered around Apurba. Those who had not witnessed the incident wanted to know what had happened. Those who had witnessed it began passing various remarks. One hawker, who had lived in Calcutta for some time and had picked up the language, soon explained to everyone that people from Chittagong came here to sell milk. They wore loose shirts and shoes. After returning from office, Apurba had discarded his European dress and had put on traditional Indian clothes. So when he came to the station, the sahibs mistook him to be a milkman and had assaulted him. They did not know that he was a clerk in some office.

Apurba somehow managed to escape from the company of these people with their excuses and misplaced sympathy. He enquired for the Station Master's room, found it, and entered. The Station Master was a sahib. He was busy in his work. Apurba showed him the imprint of the boot on his shirt, and then narrated the whole incident. The Station Master listened for a minute or so with annoyance and contempt, and then said, 'Why did you go and sit on a bench reserved for Europeans?'

'I didn't know,' said Apurba, agitated

'You ought to have known.'

'But that doesn't mean they'll assault me?'

Pointing to the door, the Station Master shouted, 'Go now, get out!' He called his attendant and, after ordering him to throw Apurba out, resumed his work.

Apurba did not remember how he managed to reach his house. About a couple of hours ago, while going out with Ramdas he had resented his unnecessary meddlesomeness. For one thing, that would not lessen his harassment and tension; it would simply increase it. Besides, whatever might have been the fault of that Christian girl, it was not proper for a man to utter such rude words to a woman, that too when she was alone. His educated, gentle heart had then felt unhappy at Ramdas's behaviour. But now, as he walked back, his sense of regret seemed to have vanished. He remembered her not as woman, but as the daughter of a Christian, the daughter of a sahib, as a sister to

49

those Anglo-Indian brutes who had insulted him, assaulted him for no reason whatsoever, who were ill-educated, vulgar barbarians. He saw her as being close to that sahib who had unjustly denied him even the basic rights as a human being and had so unceremoniously driven him out of his room.

'Your dinner is served,' said Tewari.

'Coming,' replied Apurba.

After ten-fifteen minutes, Tewari reminded, 'It's getting cold.'

Apurba said angrily, 'Don't irritate me! I won't have anything! I don't feel hungry!'

Apurba could not get any sleep that night. As the night advanced, his bed pricked him like a bed of thorns. An excruciating pain seemed to spread all over his body. He remembered the north Indian workmen at the railway station, who were there in such a large number and yet did nothing to stop his humiliation, rather helped perpetrate it. Was there any other country in the world where a native suffers so much indignity and humiliation in the presence of his own countrymen? What was the reason for this? Why does this happen?

CHAPTER 4

Two-three days passed without any fresh trouble. When the Sahib's anger did not burst out in any new form, Apurba surmised the Christian girl had not told her father about the happenings of that day. In view of her earlier attempt to appease him with a gift of fruits, her decision not to inform her father appeared not only natural but extremely logical. There was a constant flow of visitors of different shades and sizes to the flat upstairs in these two days. He had also passed her by once or twice on the staircase. Every time she would look the other way and climb up or down. But he had escaped meeting her vicious father even once. However, from the sound of his heavy boots it was clear that he was at home.

That morning, after serving him lunch, Tewari said, 'It appears the Sahib didn't lodge the complaint after all!'

'So it happens,' said Apurba. 'The dog that barks seldom bites.'

'Still, we shouldn't stay here any longer. Next time the fellow gets drunk, he'll again create trouble.'

'No need to be afraid of that.'

'Even then, with Christian neighbours eating all sorts of things. To just think of it . . . .'

'Ugh! Will you stop, Tewari?' warned Apurba. He was eating. The mere mention of their food habits was enough to cause him nausea. 'We'll shift by the end of this month. We've first to find a good house, don't we?'

Tewari realised it had been indiscreet on his part to bring up this topic at that moment. He felt ashamed and kept quiet.

That afternoon, when Apurba returned from office he was surprised to look at Tewari. The man seemed to have shrivelled up in the course of those few hours.

'What's the matter?' he enquired.

In reply, Tewari handed over a bunch of yellow-coloured printed papers. It was a summons from the criminal court. The plaintiff was Mr. J. D. Joseph, and defendants, the tenants of Room No. 3 — a Bengali gentleman and his servant. There were several charges. The court bearer had come during midday and served it. He would be back the next morning to serve another. The Sahib had come along. They were required to appear before the court the day after. Apurba went through the summons silently and then returned it to Tewari. 'We'll have to attend the court, that's all.'

Tewari was almost in tears. 'But I've never been in the dock before.'

Apurba was annoyed. 'Neither have I. If you've to start crying over every thing, why did you come?'

'But I know nothing.'

'Then why did you have to go out with that stave? You should've sat tight in your room instead!' Apurba went to his room and started changing his clothes.

Next day he received his own summons, and on the following day he appeared before the court on time, along with Tewari. He had no previous experience of such criminal cases. He was in a foreign country. He had no acquaintances here, no one to help him, and yet, strangely enough, he was not at all perturbed. It was not clear even to him from where he suddenly got such strength of mind. He hesitated to tell Ramdas anything about the case, or to seek his help in this matter. He simply took leave for a day from Mr. Rozen for attending to urgent personal work.

His case was taken up at the appointed hour. The Deputy Commissioner himself tried the case. In his deposition the plaintiff, Mr. Joseph, told all sorts of half-truths, untruths, as he pleased. There was no lawyer from the defendant's side. In his own statement Apurba gave an absolutely true version of the incident; he neither suppressed, nor exaggerated anything. The

52

only witness for the plaintiff was his daughter. In the course of her evidence, her antecedents came to light. Apurba was greatly surprised by what he heard. She was apparently the daughter of one late Raj Kumar Bhattacharya of Barisal. The girl's name was Mary Bharati. Mr. Bhattacharya had himself attained enlightenment by embracing Christianity. After his death, his wife came to Bangalore as an attendant to the daughter of a missionary. There she succumbed to the charms of Mr. Joseph and married him. The girl renounced her ancestral surname 'Bhattacharya' as it appeared old-fashioned and ugly and adopted the surname 'Joseph' instead. So she was now known as Miss Mary Bharati Joseph.

When questioned by the Magistrate, she denied having gone to Apurba's rooms with the fruits. But her tone and face betrayed the truth so clearly that it did not escape the attention of not only the Magistrate, but also of his orderly.

As no lawyer had been engaged by either party, there was no scope for making a mountain out of a molehill. The trial was over the same day. Tewari was found not guilty and acquitted, but Apurba was fined twenty rupees. This sentence in a court of law on a false charge so early in life pained Apurba greatly. He paid the amount, and as he came out of the courtroom he found Ramdas standing near the door. Apurba burst out, 'They fined me twenty rupees! What should we do now? File an appeal?'

His voice cracked under anguish and excitement. Ramdas clasped his hands and said, 'You want to spend two thousand to save twenty rupees?'

'But a fine, a punishment!'

Ramdas smiled. 'What punishment? Punishment based on false charges, on false evidence, by a false judge! But there's a higher court where the judge makes no mistakes — you've been found not guilty there. I can assure you!'

'But people won't accept that! This will remain as a

permanent blot on my name!'

Ramdas gently pressed Apurba's hand. 'Come, let's go for a walk by the side of the river.'

As they were walking, Ramdas said, 'I may be your subordinate in office, but I'm older than you in age. I'd like to tell you a few things. Kindly don't mind.'

Apurba kept quiet. Ramdas went on, 'I knew all about this case. I had also no doubt in my mind what'd be the verdict. As for public opinion . . . everyone knows what's to be expected when a case such as yours comes up for hearing before a British court. As regards the stigma caused by a fine of twenty rupees . . . .'

'But for no fault of mine?'

'Yes. I suffered imprisonment for two years for no fault of mine.'

'Imprisonment? For two years?'

'Yes, and . . . .' He smiled. Placing Apurba's hand on his own shoulder, he said, 'If I remove my shirt, you could see the scars on my back.'

'You were whipped, Ramdas?'

Ramdas nodded his head and said with a smile, 'And for no fault of mine. Yet I'm shameless enough to show my face to others. And you can't bear the loss of twenty rupees?'

Apurba continued to stare at Ramdas, dumbfounded. They had been leaning against a lamp-post. Now a man came to light the lamp. Startled to find that it had already become dark, Ramdas said, 'It's late. Come, I'll see you to your place and then go home.'

'So soon? But I had lots of things to ask you!'

Ramdas smiled. 'Want to know everything today itself? That's not possible. I'll tell everything over a period of time.' He emphasized the words 'over a period of time' in such a way that Apurba could not help looking at him in utter astonishment. But his smiling calm face gave no hint of any secret. Ramdas did not enter the lane leading to Apurba's house but took leave from the main road itself and went on straight to the railway station.

Apurba came and knocked at the door. Tewari opened it. He had come back earlier to attend to the household work. He looked grave and sullen.

'In your hurry you had dropped two ten-rupee notes,' he told Apurba.

Apurba was surprised. 'Where did I drop them?'

'Here.' He pointed to the doorway with his feet. 'I've kept them under your pillow. You're lucky you didn't drop them on the main road.'

Wondering how the notes could have fallen from his pocket, Apurba went to his room.

CHAPTER 5

After dinner that night, Tewari came to Apurba with folded hands and requested tearfully, 'Please listen to this old man. Let's go away somewhere else tomorrow morning itself.'

'Tomorrow morning itself? Where? You suggest we take refuge in some *dharamsala*?'

'Even that'd be better. Now that the Sahib has won the case, one of these days he'll break into our flat and assault us.'

It was too much for Apurba to tolerate. He said angrily, 'Did mother send you with me to add insult to my injury? You needn't stay here any longer. There's a ship leaving for Calcutta tomorrow. You go back. I'll face whatever is in store for me.'

Tewari did not say anything more and went to bed. His words had been too much for Apurba to tolerate, and had invited such a harsh reply from him. Otherwise whatever Tewari had said was not all that unreasonable; that much even Apurba had to admit. So, from the next morning, Apurba started looking around for another house. He requested almost everyone in the office, except Talwarkar, for help in locating one. Tewari made no further complaint, and Apurba also did not tell him anything. But both spent their days in apprehension and tension. Every day, while returning from the office, Apurba used to be apprehensive lest something might have happened during his absence. But nothing happened. It was expected that the Joseph family, flushed with their victory in the court case, would invent new and varied ways to torment them daily. But not to speak of any torment, sometimes one wondered if anyone at all lived in the upper storey. But neither the master, nor the servant, had any desire to discuss these possibilities. The days were passing by peacefully without any further trouble —

56

that itself was enough for them.

After a week or so, one evening, when Apurba returned from office, Tewari told him excitedly, 'Have you heard what has happened?

'What?'

'The Sahib is in hospital with a broken leg. Doubtful if he'll survive. Happened six days back . . . the very next day after the case!'

Apurba asked in surprise, 'But how did you come to know?'

'The landlord's agent belongs to our district. He had come to collect the rent today. But there was no one upstairs. The Sahib had been involved in a drunken brawl. He fell off the jetty and is now laid up in the hospital.'

'I see,' said Apurba, and went off to his room.

Since his departure from Calcutta, Tewari felt genuinely happy for the first time today. He very much wanted to discuss these new developments, but his master showed little interest. But what if he did not? Tewari went on to say that he knew this was bound to happen. He may not be familiar with all the prayer rituals, but he knew the *gayatri mantra* by heart. Since the day of the court judgment he had been reciting the *mantra* one hundred and eight times, twice a day. The young master may not have realised the real reason for the Sahib's injuries, but Tewari's belief in the efficacy of the *mantra* increased thousandfold. If a non-Brahmin dared jump about over a Brahmin's head like a horse, his legs had to break!

Next morning, Apurba told Tewari, 'The office attendant says there's a vacant house. Go and see if it's suitable.'

Tewari smiled. 'That won't be necessary. I've found out everything. The other party is leaving on the first of the next month. After all, it's not an easy job to change houses!'

Apurba knew this only too well. But he could not be sure that the peace that now prevailed in the

Sahib's absence would continue once he returned. He knew therefore that ultimately they would have to shift. As he was leaving for his office, Tewari announced that he wanted leave to go to see a programme in a Buddhist temple in the afternoon.

Apurba felt amused. He asked, 'How's it that you've suddenly become interested in Buddhist shows?'

'If I've to stay here, I feel I should know all there is to know.'

'That's right! The Sahib is in the hospital, so there's no risk in going out. Go, but try to return early. Anyone going with you?'

The man from Tewari's native district, whom he had met the previous day, had offered to take him along. The news about the Sahib's accident had pleased Tewari so much that he had readily agreed.

Apurba gave him permission and left for his office. In about an hour's time Tewari's friend came and took him out. Tewari knew that Apurba had a duplicate key with him, so he would not be put to any inconvenience even if he was late in returning. Free of all anxiety, Tewari was in a really happy mood.

When Apurba got back from his office, he found the door still locked. He took out the duplicate key from his pocket and tried to open the lock, but found that it did not fit. On closer examination he discovered that it was not his lock, but someone else's. Apurba was bewildered. Why did Tewari have to use this new lock in place of their old one? Where was its key? And how was he to enter? As he stood there, undecided as to what to do, the Christian girl called out from upstairs, 'Wait, I'll open the door.' So saying, she came down and stood beside him. Apurba was flabbergasted. It was not clear to him what had happened to Tewari and how the key had fallen into the hands of this girl.

There was not enough space for two persons to stand on that narrow and ill-lighted staircase. Apurba descended one step and stood there, looking the other way. He had no previous experience of conversing with

58

strange young girls in lonely places. So when the girl said, 'My mother was telling me that I shouldn't have locked the room and that this could land me in trouble,' Apurba was much too confused to give an immediate reply.

Bharati opened the door, and said, 'My mother is a very timid person. She's been chiding me ever since. She says that you mightn't believe me and put me in jail on a charge of theft. But I'm not frightened at all!'

Unable to follow, Apurba enquired, 'What's the matter?'

'Enter the house and see for yourself.' Bharati stepped aside.

When Apurba saw what had happened, he was dumbfounded. The trunks had been broken open, and everything — books, papers, pillows, bedding, clothes — lay scattered on the floor. He could simply blurt out, 'How did all this happen? Who did it?'

Bharati smiled. 'Whoever it may have been, it wasn't I. I might be your enemy, but you'll have to believe this.' She then recounted what had happened.

Her mother had seen Tewari leave with his new friend, from the upstairs balcony. Soon afterwards she heard some sounds coming from Apurba's flat. She became suspicious and asked Bharati to see what was the matter. There was a chink in the wooden floor through which one could see Apurba's flat clearly. Bharati peeped in through this chink and saw the burglars. She raised an alarm and the burglars ran away. She then locked the door with one of their locks, and kept a watch lest they should come back. Finally, seeing that Apurba had returned, she came down to open the door for him.

Ashen, Apurba sank down in his bed. Bharati peeped in and asked. 'Is it okay if I come in?'

Apurba nodded his head. 'Come.'

When she had entered, Apurba asked, 'Now what's to be done?' He was at his wit's end.

59

'First we've to see what's been stolen.'

'Very well. Please see.'

Bharati smiled. 'Neither did I do your packing, nor have I stolen your things. Then how can I know what's been stolen?'

Apurba felt embarrassed. 'That's true. Then let's wait till Tewari returns. He'll be able to say what's been stolen.' He looked helplessly at the scattered articles.

His utter helplessness amused Bharati. She said smilingly, 'If he can find out what's missing, why can't you? Okay, I'll teach you how to do it.'

She squatted on the floor and pulled the trunk towards her. 'Let's arrange the clothes first,' she said. 'I guess they didn't get time to take these.'

She began to fold and arrange the *dhotis, chadars,* shirts and coats that lay scattered on the floor. Apurba noticed the expert skill with which she did it.

'What's this? Silk suit, isn't it? How many did you have?'

'Two sets.'

'Right. Both are here.' She arranged and put them in the trunk.

'*Dhotis* . . . one, two, three. *Chadars* . . . one, two, three. You had three sets, no? . . . . Isn't this an alpaca coat? Where is the waistcoat and the trousers? Oh, no, this is a buttoned-up coat. You didn't have a suit, did you?'

'No, only the coat; no suit.'

Bharati arranged these in the trunk and then picked up another. 'A flannel suit . . . you used to play tennis, isn't it? There are three here, one's on the clothes horse, and you've put on one. That makes it five sets, right?'

'Absolutely right,' said Apurba. 'Indeed, I had five sets.'

Noticing something glittering under the clothes, Bharati pulled it out. 'It's a gold chain! But where's the watch?'

'Thank God, they didn't see the chain,' exclaimed

Apurba. 'It belonged to my father . . . a memento from him.'

'But where's the watch?'

'Here,' said Apurba, and pulled out the gold watch from his pocket.

'So both the chain and the watch are here. Now tell me, how many rings did you have? I don't see any on your fingers.'

'I don't have any . . . neither on my fingers, nor in the trunk.'

'Right. Gold buttons? Possibly you're wearing them.'

'No,' said Apurba anxiously. 'They were kept with the silk shirt, in the trunk, right on top!'

Bharati glanced at the clothes horse, searched amongst the clothes still on the floor, and then said with a smile, 'Both are missing. Did you have any other buttons?'

Apurba shook his head.

Bharati enquired, 'Any money in the trunk?' Apurba nodded. 'Then I'm afraid that's gone too. You don't remember how much was there, d'you? I'd guessed as much. I know you carry a purse. Come, show it to me.'

Apurba took out the purse from his pocket and handed it over to Bharati. She emptied the contents on the floor, counted the money and said, 'Two hundred fifty rupees and eight annas. D'you remember how much you had with you when you left home?'

'Six hundred,' replied Apurba.

Bharati took a piece of paper and a pencil from the table and noted down: 'Steamer fare, carriage fare, coolie charges . . . you must've sent a telegram home. One rupee for that. Then household expenses for the last ten days . . . .'

'But we'll have to consult Tewari for that,' said Apurba.

Bharati shook her head. 'We'll manage. There'll be a difference of one or two rupees at best, not more.'

She did not disclose that she had been using the

chink, through which she detected the theft today, in the past as well, so as to keep a track of each and every activity that went on in the downstairs flat, right from Tewari's shopping to the dishes which he cooked. She noted on the piece of paper some figures and then looked up. 'Any other expenses?'

'No.'

Bharati did some calculations and said, 'That means two hundred and eighty rupees has been stolen.'

Apurba was startled. 'So much? Wait, wait, deduct twenty rupees. We haven't taken the fine into account.'

Bharati shook her head. 'But that was unjustified, totally wrong. I won't deduct it.'

Apurba was surprised. 'But I don't understand. The charge may have been false, the money that I paid wasn't.'

'Why did you pay the fine? No, I won't deduct that amount. So altogether two hundred and eighty rupees has been stolen.'

'No, two hundred and sixty rupees.'

'Two hundred and eighty.'

Apurba did not argue further. The girl's extraordinary intelligence and all-round sharpness had amazed him. Her inability to realise, and her obstinacy in not accepting such a simple thing, therefore, surprised him. Regardless of whether the judgment was right or wrong, the fine had actually been paid. He realised that it was futile to argue with someone who refused to understand this simple fact.

Bharati arranged the remaining clothes and then stood up.

Apurba asked, 'D'you think I ought to inform the police?'

Bharati shook her head. 'No. That'll only mean unnecessary harassment for me. You don't think the police will actually come and return your money, do you?'

Apurba kept quiet.

Bharati continued, 'The loss, you'll have to bear. By

informing them you'll only invite further harassment.'
'But the law. . .?'

Even before Apurba could finish, Bharati retorted
impatiently 'Law or no law, I won't allow you to do
this. Wasn't there any law the day you were fined? Or
have you forgotten that so soon?'

'If someone files false charges, gives false evidence
— is it the fault of the law?'

Bharati's face did not reveal any trace of embarrassment. She said, 'So you think if no one were to tell
lies or frame false cases, the law would be perfect? No
doubt that would be ideal, but such things don't happen in real life. Even if it were to happen, it'd take
a very, very long time.'

She smiled. But Apurba did not join issue with her
and kept quiet. The first time he had met this girl,
her sweet tone, gentle, bashful nature, and specially
her compassion and solicitude had fascinated him. But
this had disappeared completely as a result of her
subsequent conduct. Bharati's eagerness not to report
the theft to the police therefore aroused Apurba's
suspicions. He could no longer accept her unasked-for
help happily. The apprehension of some unknown
deception turned everything bitter. Bharati's hesitant
and secretive offering of fruits to him, her subsequent
distorted and incorrect presentation of the whole
episode, and finally giving false evidence in the court
— all this flashed through his mind. His face became
stern and his voice heavy. Every thing she did appeared artificial and deceptive. Bharati noticed the
change in his features but could not understand the
reason. She said, 'You didn't reply to what I said.'

'What's there to say? The thief mustn't be allowed to
go scot-free. I have to report the matter to the police.'

Bharati was frightened. 'Please don't,' she pleaded.
'Neither will the thief be caught, nor will you get your
money back. I'll only be unnecessarily harassed. I witnessed the theft, I locked up the room, I even helped
arrange your things . . . I'll be in serious trouble.'

'You've only to say what actually happened.'

Bharati was very upset. 'Only the other day we had such a quarrel,' she said. 'We've not been on speaking terms even. After all that, won't they be suspicious of my sudden solicitude for you? Why should they believe what I say?'

Apurba became even more suspicious. He said sternly, 'They could believe all your false statements, so why won't they believe the truth? The money that has been stolen is quite insignificant, but I'm determined not to let the thief go unpunished.'

Bharati was completely bewildered. She continued to look at Apurba vacantly. 'How could you say that? My father isn't a good man, he has harassed you greatly for nothing, I've also helped him in doing so. I know everything. But break into your house and steal your money — how could you even think of such a thing? I couldn't dream of doing that! How can I face such a scandal?' Her lips began to quiver. Biting hard to control herself, she rushed out.

CHAPTER 6

Next morning when Apurba set out for the police station he was not sure himself what prompted him to do so. He had no doubt in his mind that it was useless to report the theft to the police. The money would never be recovered, nor the thieves apprehended — that much confidence he had on the police. But at the same time he was full of aversion and indignation towards that Christian girl. Though he could not be as certain as Tewari that she had either committed the theft herself, or if not, had acted as an accomplice, her hypocrisy and deception annoyed him. Whatever faults Mr. Joseph might have had, no one could blame him for being a hypocrite. His devilry was undiluted, the lash of his whip unpretentious, his neighbourly behaviour unambiguous, voice remorseless, talk lucid and unequivocal, drunken footsteps loud and clear — in short, one could understand him. One could not say the same for his daughter. There was a total lack of consistency between her words and deeds. The harm done by her did not irritate Apurba so much as her inscrutable conduct from the very beginning; it seemed an insult to his intelligence. It was doubtful whether, despite his anger, he could ultimately have been able to recount the whole thing before the police, but the matter did not go that far. Suddenly he heard someone calling from behind, 'Apurba, is it you? Here?'

Apurba turned around and saw; it was Nimaibabu. Though dressed simply, he was a senior police officer of the Bengal government. Apurba's father had helped him in getting the job, and had been his patron. Nimaibabu looked upon him as his elder brother, and by the same analogy Apurba and his brothers used to call him 'Uncle.' The fact that Apurba had not been arrested or punished for his activities during the *swadeshi* movement was largely due to his efforts.

Apurba bowed before him, informed him about his own appointment, and then enquired, 'But what brings you here?'

Nimaibabu blessed him, and said, 'You're still a child. If you could come here leaving your dear and near ones, can't I?' He took out the watch from his pocket, checked the time, and then said, 'I'm in a hurry. But you've ample time before your office opens. Why not come with me? We can talk on the way. It's ages since I've been to your house. How's your mother? Brothers?'

Apurba informed him that they were well, and then enquired, 'Where are you going now?'

'To the wharf. Why don't you come along?'

'All right. D'you have to go anywhere else?'

Nimaibabu smiled. 'Maybe. I've come all the way to receive and escort a great person. Everything now depends on him. I've got his photograph and detailed description. But the Burmese police still can't lay their hands on him. I doubt if even I'll succeed.'

Apurba understood the hint. He became inquisitive and asked, 'Who's this great person, Uncle? Considering that you've come, I guess he must be a Bengali. Is he a murderer?'

'I really can't say. Nobody knows for certain. There aren't any specific charges against him either, but whatever there is, takes the cake. Even the all-powerful government is at its wit's end just trying to keep a watch over him.'

'I see. Political activist?'

Nimaibabu shook his head. 'Come on, at one time even you and your friends were called political activists. No, that doesn't do justice to him at all! He's a revolutionary! An enemy of the state! A worthy enemy indeed! The person who named him "Sabyasachi" must've been really inspired. According to the *Maha-bharata*, Arjuna or Sabyasachi could wield both his hands with equal dexterity. But the intelligence reports

66

of the government reveals that in the case of this man, each of his organs is equally dexterous. He never misses a target with gun or pistol. He can swim across the mighty river Padma; nothing can stop him. We suspect he has crossed over the Chittagong hills by foot recently and entered Burma. We're not sure whether he'll come to Rangoon from Mandalay by the steamer, or whether he'll take the train — but of one thing we're certain, that is, that he has already set out for Rangoon. Nor is there any confusion regarding his intentions. His friends and foes are unanimous in their views, and we also know that there can be no change in his attitude as long as he lives. The only thing we don't know is what route he'll follow and what'll be his mode of transport. But take care, my son, don't breathe a word of this to anyone. Otherwise, not only will I be sure to lose my old age pension, I may also be honoured with some additional benefits.'

Apurba grew restive with excitement. 'Where was he all these days, and what was he doing? I don't remember having heard his name before!'

Nimaibabu laughed. 'Such great persons can't afford to have only one name, can they? Like Arjuna, he is known by different names in different regions. Also, you may have heard of him in the past, but can't remember now. Besides, I'm not quite conversant about his recent activities. Enemies of the state don't broadcast their deeds, but this much is known that he has suffered imprisonment once for three months at Poona, and again for three years at Singapore. He can speak a dozen languages so fluently that one would find it difficult to guess what was his mother-tongue. He studied medicine in Germany, engineering in France, law in England, and since he lived for some time in America, he must've done something there as well. Like playing cards, these served as recreation for him. But none of these qualifications came to any use. The burning passion he has for his country is like an inextinguishable flame coursing through his veins! Torture him, torment him, it'll not cease as long as he lives! He has neither compassion nor attachment, no faith in religion, no home, no hearth, nothing! We also belong to the same place, but he's so different from us! One wonders how such a man was at all born in Bengal!

Apurba was too excited to speak. The flow of blood seemed to quicken in his veins. After walking silently for some time, he asked in a low voice, 'Will you arrest him today?'

Nimaibabu smiled. 'Let's get him first.'

'Supposing you do?'

'It isn't as easy as that. I'm almost certain that he must've escaped by some other route.'

'But suppose he hasn't?'

Nimaibabu thought for a few moments and then replied, 'My orders are to keep him under surveillance. I'll keep a watch on him for a couple of days. Keeping a watch yields better results than merely arresting — that's the government's latest thinking.'

Apurba was not fully convinced because Nimaibabu was after all a police officer; yet he breathed a sigh of relief. 'How old is he?'

'Not much,' replied Nimaibabu. 'Maybe thirty or thirty-two years old.'

'And appearance?'

'That's the strangest thing. Such a dangerous person has the most inconspicuous appearance, just like any common man. Hence it's difficult to recognise him or to catch him. There is special mention of this in our reports.'

'Is it to avoid arrest that he has used the hilly tracks to cross over?' asked Apurba.

'Not necessarily. He may've had some other purpose . . . possibly to familiarize himself with the route . . . one can't say anything definitely. The ways of such revolutionaries are quite different from those of common people. Let's see who wins in the end . . . him or us! On the other hand, it's also quite possible that all our running around may be in vain.'

Apurba laughed. 'I hope and pray that it be so,' he said.

Nimaibabu also laughed. 'You really shouldn't say such things to a police officer, should you? Anyway, what did you say was the number of your house? Thirty, was it? Let me see, if it's possible, I'll drop in some time tomorrow morning . . . . I think his steamer will dock at this jetty . . . it's time for your office. You shouldn't be late at your new job.' He quickened his pace.

'Not to speak of being late,' said Apurba, 'I wouldn't mind even bunking office today. I don't want him to fall into your hands, but even if that were to happen, I'd get to see him at least. Come, let's go.'

Though Nimaibabu was unwilling, he did not raise any objection. However, he cautioned Apurba, 'It's understandable that you'd want to see him, but let me warn you, it's dangerous to have any sort of acquaintance with such people. You're no longer a child. Your father is also no more. You've to act responsibly, for your own future.'

Apurba smiled. 'As if you'd let anyone come near him. He has committed no crime, there's no charge against him, and yet you've come all the way to trap him!'

Nimaibabu simply smiled. That was significant enough. He said, 'Duty.'

Duty? Apurba knew that this single word covered hundreds of good and bad deeds in this world. So he did not press the issue further and kept quiet.

When they reached the jetty they saw that a large steamer was about to dock. Some policemen were already there in plain clothes. Apurba could identify them from the significant glances which they exchanged with Nimaibabu. They were all Indians who had come all the way to Burma to hunt down a revolutionary who was working for the good of India. The prey was almost in their hands now. Apurba

69

noticed a look of happiness and excitement on their faces. Overwhelmed by shame and sorrow, he turned his face away. His anguished heart went out to that unfortunate, unknown stranger.

The sailors were throwing the hawsers to fasten the ship. So many passengers leaned against the railing, watching this. On the deck there was haste, commotion, hustle-bustle. In that crowd maybe there was one who watched the shoreline with wistful eyes — Apurba's own eyes filled with tears, blurring his vision. So many people stood there, men and women, on the ship, on the dock, unafraid, unapprehensive. Why was it that imprisonment and death awaited one who had willingly sacrificed all desires, hopes and aspirations of his young heart?

The ship berthed. The gangway was lowered. Nimaibabu and his men took their stand on both sides of it. But Apurba did not move from his place. He stood, rooted to the ground like a stone statue. He thought, 'After a few minutes there'll be chains around your hands, the curious crowd will witness your humiliation and insult; they will never know that it was for them that you had sacrificed all you had, and for that you're being removed from their midst.' Tears rolled down his cheeks.

Addressing the man he had never seen before, he said to himself, 'You're no ordinary mortal like us. You've sacrificed everything for your motherland. It's because of this that the boats of your country don't carry you, and you've to swim and cross the river Padma; because of this that the highways are closed to you, and you've to cross the hills and mountains on foot. Long ago, sometime in the dim past, iron chains had been first fashioned to bind you; prison cells built to hold you in bondage. That is your glory! Who can dare to neglect you? These numerous sentries, this huge army, they are meant only for you. God has imposed upon your shoulders this heavy burden because you alone are capable of bearing it. O, harbinger of freedom, revolutionary of a subject nation, I salute you!'

Absorbed in his own thoughts, Apurba stood totally unmindful of the milling crowd around him, their movements and their curious looks. In an emotional upsurge, tears streamed down his eyes. He was oblivious of the time spent. Suddenly he was awakened from his reverie by Nimaibabu's call. Hurriedly he wiped his tears and made an attempt to smile. Nimaibabu was surprised to notice Apurba's distracted, bewildered look, but offered no comments. 'Our fears have come true,' he said, 'He has again given us the slip.'

'But how could he escape?'

'Had I known that, he wouldn't have escaped,' said Nimaibabu. 'Altogether there must've been about three hundred passengers — twenty or twenty-five Sahibs and Anglo-Indians, about a hundred and fifty Oriyas, south Indians, and Punjabis; the rest were Burmese. What disguise he put on and what language he had used to escape, even God wouldn't know, not to speak of poor mortals like us. Who knows whether he was dressed like a Sahib or a native? Jagdishbabu has taken a few Bengalis to the police station on suspicion. There's some resemblance with one of them as well. But that's about all; he's not our man. Would you like to come and have a look at the fellow?'

Apurba felt his heart pound with excitement. 'I wouldn't like to go in case you've to use third degree methods,' he said.

Nimaibabu smiled. 'I let so many passengers go away, why should I now beat up these few fellows just because they're Bengalis? The police aren't all that bad, as you seem to think. Of course there are good and bad people in every department, but if you had any idea how much unhappiness we've to suffer silently, you wouldn't have hated this uncle of yours so much.'

Apurba felt embarrassed. 'You've come to do your duty,' he said. 'Why should I hate you for that?' He

71

bowed down and took the dust from his feet.

Nimaibabu was pleased. He blessed Apurba and said, 'That's all right. Come, let's go quickly. The poor fellows must be both hungry and thirsty. I'll release them after a brief interrogation.' He clasped Apurba's hand and took him along.

On entering the police station, they found about half a dozen Bengalis seated in a hall along with their luggage. Jagdishbabu had already opened their trunks and bundles and started his investigation. Only one man who had aroused his greatest suspicion had been locked up in a separate room. The men were all workers in the Burmah Oil Company in Upper Burma. The climate there did not suit them, so they had come to Rangoon in search of new jobs. After noting their names and addresses and examining their luggage, they were all released. Then the political suspect, Sabyasachi Mallick, was produced before Nimaibabu.

The man entered coughing. His age would not be more than thirty or thirty-two, but he appeared to be thin and emaciated. He began to pant after a bout of coughing. It did not seem the man had long to live; some incurable disease seemed to be eating into his vitals. But he had the most remarkable pair of eyes. To describe them as large or small, round or slanted, bright or lacklustre, would be a futile exercise. It was like a deep, unfathomable pond. Something in it hinted of danger; it seemed safer to keep a distance. Somewhere at the bottom of this pond was hidden his frail life-force, where even death seemed afraid to enter; that was how he had escaped death so far.

Apurba could not take his eyes off him. Suddenly Nimaibabu took notice of the man's rather fashionable clothes and said with a laugh, 'The fellow's health has been shattered, but his love for stylish clothes is still intact! What'd you say, Apurba?'

Observing the man's dress, Apurba turned his face to hide his laughter. The man sported long hair in the front, but so closely was it cropped in the back

72

and sides as to make him look practically bald. It was parted in the middle, and a liberal use of lemon oil filled the room with offensive smell. He wore a colour-ful Japanese silk shirt, but had no shawl. A printed handkerchief having the imprint of a tiger's face hung out of his breast-pocket. Around his waist he had wrapped a fine English mill-made *sari* with a black border; a pair of green stockings were tied above his knees with red laces, and on his feet he wore shoes of shining leather, the soles studded with nails to make them durable. In his hand he carried a cane with a handle of horn. Everything on him was dirty after the long voyage. Apurba eyed him from top to bottom and remarked, 'You may release him even without an in-terrogation, Uncle. I can bet he's not the man you're looking for!'

Nimaibabu kept quiet. Apurba added, 'Above every-thing, consider that man's culture.'

Nimaibabu nodded and smiled. 'What's your name?' he asked.

'Girish Mahapatra, sir.'

'Really? You were also working in the oil mill, eh? Now you intend staying in Rangoon, right? They've already inspected your box and bedding. Now let me see what you've tucked in your clothes and pockets.'

One rupee and about six annas were tucked in his waist-cloth. His pockets yielded one iron compass, a wooden foot ruler, a few *bidis*, one match-box and a pipe for smoking hashish.

'So you smoke hashish?' enquired Nimaibabu.

'No, sir,' replied the man unhesitatingly.

'Then what's this thing doing in your pocket?'

'I found it lying on the way, sir. I kept it in case someone needs it.'

At that time Jagdishbabu entered the room. 'Look, Jagdish,' said Nimaibabu. 'What a kind-hearted fellow we have here! He's carrying this pipe lest someone should need it. Here, show me your palm.' So saying, the old and experienced police officer caught hold of

73

the man's right palm, looked at it for a few moments and then said with a smile, 'The stains are quite clear. You could've as well said that you smoke hashish. But how long will you live . . . your health is already shattered . . . better give it up. Listen to this old man's advice.'

The man shook his head. 'I swear I don't smoke hashish. If any friend comes and requests for a smoke, I only prepare it for him. I don't smoke it myself, I swear.'

Jagdishbabu lost his temper. 'What an ocean of kindness! Only prepares for others, doesn't smoke it himself. Damned liar!'

'It's getting late,' said Apurba. 'I'd better go now.'

Nimaibabu stood up and said, 'All right, Mahapatra, you may go now. What'd you say, Jagdish?'

When Jagdishbabu indicated his assent, Nimaibabu added, 'But we can't be very sure. I think we should continue to keep a watch for a few days more. Also check up the night train. There's no doubt that he has come to Burma.'

'That may be true,' said Jagdishbabu. 'But there's no need to keep a watch over this fellow. He has caused headache to everyone in the police station with his filthy smell of lemon oil.'

Nimaibabu laughed. Apurba came out of the police station and found Mahapatra walking almost alongside with his broken tin trunk in his hand and dirty bedding wrapped in a palm-leaf mat under his armpit. He took the road to the north and departed with slow and steady steps.

74

Strangely enough, Sabyasachi escaped. It was a stroke of good luck that nothing untoward happened. Even then, Apurba could not get it out of his mind. After he returned home, while there was no deviation from his usual daily routine — shaving, bathing, eating, offering prayers, going to office — his mind was totally absorbed by the thought of that unknown revolutionary whom he had never met. He was oblivious of all other worldly affairs.

Apurba's absentmindedness did not escape the notice of Talwarkar. He enquired anxiously, 'Received any letter from home today?'

'Why,. no?'

'Everyone okay?'

'As far as I know, they're fine,' replied Apurba somewhat surprised.

Ramdas did not question further.

They used to take their tiffin together. Ramdas's wife had requested Apurba one day that until his mother or some other female relative came over to look after him, he should partake of the sweets prepared by her. Apurba had agreed. A Brahmin attendant from the office used to fetch these things from Ramdas's house. That day also he had brought the eatables and placed them on a table in the adjacent vacant room. When they sat down to eat, it was Apurba who first initiated the discussion. He narrated about the theft — how, but for the timely intervention of that Christian girl, he would have lost everything; however, due to her prompt action everything was saved excepting a small amount; how she had later locked the door and on Apurba's return had opened it for him; how she had entered the room on her own accord and had helped him arrange all his things; and how she had prepared an absolutely correct list of the articles that had been stolen. 'The efficiency with which she did this work would've been remarkable even for a qualified accountant like you! Indeed, Talwarkar, I haven't seen a more efficient and enterprising girl than her. She has proved herself to be a very good friend!'

'Go on.'

'Tewari wasn't at home; he had gone to see a Burmese dance. The burglary took place in his absence. Tewari suspects the Christian girl. I'm also inclined to think likewise. Even if she hasn't committed it herself, she may have been an accomplice.'

'Then?'

'This morning I went to the police station to report the theft. But they were so busy showing their antics in another matter, I completely forgot about my case. Now I think, what has gone, isn't going to come back; let the police run after revolutionaries instead of trying to catch thieves!'

Suddenly Apurba remembered Girish Mahapatra and his fanciful dress and burst into a fit of laughter. When the laughter subsided, he told Ramdas about this great revolutionary, about his proficiency in science and medicine, who held a diploma in medicine from an English university, and Girish Mahapatra's health, education and taste, his emaciated condition, multi-coloured shirt, parrot-green socks, nail-studded shoes, his liberal use of lemon oil, and lastly, his total nonchalance at the discovery of his hemp-pipe which he swore was kept only for the benefit of others. Apurba burst out laughing as he recounted the whole incident. Suppressing his laughter somehow, he said, 'Never before have the vigilant police force made such asses of themselves. And yet, what a huge amount of government money is wasted in chasing the wild geese!'

Ramdas smiled. 'Well, they're meant for chasing wild geese, not for catching thieves. But tell me, were these police officials Bengalis?'

'Yes, and I'm ashamed to say their superior was an extremely close friend of my father, almost a family

76

member. In fact, it was my father who had helped him in getting the job.'

'Then you may have to make amends for it one day,' said Ramdas. Then, realising that it had not been quite proper for him to have said so, he kept quiet.

Apurba guessed the reason for Ramdas's embarrassment. Anxious to prove that he had not taken it otherwise, he said forcefully, 'It's true I regard him as my uncle. He's close to our family, is our well-wisher, but that doesn't make him dearer to me than my motherland. I'd say that, instead the man whom he's hunting down with the help of our countrymen at the expense of our country, is far more dear to one than him.'

Ramdas simpered, 'You know, you may have to suffer for uttering these words?'

'If so, I'm prepared for that. But not only in my own country, in any corner of the world. Anyone who strives for the freedom of his motherland . . . whoever else may disown him, I can't!'

As he went on speaking, his voice became sharp and his eyes brighter. He realised he should not be saying all this, but was unable to check himself. 'I may not be as brave as you, Ramdas,' he said. 'In fact, I'm rather timid; yet when I've to suffer punishment for no fault of mine, it hurts me deeply. When those Anglo-Indian boys kicked me out of the platform for no fault of mine, and when I went to the Station Master to complain against this and he drove me away from his office like a dog just because I was a native, the insult and humiliation was no less because of the colour of the skin. I'm aware that such incidents take place every day. But those who strive to free my people from such torture, how can I disown them? Whatever suffering that may entail, I'm prepared for it.'

Ramdas's handsome, fair face turned red. 'How's it you haven't told me about this incident?' he enquired.

'It wasn't easy. A number of our countrymen were

present there. And yet, none shared my humiliation; they've become so insensitive. They were happy that none of my ribs were broken. When I think of the incident, sorrow, shame and hatred makes me want to drown myself.'

Ramdas's eyes grew moist. When the clock struck three, he got up. He was about to say something, but did not. Instead, he simply pressed Apurba's hand, and quickly left the room.

That afternoon, before the office closed, Mr. Rozen came to Apurba's room with a long telegram in his hand. 'Our office at Bhamo doesn't seem to be functioning properly,' he said. 'There are problems in the offices at Mandalay, Shwebo, Meiktila and Prome as well. I'd like you to go over there and have a look. Once I leave, the entire responsibility will be on you. It may therefore be advantageous for you to be acquainted with their affairs. I'd suggest that you don't delay but push off in a day or two.'

Apurba agreed at once and said, 'I'm prepared to go tomorrow itself.'

For various reasons, Apurba wanted to get away from Rangoon. Besides, the trip would enable him to tour the country. So the following afternoon Apurba boarded the train for far-off Bhamo. He was accompanied by an orderly and a north Indian Brahmin attendant. Tewari was left behind to look after the house. Mr. Joseph being laid up in the hospital with broken legs, no further ·trouble was anticipated. Moreover, Tewari had somehow reconciled himself to Rangoon; he had no desire to visit other places. Talwarkar thumped Tewari on his back and said, 'Don't worry. In case of any problem, just come over to the office and inform me.'

The train was due to leave in a few minutes. Suddenly Apurba was startled to see someone. He called out, 'Hello there!'

Talwarkar turned around and immediately recognised the man. It was Girish Mahapatra. He sported the

78

same colourful shirt, green stockings, pump shoes and walking stick — the only difference being that the tiger-print handkerchief, instead of being tucked in his breast pocket, was today wrapped round his neck. When the man came nearer, Apurba called out, 'Hey, there, Girish! D'you recognise me? Where are you off to?'

Girish hurriedly bowed and said, 'Of course I recognise you, sir. Where are you going?'

Apurba smiled. 'Now to Bhamo,' he said. 'But where are you off to?'

'Two friends of mine were expected to come from Yenangyaung. I came to meet them . . . . Sir, I was unnecessarily harassed that day. Some people do smuggle opium and hemp. But I'm a God-fearing man. I'm not a swindler. Why should I do such things? It's dangerous. Besides, who can change one's destiny?'

'I also think the same way,' said Apurba smilingly. 'But you're making a mistake. I'm not a police official, nor do I have anything to do with opium or hemp. I happened to be there that day just to watch the fun.'

Talwarkar was scrutinising the man. He now said in Hindi, 'I'm sure I've seen you somewhere before.'

'Not unlikely,' replied Girish. 'I've been going from place to place in search of a job.' Then, turning to Apurba he added, 'Please don't entertain needless suspicions about me, sir. Otherwise it won't be possible for me to get a job anywhere. I'm a Brahmin's son, had learnt to read and write Bengali and also acquired some knowledge of the scriptures, but such is fate . . . . But, sir, you are . . .?'

'I'm a Brahmin,' said Apurba.

'My respectful regards to you. Kindly permit me to go. The Gods be with you.' Trying to suppress a violent fit of coughing, Girish Mahapatra hastily departed.

'You know, Talwarkar, Uncle has been pursuing this great revolutionary in India and abroad with all the police force,' chuckled Apurba.

Talwarkar did not laugh. The next moment there was a whistle and the train started. Ramdas waved his hand to bid farewell, but did not utter a single word. For various reasons Apurba's mind was preoccupied and he did not look at Ramdas carefully; had he done so, he would have seen a shadow darkening Ramdas's broad forehead and his thoughts wandering to some far-off place.

Apurba had a first class ticket, and there was no other passenger in his compartment. After sunset he pulled out the sacred thread from under his shirt and performed his evening prayers, without the usual ablution. He had brought with him such eatables which he knew would not get polluted. He now took them out from the brass container and finished his dinner. His Brahmin attendant had kept some drinking water and betel-leaf in the compartment, and had also made his bed. Apurba went to bed in a happy and contented mood. He had hoped to have an undisturbed peaceful sleep till the next morning. But hardly a few stations later he realised that he was mistaken. His sleep was disturbed at least thrice during the night by Burmese police officials who came to check his identity and antecedents. Once when he protested, the Burmese sub-inspector told him rudely, 'You aren't an European, are you?'

'No,' replied Apurba. 'But I'm a first class passenger. You can't disturb my sleep in this manner.'

The sub-inspector laughed. 'That rule applies only to railway officials. Besides, I'm a policeman. If I want, I can drag you out of the compartment.'

Apurba did not say anything more. However, he was not disturbed again that night and could manage to snatch three-four hours of sleep. When he woke up in the morning he had forgotten the bitterness of the previous night.

The landscape had changed. The track ran along a mountainside. The train was chugging along slowly, possibly because of the gradient. Apurba looked out of

the open window and was overwhelmed by the beauty
of the scenery. He felt he had never seen such a
beautiful sight before. The mountain range which
formed a semi-circle seemed to obstruct the path both
in front and behind. The entire face of the mountain
was covered with thick forests. From its foothills, lofty
trees soared upwards, almost touching the sky. It was
sunrise. Though the fiery orb was still not visible over
the mountaintops, its rays had already tinted the
foliage golden. Numerous streams purled down the
mountainside and settled at its feet like pools of tears.

Apurba was charmed. What a wonderfully beautiful
country! And how singularly lucky were its inhabitants!
Not fully satisfied with the feeling of an unexplicable
happiness, Apurba sought to give it a form, a shape;
sought to colour it with the colours of imagination. In
this way when his poetic mind had created a wondrous
world which overwhelmed him by its charm, he was
rudely shaken out of his reverie to find his magical
world disappear in the desert sands of reality. He
remembered the words of Ramdas Talwarkar. Ramdas
had collected a lot of information about Burma from
various sources, published as well as classified. He had
said, 'Burma is famous not only for its scenic beauty
but also for its natural resources. Very few countries
possess such abundant natural wealth. It has vast and
valuable forests, inexhaustible underground reserves of
oil, an invaluable stock of precious stones in its mines,
and those huge trees that reach up to the sky; is there
anything comparable anywhere?' This happened not
very long ago. The news of Burma's natural wealth
attracted the attention of greedy English merchants.
The consequences were inevitable. Confrontation followed. First the warships came; then the army, guns
and cannons. The weak, inefficient king was defeated
in the war and deported. The jewellery of his queens
were sold to meet the cost of reparations. Thereafter
the British took up the governance of the vanquished
country for its own benefit and for the welfare of its

people, for the sake of humanity, civilization and justice, and engaged themselves heart and soul in its all-round development. Hence the need for such tight security arrangements. Hence a police official of the defeated country has no hesitation in arousing from sleep an innocent passenger of another colony just like him and in saying, 'You're not an European, so why should I refrain from insulting you?'

'Quite so, quite so,' mused Apurba. 'How can I expect anything better from him? And why should he?'

Although the treetops were still golden from the sunrays, they now appeared to him dull and drab. The high mountains looked insignificant and the lofty trees, which had aroused his admiration only a short while back, now appeared commonplace. Remembering the lush green, fertile plains of Bengal, tears welled up in his eyes. Far away from his homeland, his anguished heart seemed to cry out again and again in constant lamentation. 'O, you weak citizens of an unfortunate land! What right have you on that rich, wonderful land of yours? If you are unable to uphold its glory, then why hanker for it at all? The birthright of freedom does not come automatically; it has to be earned. Can one deny this fact? Even the Gods cannot steal it. Can one call such weaklings men? No, no, that's impossible!'

Deeply absorbed in his own thoughts, Apurba lost track of the time. Suddenly, as the train slowed down he was roused from his torpor. He hurriedly wiped the tears off his eyes, looked out and saw that the train was entering the platform.

CHAPTER 8

Since his childhood, Apurba had no great regard for women. Indeed, one could even say that he had a sort of abhorrence for them. When his sisters-in-law cut jokes with him, he would be annoyed. If they tried to get closer, he would move away. Except for his mother, he disliked the care and solicitude of women. He did not approve of women receiving higher education and when he read in the newspapers about agitation in Great Britain for women's rights, he was full of indignation. But he had one thing in him — a soft and gentle heart. He loved everyone alike and it hurt him to cause pain to anyone. He was aware that it was this weakness that had prevented him from punishing Bharati even though he knew she was guilty. But what he did not know yet was that many other weaknesses lurked in the secret recesses of his young heart. While it may not be entirely correct to say that it would be impossible for him to ever punish this Christian girl, similarly it would be impossible to say that he could spurn Bharati simply because he was averse to women. And yet today, he was full of abhorrence for that liar of a woman.

It was a fortnight since he came to Bhamo. His work here was almost over and he was due to leave for Meiktila in a day or two. Seated on the verandah in front of his room that evening after returning from office, he was engaged in seeking a solution to a rather complicated problem — women's liberty. He had never been in favour of this. His personal instincts and traditional beliefs had convinced him against it. At the same time he could not deny the fact that the religious injunctions were sometimes terribly unjust towards women. This pained him, but he found no solution to it. Suddenly, the following incident cleared all his doubts.

A Burmese family lived in the ground floor of the house where Apurba was putting up. That day, in the morning, an unpleasant incident took place. The Burmese gentleman had four daughters, all married. All the four sons-in-law had assembled that day to celebrate some festival. During lunch a quarrel ensued, first among the daughters, and later among the sons-in-law, on the question of prestige and honour. It soon took a bloody turn. Apurba was flabbergasted to know that of the four sons-in-law, one was a south Indian Muslim, another a mixed-breed from Chittagong, the third an Anglo-Indian, and the youngest a Chinese expatriate long settled in that town and engaged in the leather trade. Such cosmopolitan relationships, though rare elsewhere, were quite common here. Although the gentleman had protested each time, his daughters, flushed with their unfettered freedom, paid no heed. It was a routine matter. One fine morning one of the daughters would be missing. She would reappear after a few days with a newly-acquired husband in tow. Thus the gentleman acquired the unique distinction of becoming the father-in-law of such an ill-assorted group of sons-in-law. Their languages differed, temperaments differed, religions differed, tastes differed; their education, traditions and customs had nothing in common. Like the Hindu-Muslim conflict in India, this posed an intractable problem. How could it be resolved?

Full of anguish and indignation, Apurba was convinced that such unfettered freedom for women was neither beneficial, nor permissible. Burma was degenerating. Europe already ruined . . . . If India also imported this alien concept, her miseries would be redoubled. The creators of our social system were aware of the frailties of women, and hence these restrictions. Though harsh, they were ultimately beneficial. In these trying times if their safety was not guaranteed, doom was certain. Sitting alone in the darkness, Apurba continued to ruminate over such

84

matters. But alas, it never struck him that the freedom which he sought to achieve with his body and soul was only a greater manifestation of the freedom of individuals, and by denying this freedom to women he was, in a way, dishonouring freedom itself. Is freedom something as shallow as a bath-tub where you could shut your eyes and relax in safety? No, it is a limitless ocean. Danger lurks in it in the shape of breakers and sharks. Boats founder in it. And yet it gives life to mankind, gives strength, value and meaning to life itself. The shallow waters of the pond may enable one to stay alive but it does not allow him to live.

'Sir, your dinner is ready.'

Apurba was startled. 'Ramsharan,' he said, 'bring a light. We'll leave for Meiktila tomorrow itself. Inform the manager.'

'But, sir, you were due to go there the day after tomorrow.'

'No, tomorrow itself. Bring a light,' ordered Apurba, to stop further discussion. He had seen one aspect of women's freedom in society, and it had confused him. That there could be another aspect whose colour and brilliance could brighten the skies was yet unknown to him.

The next day Apurba left for Meiktila. But after arriving there, he found he was feeling home-sick. There were cantonments for British and native forces. There were a number of Bengalis living there. It was a nice town. It offered many attractions to a new-comer. Yet Apurba did not feel happy. He was eager to return to Rangoon as early as possible. While at Bhamo, he had received a letter from his mother, which had been redirected from Rangoon. He had also received a couple of letters from Ramdas. Ramdas had written that there was no immediate necessity for shifting to a new house. That could wait till Apurba's return to Rangoon. Also, he had personally gone over to see Tewari. He had found him hale and hearty. But that was more than ten days ago. He had received no information since then as to whether peace and tranquillity still prevailed, or it had since disappeared. He presumed that everything must be all right. Yet, as on the earlier occasion, one day, all on a sudden, he decided to leave for Rangoon. He hurriedly packed his things and sent for a carriage to take him to the station. Nothing memorable had occurred during his stay here; the work too had been rather insignificant. Yet, fifteen minutes before the train left, an incident took place which, though apparently commonplace and of no great significance at the moment, would be remembered many a time in future by him.

A drunken Bengali passenger had been forced by railway officials to get down. He was dressed in European clothes, but they were dirty and tattered. Except for a violin, he had nothing with him. He had spent all his money on drinks and had boarded the train without a ticket. Apurba came to his aid. He not only paid his fare, but also gave him five rupees. He was about to leave when the man said with folded hands, 'Sir, take this violin with you. Sell it. Keep the money that I owe you and send me the balance.' Though his voice was slurred, it was clear that he was in his senses.

'Where should I send your money?' enquired Apurba.

'Give me your address,' the man replied. 'I'll let you know where to send it.'

'Keep your violin. I won't be able to sell it. My name is Apurba Haldar. I work for Messrs Botha & Co. at Rangoon. Send me the money when you can.'

The man nodded. 'As you say, sir. I shall certainly send you the money. That's the way to the exit, isn't it? Fairly big town, no? I presume everything should be available. Believe me, sir, I shall never forget your kindness.' He saluted Apurba again and left, clutching his violin.

Apurba observed him carefully. Though he appeared young, it was difficult to exactly guess his age. His intemperate habits made him look at least ten years older. His fair complexion had become tanned; long hair fell over his forehead, his eyes were bleary but the nose, straight and acquiline. His body was emaciated, fingers thin and long — in fact his whole appearance gave clear indications of starvation and intemperance. After he had left, Apurba was filled with pity for him. He knew that it was useless, indeed wrong, to give him more money, but if only he could have helped him in some other way! However, there was no time for that — he had to buy his ticket and board the train.

He reached Rangoon the following day by noon. It was hot and very sultry. To add to his problems, in the melee his lunch box had been touched by the Muslim porter. He had neither bathed nor eaten — hunger, thirst and exhaustion overpowered him. He wanted somehow to reach home, bathe and take rest.

It took him only ten minutes or so to hire a carriage, load his luggage and reach home. Tewari was not there to receive him. Not only did he not bother to open the door; he did not even come down on hearing the sound of the carriage. Apurba was furious. He hastened up the stairs and knocking violently on the door, shouted, 'Tewari! Tewari, open the door!'

After a few moments, slowly, cautiously, the door was opened. But, instead of angrily striding in, Apurba stood there, dumbfounded. The person who opened the door was Bharati. She looked a complete wreck! She was barefoot, clad in a black *sari* with dishevelled hair. There was a look of deep anguish over her face. She looked like a pilgrim journeying to a far-off place, trudging along tirelessly, without sleep and rest, without food, burnt by the sun, drenched by rain, tottering along unsteadily — it looked as if she would fall dead any moment. Apurba felt that no human being could ever be angry with such a person. Bharati made a bow and then said slowly, 'Now that you're back, Tewari will be saved.'

Shaken, Apurba mumbled, 'Why, what's happened to him?'

Bharati replied softly, 'There've been many cases of small-pox here. Tewari has also contracted it. However, you're much too tired. I'd suggest you go upstairs, have a bath and take some rest. He's sleeping now. I shall let you know when he wakes up.'

'Upstairs?' said Apurba, in surprise.

'Yes. It's still under our occupation, though I've moved elsewhere. It's quite clean. There's water in the tap; you can easily have your bath. There's no one there; you won't be disturbed. But where are your men? Let them take your things upstairs.'

'I've released them at the railway station. They were equally tired.'

'I see. But can we get coolies now? All right, let me see what I can do.'

'Don't bother. I can manage by myself.' Apurba started down the stairs. Just then the coachman craned his neck out and asked for his hire. Bharati beckoned him upstairs and said, 'We can't get any coolies. If you'll take the trouble of carrying the luggage, we'll pay you extra.' Satisfied with her mild request the coachman carried everything upstairs. Bharati neatly made a bed on the floor of the room facing the road and said to Apurba, 'Now please go and take your bath.'

'Not till you tell me the whole story.'

Bharati shook her head. Pointing to the bathroom, she said, 'No. First finish your bath and say your prayers.'

Apurba did not press any more. When he finished his bath and returned, Bharati said with a wan smile, 'Now bring your glass and that packet of sugar lying on the window-sill to the tap. Come, I'll show you how to make a sherbet.'

Apurba needed no persuasion. He was terribly thirsty. So he followed her directions and prepared it. 'A few drops of lime juice would've made it tastier,'

88

he remarked later.

'I've to give you some more trouble,' said Bharati and looked at him.

Apurba remembered all the help rendered by her in the past and now found it easy to talk with her freely.

'What sort of trouble?' he asked.

'On receipt of your telegram, I arranged to have your stove properly cleaned and washed by the Hindu servant of our neighbour. I've brought some coke from your flat. Rice, pulses, potatoes, green vegetables, *ghee*, oil, salt — everything is there. I'll fetch your brass cooking-pot. You just have to wash it and put it on the stove.' Bharati looked at Apurba, and added, 'Believe me, it's not at all difficult. I'll show you everything. You'll simply have to put it on the stove and take it off when the cooking is done. Please do this much today. We'll make some alternative arrangements tomorrow.'

Her anxious tone moved Apurba. He kept quiet for a few moments and then asked, 'But how d'you get your food? And when'll you take rest?'

'It's immaterial when I take rest,' said Bharati. 'And as regards my food, who bothers about it?' Thus brushing aside Apurba's query, she hurried downstairs to fetch the necessary ingredients.

After about an hour or so, when Apurba began to cook his meal, Bharati stood outside the doorway and said, 'It's okay if I stand here? I hope you don't mind.'

'I know that if it hadn't been okay, you wouldn't have done so.'

For the first time in his life Apurba was trying to cook. Innumerable mistakes were committed by him through inexperience, and Bharati began to lose her patience. But when he failed to pour out the cooked lentils into the bowl and spilt it on the ground instead, it was too much for her to tolerate. She burst out angrily, 'Did God create worthless men like you simply to punish us? Now, what'll you eat?'

Apurba felt embarrassed and said, 'How would I

89

know that it'd fall down from the wrong side of the pot? Should I try to scrape a little from the floor?'

Bharati laughed. 'Why not? That'd indeed be good, wouldn't it? No, do what I say. Scrub the floor with water. Then boil a few pieces of potato with other vegetables. Powdered spices are kept in that bottle over there. I shall tell you how much salt to add. That'd make some sort of a curry. I'm afraid you'll have to manage with that today. The excess water in the rice has not been entirely strained. Rice, taken with that curry, won't be too bad. Ugh! it's far better to be in hell than to stand here helplessly and watch you make such a mess.'

After one and a half hours when Apurba's lunch was over, he checked an emotional outburst and said softly, 'I can't find words to express adequately how grateful I am. But you may now go to your room. Henceforth I shall look after Tewari myself. I hope it won't be necessary to trouble you any more.'

Bharati kept quiet. After remaining silent for a while, Apurba added, 'Please tell me what happened. There has been an epidemic of small-pox and Tewari has also got it. That much is clear. But there's one thing I can't make out. When your family shifted, how's it that you stayed back to save Tewari's life in this friendless place. Didn't Mr. Joseph raise any objection?'

'My father is no more. He died in the hospital.'

'What, he's dead?' Apurba remained seated for several moments and then added quietly, 'Seeing you dressed in black, I should've guessed some catastrophe had befallen you.'

'A greater catastrophe fell when mother suddenly passed away . . . .'

'Your mother is also dead?' Apurba was shocked. Remembering his own mother in far-off Calcutta, he felt a wrench in his heart such as he had never experienced before. Bharati looked out of the window and attempted to check her tears. When she turned to Apurba again she found that he was looking intently

90

at her and that his eyes were moist. She was forced to revert back to her original position by the side of the window and remained like that silently for some time. She felt most embarrassed to shed tears in the presence of anyone. When she regained her composure after a few minutes, she said softly, 'Tewari is a very good man. My mother was ailing for some time and we knew she didn't have long to live. Tewari was of great help to me then. When we left, he began to weep. But I couldn't afford to pay so much rent.'

Apurba sat listening to Bharati. Suddenly she said, 'Did you know the police have caught the thieves who robbed your house and have recovered your things?'

'No.'

'Yes. It's the same gang who took Tewari out for the dance. They had committed a number of thefts. Then, possibly there was some disagreement over the share of booty and one of them reported the matter. The stolen goods had been kept in a Chetty's shop. The police have recovered everything. As I'm a witness, they came to make enquiries at my place. I came across to inform you. That's when I found Tewari down with the pox. I'm not sure when the case will be taken up, but I understand you'll get back everything.'

Had she not uttered those last few words she would have spared Apurba from a sense of shame and guilt. He blushed at the thought of all that he had said, both covert and overt. Fortunately Bharati did not notice his embarrassment and continued. 'I found the door bolted from inside and though I shouted repeatedly, there was no response. I had our apartment key. I entered. From that famous chink in the floor' — she suppressed a smile — 'I saw the door and windows bolted and barred. In the darkness someone was lying covered from head to feet by a blanket. It was Tewari. I shouted to him, "Tewari, it's me, Bharati. What's the matter with you? Open the door." Then I came down and again shouted at the top of my voice. After about twenty minutes, Tewari somehow crawled to the door and opened it. One glance at him and everything was clear. A few days before, the police had removed to the hospital from the opposite house a couple of south Indian coolies who had contracted small-pox. Tewari had himself witnessed this and heard their piteous cries and entreaties. He clasped my feet with both his hands and cried that he should not be sent to the plague hospital. He feared that he would not come back alive. It was no exaggeration; as far as we know no one has ever returned from the plague hospital alive. That's why he had closed all the doors and windows so that nobody should know that he had the pox.'

Apurba had been gazing at her like one completely bewildered. He now said, 'And since then you've been nursing him alone, day and night? Why didn't you inform me? You knew Mr. Talwarkar of our office. Why didn't you inform him?'

'How could I? Who'd inform him? I thought he'd come some day to look up Tewari, but he didn't come. How could he have guessed about Tewari's illness? Moreover, I couldn't risk others getting to know of his illness.'

'I understand,' said Apurba and heaved a deep sigh. After some time he said, 'But have you any idea how this has told upon your own self?'

Bharati smiled. 'You mean I looked better before?'

Apurba was unable to reply, but his grateful and admiring look seemed to wipe out from her face all signs of fatigue and exhaustion. After a long silence, he said, 'You've done what no one else would've done. But you're free to go now. Tewari is not just my servant, he's my friend, almost a relative. I've grown up with him. I shall nurse him from now on. I can't let you fall ill for his sake. You haven't yet had your bath or lunch. I'd suggest you go to your place. Is it very far?'

Bharati nodded her head. 'All right,' she said. 'I stay

near the oil mill, by the riverside. I'll come again tomorrow.'

Both of them descended the stairs, unlocked the door and entered Tewari's room. There was no response from him. Even when he was not asleep, he remained mostly semi-unconscious. Apurba went and sat by the side of his bed. Bharati picked up the few pots that had not yet been washed and entered the bathroom. She had intended to give some advice to Apurba before she left, particularly with regard to the precautions that were needed to be ·taken in the case of such a dreadful and infectious disease as small-pox. But when she re-entered the room, she found that Apurba was sitting like a statue, staring at the distorted, unconscious face of Tewari and that his own face had turned ashen. He had never seen a small-pox patient before and he could not imagine that the disease could be so dreadful. When Bharati came and stood before him, he looked up. His eyes were moist and like a small child, he suddenly cried out, 'No, no, I can't do it!'

CHAPTER 9

Bharati kept quiet for some time and then said, 'Can't you? Really!'

There was merely a touch of surprise in Bharati's tone. But what a reply! Was this what he had expected from her? Apurba was rudely roused from his reverie.

Bharati continued, 'Then he has to be sent to the hospital.'

There was no irony or sarcasm in what she said. Yet Apurba felt ashamed — not only because of his own inability to nurse Tewari, but also because what he had said contained a covert request to Bharati, and now her quiet refusal struck him as a rude reproach. With downcast eyes, and overwhelmed with a sense of regret, Apurba realised once again that he had not understood this woman correctly. It was not a question of unhappiness or disquiet — it was as if someone had snuffed out the light and dropped the curtain on his unfinished drama. In the ensuing darkness only he remained along with the dying Tewari.

'Something has to be done before evening,' said Bharati. 'If you want, I can ring up the hospital on my way home and ask them to send an ambulance across.'

Apurba aroused himself from his numbness and said, 'But you yourself said that whoever goes there dies?'

'I didn't say that everybody dies.'

'But,' said Apurba, with a pale face, 'most of them die.'

Bharati nodded. 'Very true. That's why no one wants to go there as long as he's conscious.'

Apurba remained silent for a few moments and then said, 'Is Tewari completely unconscious?'

'No. He regains consciousness from time to time.'

At that moment Tewari suddenly groaned. Bharati noticed that this startled Apurba badly. She came close to Tewari and, bending over, softly asked, 'What d'you want, Tewari?'

Tewari opened his lips and murmured something. Apurba could not make out what he said. But Bharati carefully turned Tewari over, poured a little water into his mouth and then whispered, 'Your master has come.'

In reply Tewari made an indistinct sound and tried to raise his right hand but failed. The next moment tears rolled down from his closed eyes. Apurba's own eyes filled with tears; he hastened to wipe them with the end of his *dhoti* but could not entirely check them. For a few minutes nobody spoke. Sorrow and grief filled the room. Bharati was the first to speak. She came closer to Apurba and whispered to him, 'What's to be done? Send him to the hospital?'

Apurba's eyes were still covered by the *dhoti*. He simply shook his head to indicate his dissent.

Bharati said softly, 'That's better. I'm leaving now. I shall come tomorrow if I find time.'

Apurba still could not look up and remained seated like one dazed.

Bharati got up to leave. 'Everything is here,' she said, 'except candles. I shall fetch a few before I leave.' Saying this she opened the door and quietly went out.

When she returned after some time, Apurba appeared to have regained his composure to some extent. He had wiped his eyes dry, though they still appeared red. As Bharati entered, he turned his face aside. She placed the candles near Apurba and was about to say something, but seeing that he was still looking the other way, hesitated. She waited for some time in silence and then opened the door to go out. Suddenly Apurba cried out, 'If Tewari wants water?'

She turned around and said, 'Give him water.'

'And if he wants to change sides?'

'Turn him over.'

'It's easy to say this. But where shall I sleep? My bedding is upstairs.' His harsh voice indicated his

95

angry mood.

Looking at Bharati's face, it was not clear what was her reaction. She kept quiet for a little while and then said softly, as before, 'There's a bed in your bedroom. You can easily use it.'

'I knew you'd say that,' Apurba replied. 'But what about my food?'

Bharati kept quiet but it seemed that these unreasonable, inconsistent questions amused her. Though she suppressed her laughter, her eyes were sparkling. After a while she said gravely, 'Am I responsible for making arrangements for your food and sleep?'

'Did I say that?'

'You said so just now, and that too angrily.'

Apurba was unable to give an appropriate reply. Looking at his pale and helpless face, Bharati said softly, 'You should've said, "Kindly make these arrangements for me." '

Without looking at her, Apurba said, 'It's not difficult to say that.'

'Then why don't you say so?'

'That's what I said,' replied Apurba sulkily and turned his face aside.

'Haven't you ever nursed anyone?'

'No.'

'And have you never been away from your home before?'

'Never. My mother didn't allow me.'

'Then how did she allow you now?'

Apurba kept quiet. He did not want to discuss with others why his mother had at last agreed to let him go.

Bharati continued, 'Such a good job! How could she possibly refuse? But why didn't she come with you?'

These sarcastic remarks of Bharati offended Apurba. He said, 'You haven't seen my mother, otherwise you wouldn't have said so. It was with great reluctance that she allowed me to leave. But she's a widow. How could she come to this barbarous country?'

Bharati remained silent for a while and then said, 'You're full of hatred for the so-called barbarians. But it's not the poor alone who suffer from illness. You could've fallen ill yourself; you still may. Won't your mother come even then?'

Apurba's face blanched. 'If you frighten me like this,' he said, 'how can I stay alone here?'

'Even if you weren't frightened,' Bharati replied, 'you wouldn't be able to stay alone. You're very timid.'

Apurba had not the courage to protest. He simply kept quiet.

Suddenly Bharati said, 'I'd like to ask you a question. Tewari has lost his caste for having drunk water from my hands. What'll he do when he recovers?'

Apurba was not aware of the scriptural injunctions in the matter. He thought for a while and then said, 'Tewari hasn't taken it knowingly. He took it when he was seriously ill. Otherwise he would've died. Presumably one doesn't lose his caste in such circumstances. Some sort of penance should suffice.'

Bharati frowned. 'Uh huh! And I believe you'll bear the expenses for that, otherwise how'll you take food cooked by him?'

Apurba readily agreed. 'Certainly I'll meet the expenses. I pray that he may recover fast.'

'And it's I who should nurse him to health, isn't it?'

Apurba took no notice of her calm but stern tone, and said gratefully, 'That's very kind of you. If Tewari survives, it'll be entirely due to you.'

Bharati said with a bitter smile, 'There's no harm if a barbarian saves his life, but penance is necessary if he drinks water from my hands, right? Well, I'm going now. I shall try to look him up tomorrow if I find time.'

She was about to leave when she turned back and said, 'But if I'm unable to come again, please tell Tewari when he recovers that I wouldn't have left him and gone away if you hadn't returned from tour But even barbarians have a society of their own. They

97

wouldn't approve of my spending a night with you alone in the same house. When your attendant comes tomorrow morning, send word to Mr. Talwarkar through him. He's an experienced man. He'll be able to make all necessary arrangements. Goodbye!'

'Will it hurt Tewari when I turn him over?' asked Apurba.

'No.'

'And if it becomes necessary to change his bed clothes during the night, how should I do it?'

'Carefully. If I, a woman, could do it, why shouldn't you be able to manage?'

Though frightened, Apurba did not say anything. But as soon as Bharati opened the door to go out, Apurba cried out, 'Supposing he suddenly gets up? Supposing he cries?'

Bharati did not bother to reply, but quietly shut the door and left. So long the sound of her soft footsteps on the wooden staircase could be heard, Apurba remained still, glued to his seat like a wooden statue. But as soon as the sound faded away, a terrible fright seized him and a dark shadow seemed to come down upon him. He felt a peculiar sensation such as he had never experienced before. Fear-struck, he ran to the verandah, opened the door and peering down, saw Bharati walking away. He called out, 'Bharati!' He was unable to bring herself to call her 'Miss Joseph.'

When Bharati glanced upwards, Apurba requested her with folded hands, 'Kindly come up for a minute.' He was unable to say anything more.

Unhesitatingly, Bharati returned. When she entered the room she found that Apurba was not there; only Tewari was lying on the cot. She advanced and peeped into the verandah; Apurba was not there either. Looking around, she found that the door of the toilet was ajar. She waited for a few minutes but when Apurba did not turn up, she opened the toilet door and what she saw alarmed her. Apurba was lying prostrate on the floor with his face downwards, perspiring profusely. He had thrown up all that he had eaten for lunch. She came closer and called out, 'Apurbababu.'

Apurba opened his eyes, looked at her once, then closed it and remained prostrate as before. After hesitating for a moment, Bharati went and sat down beside him. Placing her hand on his head, she coaxed, 'You've got to get up, Apurbababu. You won't feel better till you wash yourself.'

When Apurba got up, Bharati caught hold of his hands and led him to the tap. She opened it so that Apurba could wash himself. Then she carried him to his bed and laid him down. In the absence of a towel, she wiped his hands and feet with the end of her *sari*. She searched out a palm-leaf hand-fan and began to fan him. 'Now try to get some sleep,' she said. 'I won't go away till you come round.'

Apurba said apologetically, 'But you haven't had anything to eat yet.'

'Thanks to you,' replied Bharati. 'But now please go to sleep.'

'You won't go away when I'm asleep, will you?'

'No. I'll wait till you wake up.'

Apurba kept quiet for a while and then enquired, 'Will you be displeased if I call you Miss Bharati?'

'Certainly,' replied Bharati. 'But not if you call me simply Bharati.'

'Even in the presence of others?'

Bharati smiled. 'I wouldn't mind. But now will you please keep quiet and sleep . . . . I've lots of work to do!'

'I'm afraid to sleep lest you give me the slip and go away.'

'But I can go away even when you're awake. How'll you stop me?'

Apurba remained silent.

Bharati said, 'Even we have a code of conduct in our society. Don't I have to obey that?'

Perhaps Apurba was not in his proper senses; so he gave an astounding reply. 'My mother isn't here. If I

99

were to fall ill, then what'll you do? You'll then have to stay.'

'But do I have to?' replied Bharati. 'Wouldn't it do if your friend Mr. Talwarkar is informed?'

Apurba shook his head violently and said, 'No, no. Either my mother or you must be by my side during my illness. Otherwise I won't survive. If I should ever get small-pox, please don't forget this.'

The last part of his request sounded so touching that Bharati forgot herself momentarily. She plonked down on one end of the bed, put her hand on him and said in a choked voice, 'No, no. I'll never forget, never! How can I ever forget?' No sooner had she uttered these words than she realised her mistake and got up hurriedly. She forced a smile on her lips and said, 'But that'll only create further problems for you. You'll have to undergo a ceremonial penance. But, rest assured, nothing will happen to you. Now please try to sleep. Honestly, I've lots of work.'

'Like what?'

'Like what?' replied Bharati. 'Not to speak of eating, I haven't even been able to bathe the whole day.'

'But won't you fall ill if you bathe in the evening?'

'Not impossible. But after cleaning up the mess that you've made, can one avoid having a bath? Then I'll also have to eat something.'

Apurba felt greatly embarrassed and said, 'I'll clean it, please don't do it.' Saying this, he hastened to get up.

Bharati said with a show of anger, 'No need for such bravado. Now be a good boy and go to sleep. I wonder how your mother could permit such a delicate thing to come to such a distant land. Now, listen to me. You mustn't get up. Your mother is not present here, but if you don't listen to me, I'll surely get angry.' Having warned him in a mock serious tone, she left the place.

Worried, fatigued and weak, Apurba did not realise when he fell asleep. He woke up at Bharati's call. Rubbing his eyes, he sat up on the bed. Looking at the clock on the opposite wall, he saw that it was past midnight. Bharati was standing by the side of his bed. The first thing he noticed was her hair — its thickness and length. The freshly washed hair hanging loose across her back was jet-black and reached almost to the ground. The smell of soap filled the room with a sweet fragrance. Bharati was wearing a cotton sari with a black border. Her arms were bare; she had not worn a blouse. This was a new image of Bharati which he had never seen before. All that he could say was, 'How will so much hair dry?'

'It won't. But you needn't bother yourself with it. Here, come with me.'

'How's Tewari?'

'Okay. In any case you don't have to worry about him for this night. Come.'

Apurba followed Bharati to the bathroom and there he found a basket containing some fruits, a kitchen knife, a plate and a tumbler.

'Nothing better could be arranged tonight,' said Bharati. 'Now open the tap and wash everything — knife, plate, tumbler, everything. Then fill up the tumbler and come to the other room. I've laid out a mat for you to sit upon.'

'When did you get these fruits?'

'When you were sleeping. There's a stall nearby. I didn't have to go far. The basket is yours.' Saying this, she went to the other room; but before she left, she cautioned him to be careful while washing the knife so as not to cut his fingers.

A little later, as Apurba was paring the fruits, Bharati sat at a short distance, smiling amusedly.

'I don't mind your smiling,' said Apurba. 'Everyone knows that a man can't pare fruits with a kitchen knife properly. But I'm grateful to you for all the trouble that you've taken for arranging all this. Except for my mother, nobody else would've done all this for me!'

Bharati took no notice of the last few words. She said, 'Apurbababu, I'm not smiling simply out of fun.

101

It's true that all men aren't able to use a kitchen knife properly. But is everyone else as blissfully ignorant as you? When Tewari recovers, I shall certainly write to your mother requesting her either to come over here, or else to take back her son. Such a person shouldn't be left alone on his own.'

'Well, mother knows her son very well. But had it been my elder brothers instead of me, they would've got everything done by you.'

Bharati could not follow.

'My brothers have no scruples whatever regarding their food,' explained Apurba. 'Chicken curry and hotel food are indispensable for them.'

Bharati was astonished. 'Is that so?'

'Yes,' replied Apurba. 'My father was almost a Christian. His unorthodox ways used to cause mother much unhappiness.'

Bharati became curious. 'Really? But is your mother a very orthodox person?'

'Nothing exceptional. Only what is expected of a Hindu lady.'

Talking about his mother, Apurba's voice became tender and mellow. He continued, 'My mother has two daughters-in-law, yet she cooks her food herself. She never imposes her views on anyone, nor complains against anybody. She says, "I didn't agree to surrender my belief for my husband's sake. If my daughters-in-law aren't prepared to accept my views, I mustn't blame them. It's not necessary that my sons and daughters-in-law must follow my ways." '

Greatly impressed, Bharati felt deep reverence for Apurba's mother. 'Although your mother belongs to an old-world atmosphere,' she said, 'I find she has great patience.'

'My mother's patience,' said Apurba excitedly, 'is limitless. You haven't seen her. You'd have been astonished if you had.'

Bharati continued to listen to Apurba silently. Apurba stopped paring the fruits and went on with his narration. 'In a sense my mother's entire life has been one of misery. All her life she has tolerated silently the unorthodox ways of her husband and her two elder sons. I'm her only hope. When she's ill and can't cook herself, she takes a little boiled rice cooked only by me.'

'Then she must be facing difficulties in your absence?'

'Yes, quite possible. That's the reason why initially she didn't approve of my coming away. But I can't stay at home all my life, can I? Her only hope now is that when I get married, she'll be freed from the botheration of cooking her own food.'

With a wan smile, Bharati said, 'Then why did you come away without fulfilling her hope? You ought to have done that.'

Apurba readily agreed. 'Very true. She had even selected a girl for me. But I had to leave in a hurry. There was no time for performing the marriage. However, I've assured her that whenever she sends for me, I shall go and carry out her order.'

'That's only proper.'

Moved deeply by his love for his mother, Apurba said, 'Isn't it? I want that the girl should come from an orthodox Brahmin family, should observe fully all injunctions of the Brahminical code, including fasting on certain auspicious days, and should never cause any unhappiness to my mother. What's the use of an educated girl, accomplished in music and dancing?'

'None whatsoever!'

Apurba forgot that once he had supported his educated sisters-in-law and had told his mother angrily to resolve the matter by bringing from any Brahmin family any girl she fancied for him. He continued, 'You don't belong to our religion or society. It's not permissible to take water from your hands. I've to change clothes even if I touch you. Even then you understand the position clearly, but my brothers and sisters-in-law don't. One must follow the tenets of one's

103

religion, isn't it? What greater misfortune can there be than my mother having to lead a solitary life in her own house? That's why I always pray to God that I may not cause any unhappiness to my mother by any action of mine.' His voice choked and his eyes filled with tears.

At that moment Tewari, who had been asleep, made some sound and Bharati got up and left in a hurry. Apurba wiped his tears with the back of his hand and resumed the work of paring the fruits. He loved his mother greatly and, when at home, did everything to please her, including growing a tuft of hair on his head and not eating rice on the day of the ritual fast. He found it hateful if any Brahmin adopted heterodox ways, but even his own mother could not have imagined that he would be so fastidious and scrupulous about his food abroad. The fact was that he was greatly upset today, and his desire to have his mother by his side agitated and disturbed him. Consequently, whatever he said was highly exaggerated. He was not conscious of this, but Bharati felt insulted and deeply hurt by his words.

When she returned she found that Apurba had somehow finished paring the fruits but had not yet eaten.

'Why haven't you eaten yet?' she asked.

'I was waiting for you.'

'Why?'

'Won't you have some?'

'No. I've kept some aside for myself. If I need, I'll take them.'

Apurba pushed the plate away and said, 'How can I eat alone? You haven't eaten anything the whole day . . . .'

Before Apurba could finish, Bharati said harshly, 'Ugh! Why d'you torment me? Eat if you're hungry, or else throw it out of the window!' Without waiting for a moment longer, she left the room.

Apurba had a glimpse of Bharati as she stalked out

of the room. But there was something in it that he would remember till the day of his death. He had seen her many times, on different occasions and in different moods — during quarrel and enmity, in friendship and cordiality, happiness and sorrow — but never before had her face appeared so stern and hateful. She seemed a different person altogether.

After Bharati had left, for a long time Apurba remained seated like a wooden statue. He did not touch the fruits. However hard he tried, he could not comprehend what had gone wrong. He was completely baffled.

After one hour or so he went to the other room and found Bharati sleeping on a mat on the floor near Tewari's bed. For want of a pillow she had rested her head on her arm. He returned to his room as quietly as he had come, lay down on his bed and soon fell asleep out of sheer exhaustion. When he woke it was morning.

'I'm going,' said Bharati, and left.

Apurba got up in a hurry, but before he was fully awake, Bharati was already gone.

CHAPTER 10

More than a month elapsed since the last incident. Tewari had recovered, but still not regained his normal strength. The office attendant who had accompanied Apurba to Bhamo had been cooking for him all these days. Most of the employees of Apurba's office had worked very hard to save Tewari. Ramdas had even spent several nights at Apurba's place. An eminent physician of the city had treated Tewari and it was largely due to his recommendation that Tewari had not been removed to the hospital. From the beginning, Tewari never liked Burma. Apurba had therefore permitted him to go on leave. It was decided that he would leave as soon as he was able to stand the journey. Tewari was hopeful that it might be possible for him to leave in a week's time.

Since that eventful day, Bharati had not come even once to inquire after Tewari. Strangely enough, neither Apurba nor Tewari ever discussed her. So far as Tewari was concerned, he spent his days in anxiety lest the matter should crop up. Bharati belonged to the enemy camp. They had harassed Apurba in numerous ways; they had even tried to send him to jail by giving false evidence. Tewari felt embarrassed whenever he remembered that he had to seek her help during his master's absence. But he did not know when and why she went away. He was most curious to know this, but was unable to devise a suitable stratagem to extract the information. Sometimes he thought that as Bharati was an intelligent girl, she might have left as soon as she had heard about Apurba's return from tour. At other times he wondered if after his return, Apurba had insulted her and driven her away. Whatever might have actually happened, he was certain that Bharati would never again come to this house on her own accord. Apurba never mentioned Bharati's name, and Tewari was afraid that if he ever raised the issue, the whole episode would come to light. Despite the hostility shown by her folks, he had drunk water from Bharati's hands, had taken food cooked by her. Perhaps he had thereby committed a sin for which there was no expiation. Tewari had decided that on reaching Calcutta, he would immediately leave for his native place. There he would bathe in the Ganga, partake of the prescribed purifiers secretly and, on some pretext or the other, feed a number of Brahmins and thus absolve himself for all practical purposes. If, however, the story of Bharati's nursing him ever reached the ears of Apurba's mother, through inadvertence on his part, then he would not only lose his job in the Haldar household, but also ran the risk of being excommunicated by his village community.

Apart from the apprehension in Tewari's mind that, in his own interest, the story of his close association with Bharati should not become public, lest it brings disgrace to him, there was another aspect of the issue, the thought of which gave him pleasure as well as pain. Every day, after Apurba left for office, Tewari would pass the midday hours sitting on a cane stool in the verandah. Leaning his weak body against the wall, he would continue to gaze at the distance where the lane joined the main road. He found it difficult to believe that Bharati would not have any occasion to pass this way and would not, forced by habit, look up even once.

After Apurba's departure for Bhamo, he became close to this girl the day her mother died suddenly at noon. Tewari had not yet finished his lunch when she came weeping and knocked at the door. Mr. Joseph had passed away two or three days earlier, so Tewari had no reason to be scared any more. When he opened the door, Bharati entered and catching hold of his hands, began to cry bitterly. Who could believe that she was the daughter of a Christian? Tewari had

107

no time to finish his lunch. He spent the whole day delivering Bharati's messages to so many people. Next day, when the dead body was taken away in a coffin, he could not check his tears and remained standing in the verandah, looking at the funeral procession. Since then he began to address Bharati sometimes as *Ma* (mother) and sometimes as *Didi* (elder sister). He did not allow her to do her own cooking, and volunteered to do it for her. On the day Bharati left the apartment and moved to her new quarters with her luggage, the evening seemed to hang heavy on him. He did not know precisely what Bharati had done for him during his illness; he preferred not to think about it, as the question of his losing caste was involved. Instead, he was happy bringing back to mind other pleasant memories.

Every morning, after her bath, with her lush wet hair cascading down her back, Bharati would come to enquire after Tewari. She would not enter the kitchen or touch anything. She would squat on the floor on the other side of the door and ask, 'What did you cook today, Tewari?'

'Let me spread a mat for you,' Tewari would say.

'No need,' Bharati would reply. 'You'll unnecessarily have to wash it again.'

'Why? Does a mat become unclean if you sit on it?'

'Undoubtedly. Your master seems to believe I've made the whole house impure. Had it been his own, he wouldn't have hesitated to purify it with fire. Isn't it so, Tewari?'

Tewari would smile. 'That's what you feel. But that's because you're angry with him. Had you known him better, you'd have agreed that such a man is rare to find in this world.'

'Of course. Otherwise, would he have reported against the person who in fact prevented the theft?'

Recollecting his role in the matter, Tewari would feel piqued. He would attempt to change the topic by saying, 'But you were no better. You knowingly brought a false charge against him, so he had to pay a fine of twenty rupees.'

'Well, ultimately it was I who paid the fine, not he,' Bharati would reply, embarrassed.

'How can you say that? I saw him paying the fine with my own eyes.'

'I also saw you picking up two ten-rupee notes that were lying at your doorstep and handing them over to your master.'

Tewari would stop his cooking halfway. 'I see.'

'Your food is getting burnt. It won't be fit for eating.'

Tewari would remove the cauldron from the fire. 'I have to inform the master about this.'

'As you wish. Am I afraid of him?'

But Tewari never got an opportunity to narrate this to Apurba, nor did he know when and how he would get the chance.

Once he was scolded by Bharati for using stale spices in his cooking. On another occasion she refused to take the food because Tewari had prepared it without first having a bath. Tewari had replied angrily, 'Do Christians have such scruples? You seem to outdo even my mistress in this matter.'

Bharati had given no reply but had simply smiled and gone away. Except for his mistress, no one had ever found fault with Tewari's culinary skills. But after that he took precautions so as not to give her any opportunity for complaint. At that time Tewari had felt annoyed. He could not have guessed that recollecting it later would give him such joy and happiness. He would never return to Burma; he had no hope of seeing Bharati again before he left, no excuse to meet her, no one to share his thoughts with. His fruitless vigil, day after day, silently sitting in one corner of the verandah, gazing towards the end of the road in the hope of getting a glimpse of her, only tormented and tortured him.

One day after returning from office, Apurba suddenly asked, 'Tewari, do you know where Bharati's new house is?'

'Have I ever been there?' Tewari replied, intrigued.

'But didn't she tell you before she left?'

'Why should she tell me?'

'Well, she told me. Only I can't remember it now. I've got to see her tomorrow.'

Tewari was greatly worried and wondered whether some fresh trouble had arisen, but he did not have the courage to ask Apurba. Apurba said, 'The police want to hand over those stolen things which they recovered, but they insist on Bharati's signature.'

Tewari looked the other way and kept quiet. Apurba added, 'She had come to give this information but when she found that you were seriously ill she stayed back to nurse you. Had she not done this, you would've died even before I returned from Bhamo.'

Tewari remained silent but was most eager to hear the rest of the story. Apurba continued, 'When I returned, I found her all alone with you. There was none else to help her. . . it's difficult to say what would've happened if she hadn't been around. . . no food, no rest . . . besides she had lost her parents only a couple of days ago . . . but she's very courageous, Tewari! She didn't bother about anything!'

Tewari could not control himself any longer and asked, 'When did she leave?'

'The day after I returned. It wasn't yet morning when she said, "I'm going," and just vanished.'

'Did she leave in anger?'

'Anger?' Apurba thought for a while and said, 'Maybe. I'm not sure. It's so difficult to understand her! She took such pains for you, yet she didn't come even once afterwards to enquire whether you recovered or not.'

Tewari did not like this and said, 'She might've fallen ill herself.'

Apurba was startled. While cogitating in his mind upon the reasons for Bharati's disappearance, this possibility had never struck him. That she might have left in anger was possible, and he used to search for plausible reasons for her anger. But that there could be other possibilities as well never occurred to him. Remembering the discussion he had with Bharati that night, he could think of nothing else but small-pox. There would be none to look after her in her new house, she might have been removed to the hospital, she might not even be alive — Apurba was overwhelmed with anxiety thinking about these possibilities. He had begun his talk with Tewari while taking off his office dress — the collar, necktie and waist coat. His hands refused to act now. He remained seated on his chair, motionless and speechless like an earthen statue, overwhelmed by an unknown, inexplicable feeling, uninterested in anything else in this world.

For some time neither of them spoke. But when Apurba did not stir even after twenty minutes or so, Tewari was not only surprised but also alarmed. He said slowly, 'Sir, the landlord's agent had come today. He said that if we're interested in moving to the flat upstairs we'll have to do it within this month. I'm afraid someone might occupy it otherwise.'

Apurba looked up. 'Who'll occupy it?' he said.

Tewari continued, 'I received a postcard from your mother today. She had it written by the watchman.'

'What has she written?'

'She's very happy that I've recovered. The watchman's brother is going on leave. She has given him five rupees to offer prayers on my behalf.'

'Good. Mother loves you like her own son.'

Tewari was deeply moved. 'More than her son,' he said. 'I'll be going on leave, but your mother actually wants that both of us should go. There's so much illness . . . .'

'Isn't there illness elsewhere? Is Calcutta free from illness? You must've written all this and scared her.'

'No, sir.' Tewari had decided he would broach the topic leisurely after dinner. But he found he could wait no longer. He said, 'Kalibabu has been pressing

111

hard. Perhaps they all want to perform the auspicious ceremony in the next month.'

Kalibabu was a pious Brahmin. The orthodoxy of his family was well known. Apurba's mother had approved of his youngest daughter. She had hinted so in some of her recent letters. But Apurba did not like Tewari's talk. 'What's the hurry?' he said. 'If Kalibabu is so impatient, he can try elsewhere.'

Tewari attempted a smile and said, 'Who knows whether it's he who's impatient or your mother. People might've scared her by saying Burma wasn't a safe place; boys went astray there.'

Apurba became furious. 'Look here, Tewari, don't give me all these lectures. What's it that you wrote to mother in your letters? I'm not a child!'

Tewari was at first surprised at Apurba's outburst. But since his recent illness his own temper had been frayed. He retorted angrily, 'Why didn't you say that to your mother before coming? I wouldn't have then had to board the ship and lose my caste!'

Apurba glared at Tewari angrily and began to put on his collar and tie. Tewari knew what it meant. 'Then you won't have your tea?' he asked.

Apurba gave no reply but slipped on his coat and stomped out.

'There's a ship leaving tomorrow via Chittagong,' said Tewari indignantly. 'I'm leaving by that, take note!'

'You must!' shouted back Apurba, and went away.

An inexperienced person would have been greatly surprised at this sudden, meaningless quarrel between master and servant; he would not realise that it is through such meaningless shocks that the embittered, aggrieved human heart has forever sought to find the path to normalcy.

CHAPTER 11

The only place where Apurba could go to was Talwarkar's house. There was no dearth of Bengalis in Rangoon, but since his arrival here Apurba had to pass his time through such stress that he had not been able to get acquainted with any Bengali family. He was walking towards the railway station when he suddenly remembered that it was a Sunday when Talwarkar usually took his wife to the theatre. So he had no other alternative but to roam about aimlessly. Suddenly he remembered Bharati, and his ingratitude towards her distressed him. His guilty, wounded mind consoled itself with the argument that she must be all right; had it been otherwise she would have certainly sent information to him.

But this argument did not give him peace of mind. He recollected that Bharati had said that she now lived somewhere near the oil mill. The idea of seeing her elated him. At the same time he could not shake off a sense of humility in trying to search for one who had deliberately chosen to live in seclusion. It was possible she would not approve of his visiting her, might even be annoyed at seeing him. So, as he proceeded towards her new house, he assured himself that he was going there on business — because the police wanted her signature; otherwise he had no idle curiosity to find out where she was living and whether she was well. Certainly Bharati could not object to his visiting her after such a long time.

Apurba had never been to this locality before. A wide road ran straight towards the east. He walked along this road for quite some time and when he came to a crossing where the road branched off towards the river, he asked someone, 'D'you know which is the European locality here?'

In reply, the man pointed to the bungalows on both

sides of the road. But their size, shape and beauty convinced Apurba that he was wrong in asking that question. He corrected himself and said, 'I believe some Bengalis live here as well, such as workmen, mechanics, et cetera.'

'Many. I'm myself a workman. Fifty labourers work under me. I can do whatever I like with them. I can even report to the Sahib and get them dismissed from service. But whom d'you want?'

Apurba thought for a while and then said, 'You see, the person I'm looking for . . . . Well, where do Bengali Christians live?'

The man was astonished. 'You say he's a Bengali and again you say he's a Christian. Now, how can a Bengali be a Christian? Christians are Christians and Muslims are Muslims! I know that much.'

'But one who has come from Bengal? Who speaks Bengali?'

'Is it enough that he speaks Bengali?' the man replied, agitatedly. 'One who has renounced his ancestral religion and embraced Christianity, does he still continue to be a Bengali? Will any Bengali keep any social relationship with such a person? Now, there are some lady teachers who've come from somewhere; they teach the local children. That's all. Does any of us have anything to do with them?'

Apurba saw that he was getting closer. 'D'you know where they live?' he asked.

'Of course. Go down straight to the river and then ask for the new school building. Even a small child will direct you to it. That's because Doctorbabu lives there. He's no ordinary man, he's God! He can bring back a dead man to life.' Saying this, the man went his way.

Following the man's directions, Apurba came to a red-coloured, double-storied wooden building by the side of the river. It was already dark. The road was deserted. Light fell from the upstairs open window. Apurba stood below, waiting to enquire from someone

114

passing that way. But somehow he was convinced that Bharati lived here and would appear at that window.

Fifteen minutes later two or three persons came out of the house. They were startled on seeing Apurba standing there. One of them asked, 'Who're you? Whom d'you want?'

Embarrassed at the man's suspicious tone, Apurba replied, 'Does anybody by the name of Miss Joseph live here?'

'Yes,' the man said promptly. 'Come with me.'

Apurba had no clear intention of going into the house. Noting his hesitation, the man said, 'How long have you been waiting here? She's at home. Come, we'll take you to her.' Saying this he began to lead the way.

It was clear from their haste that they wanted to verify the veracity of his statements. Apurba realised that if he were now to return without meeting Bharati, their suspicions would increase with disagreeable consequences for him. So he said, 'Very well,' and followed them.

Shortly they entered the ground floor of that house. It was a large hall with a staircase leading upstairs. A lamp hung from a chain attached to the ceiling. It had some tables and chairs and a blackboard. A number of maps of different sizes and colours hung against the walls. It was clear that this was the new school building. Four or five men and women sat engaged in some heated argument. Suddenly, seeing a stranger enter the room, they fell silent. Apurba cast a hurried glance at them and then followed his guide upstairs.

Bharati was in her room. On seeing Apurba, her face lit up. She came near and welcomed him by taking his hands in hers, and led him to a chair. 'You didn't care to enquire about me all these days,' she pouted.

'Neither did you,' said Apurba. But he realised it was not an appropriate reply.

Bharati smiled and said, 'Tewari wants to go home; let him go. He won't recover otherwise.'

115

'That means it isn't correct to say that you didn't keep yourself informed about us.'

Bharati smiled again and said, 'Tomorrow is a Sunday. So nothing can be done. But the day after you should go to the court at noon. You'll get your money and articles back. Be sure they don't cheat you.'

'But your signature will be necessary.'

'I know.'

'You meet Tewari off and on, don't you?'

'No,' said Bharati, shaking her head. 'But please don't be angry with him for nothing.'

'There's every reason to be angry with him. You saved his life; he ought to be grateful to you.'

'He is; otherwise he'd definitely have tried to send me to jail.'

Apurba got the hint. He kept quiet with his face downcast for some time and then said, 'You must be terribly angry with me.'

'Not at all. The whole day I'm busy teaching in the school. After I return home, as secretary of this organisation, I've to write a lot of letters every day. By the time I go to bed, I'm dead tired. Where's the time to be angry with anyone?'

'So it's because you don't have the time to be angry?'

'That's right. You can come and spend a day here and see whether that's true or not.'

Unconsciously, Apurba heaved a sigh. 'What's the point?' he said.

Then, after a little pause, he asked, 'What's your salary here?'

Bharati suppressed a smile and then said gravely, 'What sort of a person are you? Don't you know it's impolite to inquire about one's salary? Isn't it insulting to the other person?'

Apurba said with a hurt voice, 'You know I didn't mean any insult. As you're working here . . . .'

'Do you suggest I starve instead?'

'This is no better. There's a vacancy in our office; the salary is one hundred rupees a month. You won't have to work for more than a couple of hours every day.'

'You suggest I do that job?'

'What's the harm?'

Bharati shook her head. 'No, I won't. You're the boss there. If I make a mistake, you'll come with a stick after me.'

Apurba did not say anything more. It was clear that Bharati had said all this in jest. Yet he was incensed at her remarks for hinting at that unfortunate incident.

For some time now a heated discussion had been going on downstairs; it now turned uproarious. Apurba said innocently, 'Perhaps your school is now starting . . . . The students are reading out their lessons!'

'In that case the noise would've been a little less,' said Bharati gravely. 'It seems their teachers are debating on the distribution of subjects.'

'Won't you go?'

'I should, but my heart doesn't permit me to leave you and go,' chuckled Bharati.

Apurba blushed. He turned his face aside to hide it. Noticing something etched on the wall with casuarina leaves, he asked, 'What's written there?'

'Why don't you read?'

Apurba turned his attention to the wall and read aloud, *Pather Dabi* — the right of way. What does it mean?'

'That's the name of our society — our motto, our objective! Will you become a member?'

'You must be a member; but what'll I have to do?'

'We're all passers-by. We believe in the right of all men to live as human beings without any hindrances. It is our aim that those who come after us may be free and not find their path obstructed. Will you join us?'

'But we're just a colony — neither are we British, nor French, nor Americans! How then can we have untrammelled freedom of movement? We haven't the right to sit on a bench on the railway platform; we're even debarred from protesting against insults inflicted on us . . . .'

As he went on, he remembered all the indignities he had faced that day — the kicks of the Anglo-Indian boys and the Station Master ordering him out of his office — and suffered afresh the insults heaped upon him.

His eyes blazing, he continued, 'The bench becomes impure if we sit on it! The air is polluted if we enter the room — as if we're not men! As if we're not human beings! We don't have the flesh and blood of men! If fighting against this is your aim, I'm with you.'

'Do you really feel for the suffering of men, Apurbababu?' asked Bharati. 'Is there really no objection in someone's touch? Doesn't the air of one's room become polluted by the presence of another person?'

'Certainly not!' cried Apurba. 'The colour of a man's skin is hardly the criterion by which he should be judged. Nor can he be condemned simply because he was born in a particular country. I hope you'll excuse me, but I was fined twenty rupees by the court simply because Mr Joseph was a Christian? Should a man be considered inferior just because he professes a separate faith? Is this justice? I tell you, they'll suffer for this. God will never forgive their hatred and malice for others.'

There is nothing like indignity and suffering to reveal the true nature of a man. It was this that made Apurba eloquent in his support for the oppressed against the indignities and tyranny perpetrated upon them by their oppressors.

Bharati had been listening to his outburst silently. When he finished, she chuckled and turned her face aside. Apurba was startled. He felt as if someone had struck him. He had not paid proper attention to Bharati's questions till then; their significance now became clear to him and struck him dumb.

When Bharati turned around after a minute or so, there was no sign of any smile on her lips. 'Today is

118

a Saturday,' she said, 'so the school is closed. We attend to the society's work instead. Why don't you come with me? I'll introduce you to Doctor and then enrol you as a member of *Pather Dabi*.'

'Is he the president?'

'President? No, he's the soul of the organisation. He remains underground; his work is not visible.'

Apurba felt no curiosity to learn more about the soul. He enquired, 'I suppose all your members are Christians?'

'No. Except for me, all are Hindus.'

Apurba was astonished. 'But I hear the voice of some ladies?'

'All Hindus,' replied Bharati.

After a moment's hesitation, Apurba said, 'I suppose they don't believe in the caste system . . . that is, in observing certain restrictions about food and drink, and in untouchability?'

'No. But if someone believes such things, we don't force him either,' said Bharati, with a smile. 'We respect individual tastes. You needn't be afraid on that account.'

'Why should I be afraid? But, tell me, are there other educated ladies like you in your society?'

'Like me?' smiled Bharati. 'Sumitra, our president, has travelled around the world alone. Except for Doctor, I suppose there's none in this country as learned as her.'

Apurba was surprised. 'And what about him whom you call Doctor?' he asked.

'Oh, Doctor? It's better not to speak about him,' said Bharati. Her eyes became moist with reverence and regard. 'Whatever I say will be an understatement.'

Apurba asked no more questions and remained silent. He loved his motherland and so was attracted to this strange-sounding organisation — *Pather Dabi*. It was difficult to resist the desire of being associated with this organisation formed by these exceptionally learned men and women in this friendless foreign country,

119

representing their hopes and aspirations, their aims and efforts, their history, their mysterious way of life and bearing the strange name of *Pather Dabi*; and yet a kind of alien, irreligious and unwholesome vapour seemed to arise from the hall downstairs and slowly filled his mind with distaste.

As the noise grew tumultuous, Bharati suggested, 'Let's go.'

Apurba readily agreed.

When they came downstairs, Bharati offered a cane sofa to Apurba to sit upon and, for want of extra chairs, squeezed in beside him.

The sofa was so small that it was dificult for two persons to sit on it without looking indecent. Bharati had never behaved like this before. Apurba felt not only embarrassed but also abashed. But it seemed that nobody had any time to notice such things. Another thing which attracted Apurba's notice was that although most of them glanced at him as he, a stranger, took his seat amongst them, there was not the least abatement in their stormy debate. Only one man, who was writing something seated at a table in one corner of the room with his back towards the assembly, continued undisturbed with his work. It seemed as if he had not even noticed Apurba's arrival.

Apurba saw that half a dozen women and eight men were engaged in the debate. All of them were strangers to him, excepting one whom he recognised at first glance. He was the same man whom Apurba had freed from police custody at Meiktila railway station by paying his fine for ticketless travel and who had promised to repay the amount. The man looked at Apurba but now being sober, did not seem to recognise Apurba as the man from whom he had borrowed money while drunk. But more than this, it pained Apurba to think how Bharati had come into contact with such undesirable elements.

Someone who had been standing in front of them now sat down. Bharati whispered to Apurba, 'She's our president, Sumitra.'

The introduction was unnecessary. Apurba could easily make out. For, if the society had to be led by a lady, she was undoubtedly the ablest. Though nearing thirty, she had a regal appearance. Her complexion was molten gold. Her hair was knotted loosely in the south Indian fashion. On her arms she wore several gold bangles and a portion of her necklace glittered around her neck. She wore emerald ear-tops which sparkled like the eyes of a serpent when light reflected upon them. Her forehead, chin, nose, eyebrows, hips, were all flawless. Her beauty was extraordinary, unparalleled! She had stood with her hand against the blackboard, and Apurba had continued to gaze at her like one mesmerised. He was a student of mathematics and had little acquaintance with poetry. But it was clear to him now why poets compared the female form with a young creeper.

An ordinary looking woman in her early twenties sat in front of them with her eyes downcast. The stormy debate seemed to centre around her. At a short distance from her sat an elderly gentleman. He was dressed in immaculate European clothes and appeared to be well-to-do. Most probably he represented the opposite side. Apurba had not paid much attention to what he had said — all his attention was directed towards Sumitra. He waited eagerly to hear her speak. He no longer regretted having come to this meeting.

Sumitra now replied to the argument advanced by the gentleman in European dress. Indeed, this was what a woman's voice should be like! Apurba leaned forward so as not to miss a single syllable.

'Manoharbabu, you're no inexperienced young lawyer,' said Sumitra. 'If your argument becomes irrelevant, how am I to decide the case?'

'To talk irrelevant matters is against my profession,' replied Manoharbabu.

'That's what we expect,' smiled Sumitra. 'Now your argument in brief is like this. You're a friend of

121

Nabatara's husband. He wants to force her to return to him. But she's not agreeable; she wants to serve her country. I don't see anything wrong in her decision.'

'But doesn't she have a duty towards her husband? It's not enough if she says that she wants to serve her country.'

'Look here. It's for Nabatara to decide what she wants to do or not to do. But her husband also had a duty towards his wife, which we all know he never fulfilled. Certainly duty cannot be one-sided.'

Manoharbabu said angrily, 'But that's no argument for the wife to become unchaste. That she'll be able to maintain her chastity while working for the country, in this crowd, and in her age . . . surely no one can give that assurance either!'

Sumitra's face turned momentarily red. Then she regained her composure and said, 'One can of course give no assurances. But we've seen that Nabatara is humane, energetic, courageous, and above all, has piety. But whether she'll be able to retain what you describe as chastity, that is for her to say.'

Manoharbabu looked askance at Nabatara's downcast face and said sarcastically, 'What wonderful piety! Perhaps this is what she'll teach other women in the name of social service.'

'We have full confidence in her sense of responsibility. It's against our creed to discuss anyone's personal character. But if Nabatara, who couldn't love her husband and didn't consider it wrong to leave him for a nobler task, wants to teach this to other women, we shall not object.'

'She'll teach this to the women of the country that produced such women as Sita and Savitri?' asked Manoharbabu incredulously.

'She should. Instead of muttering some hackneyed meaningless cliches, if Nabatara tells them that in this country once upon a time Sita had forsaken her husband and gone to the nether world in order to save her self-respect, and that the princess Savitri loved the

122

poor Satyaban so deeply that she didn't hesitate to marry him even though she knew fully well that he was destined to die soon, and that Nabatara herself had left her villainous husband for whom she had no love, and that in similar circumstances other women should also act accordingly, such teaching will certainly be beneficial to them, Manoharbabu.'

Manoharbabu's lips began to quiver with rage. For a moment he was speechless. Then he cried out, 'Then this country will undoubtedly go to dogs!'

With folded hands, he added, 'Do whatever you wish, but for heaven's sake don't preach such things to others. Much harm has already been caused by imitating the Western civilization. Let's not spread such things among our women now and bring this country to ruin.'

Sumitra's face showed signs of disgust and fatigue. She said, 'If there's any way to save ourselves from ruin, it's this. However, your knowledge of Western civilization is rather limited, so any further argument regarding this will be a mere waste of time. We've already wasted enough time . . . we've other things to do.'

Manoharbabu somehow suppressed his anger and said, 'I too don't have unlimited time. Nabatara won't return then?'

Nabatara did not raise her eyes. She shook her head and indicated her dissent.

Manoharbabu asked Sumitra, 'Then you're taking her responsibility?'

The reply came from Nabatara. She said, 'I'm capable of shouldering my own responsibility; you needn't bother about that.'

Manoharbabu glanced slyly at Nabatara but addressed himself to Sumitra, 'I ask you, can there be anything more glorious for a woman than spending her life with her husband?'

'Whatever might be the case with others,' said Sumitra, 'I can't say that Nabatara has had a glorious

123

life with her husband.'

Manoharbabu could contain himself no longer. He said rudely, 'Perhaps you'll regard her unchaste life now as glorious?'

Strangely enough, these indecent remarks of Manohar did not disturb those present. Sumitra said calmly, 'Manoharbabu, our society's rules require that we observe decorum while speaking.'

'What if I can't follow that rule?'

'You'll be thrown out.'

Manoharbabu went berserk with rage. He sprang up like an arrow from the bowstring and growled, 'I'm leaving! Goodbye!'

He stopped near the doorway and burst out in fury. Shaking his fists, he shouted, 'I know everything about you people. You want to drive the British away, eh? Forget it. I'm an advocate, not a peasant. I know where to get justice and how to put handcuffs on your wrists. Very well . . .' Saying this, he disappeared in the darkness.

This unexpected development seemed to stun everyone. None expressed it, but it was as if a shadow had fallen on their faces. Only the man who sat in the corner continued with his writing. He had not bothered to look up even once. It seemed to Apurba that either the man was totally deaf or else insensitive and impenetrable like stone. He wanted to see Bharati's reaction, but she had turned her face aside, perhaps deliberately. Whoever Manoharbabu may have been, the allegations levelled by him in anger against the society were very grave and bound to arouse suspicion. From where had so many men and women gathered together to form this society, what was its real objective and how had Bharati got involved with them?

And that man who had been arrested by the police in a drunken condition? And above all Nabatara, who had forsaken her husband to serve her country, and who had now no time even to think about her own

124

chastity? And these people not only supported such a thing, but actually encouraged it! And their President, who, though a woman herself, had no hesitation to express her utter disregard for the concept of chastity, openly and unabashedly, in the presence of so many men!

For quite some time there was complete silence in the room. Outside, the dark and narrow street was equally silent and deserted. A kind of anxiety and apprehension seemed to grip Apurba.

Suddenly Sumitra's voice could be heard. 'Apurbababu!'

Startled, Apurba looked up.

'You don't know us,' said Sumitra. 'But we all know you through Bharati. I understand you want to become a member of our society. Am I correct?'

Apurba could not bring himself to say 'No.' He merely nodded his head.

Sumitra now turned to the man who was busy writing and said, 'Doctor, please write down Apurba's name.'

To Apurba she said, smiling, 'There's no membership fee. This is a special feature of our society.'

Apurba tried to smile back, but failed. When his name was entered into the voluminous register, he felt ill at ease. Unable to remain silent any longer, he blurted out, 'But I know nothing about its aims and what I'll be expected to do.'

'Didn't Bharati tell you?'

Apurba thought for a while. 'She did say something. But, tell me one thing. Do you really approve of Nabatara's conduct?'

'At least I do. Because there's nothing greater to me than my motherland.'

Apurba said reverently, 'I too love my country with all my heart. Also, I agree that men and women have equal rights to serve their country. But certainly their field of activity cannot be the same. While men will work outside, women should try to serve their husbands and children in the purity of their households.

125

In bringing about their welfare they will be rendering a far greater service to their country than by jostling with their menfolk outside.'

Sumitra chuckled. Apurba noticed that others too were trying to suppress their smiles.

'I accept that this is an ancient theory advocated by many,' said Sumitra. 'But you'll agree that a thing doesn't become true simply because many people have repeated it over the years. This is just a hoax. Those who've never served their country, to whom self-interest is far more important than the service of their country, have propounded this theory. There's not an iota of truth in it. When you begin your work, only then will you realise that if and when women join their menfolk in the service of their country, only then will real work be done. Otherwise the work done by the men will disintegrate like sand and nothing worthwhile will be achieved.'

Apurba asked shamefacedly, 'But won't this lead to immorality? Won't there be the risk of losing one's character?'

'But will the risk be less if they're confined indoors? The fault lies not in their venturing out but with God, who created men and women, created mutual attraction between them. Apurbababu, see for yourself what's happening in other countries.'

Apurba was not satisfied with this reply. He said sharply, 'Let other countries worry about themselves. I shall consider it sufficient if I can think about our own welfare. Pardon my saying so, but I can't help noticing that none of you here have any faith in the institution of marriage. Not only that, you even look down upon the two noblest things in a woman's life — her chastity and fidelity. Will this lead to the welfare of the country?'

Sumitra looked at Apurba for a while and then said in an amused but calm voice, 'Apurbababu, you were somewhat angry when you said all this, for I'd not spoken exactly in the same vein. At the same time, I can't say you've totally misunderstood me either. As a woman I can't have any great regard for a society where the main purpose of taking a wife is to beget a son. You were eloquent in praise of chastity, but if this be the intention of marriage in this country, chastity is not ennobled, it is degraded! Chastity is not confined to the body alone, Apurbababu. The mind has also to be chaste. Is it possible for a woman to be mentally chaste if she doesn't love her husband with all her heart? Do you really believe that just because they're married, every wife can love her husband? Is it like water that you can pour it in any container and shut its lid?'

Apurba was at a loss for words. 'But this has been going on for ages,' he said.

Sumitra smiled and nodded her head. 'Of course, it has. It doesn't stop her from addressing her husband affectionately or in showing regard to him out of a sense of duty. In fact, nothing more than that is needed. You must've read the story of the sage's son who was happy drinking water with powdered rice instead of milk. But even if it's easier, one can't feel proud by deceiving oneself.'

Apurba found the argument unpalatable, but was unable to give a suitable reply. 'Do you mean one can't expect anything better,' he said.

'Oh no, I can't say that because there's always the chance factor.'

'Ah, chance! But even if you're correct, I'd still say that in the interest of the society and for the sake of our descendants, the existing system is beneficial.'

Sumitra continued in a calm but firm tone. 'No, Apurbababu, it'll not be for the ultimate benefit of either the society or its descendants. There was a time when human beings were sacrificed in the name of society and progeny, but the result was not a happy one. Today it's totally unacceptable. The greatest need for love between the married couple is really to ensure the good of the descendants. Women must overcome this fascination for a married life in which there is no love. She must understand that such a life is something of which one should be ashamed and not proud.'

Apurba was bewildered. 'But such ideas will only sow dissension and discord in our peaceful, disciplined society,' he said.

'Let it be. But discord and dissension aren't necessarily harmful. One who is diseased, decrepit and old tries anxiously to shield himself from any blow coming from any direction. He's always afraid lest the slightest movement should cause his death. And if our society has come to this pass, it's best to decide the matter once for all. A few days this side or that is not going to cause any difference, is it?'

Apurba kept quiet. Sumitra also remained silent for a while and then said, 'Perhaps I've caused you pain by citing the example of the sage's son. But you deserved the pain and there was no way I could've spared you that.'

Apurba could not understand clearly what Sumitra's last words meant. But he had heard enough, and so he blurted out, 'Standing in front of the Jagannath temple, Christian missionaries say many things which hurt, the feelings of the pilgrims. Yet none of them gives up worshipping the armless Jagannath for Jesus Christ who had both his arms. The armless God was sufficient for them — how surprising!'

Sumitra did not get angry. Later she smiled and said, 'Apurbababu, it's only because such strange things happen that men are able to live. Many people aren't able to make out the colour of the leaves without themselves being aware of it. And yet they all call it green — isn't that itself strange? If only one knew the real value of chastity . . . .'

'Sumitra!' The man who had so long been engrossed in writing now got up. All those present also stood up.

Apurba saw he was Girish Mahapatra.

Bharati whispered to him. 'He's our Doctor. You

must stand up.'

Like a mechanical doll, Apurba stood up. But remembering the last portion of Manohar's angry threat, his blood turned cold.

Girish came up to him and said, 'I believe you haven't forgotten me. These people call me Doctor.' He laughed.

Apurba found it difficult to laugh. He said in a low voice, 'But my Uncle's records contained some other dreadful name . . . .'

Girish suddenly clasped Apurba's both hands and said in a whisper, 'It was Sabyasachi, wasn't it?' He again laughed and added, 'But it's already late, Apurbababu. Come, I'll see you to your place. The road isn't quite safe. When these Pathan workmen get drunk, they seem to lose all sense. Come.' Saying this, he literally dragged Apurba out of the room.

He had not been able to bid goodbye to Sumitra, or to say a word to Bharati — but what really worried Apurba was that his name had been entered in that bound register.

CHAPTER 12

After walking a short distance, Apurba said politely, 'You're weak and unwell. There's no need for you to go further. The main road is straight ahead. I can easily manage.'

Doctor smiled. 'It may've been easy while coming; it may not be that easy when returning. The road that had been straight enough in the evening may have become crooked due to the activities of Pathans and unemployed Negroes. Come, let's not halt now.'

Apurba understood what was hinted. Yet he asked, 'What do they do? Assault?'

His companion again smiled. 'But of course,' he said. 'When they force others to pay for their drinks, they can't possibly avoid that, can they? For example, let's take that gold pocket watch of yours. If it has to go to someone else's pocket, it's but obvious that you'll resist. What follows is quite natural. Right?'

Terrified, Apurba nodded his head. 'Quite true. But this is my father's watch.'

'This is exactly what they don't understand! But that won't do today.'

'You mean . . .?'

'I mean that this won't go towards paying for their drinks today.'

Apurba remained silent for a while and then said hesitantly, 'Let's take an alternative route.'

Doctor looked at him and giggled, like a young girl. 'Take an alternative route? At this hour? No, that won't be necessary. Let's go.' Saying this, he reached out and took Apurba's hand. Apurba felt as if his bones — despite the long years of gymnastics, cricket and hockey — were being crushed.

Apurba snatched his hand back and said, 'I understand. Let's go.' He forced a smile on his lips. 'Uncle had said jokingly that day, ' "It's not for nothing that

130

we've come in such large numbers to welcome this great man. Our secret records say that if he so wishes, he can wipe off five or ten policemen with a single whack." We had laughed at Uncle's expression that day, but now it seems we were not justified in laughing. You appear to be quite capable of doing that.'

There was a perceptible change in Doctor's expression. 'That's an exaggeration,' he said. 'But who were "we"?'

'Two or three of his officials, and I.'

'Oh, they!' Doctor heaved a deep sigh. Apurba understood what it signified. He did not know what to say.

The road remained straight tonight; for whatever reason, no one came out to rob the passers-by . When they had crossed the deserted lane in silence and approached the main road, Apurba said, 'I think I can safely go alone now. Thank you.'

In reply Doctor peered ahead into the dimly lit broad highway and said softly, 'Possibly.'

Apurba bid him goodbye. As he was about to leave, he could suppress his curiosity no longer, and spoke out, 'Well, Sabya.'

'No, no, not Sabya . . . simply Doctor.'

Shamefaced, Apurba asked, 'Well, Doctor, we were lucky that there was none on the road. But supposing they were in a gang, was there nothing to fear even then?'

'They're never more than two to ten on any day,' replied Doctor.

'Two to ten? You mean to say that there was nothing to fear even if there were ten of them?'

Doctor smiled. 'No.'

When they came to the crossing, Apurba asked, 'Is it really true that your pistol never misses its target?'

Doctor shook his head. He had an amused smile. 'No,' he said. 'But why d'you ask this? I don't have a pistol with me now.'

'You came without it? Strange!'

It was the dead of night. Looking at the deserted road, Apurba said, 'It's so lonely. There are no passers-by, not even a policeman, practically no lights either. My house shouldn't be more than a couple of miles away. What d'you say, Doctor?'

'That's right.'

'Okay, goodbye. I've given you a lot of trouble already.' Apurba was about to move on, but he stopped and inquired, 'Is it possible that the rascals may be waiting on some other road tonight?'

'Not impossible.'

'Most definitely, yes! All right, goodbye. But just see the fun. Policemen are never around when they're needed most. Such is their sense of duty! It's for this that we pay taxes through the nose. This should be stopped! What d'you say?'

'Undoubtedly.' Doctor laughed again — the same soft, gentle, girlish laughter. 'Come, let me walk you to your home. We can chat on the way.'

Apurba was greatly embarrassed. With his face downcast he said in a low voice, 'I'm a very timid person. I've no courage. Anyone else would've been able to go without any fear. I've given you so much trouble so late at night.'

Apurba's unpretentious and candid confession touched Doctor. He felt ashamed for having laughed earlier. Putting his hand on Apurba's shoulder, he said affectionately, 'But I came prepared to escort you, Apurba. Or else why d'you think our President put this thing in my hand?' Saying this, he showed Apurba a thick black stave which he held in his left hand.

Apurba was taken aback. 'Can Sumitra order even you?' he asked.

'Of course,' smiled Doctor.

'But she could've sent someone else.'

'That would've meant sending the whole gang. It's better this way.'

They chatted as they walked along. Doctor said, 'Sumitra is the President of our society. She has to consider all aspects before taking a decision. She couldn't have sent just anyone where there's a risk of assault or murder. If it hadn't been for me, you'd possibly have had to spend the night there. She wouldn't have allowed you to come.'

The prospect of a possible assault on this dark and deserted road made Apurba's hair stand on end. His voice dropped to a whisper, 'But you'll have to return alone?'

'Yes.'

Apurba asked no further questions. The thought that their voices might attract unwanted persons was uppermost in his mind. He concentrated on the road and started walking with rapid strides, in silence. After walking this way for about fifteen minutes, they entered the town. It was only after they had crossed the railway station and saw human habitation, that Apurba ventured to speak.

'Doctor,' he said, 'my house isn't much farther. There isn't any harm if you stay back for the night, is there?'

Doctor guessed what was in Apurba's mind and said, smilingly, 'There may not be any harm in doing many things, but we're not permitted unless there's a real need for it. I've to go back because it's not necessary for me to stay here.'

'Aren't you permitted to do anything that's not necessary?'

'We aren't. Then, Apurbababu, let me take leave of you.'

Apurba glanced at the dark road behind them. Just the thought of this man returning alone by the same road terrified him. He said, 'Doctor, can't you let a man retain his self-respect?'

Surprised, Doctor asked, 'Why d'you say that?'

Apurba replied in a piqued tone, 'What else can I say? I'm a timid fellow. I couldn't return by myself for fear of hoodlums, so you escorted me back. And now, if you go back alone despite all the danger, shall I be able to show my face to anyone?'

133

Doctor immediately clasped Apurba's both hands and said affectionately, 'All right, let's go to your place. I'll be your guest for tonight. But should one willingly invite such trouble for nothing?'

Apurba could not understand what Doctor meant. But after walking a few steps he felt something pulling him back. Turning around, he exclaimed, 'Your feet must be hurting? You're limping!'

'That's nothing,' said Doctor, with a soft smile. 'When I approach human habitation, my feet automatically starts limping. Remember Girish Mahapatra's gait?'

Apurba stopped in his tracks. 'No, Doctor,' he said, 'you needn't come to my house.'

'But your self-respect?'

'Worth nothing, where you're concerned. There's none else as brave as you!'

Apurba had no personal knowledge about this man's life-history. Or he would have been greatly ashamed to gush over such a small matter. Crossing this road alone was merely a drop as compared to an ocean. One whom the police knew as Sabyasachi — what were ten or twelve hoodlums before him?

Doctor turned aside to hide his chuckle. He then said, innocently, 'Better let's go back. Even if someone attacks me if I'm alone, they wouldn't dare to if you were with me.'

Apurba said hesitatingly, 'Go back again?'

'What harm? There'd then be no risk involved.'

'Where shall I stay?'

'With me.'

Apurba had eaten nothing after returning from his office. He was very hungry. He said rather apologetically, 'I haven't had my food. Of course that can be . . . .'

'Come on, let's see what our luck holds for us today. But one thing. Tewari will be terribly worried.'

At the mere mention of Tewari's name, a strong urge to take revenge welled up in Apurba's mind. 'Let him worry!' he said angrily. 'Let's go.'

He almost pushed Doctor, and soon they were walking back along that dark and desolate road. This time, however, he was not assailed by any fear. As they crossed the police station, Apurba suddenly asked, 'Are you an anarchist, Doctor?'

Doctor looked at him. 'What does your uncle say?'

'He says that Sabyasachi is an anarchist.'

'Do you doubt that I'm Sabyasachi?'

'No.'

'What do you understand by the term "anarchist"?'

Apurba was unable to give a suitable reply immediately. After a little thought he said, 'One who's a rebel — an enemy of the king.'

'Our king doesn't live in India, but in England. People say he's a perfect gentleman. I've never seen him, nor has he harmed me in the least. Then why should I have enmity towards him?'

'But those who have? Why should they have enmity? He hasn't harmed them either?'

Doctor shook his head violently. 'There are no enemies of the king in this country, the accusation is totally false!'

His forceful voice and the vehemence of his denial startled Apurba. He had not the courage to disbelieve him, and yet he had no doubt that something was brewing. When he was younger he had been drawn into it himself, and had it not been for his father who was a deputy magistrate, he would have been in deep trouble. He realised this as he grew older.

He thought for a while and then said, 'If not against the king, there is a conspiracy against his officers at least. This can't be denied, can it?'

Doctor remained silent for some time and then replied, slowly, 'The officers are the king's paid servants. They receive their salaries and carry out his orders. If one goes, another comes in his place. These are the broad and simple facts. But when one makes these simple facts complicated, he commits a terrible mistake. He deceives himself into thinking that an

135

assault against them is an assault against the government. There can be nothing more futile than this.'

'But aren't there any Indians who are engaged in such futile activity?' asked Apurba, after a while.

'Maybe,' replied Doctor calmly.

'Where do they live nowadays? What do they do?' asked Apurba, inquisitively.

Doctor merely smiled at his curiosity and fervour, but gave no reply.

'Why d'you smile?'

'Had your Uncle been here, he'd have understood. You believe I'm their leader. You don't expect me to divulge this information, d'you?'

This blunt jibe at his stupidity embarrassed and annoyed Apurba. He said, 'I'd normally not have expected a reply, had I not been enrolled as a member today. Certainly you'll agree that members have a right to such information. After all it's not a game that we're indulging in, but a serious matter!'

'Of course,' smiled Doctor. His sweet smile and straightforward reply seemed derisive to Apurba. Was this the reply to the query of one who had just been enrolled into this revolutionary organisation? In his agitation, Apurba misunderstood this man. In future he would have to change his opinion on finding, not once but on several occasions, that whatever be the situation, Doctor retained his serenity and composure despite the anxiety and excitement.

Apurba continued to walk in silence, as if protesting against the brevity of Doctor's reply. But he could not retain his gravity for long. The acerbity of Doctor's reply hurt him like an arrow. He said bitterly, 'It isn't enough to simply enrol someone; it's necessary to explain to him the consequences also.'

'Haven't they done that?'

'Not at all. Just "the right of way," that's all. Who knew this was the extent of the right? You were there. Shouldn't you have ascertained my views before enrolling me?'

Doctor said awkwardly, 'It's basically a women's organisation. They decide whom to enrol, whom not to. I happen to be merely associated with it. However, it's a fact that I don't know much about the society myself.'

Apurba found this ridiculous. Anxiety and apprehension made the whole thing annoying. He could control himself no longer and said sharply, 'Why this pretence? You may make Sumitra President, or anyone anything else, but there's no doubt that the organisation is yours and you're its brain. You may have succeeded in hoodwinking the police, but you can't deceive me. Just remember that!'

Doctor seemed to be genuinely surprised. His eyes wide open with amazement, he said, 'When you say my organisation, you undoubtedly mean an anarchist one, don't you? But you're totally mistaken and unnecessarily apprehensive. Theirs is a life and death struggle. So why should they take a timid fellow like you? Are they crazy?'

Apurba was mortified, but nevertheless felt as if a heavy load had been lifted from his mind.

Doctor continued, 'Sumitra formed this small organisation named *Pather Dabi*. Men seemed to have forgotten how important and sacred are their rights. The members will try to impress upon others this truth throughout their lives. Sumitra requested that I help her in building up this organisation during my stay here. I agreed. I've no other connection with you people except for this. You're all social reformers, but I've neither the time nor the inclination to be one. I may stay here for a few days, or I may go away tomorrow itself, and we may never meet again. You may not even get the information whether I'm alive or dead.'

The words were spoken slowly, calmly; it was bereft of any excitement or emotion. Apurba suddenly remembered all that his uncle had said about Sabyasachi and he felt a pang in his heart. But then

137

he thought, the man was insensitive like stone — why feel any pain for him? After a while, he enquired, 'Doctor, who's Sumitra? How did you get to know her?'

In reply, Doctor simply smiled. Apurba realised it had not been proper for him to have expressed such curiosity. He had noticed the peculiarities that characterised this strange and mysterious organisation. So he checked his inquisitiveness regarding Bharati and kept quiet.

After a few minutes' silence, it was Doctor who spoke first. 'It's in your advantage that the road is quite safe today. It's rarely like this. But what're you thinking about?'

'Oh, a lot many things. But let that be. You talked about a man's right to go his way unhindered. Is it similar to the way we're walking today?'

'Possibly,' laughed Doctor.

'I couldn't decide what to make of that lady who deserted her husband to join this organisation.'

'I can't say; the matter is not very clear to me either. It's Sumitra who understands such things well.'

'That's possibly because she has no husband, right?'

Doctor remained silent. Apurba remembered once more, with humility and remorse, that he would give no reply to his needless curiosity. He looked at Doctor through the corners of his eyes, but what he saw astonished him. He felt as if a facet of this strange man's unknown past had been revealed to him. It was difficult to explain what exactly it signified, but it exceeded all that he had known so far. It seemed as if his thoughts had wandered away. From the nearby lamp-post a thin ray of light had fallen on his face. As they walked by, Apurba saw in that light as if a haze had descended upon the face of this extremely cautious man and that, oblivious of his surroundings, he was engrossed in a search within himself.

Apurba did not ask any further questions but continued to walk in silence. Suddenly Doctor burst out laughing. 'Honestly, I tell you I don't understand the

138

affairs of women or their show of pique. I'll be wasting much time in trying to understand these things. How can I afford to do that?'

This was obviously not the reply that Apurba expected. So he kept quiet.

Doctor continued, 'The problem is that you can't do without women; on the other hand, if you associate them, they create all sorts of trouble.'

These remarks were irrelevant. Apurba did not bother to reply.

'What's the matter? Why're you so quiet?'

'What should I say?'

'Whatever you like. You see, Apurbababu, Bharati is a very good girl. She's intelligent, hardworking and well-mannered.'

This was equally irrelevant. Though he was tempted, Apurba did not raise the usual questions, such as 'how long have you known her,' or 'how did you get to know her?' this time. He simply said, 'Yes.' Had his companion not been unmindful, this monosyllabic reply would have greatly surprised him. But it was clear he had been talking absent-mindedly.

Picking up the thread from where he had left it, Doctor continued, 'She was saying that you were an absolutely staunch and orthodox Hindu, and that she had injured your caste prejudices.'

'Maybe,' replied Apurba. He had no desire to enter into an argument with this absent-minded person.

They had almost covered the distance. The street lights at the entrance of the lane could be seen ahead. Their destination was now barely ten minutes away. Suddenly Doctor seemed to rouse himself and exclaimed, 'Apurbababu!'

The sharpness of his tone startled Apurba. He replied, 'Yes.'

'So long as I'm here, you needn't bother. But after I leave, you must help Sumitra. Even if you were to search the whole world, you won't come across another person like her. See that her organisation doesn't die for want of care. Such a grand idea — but can a few women alone carry it out? Your unstinted help is absolutely necessary.'

That this great man should have considered him indispensable, Apurba found unconvincing. 'If it's really such a grand idea,' he said, 'why don't you implement it yourself? Why d'you have to go away?'

'When dissociation appears beneficial, it's wrong to hang on. You don't need my help. You must build it up yourselves. Perhaps the motherland will be best served through this.'

'But, Doctor, I really am not convinced about Nabatara's actions.'

'But you do believe Sumitra. You won't find another one so worthy of your trust.' He added after a pause, 'I've told you before that I don't understand well the ways of women. But when Sumitra talked about the inalienable right of man to go unhindered, I could find no arguments to refute it. I know that Nabatara's life would be easier had she chosen the traditional path approved by Manohar and others in the society, and that the path she has chosen may not be easy. But I myself live dangerously. How can I judge others? Sumitra says, Is safety everything in life? A man is guided by his own ideas and propensities. But if he chooses to sacrifice his independent thinking and allows himself to be guided by others, can there be anything more terrible than that? Isn't it like committing suicide? I'm unable to find a convincing reply, Apurbababu.'

'But supposing everyone acts according to his own convictions . . . .'

'What you mean is that if everyone acts according to his whims,' said Doctor with a sly smile. 'You better ask Sumitra what happens in that case.'

Apurba realised he had framed his question wrongly. He was about to correct it when Doctor interrupted him. 'We must end our discussion here today,' he said. 'We've arrived. If you wish we'll continue the debate

140

some other day.'

Apurba looked ahead and saw the brick-coloured school building. A lamp was still burning in Bharati's room upstairs.

'Bharati!' called out Doctor.

Bharati craned her neck out of the window and said anxiously, 'Did you meet Bijoy on the way? He'd gone to call you.'

'Another of your President's orders?' laughed Doctor. 'But no order can force a man to go out so late at night. But have you seen whom I've brought back with me?'

Bharati peered through the darkness and recognised Apurba. 'You haven't done well,' she said. 'But you must go at once. Narahari has struck his wife Haimanti with an axe while in a state of drunkenness. It's doubtful whether she'll survive. Sumitra-didi has gone there.'

'He has done well,' replied Doctor. 'Let her die. But what of my guest?'

'You're exceedingly kind towards women! Had it been Narahari instead of Haimanti, you'd have rushed by now.'

'Okay, I shall rush. But what about my guest?'

'Just a minute,' said Bharati. She immediately came down with a lamp in her hand and opened the door. 'Honestly, Doctor, you must go at once. As for him, will he accept the hospitality of a Christian?'

Doctor felt slightly embarrassed. 'How can I leave him and go?' he said. 'Why haven't they arranged to send her to a hospital?'

'You do that,' retorted Bharati. 'But I beg of you, don't delay any longer! I'll look after him. I'm used to it. But for heaven's sake, go!'

Apurba had kept quiet so long. But it would not do if someone were to die for his sake. He was about to say something, but Doctor had already disappeared into the darkness.

141

CHAPTER 13

While Bharati engaged herself in shutting the doors and windows of the ground floor rooms, Apurba climbed the stairs and entered her room. Selecting an easy chair, he stretched out on it. He closed his eyes and sighed. He realised how exhausted he really was.

When Bharati came up and placed the lamp on a side-table, Apurba was not asleep. But he was suddenly overcome by such a sense of bashfulness that he could think of nothing else but to pretend that he had fallen asleep within this short period. It was not the first time he was sharing a room with Bharati at night. He had not felt embarrassed on the earlier occasions. As he sought to analyse the reasons for this, Apurba remembered Tewari. Though unconscious and dying, his presence provided Apurba with the reason he was searching for and he had felt greatly relieved.

On entering the room, Bharati cast a mere glance at Apurba and went about with her unfinished work. She made no attempts to rouse Apurba. But the racket she made in trying to close the doors and windows of this ramshackle old building was enough to arouse even a genuine sleeper. Realising this, Apurba sat up. He rubbed his eyes, yawned and then said, 'How irritating! I had to come back so late at night.'

Bharati was attempting to close a window. 'You could've said so when you left,' she said. 'I could then have asked Mr. Sarkar to send your food in advance.'

Apurba became wide awake at this remark. He said sharply, 'What d'you mean? Did I know that I'd return?'

Bharati bolted the window and then spoke in a calm voice, 'It was my mistake. I should've ordered for your food at that time itself. At least I wouldn't have had to bother so late in the night. Where were both of you sitting for so long?'

'Better ask him,' replied Apurba. 'I don't know how one can describe walking six miles as "sitting"?'

Bharati had not finished with the windows yet. While drawing the curtains, she exclaimed, 'Ah, say that you'd lost your way in a labyrinth! The walking was in vain!'

She turned round and said with a smile, 'Do you still say your prayers in the evening or have you given it up since? If you haven't, then change your clothes. I'll give you some fresh ones.'

She took out her bunch of keys and began to unlock the almirah. 'Poor Tewari will be worried to death,' she continued. 'I can see that you came here straight from your office.'

Apurba controlled his anger and said, 'I admit you can see many things that I can't, but you needn't bother to take out fresh clothes. I haven't given up saying my prayers; I don't think I can in my lifetime. But the clothes you offer will be of no use. So, just don't bother.'

'First see what they are.'

'I know they'll be of silk. But it won't be necessary . . . . Don't take them out.'

'Won't you say your prayers?'

'No.'

'And how d'you propose to sleep? Wearing your coat and pants? And won't you eat?'

'No.'

'Really?'

Apurba's voice had sounded harsh. But he now said angrily, 'Are you cutting jokes with me?'

Bharati lifted her face and looked at him. 'You're the one cutting jokes,' she said. ' You really think you'll be able to sleep with an empty stomach?'

Saying this she took out from the almirah a beautiful silk *sari*. 'This is absolutely new. I've never worn it. Go to the adjacent room and change your clothes. There's a tap on the ground floor. I'll hold the lamp, you wash your hands and feet and say your prayers. This

143

is permissible in an emergency. You won't be committing a sin.'

Her voice and manner of speaking had suddenly changed. It startled Apurba. He remembered she had spoken in a similar vein when she had left his house early that morning. Apurba stretched out his hand and said, 'Give it to me. I can carry the lamp myself. But I tell you, I can't take food prepared by just anyone.'

Bharati said softly, 'Mr. Sarkar is an orthodox Brahmin. He's poor and runs a hotel, but he's not unorthodox. He prepares the food himself, everyone takes it . . . no one objects . . . even Doctor gets his food from him.'

Apurba was still hesitant. He said with a gloomy face, 'I hate taking stale food.'

Bharati smiled, 'Can I offer you such food? I'll see to it myself. I hope you'll have no objection then,' she said.

Apurba did not argue any further. He took the clothes and the lamp and went downstairs. Bharati could make out from his face that he was extremely reluctant to eat hotel food.

After some time when Apurba was seated on a wooden bench, dressed in the silken clothes, saying his prayers, Bharati opened the door and went out saying that she was going to call Mr. Sarkar, that she would not take long, and that Apurba should wait downstairs till her return.

She returned soon enough, treading cautiously, lamp in hand, just as Apurba was finishing his prayers. Mr. Sarkar followed, carrying a plate covered with a lid made of brass. Behind him was another man carrying a glass of water and a mat to sit upon. As directed by Bharati, he sprinkled water on the floor, washed it and spread the mat for Apurba to sit upon. Mr. Sarkar then laid out the food. After they had left, Bharati closed the door and said with folded hands, in all humility, 'Doctor has paid for this food, not me. You may take it without hesitation.'

Apurba did not find it funny. It was true he believed in the caste system, refused to take food touched by other people and was reluctant to eat hotel food, but he was not that bigoted as to insist that it should have been paid for by a Brahmin and not a Christian. His brothers had caused pain to his mother by their heterodox ways. He therefore felt hesitant to go against her wishes, regardless of whether they were right or wrong. It was not as if Bharati was unaware of this, yet she taunted him every now and then. This irritated Apurba, but he said nothing. Instead, he sat down to eat and lifted the cover. Bharati was sitting a short distance away so as not to defile the food. She was upset at the very sight of the foodstuff. A Christian, she was not permitted to enter the kitchen. It had not occurred to her that Mr. Sarkar might supply her with the leftovers. The room was dimly lit; yet the sight of the food was such that it shocked her. Many times she had peeped through the chink in the wooden floor and watched Apurba taking his food and finding fault with Tewari for the slightest mistakes. So when this fastidious person sat down to eat the food which normally he would never have touched, she could remain silent no longer. 'No, no, don't eat that!' she implored. 'You won't be able to swallow it.'

Apurba looked up surprised. 'Why can't I?' he asked.

Bharati simply shook her head. 'You can't,' she repeated.

Apurba protested, 'Of course I can.'

He was about to eat when Bharati got up and came nearer. 'Even if you can,' she said, 'I won't let you have it. If you fall ill after taking this stuff, I'll again have to nurse you. So, just get up.'

Apurba stood up and asked hesitantly, 'Then what'll I eat? Talwarkar had also not come to office today. Why not let me have a bit of this? What d'you say?'

He looked at her so piteously that Bharati could immediately make out how hungry he actually was. She gave him a wan smile and shook her head. 'No,

Apurbababu, I can't for the life of me let you eat this rubbish. Wash your hands and go upstairs. I'll try to arrange something else.'

Apurba obeyed her request or rather her command, and like a good boy went upstairs. In ten minutes' time, Mr. Sarkar and his assistant made their appearance once again. This time instead of rice, one carried puffed rice and a bowl of milk, and the other some fruits and a pot of water. Apurba felt happy. He could not imagine how all these could be arranged in such a short time. After they left, Apurba settled down to eat happily. Seeing that Bharati was standing outside near the stairs, he said, 'Why don't you come in and sit down? If one is fastidious about sitting on a wooden floor, one can't live in Burma.'

Bharati laughed. 'You're saying this!' she called out from where she was standing. 'You've become very liberal in your views, I must say.'

'No, really, there's nothing wrong in it. Doctor said, let's go back. So I came back. How was one to know that we'd be confronted with the problem of a drunkard trying to kill his wife?'

'And what if you'd known?'

'If I'd known it'd mean giving you so much trouble, I wouldn't have agreed.'

'Possibly. But I thought you came back on your own.'

Apurba's face turned red. He gulped the morsel and protested vehemently, 'Certainly not ! Never! You can verify from Doctor tomorrow.'

'What's there to verify?' replied Bharati calmly. 'Isn't it enough that you say so?'

Despite the tenderness in her voice, Apurba was incensed. He remembered the remarks she had made when he returned, and said angrily, 'You may not believe it, but I'm not in the habit of lying.'

'But why shouldn't I believe you?'

'I don't know. It depends on one's nature,' replied Apurba, and concentrated on the food.

Bharati kept quiet for a while and then said gently,

146

'You're unnecessarily getting angry. There was no harm if you'd come on your own instead of at Doctor's suggestion. I was merely trying to tell you that. When you came the first time to enquire after me, was there anything wrong in that?'

Apurba said, without looking up, 'To come in the afternoon to enquire after someone, and to come at the dead of the night without any reason — both are not the same.'

'True. That's exactly why I'd said that had you told me earlier that you'd return, you wouldn't have faced such problem for your food. Everything could've been kept ready.'

Apurba did not say anything further. When he had nearly finished eating, he suddenly looked up and found Bharati gazing at him silently, in a pleasant and amused manner.

'You see what I meant,' she said. 'It was a rather unsatisfactory meal.'

'I don't know what's the matter with you today,' replied Apurba gravely. 'You don't seem to understand even simple things.'

'Maybe they aren't all that simple. That's why I don't understand,' grinned Bharati.

This made Apurba also to smile. He began to suspect that so long Bharati had simply been pulling his leg. He remembered how this Christian girl had tried to tease him from the very beginning. And yet there was no hatred in it. He knew that whatever problems he faced, whenever he needed help in this foreign land, he could turn to her. He was convinced about this.

Apurba had drained the water in his tumbler. As he picked it up once again, Bharati exclaimed, 'See what I've done?'

'Why, isn't there any more water?'

'Of course there is!' She then said angrily, 'How can a drunkard remember anything? That fellow Shibu must've left that pot of water on the stool downstairs. It's stupid of me not to have noticed it. Nothing can be done now. You'll have to wash your hands and then drink water. But, for heaven's sake, don't get annoyed!'

'What's there to be annoyed?'

'Of course there is,' said Bharati with sincere regret. 'One is bound to feel dissatisfied if there's no water while eating. It's as if it were an incomplete meal. But you mustn't waste any food. Should I run and fetch Shibu?'

Apurba smiled. 'Go out in this darkness just for that?' he said. 'Do you think I'm so inconsiderate?'

He was already full, yet he took a few more mouthfuls and then got up. Somewhat abashed, he said, 'Honestly, I wasn't at all inconvenienced. I shall drink water after I've washed my hands. You're unnecessarily feeling bad about it.'

Bharati laughed. 'Feel bad? Never. I've no reason to do so.' She looked away, and holding the lamp high, said, 'I'll show you the light. Please go downstairs and wash yourself. The pot of water is kept right in front. Don't forget to bring it.'

Apurba went downstairs. When he returned, he found that in the meantime Bharati had removed his plate and cleaned up the place. Some chairs, which had earlier been shifted to make room for him to sit and eat, had been brought back to their usual places. A small dish containing some spices such as cardamoms had been placed on the teapoy near the easy chair which Apurba had used earlier. He now took the towel from Bharati's hand, wiped himself dry, popped a cardamom into his mouth and, stretching himself on the easy chair heaved a sigh of deep satisfaction. 'Ah! I'm myself again. I really had been terribly hungry.'

Bharati was shifting the lamp to another corner so that the light would not fall on Apurba's eyes. As she did so, her own face became visible. Apurba exclaimed, 'What's this? I can see that you've caught a bad cold.'

Bharati hastily put the lamp down and said, 'Why, no.'

'How can you say that? Your voice is hoarse, eyes

148

red and swollen. There's no doubt that you've caught a cold. Strange I didn't notice it before!'

Bharati remained silent.

'It is but natural for you to catch cold,' continued Apurba. 'You had to go out so many times tonight.'

Bharati gave no reply. Apurba said regretfully, 'I unnecessarily gave you so much trouble by coming back. But who knew that Doctor would bring me back and then dump me on you and disappear himself and leave you to face this trouble.'

Bharati was standing near the window with her back towards Apurba, doing something. She now said, 'That's true. But if this was God's wish, how can I blame anyone!'

'What d'you mean?' asked Apurba, surprised.

Bharati continued as before. 'As if I know? But I do see that ever since you arrived in Burma, I've had to face lots of trouble for your sake. You quarrelled with my father, and I had to pay the penalty. You went away on tour leaving Tewari behind to guard your house; I had to look after him. Doctor invited you in, and the burden of looking after you falls on me. I fear lest I've to do this all my life! But it's already very late. Tell me, where are you going to sleep?'

'How'd I know?' asked Apurba surprised.

'I'd asked them to make your bed in Doctor's room in the hotel. I guess they must've done it.'

'But who'll take me there? I don't know the place.'

'I will. Come, let's go and wake them up.'

'Come,' replied Apurba and stood up, ready to go. Then he said with a little hesitation, 'But I'll take your pillow and bed-sheet. Indeed, I must. I just can't use someone else's bedding.'

He was about to take them from the bed when Bharati stopped him. Now, at last, a smile appeared on her sad, grave face. She turned round to hide it and then said quickly, 'This too is someone else's bed. It's strange that you don't feel bad to use this. But if this is so then what's the need for you to go to the hotel. Why don't you sleep here itself?' She did not remind Apurba that not long back, he had considered her clothes impure and unfit for use for saying his prayers.

Greatly embarrassed, Apurba said, 'But where'll you sleep?' You'll be put to difficulty.'

Bharati shook her head. 'Not at all.' Pointing to the adjacent small room, she said, 'I'll spread something there and sleep quite comfortably. You don't know how many nights I've had to sleep on the wooden floor near Tewari's bed, using my arms as pillows.'

Remembering the incidents that happened a month back, Apurba said, 'It's not as if I'm totally unaware. I was witness to at least one such night.'

Bharati smiled. 'You still remember that? Well, I'll manage the same way tonight.'

Apurba said hesitantly, 'Tewari was seriously ill then. Now it's different. People will talk about it.'

'Not at all. There's none amongst us who'd be so mean as to unnecessarily talk about others' affairs.'

'I can as well sleep on the bench downstairs,' said Apurba.

'Even if you can, I won't let you do so. Because it isn't necessary. You treat me like an untouchable. You won't do anything that'll harm my reputation, I'm confident of that.'

'I'm sure you'll never come to any harm because of me,' said Apurba emotionally. 'But it pains me greatly when you say that I treat you like an untouchable. The word "untouchable" has connotations of hatred. But I don't hate you. Our religions differ; I'm not permitted to eat food touched by you. But is it indicative of hatred? Nothing can be farther from the truth. Rather, you must be hating me for it. That morning when you left me alone and came away . . . . I still remember the expression on your face. I'll never forget it in my life.'

'I see. You'll forgive my other faults, but not that one?'

150

'Never.'

'What did my expression indicate? Hatred?'

'Certainly.'

Bharati looked at his face, smiled and then said gently, 'This shows that your ability to read others' minds is wonderfully strong — almost nil! But let that be. You'd better go to bed now. I'm used to staying awake, but if you don't sleep now, it'll mean some fresh trouble for me.' Without waiting for a reply, she picked up a couple of blankets from the rack and entered the adjacent room.

She returned after a while, rigged up the mosquito net, tucked it in carefully and then departed. But it was long before Apurba could fall asleep. A lantern glowed dimly in one corner of the room. Outside it was pitch-dark. There was silence everywhere. Possibly he alone was awake; nor was it certain how long he would remain so. And yet he felt no discomfort. It appeared to him as if there could be nothing more pleasant than to be awake in this room, on this bed, in this still night. Never before had he felt so relaxed and comfortable as at present.

The next morning he woke up at Bharati's call. Opening his eyes he saw her standing near the foot of his bed. The crimson rays of the morning sun streamed through the eastern window and fell on her freshly bathed hair, on the red border of her white silken *sari*, and on the bright, clear features of her beautiful face. It all appeared wonderfully beautiful to Apurba.

'Get up now,' said Bharati. 'Don't you have to go to office?'

'Of course,' said Apurba, and got up. 'I see you've already finished your bath.'

'You too must get ready quickly. There was much to be desired in our hospitality last night. Hence our President has ordered that you're not to be allowed to leave without being properly fed.'

'Could that woman be saved last night?' asked Apur-

151

ba.

'She's been sent to the hospital. We're hopeful she'll survive.'

Apurba had not even seen her. Yet the reassurance seemed to set his heart at rest. It seemed to him he could not bear the news of misfortune befalling anyone that day.

It was about nine by the time Apurba returned to the room after finishing his prayers and bath downstairs. In between, Mr. Sarkar had served his food. Apurba sat down on the mat and said, 'I don't see your President anywhere. Is this her way of showing her hospitality?'

'She'll definitely meet you before you leave. I believe she has some work with you as well.'

'And Doctor, who invited me in! I suppose he's still in bed?' laughed Apurba.

Bharati did not join in the laughter. 'Where does he have the time to sleep? He just returned from the hospital. Sleep or no sleep . . . nothing seems to matter to him.'

Apurba was astonished. 'Doesn't that make him fall ill?' he asked.

'Never seen him fall ill,' replied Bharati. 'Comfort and illness . . . he seems to have renounced both. You can't compare him with any other man.'

Apurba remembered about the incidents of the previous night. He said softly, 'I suppose all of you revere him very much?'

'Revere him! We revere so many other people as well.' As she spoke her voice choked, 'When he walks by, one wishes one could be part of the dust that he walks upon. Even then one doesn't feel satisfied!'

She turned aside and wiped the tears from the corners of her eyes.

Apurba asked no further questions. As he ate silently, with his face downwards, he pondered over Bharati's words. He wondered how extraordinary Doctor must really be if intelligent and educated women like

152

Sumitra and Bharati held him in such high esteem. God must have planned to get extraordinary feats performed by him!

Bharati sat silently near the doorway. Apurba too did not say anything more and concentrated on his food. Though no apparent unpleasantness had occurred, Apurba felt as if a cloud had fallen over the morning which had started off so brightly.

Before leaving for the office, Apurba said, 'Come, let's go and meet Doctor once.'

'Come. In fact, he has asked for you.'

Doctor's room was in the innermost portion of Mr. Sarkar's dilapidated hotel. There was no ventilation, nor any light. The whole place stank from the foul water which had accumulated in the neighbourhood. The floor was made up of wooden planks which had become so old and rotten that one was afraid to step on it lest it should break and fall down. When Bharati showed him into this ugly, dingy room, his astonishment knew no bounds. On entering, he was unable to see anything for a few moments.

'Do come in, Apurbababu!' Doctor welcomed him.

'Ugh! What a dungeon you've found for yourself, Doctor!'

'But how cheap! The rent is only ten annas.'

'Exorbitant! Much too exorbitant!' exclaimed Apurba. 'Shouldn't have been more than a few pice.'

'You should see how poor people like us live. To many this is a palace!'

'In that case I shall pray to God to keep me away from such palaces. Ugh!'

'I heard you were put to much inconvenience last night. You must accept my apologies.'

'I will, but only if you leave this place. Not before that.'

Doctor smiled. 'Okay, I will.'

Suddenly Apurba noticed Sumitra sitting on a stool near the wall. He was astonished. 'I'm sorry,' he said. 'I didn't notice you before.'

153

'It's not your fault,' replied Sumitra. 'It's the darkness.'

Apurba was startled to hear her voice. It was heavy and sorrowful. He apprehended that something disastrous must have happened. He peered at Doctor and remarked, 'You're dressed in strange clothes today. Are you going somewhere?'

Doctor had wrapped a turban round his head. He was dressed in a long coat and loose pyjamas and on his feet he wore a pair of pointed shoes from Rawalpindi. In his hand he carried a leather bag stuffed with some bundles. 'I'm leaving,' he said. 'They'll remain; I leave them in your care. I guess I needn't tell you anything more.'

Apurba was bewildered. 'But why so suddenly and where to?'

There was no change in Doctor's tone. He continued in the same calm manner. 'Does the word "suddenly" figure in our dictionary, Apurbababu? For the present I'm going northwards beyond Bhamo. I've some brocade with genuine silver thread. It'll fetch a good price from the soldiers,' he chuckled.

Sumitra, who had been silent so long, now suddenly spoke out, 'They've been brought from Peshawar to Bhamo. You know what a vigilant watch is kept over them. Many of them know you; don't think you can hoodwink everyone. Can't you stay back for a few days more?' Her voice sounded strange towards the end.

Doctor smiled. 'You know I have to go,' he said.

Sumitra did not say anything further. But the whole thing became instantly clear to Apurba. His whole body seemed to shiver with excitement. He asked agitatedly, 'Supposing they recognise you? Suppose you get caught?'

'I suppose they'll hang me. But I must hurry if I'm to catch the ten o'clock train.' He effortlessly slung the huge hold-all on to his back and picked up the leather bag.

Bharati had not spoken so long. She did not utter a

154

single word even now, but only bowed. Sumitra prostrated herself at Doctor's feet. She remained like that for a long while and when she slowly got up, her face remained downcast and was not clearly visible in that dimly lit room.

Doctor came out of the room. Clutching Apurba's hands as he had done the previous evening, he said, 'Goodbye, Apurbababu . . . . I'm indeed Sabyasachi.'

Apurba's tongue became parched and dry. Words did not come out of his throat. He went down on his knees and prostrated himself before Doctor just as the two women had done. Doctor placed one hand on his head and the other on Bharati's. He uttered something but it was too indistinct to be heard. He then rushed out.

When Apurba stood up, he found himself alone with Bharati. Behind the closed door of that dingy room the fearless, extraordinarily intelligent and strong-willed President of their society was engaged in some activity which they could not make out.

CHAPTER 14

Both Bharati and Apurba looked at the closed door, but neither said anything. Though not totally clear, at least this much was clear to Apurba that he should not be unnecessarily curious about someone who had deliberately locked herself inside the room. Without exchanging a single word, they came out of the hotel. Bharati said, 'Come, let's go to my room.'

'But it's time for office . . . .'

'On a Sunday?'

'Sunday? Indeed it is so,' said Apurba happily. 'Had I known, I wouldn't have had to rush through my bath and food. You usually remember everything, but even you forgot this!'

Bharati smiled. 'Maybe. But I haven't forgotten that you had no proper meal last night.'

Suddenly Apurba stopped in his tracks. 'I must go home,' he said. 'Poor Tewari must be sick with worry.'

'Not at all. He was informed about your being here even before you woke up.'

'He knows that I'm staying with you?'

Bharati nodded. 'Yes. I sent a man to him early in the morning.'

This not only eased Apurba's anxiety but also removed a heavy load from his mind. Since the previous day he had been disturbed as to whether Tewari would believe his story or not. Many rumours were heard of people's conduct in Burma — it was possible that Tewari might write to his mother against him or else spread tales on returning to India which would taint him forever — even if the stains were removed, the mark would remain. This had been like a thorn in his flesh; but now he could breathe freely again. Whatever else he might do, Tewari would never disbelieve Bharati. There could never be any greater proof of his innocence for Tewari that Bharati's clean

156

chit — Apurba was certain about this.

He said cheerfully, 'You do think of everything. I've seen my sisters-in-law, as well as others; I've also seen my mother, but none can match you. I can say unhesitantly that when you get married, your family will have a jolly good time. They can just close their eyes and relax and not worry about anything.'

It was as if a flash of lightning had hit Bharati. Apurba was walking behind her, so he did not notice this and went on as usual, 'Just imagine what would've happened to me if you hadn't been there to help me! Everything would've been stolen; Tewari would've died uncared for and his corpse removed by scavengers . . . .' The possibility of a Brahmin's corpse being thus polluted sent a shiver down his spine.

He resumed after a while, 'Could I've continued to stay here after that? Possibly I'd have had to resign and go back. And face the same music as before — my sister-in-law's taunts and my mother's tears. You've saved me from all this.'

'Yet you picked up a quarrel with me as soon as you landed.'

Apurba felt embarrassed. 'It was all because of Tewari,' he said. 'But you've no idea how much my mother'll bless you when she hears the whole story.'

'How can I? I can only hear from her if she comes here.'

'Mother, come to Burma!' said Apurba in surprise. 'You don't say that!'

'Why not? If others can come, why can't she? One doesn't lose one's caste simply by coming to Burma.'

Apurba entered the room and sat down on the same easy chair as before. As the sun hit his face, Bharati reached out and closed the window. She said, 'Your sisters-in-law don't take proper care of your mother. If you've to serve abroad all your life, who'll look after her in her old age?'

'Mother says her youngest daughter-in-law will do so.'

'But what if she doesn't? You'll be away. Like the

157

others, instead of taking care of your mother, she too may cause her pain. What'll you do then?'

Apurba was alarmed. 'That'll never happen,' he said. 'A girl coming from a pious Brahmin family will never cause her pain, I can tell you that.'

'A pious Brahmin family?' chuckled Bharati. 'If necessary I'll tell you the story of such a girl some other day.'

After a while she added, 'But don't you think you'd be doing an injustice to the girl you marry simply to look after your mother?'

Apurba looked at her and said, 'I agree.'

'And you expect her loyalty in return?'

Apurba remained silent for a while and then said, 'But is there any other alternative open to me, Bharati?'

'You may be right. But you mustn't expect the impossible from the girl, no matter how pious a family she comes from. The result of this can never be good. Regardless of your cruelty towards her, the more she's dutiful, the more you'll fall in her esteem. There's nothing more humiliating for a man than to appear unworthy in front of his wife.'

What she said was irrefutable, and so Apurba kept quiet. In his arguments with his friends on many occasions, Apurba had quoted examples from the scriptures to prove his point about a woman's duties, what constituted chastity and how meritorious it was for her to selflessly serve her mother-in-law and to carry out the wishes of her husband. He used to silence his friends with these arguments, but today on being confronted with this Christian girl, he could not bring himself to utter any of his usual arguments. After some time he said, as if speaking to himself, 'I suppose such a girl can't be found these days.'

Bharati smiled. 'How can you say that? There may be one who, though not the daughter of a pious Brahmin, may be willing to sacrifice herself totally for your sake. But where'll you find her?'

Apurba was absorbed in his own thoughts. He said casually, 'Yes, indeed.'

'When d'you plan to go home?' asked Bharati.

'I don't know. Whenever my mother sends for me,' replied Apurba unmindfully. After a while he said, 'My mother had differences of opinion with my father and was unhappy all her life. I didn't like the idea of leaving her alone at home. I don't know whether I'll be able to return once I go home.'

Looking up at Bharati he said, 'You see, others may think we're affluent, but that's not true. In reality we're not above want, same as with most others in the town. My sisters-in-law may force us to fend for ourselves. There'd be no end to our misery if I'm unable to come back.'

'But you must!'

'Should I live all my life away from my mother?'

'Why don't you bring her with you? I'm sure she'll agree.'

Apurba smiled. 'Never. You don't know her. Okay, suppose she does, who'll look after her here?'

'Why? I will,' said Bharati.

'You? She'll throw away her cooking pots, if you even enter her room.'

'How many times will she do that? I'll enter her room every day.' Both burst out laughing.

Bharati turned grave. 'You too are in the same boat,' she said. 'But if only throwing the pots would've been the solution, there wouldn't be any problems left in this world. If you don't believe me, ask Tewari.'

Apurba acquiesced. 'You're right,' he said. 'The poor fellow may throw his pots, but he'll shed tears too. He reveres you so much that one never knows, he may even agree to become a Christian if you tell him to.'

'One can't be sure about anything in this world,' replied Bharati. 'Neither about the servant, nor about the master.'

Saying this, she lowered her face to hide her smile. But Apurba turned red as a beetroot. 'One can how-

159

ever be sure of one thing,' he remarked, 'that there's bound to be a great difference in the level of intelligence of the two.'

Bharati looked up. 'Undoubtedly,' she said. 'As a result there may be some delay on Tewari's part to convert to Christianity, but not so in your case.'

Her eyes sparkled with suppressed laughter. Realising that Bharati was joking, Apurba said gaily, 'Jokes apart, d'you really believe that I can renounce my faith?'

'I do.'

'Honestly?'

'Yes.'

'On the contrary, the fact is that I can't do so even for the sake of my life.'

'You don't know how it feels like to face death. Tewari knows. But what's the point in continuing this argument? I've far more pressing things to do than enlightening you. You'd better take a nap now.'

'I never sleep during daytime. But tell me, what's the important work that you have?'

'As if I've nothing else to do except slogging for you for nothing! I've to do a bit of cooking as well. If you can't sleep, why not come down and see how I cook and what I prepare? Since you'll have to take food prepared by me one day, it'd be better to have some idea.' She giggled.

'I'll never eat anything prepared by you even if I die.'

'Well, I'm speaking about your doing so while you're alive.' Smiling, she went downstairs.

Apurba called out, 'I really must go home now. Poor Tewari will be terribly worried.'

He pricked his ears and waited for a reply. When none came, he stretched himself on the chair. His problem was not whether Bharati heard him or not, or whether, even after hearing him, she preferred not to give any reply. His problem was that he realised that he should forthwith go home and delay no longer whatever may be the excuse. And yet, the more he

160

realised this, the more lethargic and listless he felt. Finally, with his hand across his face, Apurba fell asleep.

CHAPTER 15

'It's nearly evening. Get up!'

Apurba rubbed his eyes and sat up. He glanced at the wall-clock and exclaimed, 'Good heavens! I must've slept for nearly four hours. Why didn't you wake me up? Ah, I find you've come and provided me a pillow. How could I've woken up then!'

'If you had to wake up,' replied Bharati, 'you'd have done so when I placed the pillow. If I hadn't, you'd have had a stiff neck. Anyway, go and have a wash now. Mr. Sarkar is waiting with your snack. He's got other things to do, so you'd better hurry up.'

The man who was standing outside now craned his neck and made the same request.

Apurba went downstairs and washed himself. He came back, had his snack, then popping a few corns of spices in his mouth, said happily, 'Now please permit me to go home.'

Bharati shook her head. 'No, you can't,' she said. 'I've informed Tewari that you'll return tomorrow evening, after office hours. I've found out that Tewari is hale and hearty and is taking good care of your house, so don't worry.'

'But why can't I go now?'

'Because you're our guardian now. Sumitra-didi is unwell. Nabatara has gone to the other side of the river along with Atulbabu. You've to accompany me. That's our President's order. I've kept a *dhoti* for you. Put it on and come along.'

'Where?'

'To the workmen's lines — that is, to the hellish hovels which the millionaire factory-owners have built for their workmen. Today being a Sunday, we've to work there.'

'But why there?'

'Because the society's work can't possibly be done in

162

this room.' She smiled. 'You're an important member of our society. If you don't go to the scene of action how'll you form an idea of our work?'

'Okay.' Apurba went and changed his dress. Five minutes later, he was ready to go.

Bharati opened her almirah, took out something and slipped it into her pocket.

Apurba noticed it and asked, 'What was that?'

'A country-made pistol.'

'Pistol? What for?'

'For self-defence.'

'D'you have a licence?'

'No.'

'If you're caught, it'll be the end of the road for both of us. What's the punishment for carrying un-licensed arms?'

'We won't. Come on.'

Apurba heaved a deep sigh, muttered a prayer and said, 'Okay, let's go.'

Taking the main road they crossed the Burmese and Chinese localities in the north. Skirting round the bazaar they must have walked for about a mile when they found themselves in front of a huge factory. The gate was closed but they found a gap and slipped through it. To their right were rows of corrugated-iron sheds. Beyond these were the workmen's quarters. They were made of broken planks and tin-sheets. A number of water-taps stood in front, and to the back were rows of toilets built of tin-sheets. Originally these may have been fitted with doors; now only jute cloth hung there.

These were the Indian coolie lines. Punjabis, south Indians, Burmese, Bengalis, Oriyas, Hindus and Mus-lims, men and women — nearly a thousand of them — lived in these conditions day after day, month after month, and year after year.

Bharati remarked, 'Today is a holiday for them. Else you'd have witnessed one or two brawls near these water taps.'

163

'I can well imagine that from the apparent rush even on a holiday,' said Apurba.

In the presence of all these people, one south Indian woman pushed aside the jute screen and entered a toilet. Seeing the condition of the curtain Apurba turned red with embarrassment. 'If you have to do the society's work,' he cried, 'let's do that elsewhere. I can't stand here any more.'

Bharati had noticed the scene herself but she gave no reply and merely smiled as if to say, 'Why bother about those who've been degraded to the level of animals?'

Finally they entered a Bengali workman's hut. He was an elderly man and worked in the brass foundry. He lay sozzled on the wooden floor, abusing someone.

Bharati called out, 'Whom are you abusing, Manik? Where's Sushila? Why didn't she attend her classes for the last two days?'

Manik opened his eyes and appeared to recognise Bharati. He somehow sat up and said, 'Come, *Didimoni*. Do sit down. How can Sushila go to school? She has to do the cooking, clean the utensils and even look after the boy. My heart bleeds for her. I'll kill that rascal Jodo, else I'm not a fisherman's son! I'll complain to the elder Sahib so that the fellow loses his job.'

Bharati laughed. 'Do that by all means. In fact, if you so like, I'll get it written by Sumitra-didi for you. But we have a meeting tomorrow, on the grounds of the Phaya Temple. You haven't forgotten, have you?'

Around this time a ten or eleven years old girl entered the room. She took out a bottle of liquor from within the folds of her dress and placing it carefully on the floor, addressed her father, 'I couldn't get the Horse brand stuff, so I brought the Hat brand instead. We owe him four pice. D'you know what that drunkard Ramaiyya was telling me?'

Her father responded by abusing Ramaiyya in filthy language.

164

'You shouldn't go to that place again, Sushila,' said Bharati. 'Where's your mother?'

'Mother? She went away with uncle Jadu the night before yesterday. They've moved out of the coolie lines and are staying together in a rented house.'

The girl would have continued, but for her father who thundered out, 'I'll show them! She's my wife, not a prostitute!' Saying this, he began to unscrew the fresh bottle with a broken kitchen spoon in the absence of an opener.

Suddenly, Bharati felt a forceful tug at her *sari* from behind. Turning around she saw that Apurba's face had become ashen. He had never touched Bharati before, but he seemed to have forgotten that.

'Come out at once,' he said.

'Just wait a minute.'

'No, not even for a minute.' Saying this Apurba almost dragged her out.

Inside the room, Manik continued to wrestle with the cork, the bottle and the broken kitchen spoon and to rave and rant. 'I'm ready to hang for murder. I'm Desho *Goonda*'s son. I'm not afraid of either the jail or the gallows!'

Outside, Apurba burst out, 'Bastard, rascal, drunken pig! He's made a hell out there. Don't you hate coming here?'

Bharati looked intently at Apurba's face and then said calmly, 'No. Because they've not created this hell. They're just expiating for the sins of others.'

'Who created this hell, if not they? You heard what the girl said? As if her mother has gone on a pilgrimage! Shameless rascal! If you ever come here again, you'll suffer, I tell you.'

Bharati smiled. 'I'm a Christian, not a Brahmin like you. What harm is it if I come here?'

'Of course there is!' said Apurba angrily. 'Isn't there anything like good conduct for Christians? Aren't they answerable to their community?'

'Who's there to whom I'd be answerable? Who cares

for me?'

Apurba was unable to give a proper reply. Instead, he said, 'You're merely trying to be clever. You have to go home now.'

'I've several other places to go to. If you don't like to come along, you may go back.'

'How can I leave you here and go back?'

'Then come with me. Learn to see the misery man causes to his fellow-beings. Merely by practising untouchability and remaining pure yourself, do you think you'll achieve piety and go to heaven? Never!' As she went on her face became grim and her voice sharp. Apurba had seen her like this before.

Bharati continued, 'Does the problem end by punishing Sushila's mother and Jadu for their crime? Aren't you too a part of the same system? Of course you are! Till I met Doctor, I too had the same opinion. But today I'm convinced that for all the crimes committed in this hell, you're equally responsible. You too are a part of the same hell. You can have no deliverance until you've repaid your debt to them. We come here on our own volition. This realisation is perhaps our greatest achievement. Come, let's go.'

'Okay,' said Apurba weakly. He was unable to apprehend what Bharati said; nor did he believe it.

A teak tree stood at a distance. Pointing at it, Bharati said, 'A few Bengali families live over there. Let's visit them.'

'Don't you work for other communities?' enquired Apurba.

'We do. But except for our President, others can't speak their language. When she's well she does that work herself, not I!'

'Is she familiar with all languages spoken in India?'

'Yes.'

'And Doctor?'

Bharati smiled. 'You certainly are most inquisitive about Doctor,' she said. 'Why can't you believe that he knows everything that's worth knowing and doing

166

everything that's worth doing. No one knows who gave him the name Sabyasachi — "one who wields both hands with equal dexterity" — but indeed there's nothing that he can't do or doesn't know!'

Saying this, Bharati walked on. But Apurba, who was following her, stopped and heaved a deep sigh. It hurt him to think that in this hapless subject nation such a great soul should be so uncared for. At any moment he could die like a dog. Could there be a greater injustice in this world? If it is true that God is merciful, then why was he being made to suffer and for whose sins?

They entered a room. Bharati called out, 'Panchkari, how're you today?'

Someone replied from the shadows, 'Slightly better.'

An elderly man came and stood before them. His right hand was smeared with ointment. He said, 'My daughter is ill with dysentery. I don't think she'll survive. My son is unconscious with fever since yesterday. I've no money to buy medicines for them or even to buy some sago or barley.' Tears welled up in his eyes.

Apurba suddenly blurted out, 'But why don't you have any money?'

The man looked at this stranger silently for a while and then said, 'The pulley chain fell on my hand and hurt it. I haven't been able to go out to work for over a month now. How can I have any money left?'

'Doesn't the manager of the factory offer compensation?'

Panchkari touched his forehead and said, 'Alas, what compensation for a day labourer? I'm being told to vacate this room if I'm unable to go to work. "We'll allot you a room again when you return to work," they say. Tell me, where can I go in this condition? Maybe if I plead with the younger Sahib, they'll let me stay for a week more. I've been working here for twenty years now. They're such ungrateful people!'

Apurba felt infuriated. He felt that if he could get

167

hold of the manager, he would have dragged him by his ears and shown him the miserable state of one who, in better times, had helped the factory earn millions.

There was a bullock cart stand near Apurba's ancestral house in Calcutta. He remembered that when, after life-long hard work, the bullocks became old and infirm, their owners sold them to the slaughterhouse. There was no way of stopping this heartlessness; no one tries to, and if one does, he is branded as a crank. Apurba remembered that whenever he had passed by that road his eyes grew moist, not for the hapless animals, but for the men, who in their greed for money, perpetrated this barbarous act and thereby degraded themselves.

Suddenly he remembered what Bharati had told him and said to himself, 'She was absolutely right. One cannot brush aside the question simply because it does not concern us directly, or that I'm not responsible for it, or by saying that such things happen, and have happened all along. The slaughter of the animals provided an example. Panchkari, with his broken arm, provided another. The slaughter of the defenceless, the tyranny over the weak, the shameless exploitation of the helpless — this murder of one's conscience, this slaying of the self, this celebration of madness — when will it end? How is this destructive energy to be curbed? Will man ever be enlightened?'

The children were lying half-dead on a dirty, tattered bed in one corner of the room. Bharati went over and began to examine them. Apurba felt frightened to even go near them, but the silent agony of these two poor and sick children wrenched his heart. Standing there, he thought emotionally, 'People say life's like this! This is how things have been all along! But can one accept this argument? Should we be guided only by the past? Should one cling to old superstitions and do nothing? Should he not strive to do something new? Is he incapable of progress? Should the past, the dead past, determine the future? Should it close the doors to life, to progress, and reign forever?'

'Let's go.'

Startled, Apurba saw Bharati standing beside him. Panchkari stood there, silent, distressed. In a calm voice, Bharati reassured him. 'Don't worry, they'll come round. Tomorrow morning I'll send a doctor, medicines, food, everything . . . .'

Before she could finish, Apurba thrust his hand into his pocket to fish out some money, but Bharati prevented him from doing so. Panchkari's attention was elsewhere and so he did not notice what transpired. But Apurba could not understand the reason behind her action. Bharati then took out four annas from her pocket and gave it to Panchkari. 'Buy four pice worth of candy for the children and four pice worth of sago. With the remaining two annas, buy some rice and lentils and somehow manage for today. I'll make the remaining arrangements tomorrow. We're going now.' Saying so, she came out with Apurba.

When they reached the road, Apurba said in a piqued tone, 'You're very miserly. Neither did you allow me to give him some money, nor did you give yourself.'

'But I did.'

'In his time of dire need to give him only four annas is nothing short of an insult!'

'How much were you going to give?'

Apurba had not decided anything. Most probably he would have given whatever he had fished out. Now he thought for a minute and said, 'At least five rupees.'

Bharati bit her tongue. 'Don't tell me,' she said. 'That would've been disastrous. He'd have gone and got drunk. Thereafter he'd have been unconscious the whole night and the children would've died.'

'He would've got drunk?'

'Wouldn't he? Is there any such extraordinary person who doesn't drink when he has money in his hands?'

Apurba remained silent for a while like one be-

169

wildered, and then said, 'You're joking. Is it possible that a father would've spent money meant for his children's medicines on drinks?'

'I can swear in the name of any god you like — Manasa, the serpent goddess, or Ola Bibi?' She burst into a laughter but immediately checked herself and said gravely, 'Otherwise why should I prevent a benefactor from offering donation to a poor man? Tell me, am I so mean?'

'Isn't their mother alive?'

'No.'

'I guess they've no other relatives either.'

'Even if there were, they wouldn't be of any use. About ten or twelve years ago Panchkari had been to his native place. There he managed to elope with the widowed daughter of a neighbour. These children are hers. About a couple of years back she hanged herself. This, in short, is Panchkari's story.'

'Hellish,' sighed Apurba.

Bharati nodded her head, 'No two opinions about that,' she said. 'But our problem is that they are all our brothers and sisters. One can't get away by saying that one is not connected by blood ties. We'll be answerable to God for this.'

'I agree,' replied Apurba gravely. The thoughts that had assailed him as he stood in Panchkari's room now flashed through his mind again. 'Being human, I too have a responsibility towards them.'

Bharati nodded. 'I didn't clearly understand it earlier,' she said. 'It used to upset me. But now I see clearly who're really responsible for the sins committed by these ignorant, unhappy and weak people.'

An Oriya workman lived in the room adjacent to Panchkari's. From time to time the sound of revelry and loud laughter could be heard from that room. This had been audible even from Panchkari's room. Now both Bharati and Apurba entered this room. All the inmates knew Bharati and accorded her a noisy welcome. One hurriedly brought two stools, one

170

wooden and the other cane, for them to sit upon. Half a dozen men and about eight or ten women sat on the wooden floor, drinking. A broken harmonium and a *tabla* were kept in the middle of the room. Numerous empty bottles of different colours and sizes lay scattered all around. An elderly woman sprawled drunkenly in a half-naked condition in one corner of the room. Those present in the room ranged from sixty-to-twentyfive-year-olds. It was Sunday and a holiday for the men. The stench of cheap German liquor mingled with the smell of onion and garlic curry to give Apurba nausea.

A young woman, apparently new to the place and a beginner, clutched at a glass. She pressed her nostrils, emptied the glass down her throat, and proceeded to spit repeatedly through the chinks in the wooden floor. One man got up and stuffed a little curry into her mouth. Watching Bengali women drink, Apurba felt miserable. Looking at Bharati through the corners of his eyes, he found her unmoved even by this obnoxious sight. She appeared to have got used to this. But after some time when, at the request of the master of the house, Tuni began to sing and the man sitting beside her caught hold of the harmonium, pressed a reed and began to bellow furiously, it was a bit too much even for Bharati. Addressing the workman, she said hurriedly, 'I hope you've not forgotten about our meeting tomorrow. All of you must attend.'

'Of course,' said Kalachand and drained his glass.

Bharati added, 'As children you must've read that even straw, if braided into a rope, can bind an elephant. Without unity you'll never be able to achieve anything. It's for your good that Sumitra-didi is working so hard. Don't you agree?'

All of them expressed their agreement. Bharati continued, 'Will this factory run even for a single day without your help? You are its real owners. How'll it do if you don't understand this simple thing?'

'You're absolutely right.' They were unanimous that

171

if they did not work, the factory would close down.

Bharati said, 'And yet, think how miserable you all are. The Sahibs insult you without any reason and kick you out whenever they feel like. See Panchkari, your neighbour. He broke his hand while working in the factory, and now he's starving. His children are dying for want of medicines and food and the Sahib wants to throw him out from his room! They've earned profit of millions of rupees . . . who helped them earn it? And how much do you get? The other day Shyamlal was knocked down by the younger Sahib . . . he's still in hospital. How do you tolerate such things? If all of you stand. unitedly and decide not to take such tyranny any more, they won't dare lay their finger on you again! For once, just learn to recognise your strength . . . . We want nothing more from you!'

One drunkard who had been listening to Bharati open-mouthed, now said, 'Indeed! What can't we do? I've just to loosen one bolt and — crash! Half the factory will disappear!'

Bharati was shaken. 'For heaven's sake, Dulal,' she pleaded, 'never do such a thing! That'll ruin all of you. A number of people may die, maybe . . . no, no, never even dream of such a thing! You'd be committing a great sin.'

The man laughed drunkenly. 'Don't I know that? I was just giving an example. You don't think we're sinners!'

'You must remain on the right path and act honestly. Only then will you get your dues. They owe you all lots of money — you'll have to extract it all!'

All of them grew excited and began to create an uproar.

'It's getting dark,' said Bharati. 'We've to visit another place. We must go now. But don't forget about tomorrow's meeting.' Saying so, she stood up.

The entire episode in Kalachand's room had been most distasteful to Apurba. The discussion towards the end in particular strained his nerves. When they came

172

out, he burst out angrily, 'Why did you have to tell them all those things?'

'Which things?' inquired Bharati.

'That drunkard . . . Dulal or whatever his name was . . . You heard what that bastard said? Suppose the Sahib gets to know about it?'

'How will he?'

'Why? They themselves may tell him or did you think they were all saints? In their condition, they're capable of doing anything! And the blame will come upon you! They may even say that you tried to instigate them.'

'But that'd be a lie?'

'A lie!' said Apurba impatiently. 'Under British rule hasn't anyone ever be imprisoned on false charges? Their power is itself founded on falsehood.'

'I'm prepared to go to jail.'

'No, no, this'll never do. You should never come here again.'

Bharati had business with another person, but when they reached the place they found it locked. So they returned the same way. Passing by Kalachand's room, they found Tuni's song had ended and that their drunken discussion has become more uproarious. One drunken woman was lamenting over her dead husband. Another was consoling her and advising her to forget about the past. Instead she should offer prayers every full moon day.

Others were arguing that these Christian women wanted to start a strike in the factory. Then there would be no end to their misery. They should never be allowed to enter their lines. Kalachand was telling them that he was no kid. He was simply watching the fun. One over-cautious woman suggested that it would be better to inform the Sahib without delay.

Apurba dragged Bharati away from that place and then said bitterly, 'You still want to do good to them? Ungrateful wretches! Bastards! Ugh! Two small children are dying next door — they don't even bother to help! Hellish!'

173

Bharati looked at Apurba sharply. 'What's the matter with you?'

'Nothing. I knew it. But tell me whether you heard what they said or not?'

'Nothing new. We hear it everyday.'

'Such mischievous fellows! Such ingratitude!' thundered Apurba. 'And you want to unite them, to do good to them?'

There was not a trace of excitement in Bharati's voice. Instead, with a wan smile, she said, 'Who are they after all? They're my own people. Whenever you forget this basic thing, you get confused. And so far as doing good is concerned, if anywhere there's need for doing some good, it's here. You don't need to do any good to a man like Doctor, do you?'

Apurba gave no reply.

They came out of the gate silently. Skirting the Burmese locality and the bazaar, they at last reached the main road.

It was past evening. Lamps had been lighted in the houses. Shops had sprung up on both sides of the road and were doing brisk business. Bharati pulled her *sari* down to her forehead and walked on with rapid strides, without uttering a single word.

At last they crossed the residential area and reached the marshes and the open fields. Coming to a crossing, Bharati said to Apurba, 'If you want to go to your house you've to take the road on the right. It'll lead you straight to the town.'

Apurba had been unmindful. 'What did you say?' he inquired.

'I see that you've finally got your cool back. You remembered to use the correct form while addressing me.'

'What's that?'

'In your anger you had forgotten the difference between the formal and the informal mode of address. Now you've again remembered it.'

Embarrassed, Apurba said, 'I hope you didn't mind

it.'

'A bit,' said Bharati with a laugh. 'Let's go.'

'Again to your place?'

'Then do you suggest I go alone in this darkness?'

Apurba did not argue any further. The events of the afternoon filled him with indignation. He was unable to forget the behaviour of those drunkards. Suddenly he burst out, 'This is Sumitra's work; then why do you have to go there? If someone reports against you, you'll be in serious trouble.'

'It doesn't matter.'

'Of course it does! The fact is you're fond of bossing over others! But there are other places where you can do that.'

'Pray, show me one.'

'Why should I?'

A portion of the road had been dug up for repairs. There had been no difficulty in crossing it during the afternoon. But now in the darkness, in the shadows of the *gulmohar* trees on both sides of the road, it had become almost impassable. Bharati clutched Apurba's hand tightly and said, 'I don't think I can shake off my habit. I'll have to do something. If only I could boss over a person like you, maybe I'd give up bossing over others.'

'I can't match you in arguments,' said Apurba, and began to pick his way cautiously.

CHAPTER 16

The meeting held the next afternoon in the grounds of the Phaya temple was thinly attended. Many of the speakers who had promised to address the meeting also failed to turn up. The meeting was delayed for various reasons and since no lighting arrangements had been made, it had to be wound up soon after dark. Except for Sumitra's speech there was nothing remarkable about the meeting.

However, it could not be termed a failure either. Information about the meeting spread among the labourers by word of mouth. It reached the ears of the factory owners as well. Somehow it got round that an exceptionally beautiful, powerful and widely-travelled Bengali lady had recently arrived in Burma. She was strong enough to brush aside any obstacles that came in her way. She declared openly in the meeting that she would force the Sahib to grant various facilities to the workmen and also to double their wages. Those who could not hear her speak in the last meeting for want of information should attend the meeting on the following Saturday.

This news spread like wild fire among the factory workers within a radius of about forty to fifty miles. Very few of them had actually seen Sumitra, but when an exaggerated, verging on the superhuman, account of her beauty and prowess reached the ears of these ignorant workers, it created a great stir among them. They had been terrorised, ill-treated and exploited, because they were weak. They had been denied their normal rights. Having no faith in themselves, they reposed all their faith in the various gods and in Providence. The stories about Sumitra's supernormal powers were accepted by them unquestioningly. They decided to take leave and attend the meeting the following Saturday. If, as the rumour went, she possessed supernatural powers by which she could change their lot overnight, they must not fail to take advantage of it.

In the first meeting, because of absence of other speakers, even a novice like Apurba had to stand up and speak a few words at the earnest request of the chairperson. He had no previous experience of public speaking. His speech had therefore been unsatisfactory and he was ashamed of his performance. But when he came to know that the meeting had not been infructuous — indeed it had been quite a success — and that all the factory workers had decided to attend the next meeting, his heart was filled with elation and self-satisfaction. At the first meeting he had not been able to elucidate his points clearly, but his maiden speech had given him confidence. He had also his first taste of that headiness that public speakers experience while addressing an assembly.

That day, on arriving at his office, he received a letter from Sumitra in which she had showered praises on him and had invited him to address the next meeting. He was excited and could not pay attention to his office work. He tried rehearsing mentally the main points of a longer, more powerful speech. During the lunch-break he disclosed all these to Ramdas.

It was at the instance of Ramdas that one day Apurba had insulted Bharati. He therefore felt embarrassed to reveal to Ramdas about his subsequent intimacy with Bharati. It was not long when he had been fined by the court. Since then, the roguish Mr Joseph had died, his Bengali wife, too, had died and his devil of a daughter had disappeared somewhere — Ramdas knew this much. But he had no information as to how within this short spell of time, his friend had come close to that girl and how, silently and secretly, a romance was rapidly blossoming between the two. That day when in a state of euphoria Apurba disclosed the whole thing, Ramdas sat silently looking at his face. Nor did he ask a single question as Apurba spoke of

Bharati, Sumitra, Doctor, Nabatara and even the drunkard, and then went on to describe the aims and objectives of their organisation and went on to give an account of his visit to the coolie lines.

Apurba knew that Ramdas had been to jail, had been whipped and tortured for the sake of the motherland. Though Ramdas never spoke about it except once, Apurba knew it and idolized him for that. Despite being his superior in the office, Apurba felt small before Ramdas for this. He was not mean-minded and regarded Ramdas as his friend. Nor was he envious of him; yet he could not shake off his inferiority complex. Thus, there grew up something like a wall between these two friends. Apurba now placed Sumitra's letter before Ramdas and describing himself as an important member of the organisation, devoted heart and soul to the service of the motherland; he felt he had become his equal at last.

Sumitra's letter was written in English. Ramdas read through it silently more than once and then looked up and asked, 'How's it you've never told me anything about all this earlier?'

'Suppose I had,' replied Apurba, 'could you've joined us?'

'Why d'you say that? You didn't ask me to join you.' There was an unmistakable note of pique in his tone.

Apurba kept quiet for a while and then said, 'There was a reason why I didn't. You know very well the responsibilities and dangers involved in this work. You're married. You have a wife, a daughter. That's why I didn't want to drag you into all this.'

'Haven't householders any right to serve the country?' asked Talwarkar in surprise. 'Is the motherland only yours, not ours?'

Apurba felt ashamed. 'I didn't mean that,' he said. 'I simply said that you were married and had a family. With these responsibilities perhaps it may not be proper for you to take such a risk in a foreign country.'

178

'Perhaps? Maybe you're right. But any service to a motherland which is under foreign subjugation must necessarily be fraught with danger. This is unavoidable and I'm aware of it. To us Hindus, marriage is a part of our religious duty. But service to the motherland is a far greater duty. If I had thought that one's duty would stand in the way of another, I would not have married!'

Looking at his face, Apurba said nothing more. But he was unconvinced. He knew that Ramdas had suffered a lot for the sake of the motherland, that the fire in his heart had not totally died out, and that it had been rekindled once more. He respected him for that, but nothing more. He did not believe that Ramdas would ditch his wife and child and rush to join the organisation if he was invited to, nor did he want that. His estimation of his own capabilities of serving his country had enhanced considerably in the past few days. However, he now changed the topic and while elaborating upon the aims and objectives of the next meeting, frankly confessed that apart from the last occasion, he had never addressed a public meeting in his life. While he could not possibly disappoint Sumitra, he possessed neither the command over language nor the experience to address public gatherings.

'What are you going to do then?' asked Talwarkar.

'I've had the opportunity to visit a factory only once. I know that the labourers and factory workers lead a bestial life. But I don't know what's the root cause of their misery.'

Ramdas smiled. 'And yet you'll have to speak? Better don't.'

Apurba did not say anything but it was apparent from his face that he was finding it difficult to refuse this honour.

'But I've some knowledge about these people,' said Ramdas.

'How?'

'I've spent several years amongst them. If you go

179

through my certificates you'll see that I've spent my time mostly in factories and with the workers. If you wish, I can tell you about their miseries. In fact, if we don't have a clear idea of this, we'll be ignorant of the real problem that ails the country.'

'Sumitra says exactly the same thing.'

'She has to! That's why she's the President of the organisation! That forms the basis of self-sacrifice and service to the motherland. You must realise this; else all your efforts, all your intentions, will be futile.'

This was not the first time that Apurba was hearing all this. But Ramdas's words had sprung from the depths of his heart and touched him deeply. Ramdas was going to say something more but suddenly Mr Rozen pushed aside the screen and entered the room. Both of them stood up, startled. Mr Rozen said to Apurba, 'I'm going out now. I've left a letter on your table that must be replied tomorrow.'

Saying so, he departed. Both of them looked at the clock and were surprised to see it was already four o'clock.

CHAPTER 17

After Mr Rozen had gone, Apurba closed the office early and along with Ramdas, left for the Phaya grounds. The meeting was scheduled to start at five o'clock; there was not much time left. Carriages were not available in the neighbourhood, so they had to walk fast in order to be in time. Apurba remained silent most of the way. It was an important day for him. A sense of exhilaration and apprehension excited him.

Apurba had collected some information about the condition of labourers and factory workers from a book, and some he had picked up from Ramdas. He began arranging and rehearsing these as he walked on silently. It was in 1863 that the first cotton mill had been set up somewhere in the Bombay Presidency; the number had increased to so much; how miserable was the condition of the workers then; how they had to toil day and night; how disagreement first began between the British mill-owners and their Indian counterparts; in which year and on what date the Factory Act was passed after surmounting numerous objections; what were the provisions of the original Act and how these have been subsequently amended; what was the difference in the wage structure of factory workers in England and India then and now; when and who first tried to form labour unions, and what were its results; what does a comparative study of the behavioural pattern of workers in England and India reveal and how this had affected the workers, et cetera. He cautioned himself repeatedly lest he should forget these statistics. He had a sharp memory and success in so many examinations had given him the confidence that he would not forget any in the course of his speech. He visualized that when his impressive speech, eloquently delivered would end, the applause from the

181

audience would be tumultuous and prolonged. He could clearly see how pleased Sumitra would be. And Bharati? She would wonder how he could have acquired so much knowledge and experience in such a short time. Her face would glow with happiness and surprise and her bright eyes look upon his face. Just imagining the scene made the blood flow quicker in Apurba's veins. Talwarkar found it difficult to keep pace with him.

On arriving at the Phaya grounds they found it packed with people. Those who recognised Apurba as one of the speakers in the earlier meeting made way for him; those who did not recognise him did likewise. A podium had been erected in the centre of the ground. Except for Doctor, who had still not returned, all the others were present in the meeting. Apurba somehow made his way to the podium. One bench was still unoccupied. Sumitra motioned them to sit down.

A Punjabi workman, possibly retrenched recently, stood there, breathing fire. Momentarily disturbed by their arrival, he began shouting again with renewed vigour. Audiences do not generally care much for harangue of a good speaker. Neither do they seek to know the causes of their unfortunate state of affairs. They are gratified if the speaker were to describe in great detail all their grievances. The Punjabi worker possessed this special quality in abundant measure. That his speech had greatly agitated the multitude was apparent from their expressions.

Suddenly the meeting was disrupted. From one corner of the ground was heard a muted cry of alarm, and the next moment people were seen running helter-skelter. Cutting through the crowd, trampling them, twenty-odd British mounted policemen were seen advancing towards them. They held the reins in one hand and a whip in the other, and carried pistols. The metal on their shoulders blazed in the sunlight; their florid faces, flushed with anger and touched by the rays of the setting sun, looked ferocious. The thunderous voice of the speaker had fallen quiet and before they could realise, he had jumped from the podium and melted in the crowd.

The police sergeant rode up to them and said harshly, 'Stop the meeting at once!'

Sumitra had not yet recovered from her illness fully. Her face looked pale and emaciated, but she immediately stood up and asked, 'Why?'

'That's the order.'

'Whose order?'

'The government's.'

'But what for?'

'Because it's unlawful to instigate workers to resort to strikes.'

Sumitra said, 'We've no time for all that. The purpose of this meeting is to explain to these people the necessity for forming labour unions as in Europe and elsewhere.'

The sergeant shouted, 'Form an union? Against the firm! But that's an offence in this country. That may lead to breach of peace!'

'Of course! In a country where British merchants form the government, where government is an institution set up for the exploitation of the people of this country . . . .' She could not finish her sentence.

The sergeant's eyes became blood-shot with anger. He thundered, 'If you say that again, I'll be compelled to arrest you!'

Sumitra remained unperturbed. She looked at his face, smiled and then said calmly, 'I'm ill and very weak today.' Otherwise I'd have repeated not once but a hundred times what I just said so that these people could've known the truth. But, today I'm too weak to do that.' Saying this, she smiled again and sat down.

The composed and smiling face of this frail lady possibly embarrassed the sergeant. 'All right,' he said. 'I've orders to stop this meeting, not to break it up.' He looked at his watch. 'I give you ten minutes. Ask the people to disperse peacefully. And see that this

183

doesn't happen again.'

Sumitra had been fasting most of the past few days. Though she was still running a temperature, she had come to the meeting that day against the advice of the other members. But she now seemed to be overwhelmed by fatigue and exhaustion. Leaning back on the chair she said rather indistinctly, 'Apurbababu, we've only ten minutes' time . . . maybe even less. Tell these people at the top of your voice that their salvation lies only in their unity. If they're men, they should avenge this insult that has been inflicted upon us by the factory owners today.'

She could continue no longer; her weak voice broke down. But Apurba's face turned deathly pale at this request. Bewildered, he said, 'But won't that be unlawful?'

Sumitra said softly in a surprised tone, 'Is it lawful to break up a meeting at gun-point? I don't want unnecessary bloodshed, but you must impress upon them with all the force at your command that they must not forget today's humiliation.'

Four or five other male members who sat there were apparently of no consequence, possibly factory workers. Apurba, though new to the organisation, was an educated and important member. That was why he had been asked to take up the responsibility of addressing the meeting.

'But I can't speak Hindi well.' Apurba's throat was parched.

Sumitra was too weak to say anything; yet she said, 'Say a few words as best as you can. But don't waste any more time, Apurbababu.'

Apurba glanced around. Bharati was looking the other way, so her views could not be known. However, the sergeant's views were abundantly clear. He cast a threatening glance at Apurba.

Apurba stood up to speak. His lips moved but no sound came out, either in Bengali or in English or in Hindi. His ashen face was unbecoming of a member of the society called *Pather Dabi*.

At that moment Talwarkar stood up. Looking at Sumitra he said, 'I'm a friend of Apurbababu. I know Hindi. If permitted, I can tell these people what Apurbababu wanted to say.'

Bharati turned around and looked at Ramdas. Sumitra stared back in surprise. In the presence of these two appreciative ladies, the embarrassed, nonplussed and speechless Apurba slumped down with his face downcast.

Ramdas turned round and addressed the bewildered and frightened gathering. 'Brothers!' he said, 'I had a lot of things to tell you. But these sergeants have shut our mouths by the force of their arms.'

Pointing at the mounted policemen, he said, 'Those who've set these hounds on us and against you, are your factory owners. They don't want that anyone should explain your miseries to you. To them you are just so many animals employed to bear their burden and run their factories. But you are also men like them and you have a birthright to have a full meal and to lead a happy life. This is a right which God has given you! They want to keep this truth away from you by every stratagem, every strength, and every wickedness at their command. But once you wake up from your slumber, once you realise this truth that you are also men like them, however miserable, poor and ignorant you may be, still you are men and there is none who can deprive you of your birthright on any pretext whatsoever, then what can these few factory owners do to you? They are no match for you! Won't you realise this truth? This is nothing but a struggle of the poor against the rich for their self-preservation. The differences regarding country, caste, religion and belief — the differences between Hindus, Muslims, Jains and Sikhs — don't matter at all in this struggle between the proud and rich factory owners and their exploited and starving workers. They are afraid of your physical strength. They are apprehensive of the strength which education would give you and therefore your desire for greater knowledge makes them nervous. So long you remain helpless, weak, ignorant and dishonest, they can use you as their foot-stool. So they will never of their own free will give your anything more than mere subsistence. Is it so difficult for you to understand this patent truth? And shall we be silenced by these sergeants just because we want to tell you all these things? Will you not join this struggle for existence with all your strength?'

With the little knowledge of Hindi that he had been able to acquire during his stay in India, the sergeant could not comprehend much of the speech. But noticing the agitated mood of the audience, he grew agitated himself. He drew the attention of the speaker to his wristwatch and said, 'Only five minutes more! Finish quickly.'

'Only five minutes! Not a moment more! All right, I'll try to make the best possible use of these valuable five minutes. My brethren, you've been exploited long enough. My earnest entreaty to you today is: don't distrust us, simply because we're educated, because we come from respectable families and are not factory workers. If you distrust us, you'll be ruining yourselves. In every age and every country we, the intelligentsia, were the first to give a clarion call to arouse you workers from your age-old slumber. You may not be convinced today, but remember that you've no greater friend in this country than this organisation of ours — *Pather Dabi!'*

Ramdas's voice was cracking but still he continued to shout at the top of his voice: 'I've worked for long among factory workers. You do not know me, but I know you. Once upon a time I was one of those people whom you call your masters. You can take it from me they'll never let you have your human rights. You must understand that they will deny you your natural rights by keeping you degraded, by treating

186

you as animals. You've been told by them that your misery is due to your own faults — that you are dishonest, indisciplined and dissolute people. Whenever you've claimed any concession, they've told you that your dissolute character was responsible for all your ills and have thereby hindered your progress. They've always told you this lie that unless you become good you can have no real progress. But I want to tell you frankly and without hesitation that this is not entirely correct. Your dissolute character is not solely responsible for your miseries; rather your miseries are responsible for your low character. The time has come when you must fearlessly refute this falsehood. You must prove that money is not everything!'

His voice turned hoarse, but he continued to speak. 'Nothing in this world can be produced without labour. Hence the workers are as much owners of the factories as their proprietors. They too have equal rights on the factories as the owners!'

At this point one Punjabi fellow whispered something in the sergeant's ears. The sergeant's eyes, which were already red-shot, now glowed like burning coal. He thundered, 'Ṣtop! This cannot be permitted. This'll cause breach of peace!'

Apurba was startled. He caught hold of Ramdas's shirt and tried to make him sit down. 'Stop, Ramdas, for heaven's sake! Think of your wife who'll be alone in this friendless, foreign land. Think of your small daughter!'

But Ramdas paid no heed to his entreaties. He continued to shout as before, 'They're the wrongdoers! They're cowards! They want to keep the truth away from you. But no one can ever suppress the truth. It is immortal, imperishable!'

Though the sergeant could not understand what Ramdas said, the sudden excitement among the crowd was not lost on him. He roared, 'This can't be allowed! This is treason!'

In a moment five or six policemen dismounted and

187

came up to the dais. They caught hold of Ramdas and dragged him down. Ramdas disappeared between the horses and their riders, but his voice continued to ring from one end of the field to the other: 'Brothers, you may not see me again. But if you haven't surrendered your human dignity at the feet of your masters, don't tolerate such oppression, such insult!'

Before he could finish, something terrible happened. The policemen began to strike the crowd with whips, and the terrified, bewildered and humiliated labourers ran helter-skelter, knocking down and trampling those who came in their way.

Except for those injured in the stampede, the place soon became empty. Sumitra continued to gaze at the stragglers limping away. Not so far away from her, Apurba and Bharati remained glued to their seats with their faces downcast, confused and speechless.

The man, who had been sent to fetch a carriage, soon returned with one. Sumitra took Bharati's hand and without a word, slowly went and sat in the carriage. Normally no one disturbed her thoughts unless she herself chose to speak. Moreover, today she was unwell, tired and harassed.

Bharati called Apurba, 'Come.'

Apurba looked up, thought for a moment and then asked, 'Where?'

'To my place.'

Apurba remained quiet for a while and then said, slowly, 'You know I'm unworthy of your organisation. I can have no place in it any longer.'

'Then where d'you propose to go now? To your house?'

'My place? I suppose I have to. But . . . .' Apurba's eyes became misty. However, he somehow pulled himself together and said, 'Honestly, Bharati, there's one more place where I have to go. Only I don't know how I shall be able to.'

Sumitra called out from the carriage in a feeble voice, 'Come along, you two.'

Bharati again requested Apurba, 'Please come.'

Apurba shook his head. 'No. I've no place in *Pather Dabi*.'

Bharati reached out for Apurba, but somehow checked herself. Looking at his face steadily, she said in an undertone, 'Even if you've no place in the organisation, there's another place from which no power on earth can remove you.'

Sumitra called out impatiently once again, 'Will there be delay in your coming, Bharati?'

Bharati signalled to the coachman to drive on. To Sumitra, she said, 'Go on. We'll walk down.'

As they walked along, Apurba suddenly said, 'You must come with me, Bharati.'

'Am I not?'

'That's not what I meant. I don't know how I'll be able to face Talwarkar's wife, what'll I say to her, what arrangements will I make for her. Why was I so foolish as to bring Ramdas along to the meeting?'

Bharati did not say anything.

Apurba continued, 'What a catastrophe in this foreign country! I don't know what to think of.'

Bharati offered no comments. Both of them continued to walk in silence. After a while, distraught with anxiety and helplessness, Apurba burst out, 'How am I to be blamed? After repeated warnings if he still chooses to hang himself, how can anyone save him? Did I tell him to make that preposterous speech? He has a wife, a daughter, a family to look after. If he has no sense, he must pay for that. Let him now rot in jail for a couple of years!'

'Will you be going to meet his wife now?' asked Bharati.

Apurba glanced at her. 'Of course I've to meet her,' he said. 'But what'll I tell the Sahib tomorrow? I tell you, Bharati, if he says anything, I'll resign.'

'And what'll you do after that?'

'Go back home. Is this a place to stay?'

'Won't you work for his release?'

Apurba suddenly halted. 'Come, let's go to a barrister. I've about a thousand rupees with me. Won't that be sufficient? I can raise another five or six hundred rupees by selling my watch and other things. Come, let's go.'

'But the most important thing is to meet his wife. You needn't come with me. Take a carriage and go straight to the station. It's necessary to find out if she needs anything. In any case, it's imperative to give her the news.'

Apurba nodded, but continued to walk along. Bharati said, 'I can easily go home alone. You turn back.'

Apurba hesitated for a moment or so and then said, 'I can't go there alone.'

'Take Tewari with you in that case,' said Bharati.

'No. You've to come with me.'

'But I've urgent work at home.'

'Let there be. You must come.'

'Why're you entangling me in all this?'

Apurba remained silent. Looking at his face, Bharati said with a smile, 'Okay, but let's go to my place now. Let me finish my work first.'

As they walked along, Bharati said, 'Whoever sent you here to work didn't know you well, even if she's your own mother. Tewari is going back. I'll make arrangements and send you along with him.'

Apurba kept quiet. Bharati said, 'Don't you have anything to say?'

'What can I say? If my mother had not been alive, I'd have become an ascetic.'

'An ascetic?' remarked Bharati in surprise. 'But your mother is still alive.'

'Yes,' replied Apurba. 'We have a small house in the country. I'll take mother there.'

'Then?'

'I shall open a grocery shop with the thousand rupees I've got. It'll suffice for the two of us.'

'It may be so. But what's the need for such a step?'

'I've discovered myself today. I've realised that except

190

for my mother, I mean nothing to anyone else. I pray to God that I may not depend on anyone for anything.'

Bharati looked at Apurba for a moment and said, 'Your mother loves you very much, doesn't she?'

'Yes. She has been unhappy all her life. I only hope that doesn't increase. The very thought of that fetters me. Her presence shadows me day and night. That's why I'm so timid, so unworthy of others' respect.' He sighed deeply.

Bharati gave no reply; slowly she slipped her hand into Apurba's and walked on silently.

It had become quite dark by now. 'What are we going to do about Ramdas's family?' asked Apurba anxiously. 'Except for the maid, I suppose they've none else in this country. Even if they had, would he take care of them?'

Bharati too could not think of anything. Nevertheless she tried to boost his morale by saying, 'Let's go and see. We'll be able to do something.'

Apurba knew this was empty talk. His mind refused to be comforted by this. He said, 'You may have to stay with them.'

'But I'm a Christian. I'll be of no use to them.'

'Quite so!' Her words piqued him.

When they reached Bharati's place, it was long past evening. They knew that there was little they could do for Talwarkar's wife that night. This caused them fear and anxiety.

The downstairs room was open. Stepping inside, Bharati saw that someone was lying on the easy chair near the window on the other side of the room. As the person sat up and looked at them, Bharati recognised him and cried joyfully, 'Doctor, when did you come? Have you met Sumitra-didi yet?'

'No.'

Apurba said, 'Something dreadful has happened. Our office accountant, Ramdas Talwarkar, has been arrested by the police.'

Bharati said, 'He lives at Insein. His wife and daughter are there. They don't know about his arrest as yet.'

Apurba added, 'It's so far, and in this dark night . . . . Oh, what a calamity has occurred, Doctor!'

Doctor yawned, then sat up and said with a smile, 'I'm terribly tired. Can you make me a cup of tea, Bharati?'

'Certainly,' replied Bharati. 'But we'll have to go just now.'

'Where?'

'Insein. To Mr Talwarkar's house.'

'There's no need.'

Apurba looked at Doctor in surprise. 'How can you say that? We've to make some arrangements for the distressed family. At least we've to ascertain how they are. Surely there's need for that?'

Doctor smiled. 'Undoubtedly. But that responsibility is mine. You two will only end up doing the rounds of the jungles of Insein and still fail to locate his house.' He added with a laugh, 'I'd suggest you sit down instead and let Bharati prepare some tea. But I suppose you won't take that. Very well, then let the Brahmin cook prepare something pure for you and send it across. Eat it and take rest.'

Reassured by Doctor's words, Bharati got up cheerfully to go upstairs to prepare the tea. But Apurba was not convinced. Doctor's words appeared to him to be a riddle and rather in bad taste. Addressing himself to Bharati, he said, 'You may've been spared some trouble tonight, but I have a far greater responsibility. No matter how late it may be, I'll have to go there once.'

Hearing his words Bharati halted, but a glance at Doctor's eyes relieved her, and she went with an easy mind.

Doctor lighted a candle, then took out a bundle of letters from his pocket and sat down to write their replies. After waiting silently for about ten minutes,

Apurba grew anxious and disgusted. 'Are these letters so important?' he asked.

'Yes,' replied Doctor without looking up.

'But isn't it equally important to make some arrangements for them? Won't you send someone to Ramdas's house?'

'So late at night? I don't think anyone will be available till tomorrow morning.'

'In that case you needn't bother. I can go myself in the morning. If you hadn't stopped Bharati, we would've gone tonight itself and that, I think, would've been the best.'

Doctor's letter-writing was not disturbed, for he did not even bother to raise his head. He simply said, 'That was not necessary.'

Apurba controlled his anger and said, 'Our perceptions of what is necessary are, I'm afraid, not quite similar in this case. Ramdas is my friend.'

Bharati now came down with the teapot, prepared two cups of tea and then sat down nearby. Doctor went on simultaneously writing letters and drinking tea.

After sitting silently for two three minutes, Bharati said in an aggrieved tone, 'You're always so busy. We never get a chance to even sit down and chat with you.'

Somehow her aggrieved tone reached his unmindful ears. He removed the cup from his lips and said with a smile, 'What can I do? I've to leave again by the two o'clock train tonight.'

Bharati was startled, and Apurba's doubts with regard to his friend deepened.

'Can't you rest even for a night ?' said Bharati.

Doctor finished his tea. 'I'll surely rest one day,' he said. 'But that day hasn't come yet.'

Unable to follow, Bharati asked, 'When'll that day come?'

Doctor gave no reply.

Apurba had been worrying about Ramdas. He now

said, 'Though not a member of the organisation, Ramdas's sacrifice in accepting imprisonment is something extraordinary.'

'He may not have to undergo imprisonment,' said Doctor.

'If not, he'll be lucky. But if he does go to jail, the entire fault will be mine. It was I who brought him to the meeting.'

Doctor gave an amused smile and kept quiet.

Apurba went on, 'He had already suffered imprisonment for two years earlier. The innumerable scars on his back testify to that. There's none else to look after his wife and child in this foreign country. Considering that, his bravery appears extraordinary and unparallelled.'

Apurba's exuberant praise of his friend, though genuine, contained in it a covert taunt, but it failed to achieve its objective. Doctor's face lit up. 'There's absolutely no doubt about what you say, Apurbababu,' he said. 'One whose heart is fired by the love of his country can have no respite. Neither a good job in an European firm, nor attraction for his family at Insein, can deter him from his chosen path!'

Anxiety and suspicion had clouded his thinking, otherwise Apurba would not have made the grievous mistake that he made. Mistaking Doctor's remarks to be an affront, he suddenly burst out, 'You may not appreciate his heroism,' he said, 'but a good job in an European firm does not reduce his worth. You may taunt me as much as you like, but you should realise that Ramdas is not inferior to you in any way.'

'I realise that very well,' Doctor said, surprised. 'I didn't say anything to belittle him.'

'You did. You've ridiculed both him and me. But I know that he holds his motherland dearer to his heart than his own life. He's fearless and brave! He doesn't hide himself as you do. Unlike you, he doesn't limp about in disguise in fear of the police. You're a coward!'

194

Apurba's behaviour had stunned and flabbergasted Bharati. Unable to tolerate any longer, she cried out, 'What's the matter with you? Have you suddenly gone mad?'

'No, I haven't. Whatever he may be, he's no patch on Ramdas Talwarkar! I've no hesitation in saying this! He's envious of Ramdas's power, eloquence and fearlessness. That's why he prevented you from going and also tricked me into staying back!'

Bharati stood up. Controlling herself with a great effort, she said calmly, 'I can never insult you, Apurbababu. But please leave this place at once. We made a mistake in understanding you. One who loses all sense of proportion out of fear, such a mad man can have no place over here. You were right when you said that you had no place in *Pather Dabi*. In future, don't ever try to come to my house on any pretext whatsoever.'

As Apurba got up to leave, Doctor caught hold of his hand. 'Wait a little longer,' he said. 'Don't go alone in this darkness. I shall drop you home on my way to the station.'

Apurba was now slowly returning to his senses. He sat down with his face downcast.

Doctor was stuffing the leftovers of the biscuits into his pockets.

'What's that you're doing?' asked Bharati.

'Storing provisions for future use.'

'Are you really going away tonight?'

'Do you mean to say that I detained Apurbababu on a false pretext? If all of you start disbelieving me like this, what'll I do ?' said Doctor in mock anger.

'You can't go tonight,' said Bharati in a hurt tone. 'You're much too tired. Besides, Sumitra-didi is ill. You're away most of the time. I don't have an opportunity to consult you and take your advice. How can I run this organisation alone? I too shall then go away somewhere.'

Doctor smiled. Handing over the letters to her, he

said, 'One is for you, the other for Sumitra and the third for the members of *Pather Dabi*. They contain my advice or instructions, whichever way you may look at them.'

Bharati took the letters and said sorrowfully, 'Will you be away for long?'

'Not even the gods can say,' said Doctor with an amused smile.

'Our problem is that neither your face nor your words reveal what's in your mind. Tell me definitely when'll you return?'

'But I just said that not even the gods can say.'

'That won't do. You'll have to tell me definitely.'

'Why this insistence?'

'I don't know why, but I feel afraid this time. I feel as if everything is going to break up.' Her eyes filled with tears as she spoke.

Doctor placed his hand on her head and said jocularly, 'Oh, no, dear, nothing will happen. Everything will be all right.' He grinned. 'But if you quarrel with this man you'll come to grief, I tell you this. Apurbababu may be given to bouts of anger, but he also knows how to love. His heart is not dry like ours, but still fresh like a flower.'

Bharati was about to say something, but as Apurba looked up and their eyes met, she clammed up.

At that moment a horse-driven carriage came and stopped in front of the house. Two persons alighted and entered the room. One of them was dressed in European clothes. Excepting Doctor, none else knew him. The other person was Ramdas Talwarkar. Apurba's face lit up, but he refrained from extending a noisy welcome to his friend. Ramdas came up to Doctor, bowed down and took the dust from his feet. This struck Apurba as rather unusual. But he looked at Doctor's face and kept quiet.

The gentleman in European clothes said in English, 'Getting the bail took a long time. Possibly the government will not proceed with this case.'

Doctor smiled. 'Which means you've still not understood the government, Krishna Iyer.'

'I saw you accompanying us right up to the police station,' said Ramdas, with a laugh. 'Then you suddenly disappeared somewhere.'

'Something urgent necessitated my sudden disappearance. So much so that I've to leave tonight itself.'

'I recognised you at the railway station that day,' said Ramdas.

Doctor nodded his head. 'I know. But instead of straight going home, why've you come here so late at night?'

'To pay my regards to you. You left the Poona Central Jail soon after I arrived. I didn't get an opportunity then. By the way, what happened to Nilakant Joshi? He was there with you.'

'He was hanged at Singapore,' said Doctor. 'He tried to escape but failed.'

All this appeared inconceivable to Apurba; it was like a bad dream. Unable to control himself, he suddenly asked, 'Would you've also been hanged?'

Doctor looked at his face and simply smiled. That was enough to make Apurba's hair stand on end.

Ramdas asked excitedly, 'And after that?'

'I had spent three years in Singapore. The authorities there knew me well. So I had to avoid the roads and arrived at Tavoy via Bangkok after crossing the hills. I was very lucky. In the forest I chanced upon a baby elephant. That proved to be very helpful. Finally I sold it and boarded a country boat carrying coconuts and made it to Arakan. Since then I've generally had a peaceful life. But today I came across a great friend of mine in the police station. His name is V. A. Chelia. He's very fond of me. Worried about my long absence, he has come all the way from Singapore. It appears he has got the scent. He couldn't make out in the crowd, else this ancient neck would have....' Saying this, Doctor burst out laughing.

Suddenly, looking at Apurba's face he remarked,

197

'What's the matter with you, Apurbababu?'

Apurba was trying desperately to restrain himself. But before Doctor could finish, he covered his face with his hands and fled from the room.

CHAPTER 18

The abrupt manner in which Apurba rushed out of the room surprised everyone. The room was not well-lighted, but even then his facial expression and choked voice appeared somewhat incongruous. Krishna Iyer remarked after a moment's silence, 'Who's he, Doctor? Rather sentimental!' He had a complaining tone, as if to suggest, why should such people be here in the first place?

Doctor simply smiled, but the reply came from Talwarkar. 'He's Mr Haldar — Apurba Haldar. We work in the same office. He's my superior there.' He added affectionately, but respectfully, after a little pause, 'But we're quite intimate — he's a very dear friend! Sentimental? Well . . . . By the way, Doctor, I suppose you haven't heard about Haldar's first experience in Rangoon? It was . . . .'

Suddenly, noticing Bharati, he felt embarrassed and stopped. 'Be that as it may, we've been great friends from the first day itself. Very good friends!'

Talwarkar's eagerness in defending Apurba and repeated use of the words "very good friends" dissuaded the barrister from saying anything more about Apurba's sentimentalism, but it was apparent from his face that he was still suspicious and displeased.

Doctor said with a smile, 'Sentiment is not such a bad thing, Krishna Iyer. Everyone need not be as hard-hearted as you are.'

Krishna Iyer was not pleased. 'I didn't say that,' he stated. 'But I suppose it's not wrong if I say that even if we exclude this room, there's enough place for them to move about in this wide world.'

Talwarkar felt annoyed. Krishna Iyer's repeated efforts to prove Apurba as undesirable, despite his describing him as a great friend, appeared to him to be an affront. He said, 'Mr Iyer, I know Apurbababu very well. It's true that he has been initiated not long ago. But to be slightly agitated over the unexpected release of a friend, surely is no crime. There'll be no dearth of places for Apurba in this world, and I also hope that this room will always be open to him.'

Krishna Iyer, who had watched Apurba's performance at the meeting, kept quiet. But Doctor now said in his usual calm manner, 'Of course, Talwarkar, of course!' Then, glancing at the faces of those present, he said gravely, 'How fragile is human friendship, Bharati! Sometimes, for some insignificant reason, a permanent breach occurs between two friends who had once thought their friendship was everlasting. This is not uncommon in this world, Talwarkar, and one must be prepared for that. You see, Krishna Iyer, men are so weak. It is in such times that sentiment helps us tide over the crisis.'

Doctor's remarks called neither for any reply nor for any protests. So they all remained silent. But Bharati grew increasingly perturbed. She had great regard for Doctor. She knew that Doctor never spoke a single word without reason. But she was unable to comprehend exactly what Doctor's remarks meant and to whom they were directed. Her heart was full of misgivings and apprehension.

Doctor looked at the wall clock. 'Bharati, it's time I left. I'm leaving by the train tonight, Talwarkar.'

They were not permitted to show unnecessary curiosity and enquire where and why he was going, unless he himself chose to provide the information. Waiting for the moment with wistful eyes, Talwarkar asked, 'What are your orders for me?'

'Orders indeed!' said Doctor with a smile. 'But there's one thing. Even if there's dearth of space in Burma, there won't be any in your own country. Just take care of the workers.'

Talwarkar nodded. 'Okay. When'll we meet again?'

'You were a disciple of Nilakant Joshi. Then how's it that you're asking such a question?'

Talwarkar did not reply. 'Don't delay any longer,' said Doctor. 'As it is, it'll be morning by the time you reach home. So, Krishna Iyer, you've finally decided to set up your practice here?'

Krishna Iyer nodded. The carriage was still waiting outside. As they boarded it, Talwarkar said, 'We should've seen where Apurbababu went in this darkness.' But no one thought it necessary to give a reply, and the carriage drove away.

'Do you think Apurba has gone home?' asked Doctor. Bharati shook her head. 'I don't think so. He must be hiding somewhere around here. If we look around, we'll find him. He won't go away without meeting you again. I'm sure of that.'

'Then we should finish that off within ten or fifteen minutes. I can't delay any longer.'

'He'll return before that.' This she said as much as a reply to Doctor as to assure herself. Apurba would never venture to return alone in this darkness, so he must be somewhere around. She also thought that Apurba should come and apologise to this great man for whom they all had the highest regard, before he left. Apurba had been guilty of many wrong-doings that day; unless he made up for them Bharati would feel most miserable.

But time was running out. Apurba was nowhere to be seen. Standing at the doorstep, Bharati peered in the darkness and pricked her ears to catch the sound of his familiar footsteps. He must be somewhere there! She once thought of going out to look for him, but felt hesitation to show such concern, especially today.

Doctor looked at his bundle tied to the stave, yawned, and then stood up. Bharati saw from the wall clock there were hardly five or six minutes left. 'Do you plan to walk down to the station?' she asked.

Doctor shook his head. 'Around twenty past two carriage will possibly pass along the main road. Fo few coins it'll take me to the station.'

'It'll take you even if you didn't pay anything

won't you meet Sumitra-didi once before you leave. She's really ill.'

'I didn't say she wasn't. But how'll she get well if she doesn't see a doctor.'

'If that's so, then can we find a better doctor than you?'

'Then she had it!' said Doctor jokingly. 'I've been out of touch so long that I've forgotten everything. Besides, do I have the time to treat a patient?'

He had scarcely finished when Bharati burst out, 'No time! No time even if someone dies — so important is your work for the country? Doctor, you haven't lost your learning; if you've lost something, it's love and kindness!'

Doctor's smiling face became grave for a moment before returning to its earlier mood. But the sharp-eyed Bharati immediately realised her mistake. Though she was quite familiar with Doctor, she still had not the liberty to discuss his relations with Sumitra. Indeed, she knew nothing about Sumitra — who she was, what was her relation with Doctor, when did she join the organisation. They were prohibited from showing curiosity about the personal affairs of any member. So except for guessing, she had no other way of knowing anything. Being a woman, she had been able to understand Sumitra's feelings for Doctor. But realising that she should not have said anything simply on the basis of that, she was not only embarrassed but also frightened. Frightened not of Doctor, but of Sumitra. It would not do if she came to know about this, even by chance. Though not much was known about Sumitra, one thing they all knew from the very first day was that this quiet and exceptionally intelligent woman preferred to remain in seclusion. Her reticence, stateliness, striking beauty, reserved manner and grave demeanour made her appear aloof and distant from the others even when she was in their midst. So much so that no one dared even to enquire about her illness. But one day she had shed her hard exterior and displayed her weakness in the presence of Apurba and Bharati on the departure of someone. Since then, she seemed to have distanced herself even further. Bharati knew that if Sumitra ever felt that someone had tried to destroy her seclusion by a show of unwanted sympathy, she would be greatly annoyed.

Doctor made himself comfortable in the easy chair and, stretching his legs across the table, sighed deeply, 'Aah . . . .'

Bharati was surprised. 'You're lying down?'

'Why, am I a horse that I'll become useless if I lie down?' said Doctor angrily. 'I'm feeling sleepy. Unlike you people, I can't sleep while standing!'

'Neither can we,' said Bharati. 'But if someone told me that you could sleep while running, I wouldn't be surprised. You're capable of everything. But it's time you left, else you won't be able to catch the train.'

'Doesn't matter.'

'What d'you mean?'

'Oh, Bharati, I'm feeling so sleepy. I can hardly keep my eyes open.' Saying this Doctor shut his eyes.

Bharati realised happily that Doctor had postponed his departure only at her request. Otherwise, not to speak of sleep, even thunderstorms could not have deterred him from his resolve.

'If you're really sleepy, why don't you go upstairs and lie down on the bed?' she said.

'And leave you here to wait for Apurba to return?' said Doctor, without opening his eyes.

'Not at all. I'll go upstairs and lie down in the other room.'

'You can lie down in anger, but you can't sleep,' said Doctor. 'There's nothing more painful than tossing in bed. You'd better search for him and bring him back. I won't tell anyone.'

Bharati's face turned red. But Doctor did not notice it as his eyes were shut. Bharati remained silent for a few moments as she tried to compose herself. She then said calmly, 'How d'you know that it's painful to toss in bed?'

'People say.'

'You've no personal experience?'

Doctor opened his eyes. 'Unfortunate souls like me don't even get beds to sleep on most of the time; so the question of tossing about in bed doesn't arise. That's a luxury we can't afford.' Saying this Doctor gave an amused smile.

'Doctor, is it true you never lose your temper as people say?'

'Oh, no! They spread all sorts of rumours about me out of malice.'

Bharati smiled. 'Maybe it's because they love you. They also say that you never feel aggrieved, that you have no kindness or affection, that you're as hard-hearted as stone.'

'Possibly that's also out of their love for me, eh? Anything else?'

Bharati continued, 'They say that the only thing that matters to you is your motherland. That's all there is to it. It's because we never get to see its real nature that we can be with you. Otherwise . . . .'

She paused for a while and then resumed, 'You know, Doctor, the other day Sumitra-didi and I were passing by the side of the Burmah Oil Company's plant. Their new boiler was being tested that day. So a crowd had gathered to watch the fun. It was a huge mass of iron, like a black rock, but nothing more than that. Suddenly its door was opened and we saw the fire raging inside. It seemed that if this earth of ours had been broken into lumps and tossed inside, it'd devour that as well. A single boiler, we were told, was sufficient for the entire plant. When the door was shut it again became a mass of inanimate iron. Suddenly Sumitra-didi sighed deeply. I was surprised and asked what the matter was. She said, "Remember this dreadful thing; you'll be able to understand Doctor better. This is his true image."' She looked at him.

Doctor smiled unmindfully and said, 'How everyone

204

loves me! But I can stay awake no longer. Do something. But before that, won't you search for the man even once?'

'Only if you promise not to tell anyone.'

'I won't. But tell me, don't you feel shy in front of me at all?'

Bharati shook her head. 'One feels shy only in front of another human being.' Saying this she picked up the lantern and went out.

She returned after fifteen minutes or so and said, 'It seems he has gone away.'

Surprised, Doctor sat up and said, 'In this darkness? All alone?'

'It seems like that.'

'Strange!'

'My bed is laid upstairs. Please go and sleep.'

'What about you?'

'I'll spread out a blanket and lie down on that. Come, get up now.'

Doctor stood up. 'All right. One feels shy only in front of another human. I'm just a piece of stone!'

After Doctor lay down, Bharati tied a mosquito net and carefully tucked it in. She then made a bed for herself on the floor. Doctor looked at her and said in a hurt voice, 'If you all ignore me like this, my self-respect will be wounded.'

Bharati laughed. 'We've decided to treat you as a stone idol and not as a man.'

'That means you're not afraid of me?'

'Not a bit. We can't believe that you can harm anyone.'

Doctor smiled. 'You'll get to know that one day.'

Lying on her bed, Bharati suddenly asked, 'Who gave you the name of Sabyasachi, Doctor? It can't possibly be your real name.'

Doctor burst out laughing. 'Don't bother about the real one. But this was given to me by the headmaster of our village school. He had a tall mango tree in his garden. Only I could drop the mangoes from it by

205

hurling stones at them. Once I sprained my right hand while jumping from the roof. A doctor was sent for. He bandaged it and placed it in a sling. Everyone expressed his sympathy; only the headmaster was happy. He said, "Now the mangoes in my tree will be spared. I may be able to eat some when they ripen." '

'You were very naughty,' said Bharati.

'I did have a reputation,' said Doctor. 'Anyway, from the next day I began to pluck mangoes as before. I don't know how the headmaster got to know about it, but he caught me red-handed one day. Looking at me in surprise he said, "You win, Sabyasachi. I give up all hope of eating any mangoes. You've broken your right hand, but the left one has been busy. I'm sure if you broke the left, your legs would have taken over. However, you needn't take that trouble. I'll get the remaining unripe mangoes plucked for you to eat." '

'So it's a name given to you in great anguish,' said Bharati, giggling.

Doctor laughed. 'You may say that,' he said. 'But since then people have forgotten my real name.'

After a while Bharati asked, 'Everyone says you're inseparable from your motherland. How did that happen?'

'That's also a story from my childhood,' said Doctor. 'So many things have since happened in my life, but I've never been able to forget that one event. There was a monastery for Vaishnava monks on the outskirts of our village. One night dacoits attacked it. A large number of villagers gathered near the monastery, being attracted by the shouts of the inmates. But the dacoits were armed with a gun. The villagers could not challenge them because of that. I had a cousin. He was courageous and had a helpful nature. He wanted to challenge the dacoits, but as that would've meant sure death for him, others held him back. Unable to go, my cousin began to rave and rant and hurl abuses at the dacoits. But it was of no use. With that one gun

they kept the crowd of two-three hundred people at
bay. In front of their eyes they bound the head monk
to a post and burnt him alive. I was then only a child
but his screams and cries still ring in my ears. Oh
how terrible were those dying shrieks!'

'And after that?' asked Bharati, with bated breath.

'The monk's shrieks died out. The dacoits' plunder-
ing spree came to an end. But before they departed,
their leader cursed my cousin and swore vengeance
against him. As they were tired they were going away
but he swore that he would be back after a month to
take revenge. My cousin approached the British district
magistrate for a licence to keep a gun, but his request
was turned down. Two years before that he had boxed
the ears of a tyrannical sub-inspector of police. As a
result he had been imprisoned for a couple of months.
Because of this the magistrate refused to grant the
licence. My cousin said, "Shall we die then?" The
magistrate said with a grin, "If you're so frightened,
you should leave this district and go elsewhere." '

Agitated, Bharati sat up and exclaimed, 'He didn't
give the licence? Despite knowing the impending
danger?'

'No,' said Doctor. 'Not only that, when in desperation
my cousin arranged some bows and arrows and spears,
the police came and took those away.'

'What happened after that?'

'The subsequent story is very brief. The dacoits kept
their promise before the month ended. They had
another gun with them this time. Everyone else ran
away, but no one could make my cousin budge. So he
was shot dead by the dacoits.'

Bharati's face turned ashen. She gasped, 'He died?'

'Yes. He was conscious for about four hours after
being shot. The villagers assembled and began to hurl
abuses at the dacoits and the district magistrate. Only
my cousin said nothing. No proper medical help was
available in the village; the nearest hospital was twenty
miles away. It was also night time. When the village

doctor came and wanted to bandage the wound, my cousin brushed his hand aside and said, "Let it be. I don't want to live." ' His voice seemed to falter.

Doctor continued after a while, 'My cousin was very fond of me. As I sat there weeping, he opened his eyes and looked at me. Then he said slowly, "Don't cry like a woman along with these sheep and goats. But never forgive those who've destroyed the manhood of this country to preserve their power." He did not say a single word more. Out of sheer hatred, he did not even allow a groan to escape his lips, and then he passed away from this accursed land. Only I know what a great soul passed away that day.'

Bharati sat rooted to the ground. It was just the story of something that happened in a village long ago. Two unknown, unimportant persons had lost their lives in the hands of dacoits. It was nothing compared to the sufferings caused by the numerous conflicts in this world. And still it had hurt him so much! The cruelty of these two deaths was nothing compared to the suffering of the poor. In Bengal itself, so many people die every day in the hands of dacoits and robbers. But was it simply this fact that had hurt Doctor so much? Just as a flash of lightning cuts through the darkness and reveals what is hidden, the mystery of his life was revealed to her instantly. She realised that death meant nothing to him; it did not hurt him. But what hurt him was the helplessness of the people that the death of these two insignificant persons signified. They did not have the right to prevent the certain death of his cousin; they had the right only to watch silently. It seemed to Bharati that this unbearable insult and humiliation of the entire nation had darkened the face of this man for ever.

Bharati's heart was heavy with pain. She called out, 'Dada!'

Doctor looked surprised. 'Are you calling me?'

'Yes,' replied Bharati. 'Is no reconciliation possible between the British and you?'

'No. I'm their worst enemy.'

Bharati was hurt. 'I can't believe that you can ever have any enmity towards anyone, or even think ill of anyone,' she said.

Doctor remained silent for while and then said with a smile, 'Bharati, it's good of you to say that. I bless that you may be happy in life.'

Bharati knew that the smile meant nothing. So she kept quiet.

Doctor went on, 'Always bear this in mind that I've become their enemy not simply because we lost our independence. We had earlier lost our independence to the Muslims also. But humanity has no greater enemy than the British. For their self-interest they turn humans into inhuman beings. This is their trade, their capital. If possible, teach this truth to your countrymen and women.'

The wall clock downstairs struck four. The darkness outside seemed to have become denser. Bharati sat looking at the darkness with unblinking eyes, thinking of so many things. But she could never bring herself to accept the allegations which Doctor made against an entire nation as true.

CHAPTER 19

Bharati could not sleep that night. The next day she felt indisposed physically as well as mentally. So she decided to finish her dinner early and go to bed. She was cooking when a member of their organisation came and handed her a letter. It was from Sumitra. She had asked Bharati to drop whatever work she might have in hand and come at once with the bearer of the letter.

Bharati did not dare to disobey Sumitra's order; nevertheless she was surprised. 'Has she suddenly fallen ill?' she asked.

'No,' replied the messenger.

When she came downstairs she found their familiar carriage waiting for her, but the coachman was new. He did not appear to be a coachman by profession. Besides, what was the need for a carriage? It only took three minutes to walk down to Sumitra's place. Surprised, she asked, 'What's the matter, Hira Singh? Where's Sumitra-didi?'

Though Hira Singh was not a member of their organisation, he was loyal and trustworthy. He was a Sikh from Punjab. He had earlier been a policeman in Hongkong and now worked as a telegraph boy in Rangoon. He informed her that an urgent, secret meeting was being held at a place about five miles away and that her presence was necessary.

Bharati asked no more questions. She shut the doors and windows of her carriage and set off in the gathering darkness of the evening. Hira Singh, in his official uniform, left by another road, on his official bicycle. On the way Bharati thought many times that she should turn back and collect her pistol, but she did not dare to do that for fear of being late to the meeting. And so she rushed on towards an unknown destination, unarmed and unprotected. It was apparent to her that they were taking a circuitous route, and after some time she could make out from the unevenness of the road that they were driving away from the town, but the darkness made it impossible for her to know exactly where.

She was not wearing a watch but she presumed it would be around ten in the night when the carriage entered a garden and stopped. Hira Singh, who had already arrived, opened the door. Tall trees overhead added to the prevailing darkness to make it almost impossible to see even one's own hands. Under their feet the undergrowth was so thick as to render the garden path invisible. Hira Singh walked ahead along that dreadful path leading Bharati with the light of his bicycle lamp. As she walked along it occurred to Bharati again and again that she had not done the right thing by coming to this terrible place.

Soon they came to an old and dilapidated building. Even in the darkness Bharati could make out that it was a Buddhist monastery that had been long deserted. Once upon a time, long, long ago, Buddhist monks lived there. Possibly there was no human habitation nearby.

It was quite a big building but dark, and with no sign of anyone living there. Thieves had stolen even the doors and windows. As they entered the front room the foul smell of bats nauseated her. The other rooms led through that. Possibly it was infested with a number of venomous snakes as well.

A wooden staircase in the large hall led to the first floor. Some of its steps were missing. Holding Hira Singh's hand, Bharati climbed the stairs. They then crossed the passage and reached the room where the meeting was on. A mat was laid out on the floor. A couple of candles burnt in one corner of the room and seated next to it was Sumitra. Doctor, who was sitting across the room, called out affectionately, 'Come, Bharati. Come and sit by my side.'

An unknown fear seized her. Unable to speak, she

211

hurriedly sat down, huddled up against Doctor. Doctor placed his hand on her shoulder in a reassuring gesture. Hira Singh did not enter the room but stood outside the door. Bharati looked round. Five or six of those gathered there were complete strangers whom she had never met before. Among those whom she recognised, in addition to Doctor and Sumitra, were Ramdas Talwarkar and Krishna Iyer. A fierce-looking man immediately attracted her notice. He was dressed in ochre robes and wore a huge turban on his head. His face was round as an earthen pot and his body like a rhino's — huge, fleshy and rough. His beady eyes were almost entirely shorn of lashes and the hairs of his moustache were like spikes that could be counted from a distance. His skin was coppery. Even at a glance one could make out that the man was a Mongol and not an Aryan. Bharati was terrified even to look at him.

For a few minutes there was a hush in the room. Then Sumitra spoke up, 'Bharati, I understand your feelings. So I didn't want to call you here and hurt your feelings, but Doctor was insistent. Do you know what Apurbababu has done?'

Bharati had been apprehending something like this throughout the day. Her face turned pale and her mouth dry. She sat looking vacantly, unable to reply.

Sumitra said, 'Ramdas has been dismissed by his employers today. Apurba would've shared the same fate had he not chosen to divulge everything about us to the police commissioner. And so he was not touched. After all it's a lot of money that he's getting — five hundred rupees every month, if I'm not mistaken?'

Ramdas nodded his head. 'Yes'.

'Not only that. He has also told them that ours is a revolutionary group and that we possess pistols and revolvers. What should be the punishment for this, Bharati?'

That terrible-looking man thundered, 'Death!'

212

Bharati looked at him, but did not say anything.

Ramdas said, 'They know that Doctor is Sabyasachi. Apurba has also told them that he can be apprehended in his hotel room. He has informed them that I had been a political prisoner and suffered imprisonment for two years.'

Sumitra said, 'Bharati, do you know what'll happen to Doctor if he's arrested? He'll be hanged; if not, he'll be transported for life. Gentlemen, what punishment will you decide for such offence.'

They unanimously said, 'Death!'

'Do you have anything to say, Bharati?'

Bharati was unable to speak. She simply shook her head to indicate that she had nothing to say.

That dreadful man now spoke in Bengali. It was clear from his pronunciation that he belonged to Chittagong. 'I take the responsibility of executing him. I don't use any weapons. These are my weapons.' He displayed his huge tiger-like paws in the air.

Krishna Iyer looked towards the door and addressed Hira Singh, 'There's a dry well on the northern side of the garden. Cover it up with earth and dry leaves and branches so that no smell comes out.'

Hira Singh nodded his head to indicate that this will be carried out.

'Let the sentence be told to Apurbababu,' suggested Talwarkar.

Apurba's trial was over in five minutes. The jury had given its judgement. It was brief and unequivocal. There was no ambiguity in it. Bharati heard everything but comprehended nothing. There seemed to be a barrier between her ears and her head; nothing seemed to penetrate this. Whenever someone spoke she looked at him vacantly, with incomprehension, like a blockhead. She knew only that Apurba had committed a serious offence and that these people were determined to kill him. His life was in danger in this country. But she had no idea how great was that danger.

At a hint from Sumitra a man went out and what Bharati saw next was beyond her wildest dreams. The man re-entered the room along with Apurba. Apurba's hands were tied behind his back with ropes, and a stone hung from his waist. The next moment Bharati leaned against Doctor and fainted. Everyone's attention was towards Apurba; so except for Doctor, no one noticed that she had lost consciousness.

Apurba's cross-examination was already over before Bharati had arrived. He had confessed everything. He admitted that the police commissioner and the manager of his firm had been able to pump out all the information from him, but it was still not clear to him what heinous crime he had committed against his organisation and his motherland.

Ramdas had reported the matter to Sumitra before midday. The punishment had immediately been decided upon and Apurba taken into custody in the following manner. Correctly guessing that Apurba would not venture to walk back home after office that day, Hira Singh had stationed their horse-carriage in front of the office. Apurba fell into the trap easily. After coming a short distance the coachman informed Apurba that the road ahead had been blocked by a broken roller and so they would have to take another route. Apurba had agreed. He had perhaps become unmindful after that, but when he did become conscious, Hira Singh had entered the carriage and had brought him to that place at the point of his pistol.

Sumitra now said to him, 'Apurbababu, we've sentenced you to death. Have you anything to say?'

Apurba shook his head but it was clear from his face that he had not comprehended anything.

Doctor, who had been silent all this while, now turned to Hira Singh and said, 'Where's your pistol?'

Hira Singh pointed to Sumitra. Doctor stretched out his hand and said, 'Here, let me have it?'

Sumitra slipped it out of her belt and handed it over to Doctor.

'Does anyone else have any firearms?' asked Doctor.

Those present said that none of them had any pistols or revolvers with them.

Doctor then stuffed Sumitra's pistol into his pocket and said with a little smile, 'Sumitra, you've communicated the death sentence to Apurba. But Bharati has not consented to this.'

Sumitra glanced at Bharati for a moment and said in a firm tone, 'Bharati can't possibly do it.'

'She shouldn't either,' said Doctor. 'What d'you say, Bharati?'

Bharati said nothing, but hid her face in Doctor's lap.

Doctor placed his hand on Bharati's head. He said, 'Whatever Apurbababu has done can't be undone. We have to face the consequences. It makes no diference whether we punish him or not. I suggest we take no action against him. Instead, let's hand him over to Bharati. Let her try to make a man out of him. What d'you say, Sumitra?'

'No!' said Sumitra, emphatically.

'No!' chanted the others.

The ugly man was the most vociferous. He raised his fist and said something against Bharati.

Sumitra said in a hard voice, 'We're unanimous in this. If we tolerate such things, our movement will be destroyed.'

'What can be done if it does?' said Doctor.

All seven raised their voices along with Sumitra. 'What d'you mean? For the sake of our country, for its independence, we won't tolerate this. You alone can't overrule us!'

When their shouts subsided, Doctor spoke. His voice was surprisingly mild and calm. There was no trace of agitation or excitement in it. 'Don't fan a revolt,' he said to Sumitra. 'You all know that my voice alone carries more weight than all of yours.'

Turning to the fierce-looking man, Doctor said, 'Brojendra, you'd compelled me to punish you once for your insolence at Batavia. Don't force me again.'

Bharati still lay huddled on the ground, her body trembling violently. Doctor patted her affectionately and said softly, 'Don't be afraid, Bharati. I've pardoned Apurba.'

Bharati did not raise her head, nor did she feel reassured. She clutched at Doctor's thin fingers and whispered, 'But they haven't?'

'They won't easily either,' said Doctor. 'But they won't dare touch someone whom I've promised protection.'

He added with a smile, 'I don't get enough to eat, Bharati. Most of the days I've to manage with half a meal. Yet they know that these lean fingers of mine can smash Brojendra's tiger-like paws to pieces. What d'you say to that, Brojendra?'

Brojendra's face turned a shade darker. He looked sulkily at Doctor but did not say anything.

'But Apurba shouldn't stay here anymore. Let him go back to India. He's not a traitor. He loves his motherland with all his heart, but like most of our countrymen — no, I shall not speak ill of my people — he's a weakling. Bharati, I've asked you to make a man of him, but I'm not very hopeful. He won't take long to forget today's happenings or you. But let's not talk about that now. For the present I suppose we can request the President to dissolve the meeting.' Doctor looked at Sumitra.

Sumitra used to address Doctor informally or respect-fully, depending upon the situation. She now addressed him formally, 'When the opinion of the majority is overruled by the brute force of a single individual, this cannot be called a meeting, whatever else it may be. But if it was your intention to enact this drama, why didn't you tell us so in the beginning?'

'It'd have been better if there'd been no necessity for it at all. However, considering the circumstances, you'll agree, Sumitra, we played our parts well.'

'I'd never imagined that such a thing would happen,' moaned Ramdas.

'Talwarkar, could you imagine that friendship was so brittle,' remarked Doctor. 'And yet that's the truth.'

'This puts an end to our activities in Burma,' said Krishna Iyer. 'I suppose we've to disappear now.'

'Possibly,' replied Doctor. 'But you must remember, Iyer, that to make a timely departure and to give up one's activities aren't the same thing. We shouldn't complain if we're unable to stay securely in one place for long. That's not expected of us.'

Doctor stood up and signalled Bharati to get up too. 'Hira Singh,' he said, 'set Apurba free. Bharati, come, let me see both of you to safety.'

Hira Singh advanced to carry out the orders, when Sumitra said harshly, 'As the drama comes to an end, one feels like applauding. But this is not the first time that such a thing has happened. I remember having read such a story in my childhood. But it seems there's something missing. If the union of the two took place in our presence, there'd be no flaw. What d'you say, Bharati?'

Bharati felt she would die of shame. But Doctor said, 'There's nothing to be ashamed about, Bharati. Rather I pray that He who has the power to complete the drama may remove this flaw as well.'

He took out Sumitra's pistol from his pocket and handed it back to her. 'I'm going to see them off,' he said. 'But don't worry, I've another country-made pistol with me.'

He looked at Brojendra through the corners of his eyes and said, smilingly, 'You used to joke that I can see in the dark like an owl. Don't forget that tonight.'

Throwing this terrible hint, Doctor was about to leave with Bharati and Apurba when Sumitra suddenly stood up. 'Was it really necessary to put the noose round your neck with your own hands?' she asked.

'Can I afford to be afraid of a small thing as the noose?' replied Doctor with a smile.

Realising that it was foolish of her to remind this man of the risk he faced, Sumitra was embarrassed.

217

She said anxiously, 'Everything has come to naught, but when'll I get an opportunity to meet you again?'

'Whenever it's necessary.'

'Hasn't the time come yet?'

'If it has, you'll surely get an opportunity.' Saying this he began to descend the stairs carefully, followed by Bharati and Apurba.

The carriage that Bharati had travelled in was still there. The coachman was roused from his sleep and then they left. After having kept quiet for a long while, Bharati spoke. 'Where're we going?' she asked.

'To Apurba's house.'

Doctor struck his head out of the carriage and looked ahead as far as he could in that darkness. After travelling in silence for about two miles, Doctor stopped the carriage and tried to get down.

'Why here?' asked Bharati, in surprise.

'I've to return now,' replied Doctor. 'The others are waiting for me. There're certain scores to be settled.'

'Settle scores?' Distraught with anxiety, Bharati clasped Doctor's hands and cried, 'You mustn't do that. Please come with us.'

No sooner had she said it than Bharati remembered that whenever Doctor spoke, he did so after deliberate consideration and nothing could deter him. So Bharati felt ashamed just as Sumitra had felt. Still, she continued to hold on to his hands. 'But I need your help badly,' she said slowly.

'I know. Apurbababu, will it be possible for you to catch the steamer the day after tomorrow?'

'Yes.'

Suddenly Bharati became restive. 'I've to go home at once,' she said.

Doctor shook his head. 'That won't be necessary,' he said. 'Nabatara would've already removed all your papers, the records of the organisation, your pistol, cartridges, everything. The police will come to search the place at dawn. Our artist will be present then with his bottle of hooch and violin. Apurbababu, I believe you have a claim on his violin, isn't it?' Doctor smiled. 'Nothing incriminating will be found by the police. You can return around ten o'clock and finish your cooking. You can even have a nap. I'll come around two or three in the night. Keep some food ready for me.'

Bharati was amazed. Unless one were extraordinarily alert, she told herself, one would not have ventured to come along knowing fully well the dangers that lay ahead.

To Doctor she said, 'Nothing escapes your notice. You think of everyone. I've none to call my own. Please don't ever drive me away from your organisation.'

Doctor shook his head in the darkness. 'Nobody has the right to drive someone away from God's work. But you'll have to change your mode,' he said.

'You'll have to do it for me.'

Doctor gave no reply to this. He suddenly said, 'I've no more time to lose. I'm going.'

Saying this he disappeared in the darkness.

CHAPTER 20

As the wheels began to roll, Bharati craned her neck out and called out to the coachman, 'House Number 30, please.'

Before she could finish, the coachman replied in English, 'I know.'

The carriage seat was rather narrow, so they sat huddled against each other. On hearing the coachman's words, a shiver went down Apurba's spine; Bharati could feel it.

The carriage rumbled along for about an hour. Both of them sat silently. The rumbling of the carriage wheels in the stillness of that dark night terrified Apurba. He trembled to think that it might disturb the sleep of the neighbours and that the police would soon arrive to arrest him.

But nothing of that kind happened. The carriage reached his house safely. Bharati opened the door and signalled Apurba to get down. She came up to the coachman and asked sweetly, 'What's the fare?'

The coachman smiled. 'Not a pie,' he said. He nodded his head a couple of times and called out, 'Good night to you,' before driving away.

Bharati asked, 'Is Tewari at home?'

'Yes.'

They climbed upstairs. Apurba knocked on the door and roused Tewari from his sleep. Tewari opened the door. In the dim light of the lantern he first saw Bharati. The previous day Apurba had returned home in the morning; tonight he had returned when the night was almost over. With him was Bharati. It was all too clear. Tewari's blood began to boil with anger. Without a word he went to his room, lay down on his bed and covered himself with a sheet. Tewari had a lot of affection for this girl. She had saved him when he was dying. So, though a Christian, he had the

220

greatest regard for her. But for some time past things had taken such a turn that all sorts of anxieties about Apurba's relations with Bharati were assailing his mind, including the question of Apurba's loss of caste. He was now convinced about the certainty of the catastrophe.

Seeing Tewari lie down on his bed, Apurba asked, more out of habit than anything else, 'Won't you shut the door, Tewari?'

Apurba's mind was too distracted to notice anything, but Tewari's strange behaviour had not escaped Bharati's notice. She said hurriedly, 'I'll close it.'

Apurba entered his bedroom and saw that the bed was still unmade. In fact Tewari had spent the whole evening looking out from the balcony, waiting for Apurba to return. It had not even occurred to him to make the bed.

'Please sit down for a moment on the easy chair,' Bharati immediately said. 'I'll arrange everything in a minute.'

Apurba leaned back on the chair and again called out, 'Tewari, give me a glass of water.'

A jug of water and a glass were kept on a stool near Apurba's chair. Bharati pointed to it and said, 'Why d'you disturb one who's sleeping? Why don't you pour a glass of water yourself?'

Apurba stretched out his hand to lift the jug, but could not do so. He then got up and poured himself a glass of water. He emptied it in one gulp and was about to sit down again when Bharati said, 'Not there. I've made your bed. You may lie down now.'

Apurba lay down on the bed like a good boy and closed his eyes. Bharati rigged the mosquito net and tucked it in carefully. Suddenly Apurba said to her, 'Where'll you sleep?'

Bharati was surprised. This was not the first time she was sleeping in this house, and she knew it in and out. So, in reply to this irrelevant question, she merely pointed to the easy chair and said, 'There are barely

221

a couple of hours left for daybreak. You'd better sleep now.'

Apurba stretched out and caught her hand. 'No, not there,' he said. 'Come and sit here beside me.'

'Sit near you?' Bharati was taken aback. Whatever else Apurba may do, so far as these things were concerned he never lost his self-control. She had spent so many nights in the same room with him, but he had never said anything or even hinted at anything that was dishonourable.

'Just see, they've broken my hands,' he said. 'Why did you get me involved in all this?' His voice choked with overwhelming tears.

Bharati lifted the mosquito net and sat down beside him. She looked at his hands and saw that they were bruised and swollen in many places as a result of being tied tightly for too long. Tears were rolling down Apurba's cheeks. Bharati wiped them with the corner of her *sari* and tried to cheer him up.

'Don't worry,' she said. 'I'll wrap a wet towel. The marks will disappear in a day or two.'

She went to the bathroom and fetched a wet towel. Wrapping it around his hands, she said sweetly, 'Try to get some sleep now. I'll run my fingers through your hair.' She began doing it.

'If there was a ship tomorrow, I'd have taken it.' Apurba's voice was hoarse.

'Take the one that's leaving the day after. One day's delay won't cause you any harm.'

After a while Apurba said, 'Disobeying one's elders leads to such troubles. My mother asked me repeatedly not to come here.'

'Did she?'

'Yes. She told me repeatedly not to come here, but I didn't listen to her. The result is that I've made some terrible enemies for myself here. God alone knows what's in store for me. Anyway, whatever has to happen, will happen. I only hope through the grace of God I'm able to board the ship the day after

222

tomorrow.' He sighed deeply.

He was oblivious that the other person in the room suppressed a far deeper sigh in the recesses of her heart. Apurba's only concern was to depart at the earliest. He would be relieved to board the ship the day after next. His trip to Burma had proved disastrous in every way. All that he would remember of his stay in Burma would be the enmity of a few people. But one who had showered on him her love, silently and without making a show of it — he wouldn't think of her even once.

Apurba went on, 'No sooner I entered this house, I had a quarrel with your father. I was even fined by the court — something which had never happened to me before. I should've become cautious from that day, but I didn't.'

Bharati remained silent. Apurba resumed after a while, 'Tewari had told me time and again, "They belong to a different religion. Don't mix around with them." But who can alter what is destined. I lost my job — how many are lucky to get a job with a salary of five hundred rupees every month at my age? Besides, how shall I show these hands to anyone?'

Bharati said quietly, 'They'll heal soon enough.' She could not bring herself to say anything more. She had been running her fingers through his hair, but her fingers seemed to refuse to move. She felt awfully ashamed to even think that she had once loved this man. Many of the members of their organisation knew about this. Today, in order to save Apurba's life, she had betrayed them and had fallen in Sumitra's estimation. But she felt proud of having saved them from the indignity of killing such an insignificant person.

Apurba replied, 'No, the scars won't disappear easily.' There was no response from the other person. Apurba continued, 'If someone asks me how I got these scars, I don't know what I'll say. They'll think I lost my job because I couldn't do it well. People say that Bengali boys may be able to obtain university degrees, but they aren't fit for higher posts. My college friends will make fun of me and I won't be able to say anything in defence.'

'Cook up something and tell them. Anyway, you'd better sleep now.' Saying so, she got up.

'Please run your fingers through my hair for a while longer, Bharati.'

'No. I'm very tired.'

'Okay, okay. In any case the night is nearly over.'

Bharati entered the adjacent room. The lantern was still burning dimly. Tewari was sleeping, wrapped in a sheet as before. A half-broken deck-chair stood at a little distance away. Bharati came and sat down on it. The easy chair in Apurba's room would certainly have been much more comfortable. But the idea of spending the night in the same room with that man suddenly appeared revolting to her. She leaned back on the deck-chair. A storm was raging in her mind. Bharati had suffered rude shocks in this house more than once, but they were nothing compared to today's humiliation and anguish. What struck Bharati as most extraordinary was that even before the night was over, Apurba had totally forgotten the one person who had saved him from certain death. He did not remember the grievous wrongs he had done to his friend Talwarkar and especially to Doctor. All he could think about was his fat-salaried job and the marks on his hands.

Suddenly Bharati saw through the open window the first faint rays of the morning sun. She immediately got up and made for the door. Like a drunkard who, on returning to his senses and finding himself in an unsavoury place, rushes out with his face covered, Bharati rushed down the stairs and on to the road.

CHAPTER 21

The next afternoon Bharati narrated the whole thing to Doctor in detail and said, 'I was never under the delusion that Apurbababu was a very great man, but I had no idea that he was so mean and worthless.'

Sitting on Bharati's bed, Doctor was leafing through the pages of a book. He looked at her and said gravely, 'But I knew. If he hadn't been so worthless, would he have dismissed your love for him so cheaply? However, I'd say that you've been saved. You were needlessly dying for him.'

Everything lay scattered on the floor. It was quite clear that the police had been there. Bharati was tidying the room. She now looked up and said, 'Are you joking with me, Dada?'

'Not at all.'

'Certainly.'

'How can a dangerous man like me who goes round killing people with bombs and guns indulge in jokes?' said Doctor.

'I can never believe that you kill people. You're too kind to do that. But you must've meant it as a joke! The man who can forget everything within two-three hours except the scars on his hands and the loss of his fat-salaried job is, I'd say, the most unworthy and mean fellow I've ever seen. You said that my love for him was nothing but infatuation. If that be so, then it's best that I should get over it and devote myself fully in working for the country.'

An amused smile began to play on Doctor's lips. 'You may say that you'd like to get rid of your infatuation, but your voice betrays something else,' he said to Bharati. 'Be that as it may, I don't think you'll be of any use to us anymore. It'd be better for you to stick to Apurbababu. It's possible that despite all your wrangling over what's right or wrong, you may one day get reconciled to each other. Better do that.'

'D'you mean to say that I don't love my country?' asked Bharati.

'It's difficult to say for certain unless you pass through a number of trials,' said Doctor, smilingly.

After remaining silent for a while, Bharati said emphatically, 'I can assure you that I'll be able to pass all your tests. There's no room for selfishness, meanness and hesitancy in this work.'

Her fervour made Doctor smile. He struck his forehead and said, 'Oh, my God! D'you think that a country simply means a land mass, rivers and mountains? You're fed up with just one Apurba and you want to renounce the world and become a recluse! But you must know, there are thousands of Apurbas in this world, and even worse specimens. The greatest evil of colonialism is treachery. Those whom you try to help will be suspicious of you. Those whom you save will try to betray you. Their stupidity and ungratefulness will hurt you at every step, like needles. You'll receive no regard, no love and affection and no sympathy from anyone. Nobody will befriend you, nobody will come forward to help you. Like a venomous snake, they'll shun you instead. This is the price one has to pay for patriotism. The other alternative is death. Why undergo these trials and tribulations? I bless you, be happy with Apurba. I'm certain that one day he'll be able to overcome his hesitations and beliefs that imprison him, and realise your worth.'

Bharati's eyes filled with tears. She sat still for a few minutes with her face downcast. Then, pushing back her tears with great effort, she said, 'Do you want to get rid of me because you can't trust me fully?'

Doctor was unable to give a straight reply to this plain and blunt question. He said with a smile, 'My dear, it's impossible for someone not to like a nice girl like you. But you saw with your own eyes yesterday how much intrigue, cruelty and hatred is involved. Whenever I look at you, I feel that you're not meant

226

for this type of work, that it isn't right to drag you into this. However, I shall need your help the day I decide to quit.'

Bharati could not control herself any longer. Tears began to stream down her cheeks. She hastily wiped them with her hand and said, 'You mustn't remain with them.'

Doctor laughed. 'Now, Bharati, you've spoken like a fool!'

'I know,' said Bharati, without enthusiasm. 'But they're such cruel people.'

'And I?'

'You're also very cruel.'

'What d'you think of Sumitra?'

Bharati felt embarrassed. She did not know what to say. Doctor also did not press for a reply. For a while both remained silent, but these few minutes was sufficient to give Bharati an insight into the heart of this extraordinary person.

But the next moment Doctor changed the topic. Shaking his head like a child, he said softly, 'I must say you're being rather unfair to Apurba. The poor fellow could never imagine this work entailed such terrible things. I can tell you, he's not so mean and worthless as you think him to be. He left his home, relatives and friends, and came here for work. He hoped to achieve worldly success and become a respectable member of the society. He has received good education, belongs to a respectable family and feels humiliated at being colonised. Like others, he too wants that his country should prosper. So, when you asked him to join the organisation and work for the country, he agreed. He was certain that if he did what you said, he'd never come to grief. After all, in this foreign land, you were his guardian angel. How could he have imagined that you'd expose him to such mortal danger?'

Bharati tried to hide her tears. 'Why're you pleading for him?' she asked. 'He doesn't deserve it. After what he told me last night, it's improper to have any regard for him any more.'

'Why not do something improper at least once?' said Doctor, with a smile.

He added after a pause, 'You didn't witness it, but I did. When they bound him, he looked astonished. When they asked him, "Did you say all this?", he nodded his head. They said he'd die for that; he looked around in bewilderment. I knew whom he was looking for, so I sent for you. Whatever he might've told you, Bharati . . . . He'll take some time to get over this shock.'

Bharati could control herself no longer. 'Why're you telling me all this?' she sobbed. 'You're the person whom he has harmed the most. You now face the greatest danger. And yet you saved him for my sake, and made so many enemies for yourself in the process?'

'Really? I suppose I did.'

'Then why did you save him?'

'Save Apurba? I wanted to save that priceless gift of God that existed between two ordinary human beings from being destroyed by barbarians like Brojendra! Nothing more than that. Otherwise you know how little human lives mean to us.' Doctor burst out laughing.

Bharati wiped her tears and said, 'How can you laugh? It irritates me when you laugh like this. I wish I could hide you in some jungle. Those who want to hang you don't know your worth. They don't know what a loss that'd be for mankind. Your own countrymen call you blood-thirsty, dacoit, murderer! I sometimes wonder how, with all your kindness and love, you could live amongst them so long.'

Doctor turned his face aside and did not reply immediately. When he faced her again, he attempted to smile, but his usual, carefree smile was missing. When he spoke, his voice was heavy, 'Cruelty can never . . . but let that be. Come, I'll tell you a story. There was a Maratha boy named Nilakant Joshi. You've never met

228

him, but whenever I see you, I'm reminded of him. He had a very soft heart. Even a cortege moved him to tears.'

'One night the two of us entered a park in Colombo. There was a man lying on a bench under a tree. Sensing us, he began to groan for water. He was smelling awfully. We lighted a match. One look, and it was clear that he was suffering from cholera. Nilakant started nursing him. As the day began to dawn, I said to him, "Joshi, the watchman didn't notice us in the darkness. But that won't be so in the morning. There's a warrant of arrest against us. He'll die, but we'll sink with him too. Let's go!"

'But Nilakant began to weep. "How can I leave him like this?" he said. "Better you go." I tried to make him understand, but couldn't do so.'

'What happened after that?' asked Bharati breathlessly.

'The man was considerate. So he breathed his last before day-break. And so I could finally persuade Nilakant to escape.'

After a while, Doctor added with a deep sigh, 'Nilakant was hanged at Singapore. If he had agreed to disclose the names of the soldiers who'd helped us, he would've been pardoned. The Government tried its best, but Joshi stuck to his stand that he knew nothing. Consequently, he was hanged. And that too for some soldiers whom he didn't even know personally. People like Joshi are still born in our country; otherwise I'd have agreed to give up everything as you suggest.'

Bharati sighed deeply.

'My mission is not to murder people,' said Doctor. 'Believe me, I don't want to.'

'But what if it becomes necessary?'

'If it becomes necessary? Well, what appears necessary to Brojendra may not appear necessary to me.'

'I know that. I meant what would be necessary for you.'

Doctor kept quiet for a while. It seemed as if he was

hesitant to reply. Then he spoke, slowly and somewhat unmindfully, 'I don't know when that day will come for me. But . . let me say no further, Bharati. You won't be able to stand it even in your imagination.'

Bharati understood the hint and shuddered. 'Is there no other way?' she asked.

'No.'

His unambiguous, unhesitant reply flabbergasted Bharati. She could not bring herself to accept it and said, 'It's impossible that there's no other way.'

Doctor smiled. 'There are many ways of deceiving oneself,' he said, 'but only one way that leads to truth.'

Bharati was unconvinced. She said in a gentle and pleasing tone, 'You're very wise. You've travelled widely with a fixed mission in life. You've vast experience. I'm still to see a greater man than you. I don't want to argue with you . . . . But first promise me that you won't get annoyed.'

'Why should I?' smiled Doctor.

Bharati said in her usual sweet manner, but with great humility, 'You see, I'm a Christian. I've grown up regarding the English as my friends and benefactors. It's difficult for me to hate them now. I can't tell this to anyone else other than you. And yet, like all of you, I'm equally an Indian, a Bengali. Please don't distrust me.'

Doctor was astonished. Placing his hand on Bharati's head, he said affectionately, 'Why this apprehension, Bharati? You know how much affection and trust I have for you.'

'I know that. But don't you know my feelings for you? You're fearless; nothing can frighten you. That's why I couldn't tell you not to come here. But I know perhaps never again — no, no, not that — perhaps for a long time, I won't be able to meet you again. The other day when you ranted against the British, I didn't protest. But since then, I've fervently prayed to God that your animosity towards them should not cloud your judgement. And yet I'm with you, believe me.'

Doctor smiled. 'I know that,' he said.

'Then will you renounce this path?'

'Which one?'

'The cruel path of revolutionaries.'

'Why d'you say that?'

'Because I can't see you die. Sumitra might, but I can't. We certainly want India's independence — I can say that sincerely and without hesitation! It's true we want that the diseased and famished Indians should get food and clothing. It's true that we too want to enjoy the freedom and liberty that every person aspires for. But I can't accept that there's no other way to achieve this except through cruelty and bloodshed. It may be that you've realised this truth in your travels round the globe. It's also a fact that since the beginning of creation, those who struggled for their country's independence also adopted this path. But are we to believe that with all our intelligence, we're incapable of discovering any other path than the one of bloodshed? This can never be true. I look upon you as the personification of perfection. And so I suggest, you forsake the usual path of bloodshed. It's not too late to try out new ways. We want you to chalk out a new path for us, one of love in which we may follow you.'

Doctor stood up. With a wan smile, he patted Bharati a couple of times on her head and said, 'It's time for me to go.'

'But you didn't reply to my question?'

In response, Doctor simply said, 'May God grant you happiness.'

He then went out with slow steps.

231

CHAPTER 22

A small clay-built fort stood by the river outside the town. It had possibly been built to intercept enemy warships. It was not manned heavily; the barracks housed a small artillery force for firing the battery. During peacetime, restriction on the movement of people in its neighbourhood was lax. Of course if someone happened to wander into the area unmindfully, he was challenged. But that was all.

On the side of the fort, under the shade of the trees, there was a bathing ghat. Perhaps it had been built to serve as a landing place on the occasion of the visit of some dignitary. This had long been abandoned. Bharati used to come sometimes and sit on its steps. The soldiers at the fort must have noticed her, but they never objected, possibly because she was a woman, and a respectable woman at that.

The sun had set but it had still not become dark. The river, the treetops on the other side of the river, were all bathed in gold by the rays of the setting sun. Hundreds of birds flew overhead, covering the heavens. The black of the crows, white of the cranes and grey of the pigeons mingled with the gold of the skies to make them appear out of this world. Bharati sat gazing at them. Who knew where they flew to rest, and what invisible attraction drew them? Tears wetted her eyes; wiping them with her hand, she noticed that the golden hue over the distant trees had nearly vanished and darkness descended, enveloping everything.

Suddenly a small sampan emerged from the bend in the river and approached the ghat. It was empty except for the boatman, a Muslim from Chittagong. He looked at Bharati for a moment and then spoke in his almost unintelligible dialect. 'D'you want to cross over to the other side? It'll cost you just one anna.'

232

Bharati waved her hand and said, 'No, I don't want to.'

The boatman argued, 'All right, just give me two pice.'

'I live on this side of the river,' said Bharati in exasperation. 'Why should I go to the other side? For heaven's sake, go away!'

But the boatman refused to budge. 'You needn't pay me anything,' he said smilingly. 'Come, I'll take you for a joy ride.' He brought his boat alongside.

Bharati now became frightened. The place was dark and deserted. Though she could not speak the dialect, she could understand it as a result of her long stay in Burma. She had also heard that the Muslim boatmen of Chittagong were veritable rogues. She stood up hastily and said sharply, 'Go away at once; else I'll call the police!'

Her sharp voice and angry looks seemed to frighten the boatman. He stopped short. Bharati observed that though the man was nearing fifty, he still had a fancy for garish clothes. He wore a colourful *lungi*, though it was greasy and dirty. On top of that he wore an expensive military frock-coat bordered with lace, though that too was worn out and incredibly dirty. Perhaps he had purchased it from a second-hand shop. His head was covered with a frilled cotton cap which reached down to his forehead.

Bharati looked at him angrily for a few moments and then burst into laughter. 'Dada,' she said, 'apart from whatever you've done to your appearance, how could you imitate their dialect?'

'Will you come along, or still call the police?' asked the boatman.

'Well, I really ought to hand you over to the police. That was exactly what Apurbababu wanted.'

'I've something to tell you about him. Come, the tide will retreat soon, and we've to cover about four miles.'

Bharati boarded the boat. Doctor gave it a push and then started rowing vigorously like an experienced boatman.

'Were you watching the Lama depart?' he asked.

'Yes.'

'Apurba was standing on the first class deck facing this side. Could you see him?'

Bharati shook her head.

'I couldn't possibly go to his house or his office. So I went to the jetty. I tied my boat to the pier and went up. As I was waving . . . .'

Bharati was aghast. 'Why did you take such a risk and for whom? Why do you play with your life like that?'

'That's nothing,' said Doctor. 'Why did I go? For the same reason that you're sitting here alone.'

Bharati could not check her tears. 'That's not true!' she cried. 'I come here often . . . not for anyone else. Could he recognise you?'

'Not in the least,' smiled Doctor. 'I've mastered this art well. Though I was rather keen that he should recognise me. But he was far too busy for that.'

Bharati continued to gaze at Doctor without saying anything. Looking at her eager face, Doctor was struck dumb for a moment.

'What happened after that?' asked Bharati.

'Nothing much,' replied Doctor.

Bharati attempted a smile. 'Thank God for that,' she said. 'Because if he had, he'd have handed you over to the police and I'd be left with no other alternative but to commit suicide. He must be happy that although he lost his job at least he could escape with his life!' She gazed at the distant horizon and suppressed a sigh.

Doctor continued to row in silence.

After a while Bharati asked, 'What're you thinking about?'

'Guess.'

'Well, you're thinking that Bharati could read a person better than I did. I never imagined that an educated person could behave so meanly just to save his

234

own skin, that he could be so shameless, so ungrateful and so hard-hearted, that he didn't bother to enquire about us or even inform us of his departure, that he ran away like a dog for his life! But Bharati knew for certain that he'd behave like this. Am I not correct? Tell me, honestly?'

Doctor gave no reply. He looked the other way and went on rowing.

'Dada, look at me,' said Bharati.

Doctor looked at her. Bharati's lips were quivering violently. 'How can one be so inhuman?' she said. She bit her lips hard to stop them from quivering, but from the corners of her eyes tears streamed down her cheeks.

Doctor said nothing either in support or in protest of her statement, nor did he offer a single word of consolation. Only it seemed that for a brief moment his kohl-tinted eyes became dim.

The Iravati was narrow and shallow here, so steamers and bigger boats did not ply this side. A few fishing boats could be seen alongside the bank, otherwise they were deserted. Stars had appeared in the sky but the river itself looked black. There was silence everywhere except for the lapping of the waves against the oars. The trees on both sides of the river seemed to have merged together in the distance. Bharati sat silently, her eyes fixed at the vegetation in the darkness. She did not know where they were heading to, nor was she in the state of mind to enquire from Doctor.

Suddenly she noticed that the boat was entering a narrow creek hidden behind a huge tree, surrounded on all sides by thick foliage. Startled, she asked, 'Where're you taking me?'

'To my house.'

'Who all are there?'

'None else.'

'When'll you take me back?'

'If it's not possible tonight, then tomorrow morning.'

Bharati shook her head. 'No, no. Take me back from

where you brought me.'

'But I've a lot to talk to you about.'

Bharati gave no reply but continued to shake her head. 'No, please take me back.'

'But why? Can't you trust me, Bharati?'

Bharati remained silent with her eyes downcast.

'But you spent many nights alone with Apurba. Is he more trustworthy than I?'

Bharati remained silent and gave no reply.

The creek was narrow and dark. Overhanging branches brushed against them. The tide had started ebbing. Doctor pulled out a lantern from the hold and lighted it. Dropping the oars, he began punting with a bamboo pole.

'Bharati, there's no one who can rescue from where I'm taking you tonight,' he said. 'But possibly you've already guessed what I have in mind.' Saying this he began to laugh uproariously.

Bharati was unable to see Doctor's face in the darkness, but his laughter seemed to chastise her. She looked up and said unhesitantly, 'Dada, I'm not intelligent enough to know your mind. But I know you. I said that merely because I feel it's not proper for me to spend a night alone anywhere. Please forgive me.'

Doctor kept quiet for a while and then said in his usual calm manner, 'It hurts me to leave you and go. You're very dear to me. I wouldn't have chosen the path I have if I didn't have confidence in myself. But there's none in this world who knows your real worth. If Apurba could've realised even a fraction of this, he would've been blessed in life. Sister, go back to your normal life. Leave us! It's about you that I wanted to talk to Apurba and had gone to meet him.'

Bharati kept quiet. Apurba had gone away without saying anything. He had come to Burma for employment. They had come to know each other well only recently! He was an orthodox Brahmin. He had his own home, his society, relatives, friends. She was a Christian girl, without a home, without parents, without anyone to call her own. If Apurba had broken off with her, what grievance could she have? Bharati remained rooted to her seat, in silence; only profuse tears rolled down her cheeks in the darkness.

A dim light was now visible at a distance, through the trees. 'That's where I live,' said Doctor. 'One more bend and we'll be there. I had been a free man till now. But somehow I seem to have grown fond of you. That's what worries me. I hope to see you settled somewhere before I leave.'

Bharati wiped her tears with her *sari* and said, 'I'm happy as I am.'

Doctor heaved a deep sigh. It was an unusual thing for him to do and it pained Bharati. 'How can you say that?' he asked. 'I was told that you were not at home. I thought that possibly you had gone to the jetty. But I didn't find you there either. I was sure I'd find you somewhere on the river bank. It's unfortunate that the fellow has robbed you not only of your happiness, but also of your courage.'

Bharati was unable to understand fully what Doctor meant. So she did not reply.

Doctor went on. 'The other night you offered me your bed unhesitantly and slept on the floor instead. You had said, smilingly, "You aren't an ordinary mortal that I should feel shy or be afraid of you. Go to sleep now." But you no longer have that courage today. One can't say that Apurba is exactly a very dependable fellow. And yet you never felt afraid so long as he was there. It's strange how a fellow like him could destroy the confidence of a girl like you!'

'What's the remedy?' asked Bharati softly.

Doctor shook his head. 'I really don't know,' he said. 'But if you're always suspicious of yourself even if others aren't, life will become a torture for you. How'll you live then?'

Bharati had never analysed herself in this manner. She never had the time to do it either. Her reverence for Doctor increased manifold, but she said nothing.

237

Doctor continued, 'I knew a girl like you once. She was a Russian. But let's not talk about her. I don't know when you'll be able to meet Apurba again but I feel that you definitely will one day. I pray to God that you do! I know that you love Apurba deeply; no one can take his place in your heart. But if you now decide not to have anything to do with anyone, to retain your purity for his return, you'll only end up dehumanising yourself. Alas, where a pure heart like yours is not given its due, such explanations are advanced! Those who can't appreciate the beauty of lilies without deflowering them, stress upon the chastity of women. Maybe they're right. I don't know how long I'm going to live. But if I've to see you reduced to their level, I'll be sorry. I once called you my sister!'

'What d'you suggest I should do then? You yourself said that I should go back to domesticity.'

'But I didn't say that you should go with your head hanging low.'

'But people don't like women going around with their head held high.'

'In that case, don't go.'

Bharati said with a wan smile, 'It isn't possible for me to go back either. I have myself closed all doors. Only one was open; that too has closed today. You've seen it with your own eyes. From now on I'll follow the path that you chalk out for me. But, for heaven's sake, don't ask me to tread on your blood-stained path! If there can be so many paths leading to salvation, is it possible that there is no other way to achieve your goal except through bloodshed? I believe that human intelligence has not become so denuded as to be unable to discover an alternate way. Henceforth it shall be my constant endeavour to discover exactly that. I suffered such anguish that night when all of you decided to put him to death!'

Doctor smiled. 'Here's where I live,' he said. Getting down from the boat, he pushed it up the bank. Then, holding up the lantern, he called out to her, 'Take off your shoes before you alight. It's muddy here.'

Bharati stepped down in silence. Before her, on four sturdy teak posts and built with rotting wooden planks, stood a hut. The tide had receded and the whole place was full of knee-deep mire. The stench of rotting leaves, branches and creepers filled the air. Except for a narrow path the place was covered with undergrowth dense enough to hide not only snakes and tigers but also elephants. Had Bharati not seen it with her own eyes she would have found it impossible to imagine that anyone could live in such a place. But for this extraordinary man everything was possible.

Holding a rope they climbed the crumbling wooden stairs and came up. An eight-year-old boy opened the door. Bharati was dumbfounded. When they stepped inside, Bharati saw a youngish Burmese woman lying on a mat on the floor. Three or four children were lolling about her. One of them had shat in a corner of the room; it had not yet been cleaned, perhaps it was not considered necessary. The stench made it impossible to breathe. Cooked rice, fish bones, onion and garlic shells lay scattered on the floor. A few earthen pots used for cooking and black with soot lay nearby. It was clear that the children had dug in with their fingers and eaten whatever rice and vegetables they could lay their hands on.

Bharati followed Doctor and entered another room. Except for a mat on the floor, the room was devoid of any furniture. A cotton rug was stacked in a corner. Doctor rolled it out and beckoned Bharati to sit down. Bharati sat down without a word. She saw Doctor's familiar bundle in one corner of the room. This convinced her that this was actually Doctor's present dwelling. The Burmese woman called out from the other room and said something in Burmese. Doctor replied in the same language. Immediately thereafter the little boy brought some rice on an earthen plate, a bit of gravy in a cup, and some roasted fish on a leaf. He placed them before Doctor and left. Doctor had

239

brought along the lantern from the boat. In its light, Bharati saw the articles of food and immediately felt a stir of nausea.

'You must also be hungry, but these things . . . .'

Bharati did not say anything but simply shook her head violently. She was a Christian and had no caste scruples, but she had just seen with her own eyes where these had been brought from.

'But I'm awfully hungry,' said Doctor. 'I've to fill up my belly first.' Saying this, he washed his hands and sat down to eat happily.

Bharati turned her face aside. Repugnance and anguish filled her soul. A wave of deep sorrow swept across her; she felt she would burst into uncontrollable tears. Oh, this country! This love for its independence! To this man nothing else in this world mattered! This room, this inedible food, this hateful company, this life of an animal — even death was preferable to this sort of life, thought Bharati. It was easy to die — but this constant torture of body and mind, this slow death, faced willingly and with fortitude — this was something never seen before! The anguish of subjugation had inured him to all other sorrows.

Bharati thought of Apurba. She remembered his grief at losing his job, his anxiety lest his friends questioned him about the scars on his wrists — the majority of her countrymen were like that! They received education, got jobs, earned money and lived happily. That was all that mattered to them! And here was this man gulping this obnoxious food with such contentment! Compared to him they were like pygmies! And to think that she had fallen in love with one of them and that her inability to lead a happily married life with him had hurt her so!

Suddenly she spoke out, 'No, your path of bloodshed can never be good! No matter how many examples you cite from the past, I can never accept it as determining our present and future. I can never bring myself to follow your path of bloodshed, but I promise

240

to devote myself to serve my country wholeheartedly just as you do. Let Apurba be happy wherever he is! I won't grieve for him any more. I've found my life's mission today!'

Surprised at Bharati's outburst, Doctor looked up and mumbled through the rice in his mouth, 'What's the matter with you, Bharati?'

CHAPTER 23

After Doctor had finished his meal, he washed his hands and came and sat down on his baggage. Soon afterwards the boy, who had earlier brought his food, entered the room with a large Burmese cigar sticking out of his mouth. He continued to puff at it for a few minutes. Then, handing it over to Doctor, he left. Noticing the surprised look on Bharati's face, Doctor said smilingly, 'I usually don't reject anything that comes to me free. The other day when Apurba's uncle arrested me on the jetty at Rangoon, if it hadn't been for the bowl of hemp in my pocket, I wouldn't have been released.' Saying this he began to laugh slyly.

Bharati had heard this story before. 'I know all that,' she said. 'I also know that you've never smoked in your life. But tell me, whom does this house belong to?'

'Me.'

'And the Burmese woman and those children?'

Doctor burst out laughing. 'No,' he said, 'They aren't mine. They belong to a Muslim friend of mine. Like me, he's also condemned to the gallows, but for different reasons. He's away at the moment, so you won't get a chance to meet him.'

'I'm not at all anxious to meet him,' said Bharati. 'Please take me away from here. This place suffocates me.'

Doctor smiled. 'Even before I brought you here, I knew that you wouldn't like this place. But I've a lot to talk to you about and there's no other safe place excepting this house. I'm afraid you'll have to put up with a little discomfort tonight.'

'Are you thinking of going away somewhere?'

'Yes. I've got to visit the countries in the north and in the east once again. It may take a couple of years for me to return. You suffered a lot of mental agony

242

today . . . . I feel bad talking to you about these things. But it may not be possible for me to meet you again after tonight.'

'Does that mean that you'll be leaving tomorrow itself?' asked Bharati anxiously.

Doctor did not reply. Bharati understood that his decision was irrevocable. From tomorrow morning she would be all alone in this world; there would be none even to inquire after her.

Doctor continued, 'I'll proceed on foot through Canton in southern China. If my work does not take me to America, I'll return to Burma after visiting the islands in the Pacific. Then I'll stay here until the conflagration starts.'

He added with a smile, 'And in case I'm not able to return, I guess you'll get the information sooner or later.'

His calm manner appeared to be deceptively simple, but Bharati realised its serious implications. After keeping quiet for a while she said, 'I've heard it is dangerous to travel through China on foot. No, don't smile at me. I didn't mean to frighten you. After all, I don't know much about you, do I? But, why d'you want to return to Burma? Don't you have any work in your motherland?'

'It's for her sake that I propose to stay on. Here women are free; they realise the value of freedom. So I need them. If ever you hear that there has been a revolution, wherever you may be at that time, know that it is the women of Burma who started it. Will you remember?'

Bharati understood the hint. 'But I don't believe in your path,' she said.

'I know that. But whatever may be your path, there's no harm in remembering these words,' said Doctor. 'At least they'll remind me of you.'

'There are hundreds of other things that will remind me of you,' replied Bharati. 'But is this how you draw people to your path? However, you won't succeed with me.'

She stood up. Picking up a cotton rug from the corner, she dusted it and then rolled it out on the floor. She then fetched the blanket and pillow and started making Doctor's bed.

'My path has been chalked out for me today by the steering wheel of Apurbababu's ship,' said Bharati. 'This will be my path for the rest of my life. When we meet again, even you will be forced to admit this.'

'What's this you're doing, Bharati?' said Doctor, embarrassed. 'Certainly I could've spread out this torn blanket myself. There was no necessity for you to do it.'

'It may not be necessary for you; it was for me,' replied Bharati. 'In future, whenever I make the bed for anyone, I'll never forget this torn blanket of yours. If this is not necessary for a woman, what else is, tell me?'

Doctor smiled. 'I don't have any reply to that,' he said. 'I accept my defeat. But I've never accepted defeat from any other woman before.'

'Not even from Sumitra-didi?' asked Bharati smilingly.

Doctor shook his head. 'No.'

When the bed was ready, Doctor got off his baggage and sat down on it.

Bharati, who was sitting on the floor a little distance away, said, 'Will you pardon me if I ask you something before you leave?'

'Yes.'

'Then tell me, what's your relationship with Sumitra-didi? Where did you find her?'

Doctor kept quiet for a long time and then said slowly, with a smile, 'That's a question you should have asked her. But once upon a time when I hardly knew her, I had to declare that she was my wife. Her name, Sumitra, was also given by me. Perhaps, that's the evidence she uses in support of her claim.'

Though extremely curious, Bharati kept quiet.

Doctor continued, 'I've heard that her mother was

244

Jewish, but her father was a Bengali Brahmin. She first went to Java with a circus troupe and later got a job in the railway station at Surabaya. As long as he was alive, Sumitra received her education in a missionary school. But after his death — there's no need for you to hear the rest of the story!'

Bharati shook her head, 'No, no, that won't do. You have to tell me the full story.'

'I myself don't know the full details. I only know that she and her mother, along with two of her maternal uncles, one Chinese and two Muslims from south India, started a business in importing and exporting smuggled opium. In the beginning I was not aware of her activities. I only remember seeing her often on the train between Batavia and Surabaya. As she was very beautiful, she attracted my attention as of others. That was all. But one day I was introduced to her at the waiting room in Teg railway station. That was the first time I learnt that she was a Bengali girl.'

'I see you were captivated by her beauty.'

'Be that as it may, one day I left Java for elsewhere. I possibly even forgot her. But after a year or so, I suddenly met her again at the jetty at Bengkulen. She was sitting on a trunk full of opium, surrounded by the police. As soon as she saw me, she began to cry. It was clear that I had to save her. I told the policemen that she was my wife. Sumitra was startled. She hadn't expected that. Because this happened in Sumatra, I gave her the name, Sumitra. Her own name was Rose Dawood. At that time cases pertaining to Bengkulen used to be tried at Padang. I had a friend living there, one Paul Kruger. I took Sumitra to his house. Though the magistrate released her, she was no longer prepared to release me.'

Bharati smiled. 'Possibly she'll never release you.'

Doctor went on, 'The members of her group got the information about her whereabouts and started harassing us. I also noticed that her beauty was making my friend Kruger restive. So, leaving her in his custody,

I disappeared from Sumatra.'

Bharati was stunned. 'You left her alone and disappeared? That was cruel of you.'

'Yes, somewhat like Apurba. One more year passed. I was then staying in a small seedy hotel in the town of Macassar in the island of Celebes. One evening, on returning to my room, I found Sumitra waiting there. She was wearing a silk *sari* in the fashion of Hindu women and for the first time she bent down and took the dust from my feet as Hindu women do.'

'I've left everything and have come to you,' she said. 'I've wiped out my past. Please take me in your organisation. You'll find me worthy of your trust.'

Bharati asked breathlessly, 'What happened after that?'

'Well, I can tell you this much that since then I've never had any occasion to complain against her. A person who can give up her way of life which she was used to for twenty-one years deserves my admiration. But she's very cruel.'

Bharati kept quiet. She wanted to say, 'She may be cruel, but you love her even so.' But she could not bring herself to say it.

Still she seemed to get an insight into the heart of that strange woman today. Her cruel silence and ruthless indifference — everything seemed clear to Bharati.

Suddenly an unexpected sigh escaped from Doctor. He felt momentarily embarrassed. But by long practice he had attained complete control over his body and mind. So the very next moment he was his usual self again. 'After that I came to Canton with Sumitra,' he said with a smile.

Bharati hid a smile and said innocently, 'But why did you have to come away? Who told you to do that? At least none of us did!'

Doctor kept quiet for a moment and then said smilingly, 'I can't say there was no compulsion. I had thought that nobody else should know about this matter. But you people are so curious that you won't be satisfied until you hear it fully. And if I don't tell you, you'll start imagining things. So it's better that I tell you everything.'

'I too think the same,' said Bharati. 'It's better for you to tell me the whole story.'

'What happened next was that Sumitra shifted to an upstairs room in the same hotel. I forbade her again and again not to do so, but she **didn't** listen to me. When I told her to shift to some other place, she began to cry. She begged me to protect her. The matter became clear the next morning. The entire Dawood gang arrived at the hotel. They were about ten or twelve. One of them, half Arab and half Negro, and as fat as an elephant, claimed that Sumitra was his wife.'

'He said that in your presence?' asked Bharati. 'Then the two of you must have had a big fight?'

Doctor nodded his head. 'Though Sumitra denied it as part of a conspiracy against her, it was clear that they wanted to take her back for smuggling opium. They were a band of ruffians, capable of doing anything. They had their outposts in all the islands in the Pacific. It became clear to me why Sumitra had not agreed to leave the hotel and go away somewhere. I protested and said that I would send for the police. They left, but before doing so they threatened me that nobody had ever escaped from their clutches. Subsequent events proved that it was not an idle threat.'

Alarmed, Bharati asked, 'What happened after that?'

'I was on my guard throughout that night. I knew that they would come back with full strength and attack us.'

'But why didn't you leave immediately?' asked Bharati anxiously. 'Why didn't you inform the police? Didn't they have a police force?'

'Almost negligible,' replied Doctor. 'Moreover, it was not quite safe for me to call the police. However, the night passed without any mishap. The next morning I arranged for a boat to take us away. But unfortunately

Sumitra was laid up with fever and could not move. That night I was awakened with the sound of a door opening. I peeped out and saw the hotel-keeper had opened the door and let in about a dozen people. It was apparent that they intended to lock my door somehow and go upstairs to Sumitra's room by the staircase.'

'Then?' Bharati asked anxiously. 'How did you escape?'

'There was no time to escape. So I opened the door of my room and came out and stood in the passage leading to the staircase.'

'Alone? What happened then?' asked Bharati, looking pale.

'The subsequent events took place in darkness. So I can't give you an authentic account. I can only say what happened to me. One bullet entered my left shoulder and another just below the knee. In the morning the police came. The ambulance arrived and carried away half a dozen bodies. The hotel keeper said in his deposition that a band of dacoits had raided the hotel. It's difficult to say what would've happened if it had been a British territory. But presumably the Celebes islands have different rules and regulations. When the bodies could not be identified, they were probably buried.'

This story filled Bharati with fear and astonishment. For a while she could not bring herself to say anything. Then she whispered, 'They were buried! Does that mean you killed so many people?'

'I just happened to be there,' replied Doctor. 'Actually they killed themselves.'

Bharati did not say anything. She heaved a deep sigh and kept quiet.

Doctor continued after a while. 'Partly by boat, partly by steamer, we reached Minado. There we took new identities and boarded a Chinese ship and at last reached Canton. But perhaps you aren't interested in hearing the rest of the story. Isn't it so? You must be thinking that even my hands are stained with blood.'

Bharati, who had been unmindful, now looked at Doctor and said, 'Won't you take me back to my place?'

'Do you want to leave immediately?'

'Yes.'

'All right,' said Doctor.

He removed a plank from the floor and took out something and put it into his pocket. Bharati realised that it was a pistol. She too had a pistol and, as instructed by Sumitra, often carried it with her when she went out. But for the first time she realised that this was a weapon to kill a man. She suddenly wondered whether the pistol in Doctor's pocket might have been used for killing innumerable people in the past.

After she took her seat on the boat, Bharati said slowly, 'Whatever you might have done, you're my only shelter in this world. Till I get back the peace of my mind, promise that you won't leave me and go away.'

Doctor smiled. 'All right,' he said. 'I promise that I'll take leave of you before I go.'

CHAPTER 24

Throughout the return journey Bharati remained absorbed in her own thoughts. Most of it was desultory, but one particular thought that moved her the most concerned Sumitra — her past, and especially the strange and sad story of her youth. She did not consider Sumitra as her friend — indeed, no woman could! — she also did not love her; but still she respected Sumitra for her excellence in every field. But her reverence had turned into terror that day when, despite being a woman, Sumitra had unhesitantly sentenced Apurba to death. Apurba's offence might have been grievous, but Sumitra's cold-blooded manner terrified Bharati, just as a sacrificial animal would be on seeing the blood-stained sword! Sumitra was aware that Bharati loved Apurba. Besides, she herself knew what it was to love someone. And yet she had no hesitation in sentencing to death another woman's lover, despite being a woman herself! In the past whenever such doubts assailed her mind, Bharati sought to justify it by telling herself that had it not been for her intense, though pitiless at times, devotion to duty, how could Sumitra function as the President of their organisation? How could those revolutionaries rely on her otherwise? But today she was able to discover a relationship between Sumitra's birth, her upbringing, the strange history of her adolescence and youth and her ruthlessness, her terrible possessiveness and her obsessive patriotism. The sense of hurt which she had harboured against Sumitra all these days, as one woman against another, lost its edge today. She could not think of Sumitra as belonging to the same sex as her. Indeed, she felt that there could be nothing more ludicrous than to expect leniency from Sumitra on account of mere affection.

As their boat came to rest against the river bank,

someone stepped out of the shadows. Bharati was about to alight, holding Doctor's hand, but glancing at the man, she seemed to become paralysed with fear and stepped back.

'It's Hira Singh,' said Doctor softly. 'He's waiting to escort you back. Hey there, Singh-ji, I hope everything is okay!'

'Everything is fine,' replied Hira Singh.

'Should I accompany her?'

'Who can stop you?' replied Hira Singh with a little smile.

It was clear that the police were keeping a watch over Bharati's place and that it was not safe for Doctor to go there.

Bharati clutched at Doctor's hands and whispered, 'I won't go.'

'But there's no need for you to hide,' said Doctor.

'Even if it were necessary, I wouldn't be able to do it,' replied Bharati. 'But I won't go with that man.'

Doctor understood the reason for Bharati's reluctance. On the day of Apurba's trial, it was Hira Singh who had deceived her into attending the meeting. He thought for a moment and then said, 'But you know how unsafe that area is. You can't possibly go alone at this late hour. And I . . . .'

Before he could finish Bharati said anxiously, 'No, no, you needn't come with me. I haven't become crazy that I should . . . .'

She stopped in the middle of the sentence. Who knew better than her that it was impossible for her to venture alone so late at night? Observing that she showed no inclination to release his hand or to get down from the boat, Doctor said affectionately, 'I feel hesitant to take you back to my place. But are you willing to go somewhere else — our poet's house, for example? It's just across the river. Will you?'

'Who's this poet?' she asked.

'Our great musician . . . the one who plays the violin,' replied Doctor.

Bharati like the idea. 'But will he be at home?' she inquired. 'And even if he is, he'll probably be roaring drunk!'

'Quite possible,' replied Doctor. 'But he usually comes to his senses on hearing my voice. Besides, Nabatara lives nearby. I might be able to get you something to eat from her house.'

'For heaven's sake, don't try to feed me at this hour!' said Bharati anxiously. 'But, nevertheless, let's go there. We can get back in the morning.'

As Doctor pulled away from the shore, Hira Singh melted into the shadows, as mysteriously as he had appeared.

'How's it that this man has escaped suspicion till now?' asked Bharati curiously.

'Well, for one thing he's a telegraph peon,' replied Doctor. 'It's his job to deliver urgent telegrams. So he doesn't appear out of place anywhere and at any time.'

The tide was coming in. It was therefore necessary to get out of the creek and into the mainstream and then to row upstream for some distance; else it would be difficult to cross over to the exact place. Noticing Doctor straining to punt along the river bank carefully, Bharati said, 'There's really no need to go to the poet's house. Let's go back to your place With the tide in, it shouldn't take us more than half an hour.'

'I've some work with him as well. It's necessary for me to meet him.'

Bharati laughed. 'I find it difficult to believe that anyone can have any work with him,' she said jocularly.

Doctor kept quiet for a while and then said, 'None of you know him well. It's difficult to find a true artist like him. Clutching at his broken violin he has travelled all over the world. Besides, he's a great scholar. He can talk on any subject. I consult him whenever in doubt. I'm really fond of him.'

Bharati felt embarrassed. 'Then why don't you help him get over his alcoholism?' she asked.

'But then I never ask anyone to give up anything,'

he added after a while. 'Besides, he's a poet, an artist. He belongs to a different tribe of people. Their understanding of good and bad isn't the same as ours. But society doesn't accept this. Everyone enjoys the fruits of his good qualities but he alone suffers the punishment for the bad ones. Whenever he's anguished, if there's anyone else who shares his sorrows, it's me.'

'You share the griefs of everyone,' said Bharati. 'You've a heart as tender as a woman's. But how can you trust the artist? He might divulge everything while drunk.'

'Even while drunk he has that much sense. Besides, no one ever takes him seriously.'

'What's his name?' asked Bharati.

'Atul, Suren — whatever pleases him at that moment. But his real name is Sashipada Bhowmik.'

'I think he has a great regard for Nabatara,' said Bharati.

'I agree,' said Doctor, with an amused smile.

He headed the boat towards the opposite bank. The force of the current soon took the boat to the other side. The area was full of wooden logs belonging to different British timber companies. The pools of water that had accumulated between these logs turned silver under the powerful beams of light from the ships in the distance. Doctor guided the boat through these logs. Then, stepping out, he helped Bharati to alight. They walked gingerly over the slippery logs for some distance and then came upon a narrow path. The place was full of ditches, shrubs and thorny bushes. It was difficult to keep to the path through all the undergrowth in the darkness.

'You've brought me from one terrible place to another equally terrible place,' said Bharati in a terrified voice. 'Must you people live in jungles like bears and tigers? Why can't you choose a better place to live in? Even if you aren't afraid of wild animals, you must surely be scared of snakes?'

Doctor laughed. 'The snakes haven't been imported from England,' he said. 'They're quite well-bred; they don't bite unless provoked.'

This reminded Bharati of another incident. On that occasion as well, Doctor had given vent to his great hatred for the Europeans.

Doctor continued, 'You referred to bears and tigers. I sometimes think that if India had been full of only such animals instead of men, it'd have been better for us. Foreigners might have come to India even then, but they'd have come only for hunting. At least they wouldn't have stayed on to exploit us.'

Bharati remained silent. Such expressions of hatred against an entire nation used to hurt her greatly. Her eyes would become moist with tears to see such malice pour out of the heart of this man who was by nature warm-hearted and tolerant. She would repeatedly tell herself, 'This can never be true, never!'

For some time now a mellifluous tune had been audible. Doctor stopped in his tracks and said, 'It seems our artist is awake and in his proper senses. I'm sure you've never heard anyone play the violin like this before.'

After a few paces, Bharati also halted. It seemed to her as if a plaintive cry was wafting towards them, piercing the darkness. It was without beginning or end and beyond comparison with anything in this world!

For a while Bharati stood rooted to the ground, lost in the melody. Suddenly she felt Doctor's gentle touch on her arm and heard him say, 'Move on.'

Bharati was startled. 'Yes, of course,' she said. 'I've never heard anything like this before!'

'There are few places on this globe that I haven't visited,' replied Doctor calmly, 'but I don't recollect having heard anything like this anywhere.' He added with a smile, 'But this poor violin has been through all sorts of trouble in the hands of our artist. I myself have had to retrieve it at least ten times. Even now I believe it's pledged to Apurbababu for five rupees.'

'That's true,' said Bharati. 'However, I'll send the amount to Apurbababu on behalf of the artist.'

A double-storied wooden house stood half-hidden by the trees. The ground floor was full of mire and slush and undergrowth. A wooden staircase led to the first floor. A huge coloured Chinese lantern hung from the arch of the landing. In its light Bharati read the words "Sashi-Tara Lodge" written in large black letters on a signboard in English.

'So he has given the name of "Sashi-Tara Lodge" to his house,' said Bharati. 'The meaning of the word "lodge" is quite apparent, but what does "Sashi-Tara" mean?'

Doctor laughed slyly, 'I suppose he has taken "Sashi" from his name "Sashipada" and joined it to "Tara" from "Nabatara" to coin the name "Sashi-Tara Lodge".'

'But this is highly improper,' said Bharati gravely. 'How can you permit such things?'

'D'you think I'm all powerful?' laughed Doctor. 'If someone chooses to call his house "Sashi-Tara Lodge" or "Apurba-Bharati Palace", what can I do?'

'This can't be allowed,' said Bharati indignantly. 'Tell that to him; or else I won't enter his house.'

'I hear they're going to get married soon,' replied Doctor.

'That can't be permitted,' cried Bharati. 'Her husband is still alive!'

'If one is lucky, that small problem might disappear as well. I hear he died a fortnight back.'

Despite her annoyance, Bharati burst into laughter. 'Maybe that information is wrong,' she said. 'In any case, they'll have to wait for at least an year. Otherwise it'll look improper.'

Noticing her anxiety, Doctor said solemnly, 'All right, I'll tell him. But it's worth considering which is more unseemly — if they wait, or if they don't.'

Bharati kept quiet after this. As they climbed the stairs, Doctor said in a low voice, 'I feel sorry for the poor fellow. I believe he loves that woman deeply. If

255

only he had loved someone else!' He heaved a sigh. 'Everything is insignificant,' he said. 'Whether it is one's reputation or what others think about him. I sincerely feel that if his love is true, it'll redeem him.'

Bharati was surprised. 'But is that possible?' she asked.

Doctor turned round and glanced at her once. Then, without another word he ascended the stairs and standing before the closed door, called out to the artist.

The music stopped. Shortly the door opened and the artist came out. He recognised Doctor immediately; then peering through the darkness he was able to see Bharati as well. 'Is it you, Bharati?' he said ecstatically. 'Come, come inside the room!' Saying this he caught hold of Bharati's hands and led her in. His delighted face, sincere invitation and genuine and enthusiastic reception mollified Bharati.

Pulling out an envelope from under his pillow, he handed it over to Bharati. 'Go ahead, read it,' he said. 'I'll be getting a draft for ten thousand rupees the day after tomorrow. Not a pie less! Hadn't I always said that I'd inherit a large sum? Swindler, liar, drunkard, they used to call me! And now? Ten thousand! Not a pie less!'

There was a story behind this draft for ten thousand rupees that needs to be recounted here. Sashi's friends, acquaintances and even his enemies, there was none who had not heard from him that one day he would receive a large sum of money. No one took him seriously and indeed, many of them ridiculed him, but this was his trump card. He would merrily go about borrowing money from everyone, promising to repay the amount along with interest as soon as he received the money. How many dreams he had woven around this very uncertain source of income! About five or six years ago when his wealthy grandfather died, he inherited a share of the property along with his other cousins. Negotiations had been in progress for the sale of the property; the matter had been finalised about a month back. The envelope contained a letter from a well-known attorney of Calcutta. He had assured Sashi that the amount would be sent in a day or two.

When Bharati finished reading the letter, Doctor remarked, 'But you were expecting twenty thousand, weren't you?'

Sashi waved his hands. 'Even ten thousand is a lot of money,' he said. 'Besides, it's my cousin who has purchased the property from me. So, in a way, the property has remained within the family. That's exactly what my cousin has written. That is what he writes . . .'

But Doctor stopped him. 'There's no need for that,' he said. 'I'm not curious to know what he has written.'

Turning to Bharati, he said, 'If only we had such eccentric cousins!' and started laughing.

This did not please Sashi. He tried to prove that in a way he was receiving so much money without actually selling his property, and it was all because his cousin was such a nice man.

Bharati laughed slyly. 'You're right,' she said. 'Your cousin's goodness is quite clear to me. You don't have to prove it.'

Sashi said at once, 'But you'll have to lend me ten rupees tomorrow. I borrowed ten rupees from you the other day. That, along with the ten that you're going to give me tomorrow, and the eight and a half that I owe Apurbababu makes a total of thirty rupees. I shall repay it in two-three days' time. You'll have to accept the money back, I won't take a "No" for an answer!'

Bharati smiled.

Sashi continued, 'I'll deposit the draft in the bank as soon as I receive it. They've called me drunkard, swindler, spendthrift — whatever they liked — but now I'll show them! I'll deposit the money in the bank and manage with the interest alone. Why manage, I'll save something out of that as well! I'll open an account in the post office also. I won't keep any cash at home.

Maybe I'll be able to buy a house in five years' time. That's necessary now that I've decided to settle down. It's not easy to manage these days!'

Doctor glanced at Bharati and burst out laughing. But Bharati turned her face away. She was looking grim.

'I suppose you've heard that I've given up drinking?' asked Sashi.

'No.'

'Yes. Once and for all! Nabatara made me promise this.'

They could have carried on a discussion over this latest development, but Bharati was becoming increasingly distressed at one's amused questions and the other's enthusiastic replies. Noticing this, Doctor changed the topic. Addressing Sashi, he said, 'I take it then that you won't be leaving this place in the near future.'

'Leave this place? Impossible!'

'Very good. Then we can use this place as our rendezvous.'

'That's not possible,' said Sashi. 'I won't have anything to do with you in future. I can't risk my life!'

Doctor smiled. Turning to Bharati, he said, 'Whatever other faults our friend may have, even his worst enemy can't blame him for being needlessly scrupulous; it's a trait worth emulating.'

'It's far better to be plain-spoken than to give false hopes,' replied Bharati innocently. 'I can't do it myself, but if only I could've learnt it from our artist, I would've been a free woman today.'

Her voice sounded rather sad towards the end. Sashi did not notice it; he would not have realised the significance even if he had. But Doctor understood its meaning.

For a couple of minutes nobody spoke. Then Doctor said, 'I'm leaving in a day or two. I plan to press on ahead from China on foot and tour the Pacific islands. I may even go to America from Japan. I can't say when I'll return — I may not return at all — but supposing I do return one day, I take it that there'll be no room for me in your house.'

Sashi looked at him steadily for a while and his expression and voice seemed to change. Then, shaking his head he said, 'No, my house will always be open for you!'

Doctor said jocularly, 'How can you say that? Don't you know you'll be in grave danger if you do that?'

'I may be arrested. I know that. But I don't mind it,' replied Sashi unhesitantly.

He kept quiet for a while. Then, turning to Bharati, he said, 'I've no greater friend in this world than Doctor. In 1911, when Kotaku and his entire group were hanged in Tokyo for hurling bombs, Doctor was working there as a sub-editor of an English newspaper. The police had cordoned off the entire front of the building where we were living. I was frightened and almost in tears. But Doctor told me, "We can't afford to die; we must escape." Tying a rope to the back window he first lowered me and then climbed down himself. Ugh! . . . d'you ever remember it?' he asked Doctor. The memory of that past incident sent a shiver down his spine.

'I remember it,' smiled Doctor.

'You've every reason to,' interjected Sashi. 'But if Aakim hadn't helped us that night, we'd surely have died. We could never have been able to board the boat to Shanghai. Oh, there aren't greater rogues in this world than those short-statured fellows! I had nothing to do with bombs; I just lived there and learnt how to play the violin. But they wouldn't have listened to what I had to say, would they? They had no regard for laws or law courts. They'd surely have butchered me if they could. The fact that I'm alive today to recount all this is all because of him,' he said, glancing at Doctor through the corners of his eyes.

To Bharati he said, 'It's true, there can't be a truer friend in this whole world than Doctor, nor one with a kinder heart.'

Bharati's eyes grew moist with tears. She said to Doctor, 'One day you'll have to tell us about all your experiences. God gave you so much intelligence, but why did He forget to give you the wisdom to realise the value of your life? And you still want to go to Japan once again?'

'I told him exactly the same thing,' said Sashi. 'You can't expect anything from those selfish, greedy and mean fellows. They'll never give you any help.'

Doctor laughed. 'Sashi could never forget that he had to escape with the help of a rope. He could never forgive the Japanese for that. But there's more to it. They're a really remarkable people! They were able to understand the true nature of the whites from the beginning. Two and a half centuries back they passed laws that as long as the sun and the moon existed, no Christian would be allowed to set foot on their soil. Whatever faults they may have, for this alone they deserve my admiration!'

Doctor's eyes seemed to blaze with fire. Sashi was overwhelmed by its terrible brightness. He continued to nod his head fearfully and repeat, 'Quite right, quite right!'

Bharati felt her mouth turn dry and her heart beat violently. On the eve of his departure, even if it were for a brief moment, she felt she had seen the true self of this extraordinary man.

Doctor poked at his chest with his finger and said, 'What was it that you said, Bharati? That God had not given me enough intelligence to realise the value of my life? Well, you were wrong. D'you want to hear the story of my life? At a secret meeting at Canton, Sun Yat Sen told me once . . . .'

Bharati cried out in fear, 'I hear some people coming up!'

Doctor immediately pricked his ears and slowly pulled out the pistol from his pocket. 'There's none in this world,' he said, 'who can catch me in this darkness.'

260

He stood up, but his face was clouded with anxiety.

Sashi alone was not perturbed. He looked up and said, 'Nabatara and the others were supposed to come today. Most probably . . . .'

Doctor laughed. 'Not probably, it's definitely she. Hear the soft footsteps. But who are the others?'

'Can't you make out?' said Sashi. 'I suppose 'it's our President who has . . . .'

'Whom d'you mean?' asked Bharati in surprise. 'Sumitra-didi?'

Sashi nodded his head and rushed to open the door. Bharati glanced at Doctor. She felt she now understood Doctor's purpose in coming here. This night promised to be a fateful one. In view of the impending revolt within the organisation, it was inevitable that the final drama would be enacted here this night. Probably those who were coming up included Iyer and Talwarkar; possibly Brojendra was also hiding in the jungles thinking it to be safer than the city. Doctor did not stash away his pistol as he normally did in such circumstances, but continued to hold it in his left hand. His expressionless face did not reveal what was going on in his mind, but Bharati's face turned paler than before.

CHAPTER 25

Those who entered the room were all known faces.
Doctor looked up and said, 'Come in.' From his expression it was apparent to Bharati that he was not
prepared for this.

While Sumitra's views on the matter were known,
they were unaware that along with her, the others had
crossed over as well. It could not have been a mere
coincidence. It was clear that, unknown to Doctor, they
had held a secret meeting and taken certain crucial
decisions. The members of the party entered one by
one and took their seats on the floor. None of them
exhibited the least surprise or excitement. It was apparent they knew of Doctor's presence here, if not
Bharati's. She had had an apprehension that the incident concerning Apurba might result in a split in the
organisation. Her heart quaked in fear that this issue
might be sought to be settled that night.

Sumitra looked morose and grim. She did not speak
to Bharati or even looked at her. Brojendra removed
his huge ochre turban from his head, kept it on the
floor beside him and placed his thick stave on it. He
leaned back against the wooden wall and sat down
comfortably. The cruel glance of his round eyes
scanned the faces of Bharati and Doctor repeatedly.
Ramdas Talwarkar sat silently, while Barrister Krishna
Iyer lighted a cigarette and began to smoke. Nabatara
sat in one corner, away from the others, as if to imply
that she had nothing to do with them. She appeared
to be unable to even recognise Bharati. All of them
looked grim and unsmiling. They sat silently; it was
like a lull before the storm.

Bharati came and sat down beside Doctor, as she had
done the other night. 'Bharati seems to be afraid of
all of you,' said Doctor, smilingly. 'I'm the only one
she doesn't fear.'

The remark was unwarranted. Excepting Bharati, no one noticed Sumitra cautioning Brojendra, with her eyes, to exercise restraint. But either he did not get the hint or else chose to ignore it, so he startled everybody by saying harshly in his cracked voice, 'We condemn your despotism and register our protest against it! If ever I catch Apurba, I'll . . . .'

'Kill him,' said Doctor, completing his sentence for him. He fixed his glance at Sumitra and asked, 'Do all of you support him?'

Sumitra looked down and did not reply. The others too remained silent. Doctor kept quiet for a few moments and then said, 'It appears that all of you support him and that you've discussed this matter between yourselves before coming here.'

'Yes, we have,' replied Brojendra. 'And we feel something needs to be done about it.'

Doctor looked at him and said, 'I too think the same. But before that I'd like to remind you of certain consequences which you've possibly lost sight of in your anger. Ahmed Durrani was our Secretary for the entire northern China. He was the most courageous and efficient member in our organisation. In 1910, a month or so after the Japanese invasion of Korea, he was arrested at a railway station in Manchuria. He was subsequently hanged at Shanghai. You've met Durrani, haven't you Sumitra?'

Sumitra nodded her head to indicate that she had.

Doctor continued, 'I was then at Chita trying to reconstruct our splintered organisation. I had no idea that one of my trusted lieutenants had died in the meantime. It shouldn't have been difficult to save Durrani when the farce of trial was being enacted in the court against him. So many of our men were present there. And yet this happened. Do you know why? It was because Mathura Dubey of Faizabad had poisoned the minds of the party men on flimsy grounds against him. Durrani's death seemed to relieve everybody. When I got back, I came to know every-

263

thing at the meeting at Canton. By then Durrani was dead and Mathura Dubey had also died of typhoid. Nothing was left to be done, but two important decisions were taken at that secret meeting. You were present there, Krishna Iyer. So why don't you tell them what those decisions were?'

Krishna Iyer turned pale. 'It's not clear to me whom you're hinting at,' he said to Doctor.

Doctor said, without the slightest hesitation, looking at Brojendra. One of the decisions was that nobody should criticise my actions in my absence.'

'Even discussion is forbidden!' said Brojendra sarcastically.

'Yes, it is. In my absence,' replied Doctor. 'But I know it goes on all the time. I've been ignoring it so long because unlike those who were present in the meeting at Canton, I was not needlessly perturbed by Durrani's death. But the second offence is more serious, Brojendra.'

'Go ahead, tell it,' said Brojendra nonchalantly.

'I will,' replied Doctor. 'It's fomenting a revolt against me. It's a very serious offence. I have to be more careful after Durrani's death.'

Brojendra said grimly, 'The same thing applies to others as well. You're not the only person in this world for whom it's necessary.' He looked at the others but they remained silent; no one joined him.

Doctor himself kept quiet for a while and then said calmly, 'The punishment for this offence is death. I had thought that I wouldn't have to take any action against you before I leave. But you seem to have become impatient, Brojendra. You're always itching to kill others; how would you like if the same were to happen to you?'

Brojendra's face turned dark. However, he gathered himself and said haughtily, 'I'm an anarchist, a revolutionary! Life is of no consequence to me. I'm prepared to give it as also to take it.'

'Then you better get prepared to give it tonight,' said

Doctor in a calm voice. 'But you won't have time to pull that thing out of your belt. I'm not blind; besides, I know you only too well.' Saying this he levelled his own pistol at Brojendra. Terribly nervous, Bharati tried to prevent him by clinging to his arm. Doctor pushed her aside and cried, 'Shame on you, Bharati!'

All were thunderstruck. It seemed as though in an instant lightning had struck the room.

Sumitra's lips began to quiver. 'What's all this amongst ourselves?' she said.

Talwarkar had been silent all this while. He now said slowly, 'I don't know all the rules of your organisation. But is difference of opinion punishable by death? I may personally be happy that Apurba is alive today, but I must say your action that day was improper.'

Krishna Iyer nodded his head in agreement. Brojendra was no longer as defiant as before, but gathering strength from the support of others, he said, 'If someone has to die, then let me die. I'm ready.'

Sumitra said, 'If you must have the blood of a trusted comrade instead of a traitor's, take mine.'

Doctor kept quiet and did not give any reply to this emotional outburst. After some time, he said with a wry smile, 'I've known this "trusted comrade" since long, when you weren't even around. But let that be. Sun Yat Sen once said to me in a hotel in Tokyo that those who can't face disappointments should leave this path. So I'll have to put up with it. But, Brojendra, don't think I tried to frighten you for nothing. I'm going away, but I can't allow any breach of discipline. If you're able to get Sumitra's loyalty, I wish you good luck. But you'd better quit from my organisation. You attempted once at Surabaya and again the day before yesterday. If we meet in future, well, you know . . . .'

'What's all this?' said Sumitra agitatedly. 'What does "attempt" mean?'

But Doctor did not bother to reply to any of these questions. Looking at Krishna Iyer, he said, 'Krishna Iyer, I'm sorry.'

Iyer lowered his face and gave no reply. Doctor pulled out his watch from his pocket and glanced at it. He said to Bharati, 'Come, I'll reach you to your place and then go. Get up.'

Bharati had been sitting silently all this while, as if in a trance. She now stood up. Leading her ahead, Doctor came out of the room. Then, stopping at the landing, he called out to the others, 'Good night.'

None of them responded; they remained rooted to their seats in bewilderment.

After Bharati had climbed down, Doctor began to descend the stairs one by one, his eyes on the door of the room upstairs. Suddenly the door flung open. Sashi thrust his face and called out, 'But I need you, Doctor.'

He hurried down. Approaching Doctor, he said breathlessly, 'I know I'm good for nothing. I can be of no use to you. But I'll always remain indebted to you. I shall never forget it!'

Doctor clasped his hands affectionately and said, 'Who says you're good for nothing, Sashi? You're a poet, an artist, you're greater than the others! And if you really feel indebted to me, it's better not to forget it.'

'I'll never forget it,' replied Sashi. 'But wherever you may be, whatever I have is yours. You too must never forget this.'

When they caught up with Bharati, she inquired, 'What was the matter?'

Doctor replied with a smile, 'As long as Sashi was penniless, he wasn't worried. But now that his position has improved, he's worried lest he forgets his debt to me. And so he has come running to assure me that whatever he owns is mine.'

'Is that so?' asked Bharati.

Sashi kept quiet and did not reply. Doctor said jokingly, 'Rest assured, I won't forget it. This is something so rare that one can't afford to forget it.'

'When d'you propose to leave?' inquired Sashi. 'Will

266

it be possible to meet you again before you leave?'

'I don't think so,' replied Doctor. 'You are younger to me in age. So before I go, let me bless that you may be happy in life!'

'Can't you stay back till next Saturday?' asked Sashi.

'He's getting married that day,' informed Bharati.

Doctor smiled amusedly but said nothing.

They had reached the river bank. The dinghy had tilted to one side and now lay in the mud left by the receding tide. Doctor straightened it; he helped Bharati board it and then got in himself.

'You must stay back till Saturday,' pleaded Sashi. 'You've accepted all my requests in the past. Please do so once again. Bharati, you too must come.'

Bharati remained silent. 'She may not be able to come,' said Doctor. 'But if I happen to stay back, I promise I'll definitely come after it's dark and give my blessings to both of you. And if I don't come, know that it wasn't possible even for me. But wherever I may be that day, I shall surely pray to God for your happiness.'

He struck the pole against the logs and pushed hard. The boat slid down the mud and into the river.

The tide had still not come in. In the weak current their little boat glided past slowly in the darkness of the shadows of the river bank. They had to wait for a while before they could cross over to the other side, and so Doctor put down the oars and sat quietly.

Bharati was fatigued. She rested her elbow on Doctor's lap and leaned back against him. 'If I had been alone today,' she proclaimed, 'I'd have shed such copious tears as to raise the level of water in the river. Except for you, everyone else seems to be entitled to be happy in life. Sashibabu is doing something grossly improper and yet you've given him your blessings! But there's none in this world who can wish you happiness. I don't care if you're elder to me, I bless you that you too may be happy in future!'

Doctor smiled. 'The blessings of someone younger in

age isn't very effective,' he said. 'It usually has the opposite effect.'

'Rubbish!' said Bharati. 'I may be younger than you in age, but I'm your senior in another respect. You want to break up with Sumitra-didi and to create havoc before you leave, but I won't let you do that.'

After a while she added, 'You say that you don't love Sumitra-didi. That doesn't matter. A man's love is so fickle in any case as to be of no consequence. Apurbababu rejected me, but I still love him. That's all that matters. If a bee is incapable of sucking honey, whom should we blame? But let me tell you this much that if there's one who determines our destinies, He will have to restore Apurba to me one day!'

Bharati kept quiet, expecting a reply from Doctor. But he said nothing.

'You must be laughing at me,' she said.

'Not at all.'

'Definitely. Or else you would've said something.' She peered at Doctor through the darkness.

Doctor lowered his head and looked at her. 'I had nothing to say,' he replied with a smile. 'If your dispenser of justice had to accept this absurd proposition, d'you know what'd have happened to Sumitra? She'd have had to surrender herself body and soul to Brojendra!'

Bharati was not surprised. After tonight's incident, such a suspicion had in fact arisen in her mind. 'But does that mean that Brojendra loves her more than you do?' she asked.

Doctor was unable to give an immediate reply. After a while he said, 'It's difficult to say. If it's simply a passion, then it's without any parallel in this world! It knows no shame, no decorum, no decency — it's a bestial lust! One who hasn't seen it will never understand the intensity of his passion. Had I not been there to protect her, Sumitra would've committed suicide long ago. Even Providence must respect these two hands of mine.' He patted Bharati on her head.

Realising the gravity of the situation, Bharati grew agitated. 'Knowing everything, how can you think of going away leaving her at his mercy? I never imagined you could be so cruel!'

'That's why I wanted to finish him before I left. But Sumitra didn't let me do it.'

'What d'you mean?' cried Bharati in alarm. 'Did you really mean to kill Brojendra?'

Doctor nodded his head. 'Yes. If the police doesn't send him to jail in my absence, I'll have to kill him after I return.'

Bharati, who had been leaning against Doctor, now sat erect. Though she did not say anything, it was clear to Doctor that she had been greatly shocked. But he said nothing and picked up the oars so as to make the crossing.

After a while Bharati said softly, 'Suppose I had been Sumitra, would you've deserted me even then?'

'But you're not Sumitra; you're Bharati,' laughed Doctor. 'So I won't desert you. I'll entrust you with my work instead.'

'Please don't do that,' cried Bharati. 'I don't want to be associated with all these murderous activities. I can't work for your secret society any longer.'

'Then you'll also leave me in the lurch like the others,' said Doctor.

'How could you say such a thing?' said Bharati, terribly upset. 'Whatever you do, I can never leave you. I'll die before I do that. No, I'll continue to work for you until you choose to release me.'

She added after a pause, 'But I know that killing people isn't your mission in life. Rather it's making them learn how to live like men. I'll continue to help you fulfil that mission. That's why I had joined your organisation.'

Doctor stopped rowing for a minute and asked, 'And what is this mission?'

'It was not necessary for Pather Dabi to become a secret organisation. I've seen with my own eyes the

269

miserable condition of the factory workers — their sinful lives, their evil habits, their inhuman condition. If I can reduce even a fraction of their misery, I shall consider my life well-spent. Tell me honestly, isn't this your work?'

Doctor did not reply immediately. He remained absorbed in his thoughts for a long, long while. Then suddenly he stopped rowing and said slowly, 'That's not your work, Bharati. Your duty lies elsewhere. That is Sumitra's job and I've entrusted it to her.'

The tide was rising, though it had still not reached them. In the still waters their small boat began to glide along slowly.

Doctor said calmly, as before, 'It'll be proper to tell you, Bharati, that I didn't establish Pather Dabi for the betterment of a few factory workers. It has a much higher aim. To achieve that aim it may even become necessary to sacrifice these people one day like so many sheep and goats . . . . You'd better not be associated with this work; you won't be able to tolerate it!'

Bharati was startled. 'How can you say that?' she cried. 'What d'you mean by sacrificing men?'

'They are no men,' he replied. 'They are no better than animals.'

Bharati was scared. 'Don't say such things even in jest,' she said. 'I confess I can't always clearly understand what you say. But I understand you much better than you think. Don't try to unnecessarily frighten me.'

'You're mistaken,' Doctor replied. 'I'm not unnecessarily frightening you. I'm serious. You mustn't waste your time trying to improve the lot of the factory workers. Nothing worthwhile can be achieved that way. Their true emancipation can come only through revolution. The aim of my Pather Dabi is to bring about such a revolution. You must remember that revolutions can't be achieved through peaceful means. Violence is essential for its success — this is both its curse as well as its boon! Look at Europe. It has happened in Hungary. It has taken place in Russia, not once but several times. The French Revolution of June 1848 is still a landmark in the history of revolutionary movements. That day the streets of Paris were drenched with the blood of peasants and workers! Even in present-day Japan the miseries of the factory workers is the same, Bharati. No Government has given in peacefully to the right of the people for self-determination.'

Bharati shuddered. 'I don't know all that,' she said. 'But d'you want such terrible things to happen in our country? Do you want to bathe the streets with the blood of those for whom we have been labouring ceaselessly day and night?'

Without a moment's hesitation Doctor replied, 'Certainly, I do. It has always been my dream to bring about human emancipation through such sacrifice. How will we wash away the sins of generations except with their blood? And if in the process I have to shed my own blood, I won't mind even that.'

'I know that,' replied Bharati. 'But have you set up this organisation just to create disturbances in the country? Don't you have any beter aim in life?'

'I haven't been able to find another,' replied Doctor, 'though I've travelled widely, read a lot, and thought deeply. But I've already told you, Bharati, violence is not necessarily evil. Peace! Peace! Peace! I'm fed up with this constant talk of peace! Do you know who are the people who've been preaching this falsehood for so long? They are the same people who've robbed the peace of others, who've usurped what was rightfully theirs. They are the preachers of the cult of peace! They've dinned this into the ears of the deprived, diseased and oppressed populace so that they now shudder at the very thought of unrest. They are convinced it's harmful, it's evil! Tell me, have you ever seen a cow die at the place where it is tethered? It prefers to die than to tear apart the tattered rope lest it should disturb its master's peace! It's the same with

271

these poor people. That's what has been holding up their progress. And if you too think the same way, then how'll it do? No, that won't do! However ancient and sacred may be the concept of peace, it can't be greater than man! We'll have to demolish everything today. No doubt it'll create an upheaval, may even hurt a few, but that's only natural, isn't it?'

'If that's so, then why give up the path of peace and adopt violence instead?'

'That's because the path of peace is obstructed by an ancient, sacred and accepted tradition of good conduct. Only the path of revolution is still open to us.'

'But tell me,' asked Bharati, 'was our endeavour to unite the factory workers with the purpose of calling a peaceful strike also not in their interest? After you go away, should we abandon that experiment as well?'

'No, but that's Sumitra's job, not yours. Your work is different. You see, Bharati, while there's something called a strike, there's no such thing as a peaceful, non-violent strike. No strike can ever be successful if it isn't backed by violence. One has to turn to it as a last resort!'

'Who? The workers?' asked Bharati in surprise.

'Yes,' replied Doctor. 'You may not know, but Sumitra knows the difference between the financial loss of the rich and the starvation of the poor. Day by day the helpless, unemployed worker is forced towards starvation. His wife and children cry of hunger . . . their unending cries drive him insane . . . he sees no other way of stopping their cries than by snatching the food of others. The rich wait for exactly such an opportunity. He has money, power and arms — in fact he has the power of the state behind him. He uses this power to crush the unarmed, famished strikers. The streets fill with blood, their blood, thanks to your ancient and sacred peace!'

'Then?' asked Bharati breathlessly.

'Then? And so once again the oppressed, vanquished, famished workers queue before their murderers with

272

begging bowls.'

'And after that?'

'Afterwards the workers again organise a strike in the hope of getting redressal. And so the cycle goes on.'

Bharati was momentarily filled with despondence. 'Then what do we gain from organising such strikes?' she asked slowly.

Doctor's eyes glowed in the darkness. 'Gain? You want to know what's the gain?' he asked. 'This'll bring about the revolution! That's the greatest gain! The strike ends in an apparent defeat for the impoverished, illiterate, famished workers, but this defeat leads to a sense of anger and hatred that erupts one day! This brings about the revolution! That's the gain! Nowhere in the world are revolutions brought about just for their own sake. It needs some long-standing grievance to sustain it. One is a fool if one doesn't realise this and instigates the workers to go on strike simply for an increase in their wages. That way he harms both the workers as well as the country.'

Suddenly Bharati said, 'We've come a long way downstream.'

Doctor laughed. 'I'm aware of that,' he said. 'I haven't forgotten our destination.'

'I now see why you want to get rid of me,' said Bharati. 'I'm weak, just like him. I mean nothing to you. Even now it's Sumitra-didi who matters to you. But I'll never accept that all our efforts were futile, that there's no other way of achieving emancipation except through violence. I can never believe that to help someone you've to hurt another, not even if you say it!'

'I know that.'

'But how can I leave your organisation? What shall I do then? And, if you don't come back . . . how'll I live then?'

'I realise that as well.'

'You know everything. Then what's the solution?'

No one spoke for a while. Then Bharati said quietly,

273

'I could never understand what you meant by a revolution, nor why was it so necessary. Still, whenever I hear you speak of it, my heart seems to bleed. You must surely have witnessed instances of terrible suffering and human misery. What else could've made you so uncompromising and determined? But can't you take me along with you when you go?'

Doctor laughed. 'Have you gone crazy?'

'Maybe I have.' After a while she added, 'It seems I'm a liability for you. That's why you're gradually easing me out from your group. But is there nothing I can do? Am I so very useless?'

'There's a lot you can do,' said Doctor. 'But you'll have to create the opportunities yourself.'

'I can't do that,' coaxed Bharati. 'You do it for me.'

Doctor remained silent for a while. His smiling face suddenly seemed to have turned grave, though Bharati could not see it in the darkness.

'There are so many institutions, big or small, that are doing good work in the country, like nursing the sick, performing acts of piety in the society, providing medical assistance to the ailing, rescuing those affected by floods and consoling them. They'll show you the path. But I'm a revolutionary. I've no love, no affection, no compassion; good and bad are both meaningless to me. Those acts of piety appear to me to be a child's play. The independence of India is my sole aim in life, its achievement my only dream; apart from this nothing holds any meaning for me! Don't try to detract me from my chosen path, Bharati.'

Bharati had continued to look at him steadfastly through the darkness. She now heaved a deep sigh and fell silent.

274

CHAPTER 26

It was Saturday, the day of Sashi and Nabatara's marriage. Sashi had repeatedly requested Doctor to come once that night, secretly, under cover of darkness, along with Bharati, and bless him and his bride.

The thin moon had disappeared behind the trees. Bharati, wrapped from head to foot in a black shawl, came and stood silently on the steps of the solitary ghat. Doctor was waiting for her in his boat. Bharati boarded it and said, 'While coming here I was thinking of so many things. I know that you won't go away without telling me, and yet I just can't seem to shake off the fear. It was only a few days back that I'd seen you, and yet it seems like eternity. I tell you, I shall certainly go to China with you.'

Doctor replied with a smile, 'Let me also tell you that you must never do such a thing.'

He let the boat float along with the current of the river. 'This stretch is easy,' he said. 'But once we are in midstream and have to row against the current, it'll take longer.'

'Does it matter?' responded Bharati. 'As if it's some auspicious function you're going to attend that it can't brook delay? Honestly speaking, I had no desire to come. It's only because of you that I agreed to come along. What a nasty affair!'

Doctor remained silent for a while and then said, 'Sashi's marriage with Nabatara might offend the susceptibilities of some people, might even be violation of the law. But Sashi is not responsible for it. Those who've framed the laws are responsible. You know Bharati, my only regret is why couldn't Sashi love someone else?'

Bharati laughed. 'Even if he had,' she said, 'who would love him? I refuse to believe that any woman in her senses can love him. What d'you feel?'

275

'I agree it's difficult to love Sashi,' smiled Doctor. 'Which is why I postponed my departure, so that I could come and bless him. If wishes have any value, I hope it does him some good.'

Bharati noticed the change in Doctor's tone. After keeping quiet for a while, she said, 'You are rather fond of Sashibabu, aren't you?'

'Yes.'

'Why?'

'Can I say why I'm so fond of you? Maybe it's without any reason.'

'Does that mean you find no difference between Sashibabu and me?' said Bharati light-heartedly. 'At least I now know my real worth.' She laughed. 'Okay, let me also go and bless him . . . oh, no, I'm sorry . . . bow before him!'

Doctor smiled. 'Okay, let's go.'

It was not safe to wait for the tide to recede. So, despite difficulty, Doctor had to continue rowing against the current. A Japanese ship was anchored in the mouth of the river. They kept quiet till they had crossed it. Then Bharati spoke. 'It struck me many times during the past few days,' she said, 'that you're bottomless like the sea. Affection or love — nothing seems to any meaning for you.'

'But the sea has a bottom,' replied Doctor. 'So the metaphor you chose is inappropriate.'

'I've told you on numerous times that except for you I've none else in this world whom I can call my own. Who'll shelter me when you're gone? But my words mean nothing to you. How can they when you're so heartless? I know for certain that you'll forget me as soon as you leave.'

'No, I won't,' replied Doctor.

'How'll I live?' cried Bharati.

'Why? With your husband, children, your house, material possessions, like all other women!'

'I never concealed from you that I loved Apurba with all my heart,' said Bharati reproachfully. 'It's equally

276

true that I'd have considered myself blessed if I could've had him. There's nothing that you don't know. But does that mean that you should insult me this way?'

'Insult you?' asked Doctor, surprised. 'But I didn't mean to insult you!'

'Of course you have.' Bharati's voice was choked with tears. 'You know the problems. You know that he'll never agree to accept me. And yet you say all these things?'

'That's the problem with you women,' smiled Doctor. 'You say all sorts of things to others, but if someone were to apply them in your case, you're furious. The other day you made certain observations about Sumitra. Now when I repeat them to you, you're ready to burst into tears!'

Bharati wiped her tears and said, 'You must never say such a thing to me again.'

'Okay, I won't say,' replied Doctor. 'But if I come back alive, I bet you'll bow down before me and confess that you were mistaken. You'll say, "I was wrong; please forgive me. You must have known how to read the future, or else how could you predict my good fortune?" '

Bharati said nothing. After keeping quiet for a while, Doctor spoke again. This time his voice sounded strangely mellow. 'Bharati,' he said, 'when you spoke about Sumitra the other night, I was unable to give a suitable reply. I've no experience of such affairs; yet your understanding of Sumitra's predicament shook me. During my travels round the world I've learnt many things, but somehow I have always been out of my depths when it came to matters of the heart. Perhaps the word "impossible" doesn't exist in the dictionary of lovers.'

Bharati appeared to be uninterested in this talk. She said dispiritedly, 'I hope what you say comes true. Let the word "impossible" disappear from your lexicon. Let Sumitra-didi be happy one day.'

277

After a pause she added, 'As for me, I don't desire it any longer. It's true that I still love Apurbababu very much. It doesn't matter whether he's good or bad; I can never forget him. But at the same time I can't say that my life will be meaningless if I can't marry him and be his wife. It's not out of frustration or sorrow that I'm saying all this. Honestly, do guide me and give me your blessings. I too want to devote my life to the service of others just like you. I entreat you, do associate me in your work.'

Doctor gave no reply to her earnest request and continued to row the boat in silence. Bharati could not see his face in the darkness but his silence filled her with hope. When she spoke her voice was warm and hopeful. 'Then will you take me with you?' she asked. 'You're my only hope. Everything else seems shrouded in darkness.'

Doctor shook his head slowly. 'That's impossible,' he said. 'You know, Bharati, you remind me of Joan. Like you, her life too turned to ashes. My sole aim in life is to achieve the independence of India, but I've never made the mistake of thinking that there can be nothing greater in life. Independence is not an end in itself. Religion, peace, literature, happiness, are all greater than that. It's for their fullest development that freedom is essential; else of what use is it? Your heart, which is full of love, affection, compassion and sweetness, is far more valuable than freedom. It's far greater than anything I've ever strived for. I can't sacrifice it for the sake of independence!'

Bharati was filled with joy. This was an entirely different facet of Sabyasachi's personality that was now revealed to her. She said reverently, 'I feel that there's nothing that you don't know. But if this is so, why should you be engaged in conspiracy? Why go round setting up secret societies in different countries? Certainly no good can come out of that.'

'That's right,' said Doctor. 'But we've left the greatest good of man in the hands of God. We try to achieve only what's possible for ordinary mortals like us. Freedom of speech and freedom of movement — these are the only two things we seek for our people. Nothing more than that at present!'

'That's what everyone wants,' said Bharati. 'But does that call for intrigue and murder?'

As soon as she uttered these words, she felt ashamed. Because the accusation was not only harsh, but also untrue. 'Forgive me,' she said with repentance. 'I said that out of anger. I can't reconcile myself to the thought that you'll go away leaving me behind.'

'I know that,' smiled Doctor.

Both remained silent for a long while.

Around this time the Swadeshi movement was at its peak in India. The leaders of this movement were going around delivering inflammatory speeches during their spare hours, exhorting the people to fight for the freedom of their country without violating the provisions of the law. The summation of these speeches used to appear in the daily newspapers. Bharati used to read these reports occasionally and was full of admiration for these leaders. On the previous night she had read one such inspiring report in the newspaper. This had made quite an impact on her mind and consequently left her agitated throughout the day.

Recalling this, she now said, 'I know that there's no place for you in the entire British empire, but the whole world is not under their domination. Why don't you go to a place not under their control and carry on your agitation openly for achieving your goal?'

After waiting for a few moments for a reply, she added, 'Although I can't see your face in the darkness, I've no doubt you're laughing at me. But you and your party aren't the only people engaged in the freedom struggle. Those who are veterans in the political field . . . . By the way, did you read yesterday's Bengali newspaper?'

Before she could finish, Doctor burst out laughing.

279

'Please, for heaven's sake, Bharati, don't show disrespect to those venerable persons by comparing them with us.'

'It's not I, but you who's making fun of them.'

Doctor shook his head violently. 'Not in the least. I've the greatest respect for them. Besides, no one enjoys their speeches more than I do.'

Bharati was unconvinced. 'Your methods may be different,' she said, 'but certainly your objectives are the same.'

Doctor kept quiet for a while and then said, 'It's true I was laughing so long, but now I shall be angry. It's well known that our methods are different, but didn't you realise all this time that our objectives were even more dissimilar? There are many countries in this world which are independent. Freedom is the greatest glory of mankind. But according to the laws framed by the British, it is seditious for Indians to ask for independence, it is seditious even to wish for it, leave aside striving to achieve it. I'm guilty of that sedition. British law presupposes that India will forever remain under their domination. So your veteran leaders don't claim anything that may be construed as a transgression of the law. Supposing like the Manchu rulers of China, the British had passed a law requiring every Indian to sport a two-and-a-half-foot-long pigtail, our veteran leaders would never have protested against this irrational legislation. Instead they would've started an agitation proclaiming that a grave injustice had been committed and that the length of the pigtail should be reduced to two and a quarter feet only.' Amused at his own joke, Doctor burst into a loud guffaw, disturbing the stillness of the placid river.

When Doctor's laughter subsided, Bharati said, 'Whatever you may say, I can't agree with you that these leaders don't deserve our respect. I'm not referring to everyone, but it's difficult to agree that all the efforts of those who're truly experienced and who genuinely love their country are futile, useless. We

280

shouldn't scoff at someone merely because his political views and methods are different from ours.'

Doctor could make out from Bharati's voice that she was upset. So he kept quiet. A steam launch overtook them with a lot of noise and rocked their small boat violently as it did so.

'I don't want to hurt your feelings, Bharati,' Doctor said calmly, 'nor do I want to make fun of your revered leaders. My regard for their political wisdom is no less than yours. But the fact remains that when the owner of a cow tethers it with a short rope, he has only one object in his mind. I know this much. If the cow tries to stretch its neck and lolls out its tongue in an effort to reach something lying at a distance, there's nothing unnatural or illegal in it. The law doesn't debar it either, but those who watch the cow's desperate attempts often find it difficult to check their laughter.'

Bharati laughed. 'You're indeed naughty,' she said.

She checked herself immediately and added, 'But I'm surprised how someone whose own life is on tenter-hooks can indulge in jokes about others.'

'The reason is very simple,' said Doctor in a calm voice. 'The matter was decided once for all the day I joined this revolutionary movement. I've nothing to worry about, nor anything to complain of. I know this much that if ever the police are able to catch me and don't kill me, they must either be incompetent or insane or lacking even the rope to hang me with.'

'That's exactly the reason why I want to accompany you,' replied Bharati. 'There's none who can kill you as long as I'm with you. I'll never allow it.' Her voice grew hoarse.

Doctor noticed it. He sighed silently and said, 'The tide is coming in. It shouldn't take us long to reach the other side now.'

'Dammit. I'm fed up with everything!'

After a minute or so, Bharati asked, 'Do you really believe you'll be able to drive away the British by

281

force?'

'Yes, I believe it wholeheartedly,' Doctor replied without a moment's hesitation. 'If I didn't, I couldn't have continued with my mission.'

'That's the reason why you're slowly easing me out of your group, isn't it?' asked Bharati.

Doctor smiled. 'That's not entirely true,' he said softly. 'But at the same time, it's a fact that one derives strength only from one's convictions. Unless you've faith in your work, your doubts and hesitations will only serve to retard it. There are other types of work — beneficent and peaceful — in which you have faith. I'd suggest you do that instead.'

Bharati realised that it was out of his great affection for her that Doctor was trying to keep her away from his dangerous revolutionary activities. Her eyes filled with tears. Wiping them in the darkness, she said, 'Don't be angry with me, but you know how powerful the British are. They've got arms and equipment, they have a huge army. Compared to them, you're nothing! You're as insignificant as a pug mark when compared to the ocean. What can be your justification in locking horns with such a powerful adversary? Die if you must, but I tell you it's sheer madness! You'll ask, then is there no hope for the motherland? Should one do nothing for fear of dying? I don't say that. I've learnt that there can be nothing greater in life than to die for her sake. But has any country ever been free by committing suicide? However, don't misunderstand me. I'm not advocating this simply to avoid death.'

Doctor sighed, 'Undoubtedly.'

'What d'you mean by that?'

'I see I was wrong about you,' said Doctor. He added after a while, 'You see, Bharati, revolution doesn't mean just war and bloodshed. It means a rapid and radical transformation. I know that they have a well-equipped huge army. But my objective is not to wage a war against them. Who knows, those who are our enemies today may become our allies tomorrow.

282

Nilakant died trying to win them over. Poor Nilakant! Who remembers him today?'

Even in the darkness Bharati could make out the momentary excitement that the memory of an unknown youth who had died in the cause of his motherland in some foreign country, far away from his native shores, had brought about in the mind of this man who was normally composed and unruffled.

Suddenly he sat erect and said, 'What was it you said? Pug mark! Maybe you're right. But what is the size of the tiny spark that in course of time becomes a conflagration, consuming everything that stands in its way? When a city burns, it feeds itself. This is an universal law which no power can refute.'

'Your words terrify me,' said Bharati. 'You talk of setting the country ablaze, but d'you realise it'll be your own countrymen who'll perish in the holocaust. Don't you feel any pity for them?'

'No,' replied Doctor without any hesitation. 'Did you think I didn't mean it when I talked about their penance? How else shall we expiate for the sins committed by our forefathers over the ages? Justice is far more important than compassion, Bharati.'

Bharati felt miserable. 'You're merely repeating your old arguments,' she said. 'I can't conceive how cruel you can become when it comes to the question of India's independence. You can't think of anything other than bloodshed. But if bloodshed begets only bloodshed, where will it all end? Is human civilization incapable of providing any alternative to bloodshed? Nations may disappear but humanity, which is greater than everything, will persist. Can't men live in harmony with each other without bloodshed?'

'A great English poet once said, "The East is East and the West is West, and never the twain shall meet." '

'Hang him!' said Bharati in exasperation. 'I don't care what he says. But you're a knowledgeable person. And so I ask you, as I've asked you many times in the past,

283

tell me — aren't the British, the Europeans, also human beings? Then why can't we live in harmony and friendship with them? You know that I'm a Christian. I'm indebted to the British in many ways. I've seen with my own eyes their numerous good qualities. It pains me to think of them as evil. Please don't misunderstand me. I'm also a Bengali, just like you. I love my motherland and my people with all my heart. Who knows whether I'll be able to meet you again. Before you go, you must answer this question of mine. You must advise me what I should do to rely on it as a guiding principle throughout my life.' Her voice broke down completely towards the end.

Doctor did not reply immediately and continued to row the boat in silence. Bharati felt that possibly he did not want to reply. She dipped her hand into the river, scooped up some water and proceeded to wash her eyes and face. Wiping it carefully, she was about to ask him another question when Doctor spoke. His voice was soft and mellow. There seemed to be no trace of anger or excitement in it — it was almost as if he were discussing some other topic, so easy was his manner. Bharati remembered their first encounter. She had taken him to be a timid and stupid school teacher. She remembered having controlled her laughter with difficulty at his faulty English and funny pronunciation. Later she had been angry with him for having fooled her. He now spoke in the same dispassionate and calm manner.

'There's a type of snake that feeds on others. Have you ever seen it?' he asked her.

'No, but I've read about them.'

'They can be seen in the zoo. When you visit Calcutta, ask Apurba to take you to the zoo and show them to you.'

'Now don't start that again, I warn you,' she said.

'No, seriously. They find it inconvenient to live amicably, but can do so most comfortably when one is devoured by the other. If you don't believe me, ask the zoo keeper.'

Bharati remained silent.

Doctor said, 'You profess their religion. You're indebted to them for various acts of kindness. You've seen their numerous good qualities. But have you seen their greed, their voracious appetite that seeks to devour everything? They now lord over this land of ours, but d'you remember when they first came to our country? Today they've enormous wealth. They own innumerable warships, factories, mansions, arms and ammunition with which to kill people. Even after meeting all their needs they are able to lend as much as three thousand crore rupees within a period of seventy years starting from 1810. Have you ever tried to know the source of this wealth? You claim to be a Bengali. The soil of Bengal, its air, its water, its people, are all dearer to you than your own self! Every year at least a million Bengalis die of malaria. Tell me, do you know how much a warship costs? With that amount of money one could wipe the tears from the eyes of a million mothers every year! Have you ever thought over these things? Have you tried to see the real picture of your motherland? We've lost our art and craft, our trade and commerce, our religion, our age-old wisdom. The rivers have dried up and turned into deserts. The farmer doesn't get two square meals a day. Our craftsmen work as labourers for the foreigners. Today we don't have water to drink or enough food to eat. The cattle — which was the greatest wealth a householder could have — are no more. Bharati, have you ever seen little children dying for want of milk?'

Bharati felt like crying out to him to stop, but only an indistinct sound escaped her lips.

When Sabyasachi resumed from where he had broken off, the calm and dispassionate tone was missing. He said, 'You're a Christian. I remember one day, out of curiosity, you had wanted to know about the true nature of European civilization. That day I didn't

285

say anything, lest I should hurt you. But I'll explain it to you today. I don't know what's written in the books. I'm told all the references are favourable. But as a result of my long association with them, I know the reality is vastly different. Unscrupulous, naked selfishness and brute power form the bedrock of this civilization. In the name of civilization, they have exploited the weak and the powerless in every country. Look at the map of the world. No weak nation has been able to withstand the onslaught of their invasions, their insatiable hunger for greater acquisitions. Do you know the reason why the natives have been denied their rights, denied their due share of the wealth of the country? Their only fault was that they were weak, they lacked the ability to resist the foreigners. And yet they assert that they never act unjustly! They proclaim that it's for the ultimate good of the country that they've conquered it. They spread the myth of the white man's burden. These untruths they preach through their writings, their speeches, their missionaries, and their textbooks. This is their policy, the politics of the Christian civilization!'

Bharati had received her education from Christian missionaries. She had herself seen the nobleness of many of them. So Doctor's attack on her religion pained her greatly. She said, 'For some reason you appear to be disturbed today. I know the Christian missionaries much better than you do. You're prejudiced against them. Do you really mean to say that European civilization has done India no good? *Sati*, human sacrifice . . . .'

Doctor interjected, 'Inhuman practices like *Charak*, the various tortures that mendicants and sanyasis inflicted upon themselves like walking on swords, armed robbery, crimes by highwaymen or thugs, atrocities committed by the Bargis or Marhatta horsemen, human sacrifices by tribesmen like Khasis and Garos — that's all I can think of at the present.'

Bharati kept quiet.

Doctor continued, 'No, wait a minute. There are two other things. During the Muslim rule, women were not safe — the Nawabs used to slit open the bellies of pregnant women to see whether it carried a male or female child. Oh, God! Such trivialities are given prominence in the history books written by foreign authors with the sole purpose of poisoning the minds of the people against their forbears. I remember having read, when I was a schoolboy, that the Prime Minister of England had developed insomnia and lack of appetite from pondering over ways to improve the condition of the Indians. Students are forced to mug up such untruths and the teachers are compelled to force the students to do so for the sake of their own livelihood. This is the politics of civilized countries. It's useless to blame Apurba!'

Bharati felt hurt at this jibe against Apurba. She said, 'What you say may be partially true. Somewhere some overzealous government officials might have behaved in this manner. But falsehood cannot be the creed of such a vast empire. An empire dependent on untruth would not have lasted even for a single day. You may say, compared to eternity, what is the life of an empire? Such empires existed in the past as well — were they ever-lasting? If what you say is correct, the British empire too will die one day. But no matter how much you denounce this well-organised, disciplined government, can we say that we've derived no benefits from the unity and peace it has given us? We lost our independence long ago. Rulers have changed, but has there been any change in our lot? Don't think me otherwise just because I'm a Christian, but if your idea of patriotism is simply to find fault with the foreign rulers and hold them responsible for all our ills, I'm not prepared to accept this thesis even from you. With so much malice in your heart you may be able to do some harm to the British, but you definitely won't be able to do any good to your people!'

Her agitated and strident voice ruffled the silence of

287

the river and startled Sabyasachi. This image of
Bharati was unknown to him, her reaction totally unexpected. He realised that she found it difficult to
tolerate his attacks on the Christian religion and
civilization under the influence of which she had been
brought up from her childhood. And yet her fearless
and unrestrained protestations, however hostile and
intolerant they may have been, earned her greater
regard in his eyes.

Seeing that Doctor was saying nothing, Bharati said,
'Why don't you retort? But let me tell you this much,
that with all that hatred in your heart, you won't be
able to do any good to your country, whatever else
you may succeed in doing!'

Doctor replied, 'I've told you many times that those
who want to work for the good of the country raise
subscriptions and build orphanages, monasteries and
hostels. They try to help the poor and perform many
such beneficent tasks. They are good men and I revere
them. But my aim is not to do good to the country;
it is to liberate the country.'

He added after a little pause, 'The fire raging in my
heart can only be extinguished by two things — when
this body of mine is reduced to ashes, or when I hear
that the religion, the civilization and the politics of the
Europeans have disappeared from this country!'

Bharati remained silent.

Doctor continued, 'When the Europeans first came to
the east with their ships full of merchandise and their
hearts full of malice and hypocrisy, the only country
which could understand their real intentions was
Japan. That's why Japan is so prosperous and can talk
to them on equal terms. But India could not understand their real intentions, nor could China.'

'At that time the Spanish empire was at its peak. A
Japanese once asked a Spanish sailor, "How did you
acquire such a vast empire?" The Spaniard replied,
"Very simple. We first located a weak country. Thereafter we went there with our merchandise. We begged

the local ruler and obtained a small plot of land. We then brought in the missionaries. Whether they succeeded in converting the locals to Christianity may be disputable, but they did succeed in enraging the local populace by their constant attacks on their religion. The result being that a few missionaries would get butchered in the bargain. This would give us the excuse we wanted to bring in our army, bring in arms and ammunition. We'd soon prove that our war-machine was far superior to that of the barbarians." '

'When the Japanese heard this story, they said, "You may depart. We'll have no business dealing with you." They then passed a law that as long as the sun shone and the moon shed its light, no Christian be allowed to set foot in their country. If they did, they'd be executed.'

This sharp criticism of her religion and its preachers made Bharati unhappy. 'I've heard this story from you before,' she said. 'But how praiseworthy are the Japanese whom you seem to adore?'

'Adore the Japanese? Me? You're mistaken. I hate them! Despite their repeated assurances to the Koreans, when they imprisoned the Korean monarch and annexed the country in 1910, I was then at Shanghai. It's impossible for me to forget the atrocities committed by them in Korea. But assurances of protection had been given not only by Japan, but also by England. But England did not protest against the Japanese action. They simply said, "We're bound by the terms of the Anglo-Japanese treaty." The American President said in clear terms, "Do assurances matter? A weak and worthless nation which can't defend itself deserves to be invaded! And you expect us to come to its aid? Impossible! Sheer madness!" '

Sabyasachi added after a brief silence, 'I too say it's impossible, unreasonable, sheer madness! The concept of justice which the civilized nations of Europe believe in, cannot conceive why a powerful country should not seize what rightfully belongs to a weaker nation.'

Bharati kept quiet.

Doctor continued, 'Towards the later part of the eighteenth century, the British ambassador, Lord Mc-Artney, arrived in the Chinese court to secure some concessions for trade in China. The Manchu ruler, Sun Lung, was the Emperor of China at that time. He was very kind-hearted. He was pleased with the ambassador for his humility and said, "In this heavenly kingdom of ours there's nothing that we lack. But since you've come from so far facing so much hardship, I'll not disappoint you. You may conduct your trade in Canton and may you prosper!" The Emperor's blessings were not in vain. They did prosper. Fifty years later, England declared war on China.'

'But why?' asked Bharati in surprise.

'Well, the Chinese were at fault. They were impertinent enough to say that the British should stop importing opium into China as that was ruining their country.'

'What happened after that?'

'The subsequent history is rather brief. In two years' time the Chinese agreed to again import opium. They gave the British the right to trade in five more ports on payment of customs duty at a meagre five per cent of the value of all merchandise sold, and finally ceded the port of Hongkong to England in 1842. Thus ended the Anglo-Chinese conflict. The Chinese were rightly served. Any fool who refuses to take opium that's offered to them so cheap, deserves no better treatment.'

'That's your interpretation,' said Bharati.

'Maybe,' replied Doctor. 'But it's interesting all the same. Encouraged by the British example, the French said, "We may not have any opium to sell, but we still have our war machine. Hence, why not have a war?" And so they had a war. The French seized the province of Anam from the Chinese. In addition, they extracted other advantages as well — reparations, greater trade concessions, port facilities, et cetera. But let's not bother ourselves with these details.'

'But it takes two to start a fight. Were the Chinese absolutely blameless?'

'Maybe not. But the beauty is that the European's sense of outrage always results in aggression against others, never against themselves.'

'Then?'

'I'm coming to that. The Germans now felt they had a grouse against the Chinese for having denied them their share of the cake. And so they let loose on Chinese soil a thousand Christian missionaries. In 1897, when these missionaries were busy singing the glory of your saviour, Jesus Christ, and in spreading his message of peace and justice, some Chinese peasants became infuriated and chopped off the heads of a couple of pious preachers. It was certainly the fault of the Chinese! So they lost their Shantang province to the Germans.'

'Then came the Boxer rebellion. All the European powers joined hands to teach the Chinese such a lesson that it remains unparalleled in its severity. Jesus Christ alone knows for how long the Chinese will pay the reparations. In the meantime the English lion, the Russian bear, and the Japanese sun-god — no, I must stop! My throat is absolutely parched! Excepting India, there's none else in the world who've suffered as greatly as the Chinese. May the Emperor Sun Lung's soul rest in peace, his blessings did bear fruit!'

Bharati sighed deeply and kept quiet.

'Bharati?'

'Yes?'

'Why're you so quiet?'

'I was thinking about your story. Is this the reason why you've chosen China to carry on your activities? It will not be difficult to excite those who've suffered such oppression. But have you considered one thing? These poor, illiterate peasants have their cup of misery already full. If you introduce them to warfare and bloodshed, there'll be no end to their anguish.'

291

'Don't worry too much about the poor peasants. In no country have they ever played a role in fighting for independence. It's often quite the reverse. I don't have time to waste in trying to incite them. My work is with the educated middle class gentry. If you ever decide to join me, don't forget this. It's futile to expect that the peace-loving, unresistant, innocent peasants will be prepared to lay down their lives for the sake of an idea, a dream. They don't want independence; they want peace. Peace that is cherished by the weak and the incapable, is far more preferable to them.'

'I too want such a peace,' said Bharati agitatedly. 'Engage me in some work that brings such peace. The atmosphere of intrigue that exists in your secret organisation chokes me!'

Sabyasachi laughed. 'All right.'

'Don't you have anything more to say that a mere "All right?"' asked Bharati, as excitedly as before.

'But we've reached our destination. Be careful that you don't hurt yourself.' Saying this Doctor deftly manoeuvred the dinghy into a crevice. He jumped out and hurried to help Bharati disembark. 'It's dry over here. You can place your foot on this log.'

Bharati was at first apprehensive of alighting at an unknown place in the darkness. But having stepped down, she heaved a sigh and said, 'Honestly, there's nothing more reassuring than to leave oneself completely in your hands.'

But there was no response from Doctor. After advancing a short distance in the darkness, Doctor said in a surprised voice, 'I wonder what the matter is. Is this the house where a marriage is supposed to be performed? There's no light, no commotion, not even the sound of the violin! Or have they all gone away somewhere?'

After walking a few more steps, they could spot the decorated Chinese lantern dangling at the head of the stairs. Reassured at this sight, Bharati exclaimed, 'There's their Chinese lantern! The economy which

Sashi and Nabatara have practised is quite remarkable.'
Saying this, she laughed.

They climbed upstairs. Through the open door they
could see Sashi engrossed in the newspaper. Bharati
called out cheerfully, 'See, we've arrived! Where's the
party? Where's Nabatara? Nabatara! Nabatara!'

Sashi looked up. 'Do come in,' he said. 'Nabatara is
not here.'

'A house without the housewife? How's this, poet?'
smiled Doctor. 'Call her. Tell her to come and receive
us. Or else we've to remain standing here. We may
even choose to go away.'

'Nabatara is not here,' replied Sashi sorrowfully.
'They've gone.'

His unhappy face made Bharati apprehensive. 'Gone
somewhere? Today? What's the sense!'

'After their marriage they've gone to Rangoon,'
replied Sashi. 'You see, Nabatara got married today,
in the afternoon. No, no, not to me. To Ahmed —
that time-keeper in Mr Coot's mill. You must've seen
him . . . fair-complexioned fellow . . . very handsome.
Everything had been settled beforehand; only I was
not told.'

Doctor and Bharati both continued to gaze at Sashi
blankly. 'What are you saying, Sashi?' exclaimed Doctor.

Sashi got up and fetched a cotton bag from inside
the room. Placing it at Doctor's feet, he said, 'I got
the money. I had promised to pay Nabatara five
thousand; I've paid her. A balance of four and a half
thousand remains. I've kept fifty rupees for myself,
but . . . .'

'Are you giving the rest to me?' asked Doctor.

'Yes,' replied Sashi. 'What'll I do with money? Take
it. It may be of some use to you.'

Bharati asked, 'When did you give the money to
Nabatara?'

'Yesterday. As soon as I got it.'

'She took it?'

293

Sashi nodded his head. 'Yes. Ahmed gets only thirty rupees a month. They'll buy a house with that amount.'

'No doubt they will!' Doctor turned round and saw that Bharati had covered her eyes with her *sari* and had moved to one corner of the verandah.

'Our President wanted you to meet her once,' said Sashi. 'She's leaving for Surabaya.'

Doctor did not express any surprise. 'When's she going?' he asked.

'Shortly. Some people have come to take her there.'

His words reached Bharati's ears. She came back and asked, 'Is Sumitra-didi really going away?'

'Yes. Her mother's uncle was an extremely wealthy man. He had died recently. She is the only heir. Therefore she has to go.'

'If that's the case, then she must go,' said Doctor.

Sashi looked at Bharati and said, 'Will you stay for dinner? There's lots of food.'

Before Bharati could say anything to the contrary, Doctor said enthusiastically, 'Of course we'll stay. Come, let me see what you've prepared.' Saying this, he almost dragged Sashi into the room.

'There's another piece of news,' whispered Sashi to Doctor. 'Apurbababu has returned.'

Doctor was taken aback. 'Who told you that?' he asked.

'I came across him in the bank yesterday. It seems his mother is seriously ill.'

CHAPTER 27

Sashi had not exaggerated. On entering the room they found that half of it was stacked with foodstuff. Cauldrons of different sizes, plates, paper containers, earthen vessels — all were overflowing with food. Hoteliers had prepared these according to their own taste and choice, had ferried them across the river and dumped them in this room. The arrangements were all flawless, except for one vital thing — there were no guests for the feast!

Doctor cast one glance at the spread before him and exclaimed, 'Excellent! Wonderful! Bharati, see what a methodical man Sashibabu is. He has made arrangements to suit everyone's tastes! Excellent!'

Bharati turned her face aside and Sashi made an unsuccessful attempt to smile. Despite the lack of response from the others, Doctor burst into uproarious laughter. 'Ha! Ha! Ha!'

Bharati could tolerate no longer. She turned around with tears in her eyes and said angrily to Doctor, 'What's all this? Don't you have a trace of kindness in your heart?'

'Bah! Shouldn't I bless one who has arranged such a sumptuous feast for us? Ha! Ha!'

Bharati left the place in exasperation. After a few minutes, Sashi went in search of her and persuaded her to return. She served the meat, pilau, fruits and sweets in different plates, laid it out in front of Doctor and said in mock anger, 'Now eat, you glutton! That'll at least stop your laughter and let the neighbours sleep in peace.'

Doctor sighed. 'Excellent food! It's ages since I tasted such preparations.'

The words seemed to pierce Bharati's heart. She remembered the dry rice and roasted fish which Doctor had the other night.

Doctor addressed her, 'Won't you give the poet something to eat as well?'

'Yes. In a minute.' She placed a plate in front of Sashi. Then, squatting in front of Doctor, she said, 'You'll have to finish everything. You can't waste even a morsel.'

'I won't,' replied Doctor. 'But what about you? Won't you eat something?'

'Me? Can any woman have the heart to eat these things? Tell me?'

'Well . . . but all the dishes taste wonderful. Like nectar!'

'I can cook tastier things for you every day,' replied Bharati.

Doctor beat his forehead and said, 'Sheer ill-luck! The person for whom you should actually be cooking refuses to eat food prepared by you. And one who will eat — you'll be famous in no time if you continue to feed him! Strange are the ways of God! What d'you say, poet? Am I not correct? Ha! Ha!'

This time Bharati could not help but laughing. But she checked herself immediately and said, 'You're extremely naughty. But tell me, after eating your fill, do you plan to take the bag of money and depart?'

'Most certainly,' replied Doctor. 'Half the amount has gone towards Nabatara's building fund. Do you suggest I leave the other half for Ahmed Sahib to buy a carriage? Not that it'd be such a bad idea. That'd complete the drama. What d'you say, Sashi? Ha! Ha!'

'I've seen you cutting jokes before,' said Bharati, 'but I've never seen you laughing like a crazy person before.'

Doctor started to say something, but looking at Bharati's face, he stopped.

Bharati said, 'Everyone doesn't take love as lightly like you, so as to be able to laugh it off as you do. Other than being subjugated, can't there be any other sorrow in a man's life? Look at Sashibabu. See how he has changed in just half a day. The day Apurbababu left me and went away, possibly that day too you must've laughed at me like this.'

'No, no, that was . . . .'

'No, don't try to evade the issue. I know you're fond of Sashibabu. It's also true that Nabatara used to cause him a lot of pain. You're happy that he'll be spared of that in future. But is one's future everything? That the agony he has suffered today far exceeds everything that he may face in future is of no consequence to you. You wouldn't even be able to comprehend it, because you've never loved anyone yourself.'

Sashi felt embarrassed. He tried to say that it was all his fault, because he lacked common sense, but Bharati interrupted him.

'Why should you feel ashamed?' she said. 'Are you the only person in this world to have made this mistake? Didn't I make a mistake that was hundred times worse than yours? And what about another who committed a mistake that was far greater than both of ours and is today going away for ever? Doesn't Doctor know her? You say that Nabatara deceived you? Let her. Yet half the literature of the world has become immortal recounting the tales of persons like us.'

Doctor gazed at her with wonder in his eyes, but Bharati paid no heed to him. She continued. 'Sashibabu, you say that you lacked common sense. But what about me? I did not lack it. What about Sumitra-didi? She's so intelligent. Yet what use was her intelligence? She had to concede defeat before you,' she said to Doctor. 'She, who had always been unconquerable, who had never tasted defeat, was finally shattered by your heart of stone.'

Doctor did not give any reply to her accusations and merely smiled.

Bharati turned to the artist. 'Sashibabu, I've said many unpleasant things about you. Please forgive me for that.'

Sashi could not understand what she meant, but nevertheless felt embarrassed.

297

Bharati resumed after a pause, 'I once told Doctor that no woman could possibly love you. I didn't know you well then. Today it seems to me that one who gave her heart to Apurbababu would've been redeemed if she could've received your love instead. Except for Doctor, no one ever realised your real worth.'

Doctor was busy extricating the meat from a bone. He did not have the time to look up. Bharati now addressed him, 'You never make a mistake in assessing a person. That was the reason why you remarked the other day that Sashi should've loved someone else. But why couldn't you have cautioned me also? Why couldn't you've said, "Bharati, be careful; don't make a mistake?" I feel disgusted with myself when I compare myself to both of you.'

'Sashi, what did Apurba say?' asked Doctor, stuffing the piece of meat into his mouth.

The reply came from Bharati. 'He said, "My mother is ill. I need money for her treatment." He thinks that if he joins in his old office secretly, no one will come to know. He apprehends danger from two persons — Talwarkar and Brojendra. But then his uncle is a police officer — he must've made necessary arrangements to take care of them. We too may not be spared. Mean, greedy wretch! Coward! I hate him!'

Doctor smiled slyly and said, 'She must be genuinely in love with him to sing his praises in this fashion! Sashi, you too should say something similar in praise of Nabatara for our benefit.'

Bharati was taken aback. 'Did you say that to deride me?' she asked.

Doctor nodded his head. 'Could be.'

Overwhelmed by a sense of pique, sorrow, and anger, Bharati's face turned crimson. 'You must never do that,' she said. 'D'you think everyone can bear their grief as silently and with the same fortitude as Sashibabu? D'you know how it feels to be hurt?' Her voice grew hoarse. 'Now that he has come back, you must take me away somewhere from here. How could

I've even loved such a person?' She huddled over the floor and started sobbing like a child.

Doctor went on with his meal unperturbed. Looking at his utter indifference one would think all this high drama had made no impact on him. After a few minutes, Bharati went to the adjacent room, washed her face, wiped it dry and returned.

'Would you like another helping?' she asked Doctor.

Doctor fished out a handkerchief from his pocket and said, 'I'm a Brahmin's son. I'll not only eat, but also carry some home. You'd better pack some for me so that I don't have to worry for a couple of days.'

Returning his dirty handkerchief, Bharati fetched a clean towel, made out a small bundle of different delicacies and placed beside Doctor. 'The Brahmin's bundle is ready. Now what about the bag of money?'

Doctor laughed. 'That's the Brahmin's fee for having eaten here,' he said.

'That means except for the minor detail of the marriage itself, the rest of the functions are over now,' commented Bharati.

Doctor burst into a guffaw. The next moment he checked it by putting his hand to his mouth. He then said gravely to Bharati, 'This is my problem. I just can't seem to be able to laugh softly. If you hadn't come with me and shed bitter tears, Sashi would've been scandalised.'

'Are you again pulling my leg?' queried Bharati.

'Pulling your leg? Not at all. I'm trying to express my gratitude to you.'

Bharati turned her face aside angrily and did not say anything.

Sashi had been quiet all this while. He now said solemnly, 'If you don't get angry with me, Doctor, I'll tell you something. Lots of people feel that one day you'll marry Bharati.'

Doctor was momentarily taken aback. But the next moment he regained his composure and made light of the situation by saying, 'Really! How wonderful that'd be! I'd bless you! But can I even dream of such good luck?'

'But many think it's quite likely,' replied Sashi.

'Alas! If instead of many people thinking that way, only one person had done so.'

Bharati laughed. 'Who knows, your luck might change in a moment. You've only to say that I've to marry you tomorrow; I swear I won't ask you to wait even for a day.'

'But what about poor Apurba who risked his life in coming back?'

'He's got a child bride fixed up for him back home. You needn't worry about him. He won't die of heartbreak!'

'How can you agree to marry a man like me?' said Doctor earnestly. 'I must say you've lots of guts.'

'What's the big deal in agreeing to marry you?' replied Bharati.

Doctor turned to Sashi. 'Just listen to what she says. If she denies it tomorrow, you'll have to intercede on my behalf.'

'That won't be necessary,' interjected Bharati. 'I won't go back on my word. The only thing that remains to be seen is whether you will.'

'We'll see that when the time comes.'

Bharati laughed. 'What to speak of me or Sumitra-didi, even if Indra, the king of the gods, were to order the three celestial nymphs — Urvasi, Menaka and Rambha — to break the vow of the modern Sabyasachi, instead of disturbing the religious austerities of the ancient sages, I'm sure they would've had to go back disappointed and disgraced. One can win the heart of a man of flesh and blood, but what can one do with one who has a heart of stone? Your anger against foreign domination has turned your heart into stone!'

Doctor chuckled. Bharati's eyes were full of reverence for Doctor. She said, 'If I hadn't that much faith in you, I'd never have agreed to come with you. I'm not like Nabatara. I know that I chose the wrong man. But that, I suppose, can't be undone. One whom I'd once thought . . . .'

She began to sob again. Wiping her tears, she said, attempting to smile, 'Shouldn't we be going now? When will the tide recede?'

Doctor glanced at the wall clock. 'There's still time for that,' he said.

He stretched out his hand and placed it on Bharati's head. 'Strange,' he said, 'that despite all her miseries, Bengal continues to produce women like Bharati. There may be people like Nabatara, but there are Bharatis as well. Isn't it wonderful that even a hundred Sabyasachis can't take the place of one unworthy Apurba? By the way, Sashi, where's your bottle today?'

Sashi felt embarrassed. 'I haven't got one,' he said awkwardly. 'I've given up drinking.'

Bharati said to Doctor, 'Don't you remember, he promised Nabatara that he'd never touch liquor again?'

'That's correct,' said Sashi. 'I had promised Nabatara that I'd give up drinking. I will never break that promise.'

'But how'll you live then?' laughed Doctor. 'You've given up drinking, Nabatara has left you, the money which you got by selling your property is gone — how'll you bear all these losses at the same time?'

Touched by Sashi's plight, Bharati said to Doctor, 'It's easy to make fun of him. But think for a moment what it all means to him?'

'I said that after considering everything,' replied Doctor. 'No one knows better than me what dreams Sashi had woven around that money. Amongst his acquaintances there was none who hadn't heard that he'd inherit a large sum of money. Then came Nabatara. For six months or so he was completely absorbed with her. And liquor? That was his only companion in life. Till yesterday he had everything; today, suddenly, everyone seems to have forsaken him. He seems totally alone. Yet he has no grievance against anyone, no

301

malice against anybody. He doesn't even raise his face towards the heavens and cry, with tears in his eyes, "God, I never wished anyone ill. Then why this injustice towards me?" '

Bharati sighed deeply. 'I understand now why you love him so much,' she said.

'Not only love, but also respect,' replied Doctor. 'Sashi is an honest man. His mind is pure like the waters of the Ganga. Bharati, when I'm gone, look after him. I place him in your hands. He'll suffer, but he'll never make others suffer.'

Sashi felt greatly embarrassed. His face turned red. For a while, possibly for want of anything to say, the three of them kept quiet.

'What are your plans for the future?' Doctor asked Sashi. 'You've only your violin left with you. Do you intend becoming a roving minstrel as before?'

'Take me into your group,' said Sashi cheerfully. 'I promise I'll never touch liquor again.'

His words, and the way he said it, evoked Bharati's laughter. Doctor also smiled. 'No, poet, it's better you stay away from it,' he said affectionately to Sashi. 'You'd better stay with this little sister of mine. That'll be of greater use to me.'

Sashi nodded his head. After a while he said somewhat diffidently, 'At one time I used to write poetry. Maybe if I try, I can start writing again.'

'That'd be wonderful,' said Doctor. 'It'd be a positive contribution if you can do that.'

'Yes, I shall. But this time I shall write for the peasants and workers.'

'But they won't be able to read it,' observed Doctor.

'Doesn't matter. I'll still write for them.'

Doctor smiled. 'But that'll be unnatural, and nothing that's unnatural ever lasts. You can offer food to the poor, because they're hungry, but you can't offer literature to them. Mere narration of their joys and sorrows will not make it their literature. They'll have to create their own literature in future, if that's at all possible

302

for them. But the songs that you'll write for them will never be part of their representative literature. It'd be better for you not to attempt such an impossible thing.'

Sashi could not understand what Doctor exactly meant. He asked doubtfully, 'What shall I do then?'

'Write songs in praise of the revolution! But in the idiom of those among whom you were born and brought up. Your writings must cater to that class alone.'

Bharati was surprised and pained. 'Do you too believe in the class system?' she asked Doctor. 'You too want to serve only the upper classes.'

'You're mistaken,' replied Doctor. 'I didn't refer to social stratification. Nor did I talk about the class struggle. I don't believe in such stratifications. But I have to admit that there's a distinction between the educated and the uneducated. If you ask me, that's the only true stratification that exists, and one that was created by God himself. You're a Christian, but have I ever shunned you? On the contrary, who can be closer to me than you?'

Bharati's eyes filled with reverence for him. 'But will it be appropriate for Sashibabu to write about your revolution, your secret society?' she asked.

'My secret society is my responsibility alone,' said Doctor, interrupting her. 'The strength to bear that burden — no, no, let that be with me!'

He took a few moments to collect himself. Then he added, 'I've explained to you before, revolution doesn't necessarily mean bloodshed. It signifies radical and total transformation of the society instead. Poet, you needn't bother yourself about the political revolution — that's my work. Try to sing about the social revolution instead. Whatever is rotten, decayed and decrepit, whether in our religion, society or beliefs, let all these be destroyed . . . let all these be swept away! If you can't do anything else, at least enlighten the people about this. Tell them that this is our greatest enemy. As far as independence of the country is concerned,

303

that's my headache. But . . . who's there?'

Sashi pricked his ears. 'Someone seems to be coming up the stairs.'

Doctor had already thrust his hand into his pocket. Silently and swiftly, he went out to the verandah. But he returned in a minute. 'It's Sumitra,' he said.

CHAPTER 28

Sumitra's arrival so late at night was both unexpected and unwelcome. Bharati felt distressed and uneasy. When she entered the room, Doctor welcomed her warmly. 'Do sit down,' he said to her. 'Have you come alone?'

'Yes,' replied Sumitra. She glanced at Bharati and said, 'How are you, Bharati?'

So many thoughts flashed through Bharati's mind within that one minute. She had taken it for granted that Sumitra would totally ignore her, as she had done on the last occasion. But now her query about Bharati's well-being, and specially the warmth in her voice, filled her with happiness. She replied gratefully, 'I'm fine, Didi, how are you?' She could not bring herself to be informal with Sumitra today.

'I'm fine,' said Sumitra, and sat down in one corner. She was reticent by nature and had a natural, quiet gravity about her that precluded friendliness. She did not deviate from her normal practice today also. Bharati realised that her reticence did not denote either anger or irritation, yet she could not gather the courage to ask any further questions.

Doctor spoke, 'I hear that you've inherited immense property in Java and that you're going there.'

'Yes,' replied Sumitra. 'They've come to fetch me.'

'When will you be leaving?'

'By the first available steamer . . . on Saturday.'

Doctor smiled. 'So you've become rich?'

Sumitra nodded her head. 'I suppose so . . . that is, when I do get all the property.'

'You will. Take the advice of an attorney. And be careful. Those who've come . . . are they known to you?'

'Yes. They're trustworthy . . . . I know them well.'

'Then there's nothing to worry.' Turning to Bharati,

305

Doctor was about to say something, when Sashi intervened.

'Isn't it interesting?' he said to Doctor. 'You inducted three Bengali ladies into your organisation. Out of them Nabatara has already left, our President is about to leave. Only Bharati . . . .'

Doctor laughed. 'Don't worry about Bharati. She'll soon follow the others. That's certain.'

Bharati glared at Doctor but said nothing.

Sashi sensed the hurt lay beneath the surface of Doctor's words. 'You too are going away,' he said to Doctor. 'That means an effective end to the activities of Pather Dabi. Who'll run the organisation?'

He sighed deeply. Though this was expressive of his genuine sorrow, strangely enough it failed to move Doctor. He said with his usual smile, 'How can you even bring yourself to say such things? After having been associated with me for so long, is this the certificate that you give me? How can you even imagine that Pather Dabi will be wound up simply because three women decide to go away? Is this the effect of your having given up liquor? If so, you'd better start drinking again!'

Though Doctor sounded light-hearted, Bharati was sure that the words were not spoken in jest. But she failed to understand its full significance. Glancing at Sumitra through the corners of her eyes, she saw her sitting silently with her eyes downcast. Turning to Doctor she said, 'I may not need liquor to clear my vision, but I must confess I too could not understand what you meant. Nabatara may be insignificant. I too am not of much consequence. But what about Sumitra-didi whom you yourself appointed President of the organisation? Do you mean to say that even her departure will have no effect on the organisation? Tell me honestly, not out of anger just to spite someone.' She glanced at Sumitra. She was sure Sumitra would be looking at her. But Sumitra continued to sit silently, with her eyes downcast, like a statue.

Doctor kept quiet for a few moments and then said calmly, 'I did not speak in anger, Bharati. I don't say that Sumitra is unimportant. You may not be aware, but Sumitra knows very well, in our type of work we learn to take such things in our stride. Besides, when life itself is so uncertain, how does one determine its value? It's inevitable that people will depart. Not to be upset over the loss of any member, however important he or she may be, and to find a substitute who can take his place as easily and as automatically as water fills up a void — this is the first and foremost lesson that we are taught.'

'But this doesn't happen in real life,' remarked Bharati. 'Take your own case. I just can't imagine how someone can take your place.'

'Your way of thinking is different,' replied Doctor. 'Ever since I realised this, I've distanced you from our organisation. It seems to me that some other work awaits you.'

'And I thought that you were dissociating me because I'm unfit. If some other task awaits me, I shall prepare myself for it. But that was no answer to my question. Basically it's a simple question — can the void created by you be filled up as easily as you say? You say it's possible; I say it is not. I'm certain it is impossible. For one thing, men are not like water; in any case, you definitely are not.'

She added after a moment, 'I wouldn't like to press on just to prove my point. But at the same time, why should you try to say something which you know fully well is not correct?'

Doctor could not give a prompt reply. Bharati too did not wait for one. She continued, 'I realise it's not possible for you to stay here any longer. You too are eager to leave. My heart sinks when I think I may never see you again. I try not to think about it, but can't. My only regret is despite having worked closely with you, I still failed to understand you. I remember whenever I asked you a question, you'd sometimes tell

307

me the truth, sometimes untruths, and sometimes half-truths. But you never told me the plain and naked truth. I was secretary of your organisation, yet I never had any faith in your activities. I didn't hide this fact from you. You were not angry with me, nor did you distrust me, but very cleverly you distanced me from your work. I've not forgotten that you saved Apurbababu's life. I feel that you alone can guide me and tell me what's beneficial for me. And so I pray, before you go away, disclose everything to me. Don't hide it from me any longer.'

The meaning of this strange entreaty was not clear to Sashi and Sumitra. So they continued to gaze in surprise. But looking at their anxious faces, Bharati felt awkward. Her embarrassment was not lost on Doctor. He said with a smile, 'Everyone speaks a mixture of truths, untruths and half-truths. So what if I do as well? And in any case, if someone ought to be ashamed, it's I. Why should you feel embarrassed?'

Bharati lowered her head and remained silent. Sumitra piped in, 'Supposing you've no sense of shame, what then? But most women feel shy to reveal their minds; some indeed are quite incapable of doing it.'

It was clear towards whom this remark was directed and what was its purpose. But out of deference for her, and for the position she had so long occupied, everybody remained silent.

After a few minutes, Doctor addressed Bharati. 'Sumitra said just now that I've no sense of shame. You said that I speak truth and falsehood to suit my own convenience. I could've evaded the issue today also by replying something in the same vein, if it hadn't concerned my organisation, / Pather Dabi. My truths and falsehood are determined by its interests alone. This is the guiding principle in my life, my true image!'

Bharati was stunned. 'What are you saying?' she exclaimed. 'This is your guiding principle in life, your true image!'

'That's right,' said Sumitra. 'This is indeed his true image — bereft of kindness, of love, of scruples. I know this image of stone.'

Though Bharati did not completely believe what Sumitra said, she was too bewildered to say anything.

Doctor spoke again. 'You people talk of the ultimate truth, the supreme truth! These meaningless, pompous words appear to be of great significance to you. But these words are used only to beguile the fools. You think that one creates falsehood, while truth is eternal and divine. Sheer nonsense! Man creates truths in the same way as he creates lies. Truth is not eternal or ever-lasting. Like everything else in this world, it is also born, and it too dies. I don't tell a lie; I create truths to suit my convenience, as and when necessary.'

It was clear that this was no joke; this was indeed Sabyasachi's creed. Bharati turned pale. She asked, rather indistinctly, 'Is this the principle of your Pather Dabi?'

'Pather Dabi is not an instrument for propagating my philosophy,' said Doctor. 'It represents a way of life for me. Do you really mean to say that some obsolete dictum coined by someone at some point of time, for some specific purpose, should hold good for my organisation, and not the beliefs of one who is prepared to hang for it? I don't know what is your concept of truth, but if there's anything like supreme falsehood, it's indeed this!'

Sumitra's eyes blazed with excitement, but Bharati was overwhelmed with apprehension and misgivings.

'Poet!'

'Yes, sir.'

'See how respectful is our Sashi,' laughed Doctor. But none else joined in the laughter. Doctor glanced at the wall clock and said, 'The tide must have receded by now. It's time for me to go. I don't suppose I'll be coming to your Sashi-Tara Lodge again.'

'I too will be moving out soon,' said Sashi.

'Where d'you propose to go?'

'Why? To Bharati's place, as ordered by you.'

Doctor laughed. 'You see how obedient Sashi is,' he said to Bharati. 'Now, poet, what are you going to call your new home? Sashi-Bharati Lodge? I've seen your plans misfiring thrice already. But this time you may be lucky. Bharati is a good person. She has a kind heart.'

Despite being troubled, Bharati could not help bursting into laughter. Sumitra also smiled coyly.

'I'm taking your bag of money with me,' said Doctor. 'I'll leave it with Bharati. She can buy a house with it.'

'Do stop adding insult to injury,' cried Bharati.

Sashi said, 'Take it away. I'm giving it to you. Let the money which I've got by selling my property be of some use to you.'

Doctor laughed, but his eyes were moist. 'Sashi,' he said, 'I don't need it at present. Maybe, I won't need it in future either.' Saying this, he glanced at Sumitra, with a smile on his face.

Sumitra's eyes were full of gratitude. Though she said nothing, her entire being seemed to cry out, 'Whatever I have is yours, but will you touch it?'

Doctor looked away and remained silent for a while. He then called out, 'Poet!'

'Yes.'

'I've feasted in advance. But don't feel sorry for that. Because when the auspicious moment actually comes for you, I may not be able to be present. But I assure you, it'll definitely take place one day. Satisfied with the feast which you've laid out for me, I bless you. May God give you happiness! But you must never do two things. Never start drinking again! And never get involved in political activity. You're a poet, an artist, you're greater than a politician. Never forget this.'

Sashi was unconvinced. 'Why can't I be associated with your work? Am I greater than you?'

'Of course,' replied Doctor. 'It is the artist who gives

310

a nation its identity, its stature. A day will come when this struggle of ours will come to an end. These sufferings will then appear insignificant, just one more episode crowding the pages of history. But who'll deny the significance of your work? You alone will synthesize the different streams and weave it into a single garland.'

Sumitra said with a gentle smile, 'God alone knows when he'll do all this. But the way you're puffing him up, won't Bharati have a tough time managing him?'

Everybody laughed. Doctor said, 'Sashi will become our national poet. Not a poet of the Hindus, or the Muslims, or Christians, but a poet of all Bengal — a land of plenty, of rivers and rivulets, a fertile land of green fields and rich harvests, free from the ravages of disease, unaffected by droughts and famines, free from the pain and indignity of foreign domination! You will be the voice of this wonderful land of ours, won't you, my brother?'

Doctor's words sent a thrill through Bharati. Euphoric at the honour bestowed upon him by Doctor, Sashi said, 'If I try, I can write poems in English, even in . . . .'

Doctor cut him short. 'No, no, not in English! You'll write only in Bengali, only in your mother-tongue! Sashi, I know most of the languages in the world, but I can tell you there's no sweeter language, no language more developed than Bengali. I sometimes wonder, Bharati, who introduced this sweet tongue in our land.'

Bharati's eyes were moist with tears. 'And I wonder,' she said, 'who taught you to love your motherland so passionately. It seems to be limitless.'

Echoing these sentiments, Sashi said in a voice charged with emotion, 'I'll sing of her past glory and about our love for the motherland. I'll teach the people to love their country as before.'

Doctor looked surprised. He glanced at Sashi and then at Sumitra. Both of them laughed. But the other two could not understand its significance and felt hurt.

311

Doctor said to Sashi, 'What d'you mean by saying that you'll teach them to love their country as before? Bengalis never loved their country that dearly. If they had even a fraction of that love, could they have conspired with the foreigners and handed over the country to them? "Love for one's motherland" was never seriously meant — it was just an empty slogan! The Hindu general, Raja Man Singh, hunted the Hindu ruler, Rana Pratap, like an animal and presented him bound hand and feet as a tribute to the Moghul Emperor. And the people who helped Man Singh in his efforts were his own fellow men. When the Bargis ransacked Bengal, no one opposed them. Instead the people ran and hid in the lakes and ponds. When the Muslim marauders invaded the country, they desecrated and demolished the temples and vandalised the images of the deities. But what did our forefathers do? They simply ran away. They never attempted to protect their land at the cost of their lives. There's nothing to be proud of them. They mean nothing to us, poet. We'll disown them — their religion, their laws, their cowardice, their treachery, their social structures. That will be the theme of your songs, your gift to your country!'

Sashi looked bewildered; he could not understand the meaning of Doctor's words.

Doctor continued, 'It's because of their cowardice that the world treats us so meanly; because of their selfishness that we're over-burdened, crippled! And was it only the country which they harmed? In the name of a religion which they did not practise, gods in whom they themselves had no faith, they have created hideous and illogical rules and regulations in which we find ourselves circumscribed today. These restrictions are at the root of all our evils!'

Sashi managed to blurt out, 'What are you saying, Doctor?'

Bharati was also greatly upset. She said, 'I may be a Christian, but they were also my forefathers. They may

312

have had many faults, but they never practised deception in the name of religion. Don't make this false accusation against them!'

Sumitra had been silent all this while. She now addressed Bharati, 'It's undoubtedly improper to level false allegations against anyone. But it's equally improper to revere someone who doesn't deserve it, even if they are our forefathers. It may be the accepted thing, but there's no justification for it. You must learn to discard these shibboleths.'

Bharati kept quiet. Doctor said to Sashi, 'Nothing becomes venerable just because it is old. It's futile to sing praises of the past. Besides, we're revolutionaries. We've nothing to do with the past. Our outlook, our actions, our aims, are all progressive. We've to forge ahead only by demolishing the old barriers. Where's the scope for sentimentality in it? How can we discover the right of way if the old and decrepit and dead continue to obstruct our path?'

'I don't want to argue with you just for the sake of argument,' said Bharati to Doctor. 'I want to seek your help to arrive at the truth. You're a rebel, but tell me, does any tradition or custom become useless and redundant just because it is old? If that's so, then what will be the foundation for the society to rest upon?'

'I really don't know if there's anything solid enough to act as a support,' replied Doctor. 'But I know this much that with the passage of time everything becomes obsolete, worn out and useless, and has hence to be discarded. Man progresses each day, but the ancient customs and traditions remain static. This is something that's anachronistic. One problem that we face is that the utility or otherwise of any old custom cannot be judged simply on the basis of its age. Or else you too would've agreed that all that is obsolete and useless should be demolished so that a new race, a new order may rise from its ashes!'

'Can you do that single-handedly?'

'Do what?'

'Demolish whatever is ancient, whatever is sacred?'

'Yes,' replied Doctor. 'That is our aim. Nothing becomes sacred just because it is ancient. An old man of seventy is not necessarily purer than a ten-year-old boy. Take your own case. The social distinctions of the ancient times no longer hold good today. The people of the different castes — Brahmins, Kshatriyas, Vaishyas and Sudras — no longer follow the professions prescribed for them. They would perish if they were to. The old order has broken down. And yet, do you know who still continues to believe it's sacrosanct? It's the Brahmin. And, who continues to cling to the system of permanent settlement as inviolable? It is the landed aristocracy. Their motives in doing so are quite clear! Can anything be more illogical than the archaic beliefs that have led Apurba to spurn a woman like you? Why only Apurba? Even Christianity is no longer relevant today. You have to give up your blind faith in it, Bharati.'

Bharati was appalled. 'You're telling me to give up the religion I love, in which I've great faith?'

'That's right. That's because religion is basically a sham, just an old superstition. Religion is man's worst enemy!'

Bharati's face turned pale. For a long while she sat rooted to the ground, unable to say anything. Then she said slowly, 'Wherever you may be, I'll always love you. But if this is the way you feel about religion, then our paths can never be the same. I had never thought even for a day that the path of your organisation was such a sinful one!'

Doctor smiled.

'Your cruel and pitiless path can never yield any good,' said Bharati. 'I'm sure of that. I shall follow the path of love, compassion, and faith. This is not only superior, but it's also the path of truth.'

'That's the reason why I never wanted you to be in our organisation in the first place. Sumitra misjudged you, but I did not. You should do only what you

314

believe in. You'll find many organisations engaged in charitable work, but you'll never find one like our organisation . . . you'll never find . . . .' For a moment his eyes blazed with fire, but only for a moment. His voice was calm and grave. Both Bharati and Sumitra realised that Sabyasachi was most dangerous when apparently calm and unperturbed.

He raised his face and looked at Bharati. 'I've told you many times, my aim is independence, not the welfare of people. When Rana Pratap turned his kingdom desolate, he caused great misery and harm to his people. That happened many centuries back, and yet this act of misery and harm is remembered with greater reverence today than many acts of welfare that were performed by others. But it's futile indulging in such fruitless arguments — I can never accept as harmful or untruthful anything that helps me in achieving my goal.'

Bharati kept quiet. She had had differences of opinion with Doctor in the past also, but it had never affected her so deeply before. Her heart felt heavy and unhappy.

Doctor glanced at the wall clock and then said to her with a smiling face, in his usual soft voice, 'Soon the tide will be in. Come, let's go.'

Bharati stood up and said, 'Okay.'

Picking up the bundle containing the foodstuff, Doctor asked Sumitra, 'Where's Brojendra?'

Sumitra gave no reply, but continued to sit with her face downcast.

'Shall I escort you home?'

Sumitra shook her head. 'No.'

Doctor was about to say something more, but checked himself. 'Very well.'

To Bharati he said, 'Let's not delay any longer. Come.' Saying this, he came out of the room.

Sumitra continued to sit as before. Bharati wished her goodbye and followed Doctor.

CHAPTER 29

As if in a trance, Bharati came and sat in the boat. Throughout the journey she did not say a single word. It was past midnight when they reached the other bank. Innumerable luminous stars filled the night sky and bathed the landscape with a soft light.

Doctor helped Bharati alight and was about to get down himself when Bharati stopped him. 'You needn't come,' she said. 'I'll be able to go on my own.'

'Won't you be afraid?'

'I will. But you needn't come.'

'The distance is not much,' said Sabyasachi. 'I can see you to your place and return in no time.'

As he attempted to step down, Bharati said with folded hands, 'For God's sake, don't do that! That'll only go to increase my anxiety. Go to your house, I beg you.'

It was no doubt risky for Doctor to accompany Bharati; so he did not insist. But, after Bharati had gone, he continued to remain standing on the river bank for a long time.

Reaching home, Bharati unlocked the door and entered. She lighted a lamp and scouted the whole place carefully. Then she made her bed somehow and lay down on it. Physically, she felt exhausted and mentally depressed. Her eyes were heavy. But though she lay down and shut her eyes, she could not sleep. Sabyasachi's words came back to her again and again, 'In this ever-changing world there is nothing like unchanging, inviolate truth. Truth too has its births and deaths; in every age, every generation, it adapts itself to the needs of the people. To believe that what was true for the past ages would be true in today's world would be an error of judgement, like a blind superstition.'

Need of the times? What he meant, Bharati told

316

herself, was that we had to reinterpret truth in terms of the struggle for the country's independence. In other words, for the attainment of this goal no path was ignoble, no intention mean, no endeavour lowly. The efforts to rescue the dissolute factory workers from their evil ways, to educate their children, to establish a night-school — all these were just means to an end. Sabyasachi had no hesitation, no shame, in confessing that. Can an oppressed people be discriminating in deciding which path to follow in their struggle for independence?

Sabyasachi had remarked one day, 'It'll be an evil day for the country when the ethics of the ruled become the same as that of the rulers.' Bharati had not understood the significance of Sabyasachi's remark that day, but it seemed clear to her today.

The clock struck three. She did not recollect when she fell asleep. But she remembered repeating to herself, 'You're a great man, Doctor. I shall always revere and love you. But I'm unable to accept your views. I pray to God that you may be successful in your efforts to free the country from foreign rule. But you must never delude the people by equating what is just with what is unjust. You're a wise man, erudite and intelligent. It's no use trying to defeat you with arguments. The ignominy of being under colonial rule, the necessity of suffering to shake off the foreign yoke — do you think as an Indian, I'm not aware of these things? And yet if you give primacy to this need alone above everything else, if you preach irreligion as religion to the weak and ignorant masses, you'll only create endless sorrow.'

It was late when Bharati woke up from sleep the next morning. The students had already arrived and were calling her. She hastily washed herself, came down and opened the door. Some boys and girls entered, holding their books and slates. She asked them to sit down and was about to go upstairs to change her clothes when the hotel keeper, Mr Sarkar, appeared. 'Apurbababu has been searching for you since last night,' he told her.

Bharati turned round. 'Did he come here last night?'

'Yes, and again this morning. He's waiting for you. Should I send him in?'

Bharati's face turned pale for a moment. 'What does he want to see me for?' she asked.

'I don't know,' replied Sarkar. 'Possibly he wants to talk to you about his mother's illness.'

Bharati flared up. 'What's that got to do with me?' she asked irritably.

The hotel keeper was surprised. He knew that Apurbababu was a man of position and that he had previously always been treated with the greatest courtesy and hospitality by Bharati. He himself had been called upon to provide food to Apurba on several occasions, at times even at late hours. As such, he could not understand the reason for the sudden change in Bharati's attitude.

'I don't know all that,' he said to Bharati. 'Let me send him instead.'

He was about to leave when Bharati stopped him. 'I'm busy at present,' she said. 'The students have already arrived. I've to go to my class. Tell Apurbababu I can't see him now.'

'Then should I ask him to come later?'

'No. I don't have any time,' said Bharati, ending the conversation. She climbed the steps rapidly and went upstairs.

When she came down an hour or so later after finishing her bath, the classroom was already filled with students who were busy disturbing the peace of the neighbourhood with their shouts and shrieks. Previously the school used to be held in two shifts; now, for want of teachers, the night school had almost closed down. Sumitra did not attend, Doctor had gone underground, and Nabatara had gone away. Because she held the classes in her house, Bharati somehow managed to keep the morning shift going. Today,

318

while she started teaching as usual, she could not concentrate on it. It all seemed so futile, an act of self-deception almost. After a couple of hours, when the students had left, she was at a loss to think of how to spend the rest of the day.

The thought that was foremost in her mind concerned Apurba. Though she realised it was discourteous to have turned him away, she had no doubt in her mind that it would have been far worse to have granted him indulgence any further. It was apparent that he wanted to renew their earlier relationship on any pretext. Otherwise what business did he have to be here, if his mother was really ill? It was his mother who was ill, not Bharati's. Didn't he know that it was his first and foremost duty as a son to be by her bedside on hearing about her illness? Or did he have to discuss this with others?

She remembered his irrational fear when it came to handling sick people. Howsoever anxious he might be, he had neither the strength nor the courage to nurse a patient. He was bound to have trouble if entrusted with this responsibility. Bharati knew all this. She also knew how dearly he loved his mother. There was nothing he would not do for her. While on the one hand her heart filled with compassion to think of the agony which Apurba must have faced in being unable to rush to his ailing mother's bedside, on the other hand his insufferable cowardice filled her with indignation. Even if he was incapable of nursing her, shouldn't he have been with his ailing mother, Bharati told herself. Did he expect such advice from her?

It was on these lines that all her thoughts revolved. It never occurred to her that Apurba could have had anything else to talk to her about, nor that something else might have happened which prevented his return to Calcutta.

Bharati had no appetite, so she was not inclined to cook anything for herself. It was late in the afternoon when a hackney carriage came and stopped in front of the house. Bharati peered out of the upstairs window. What she saw filled her with surprise and anxiety. Sashi had arrived with all his belongings. She had never imagined that anybody could have taken seriously what Doctor had said in jest the previous night. But nothing was impossible for Sashi. And so here he was, in person, with his bag and baggage!

Bharati hurried downstairs. 'What's the matter, Sashibabu?' she asked.

'I've come to stay here,' replied Sashi smilingly. He ordered the coachman, 'Take these things upstairs.'

Bharati controlled her anger and said, 'Where's the space upstairs?'

'Never mind. Then let him dump these things in the room downstairs.'

'But that's the classroom,' said Bharati. 'That can't be spared.'

This worried Sashi. To put him at ease, Bharati said, 'Let's do one thing. Doctor's room in the hotel is lying vacant. It'd be better if you shift there. You won't face any problem for your food also. Come, let's go.'

'But what about the rent?'

Bharati laughed. 'You needn't bother about that. Six months' advance has already been paid for by Doctor.'

Though not happy with this arrangement, Sashi had to give in. It was dark by the time Bharati returned after having made the poet comfortable in the hotel room. It had been a tiring day for her. To ensure that neither Sashi nor anyone else disturbed her at night, she bolted all the doors and windows, both downstairs and upstairs, and then entered her bedroom.

As was her habit, she got up early the next morning. But she felt so weak from having starved the previous night that she found it difficult to get up from bed. Her throat was dry and parched from thirst. She realised that in order to sustain herself she would need to eat soon.

It would perhaps be wrong to say that though a

Christian, Bharati was too fastidious about her food. But the fact remained that she had still not been able to free herself completely from her old beliefs and prejudices. Her stepfather had no scruples when it came to food. While she had to eat from the same table, she refrained from taking those items which she had all along regarded as unfit for consumption. And though she was not fastidious to the extent of not eating food that had been touched by someone, she was reluctant to eat food prepared by someone who was unclean. After her mother's death she used to cook her own food for it was economical. Only when she was unwell or fatigued or did not have time for cooking, would she order some barley or bread from the hotel.

After getting up from bed she washed herself, changed her clothes and got ready as usual. But she did not have the strength or the inclination to cook for herself. So she sent word to the hotel keeper to send across a few pieces of bread along with some vegetable curry. Monday was a holiday for the school, so she did not have to worry about that.

After considerable delay, the maid brought the food. 'I'm sorry for the delay,' she said regretfully.

Bharati brought an empty plate and bowl and placed them on the table. Observing the scrupulousness of a Hindu, the maid poured out the lentils into the bowl and served the bread and curry on Bharati's plate. 'Now sit and eat that,' she said.

Bharati glanced at her but said nothing. The maid went on, 'After coming back, I heard that you were unwell. I was awfully worried, but there was none to help me prepare the bread. Now, don't delay any longer. Sit down and have your food.'

Bharati said softly, 'You may go now. I'll have my food.'

'Yes, I'm going. His servant had gone with him. I had to do everything single-handedly. When he returned, the Babu placed twenty rupees in my hand

321

and said, "What you've done for her in the last stage of her life, even her own daughter wouldn't have done." He began to shed bitter tears; I too wept with him. How unfortunate! He had none to call his own in this foreign land. He had sent a cable but nevertheless his eldest brother couldn't come. But then, one can't blame them also, can one?'

Bharati turned numb with anxiety. An unknown fear seemed to seize her. She could not bring herself to ask any questions but continued to gaze at the maid with unblinking eyes.

The maid continued, 'The master said to me, "Khanto, the Babu's mother is seriously ill. You'll have to be with her." I could not bring myself to say "No." She was suffering from pneumonia. On top of it the boarding house where she was putting up was horribly crowded. Its doors and windows were all broken; none of them would close. Oh, what distress! She died at five in the evening, but the people at the hostel had to be informed. By the time they could take the body for cremation, it was past midnight. It was late by the time they returned. I had to do everything myself . . . cleaning up the place . . . .'

Everything was now clear to Bharati. She asked slowly, 'So Apurbababu's mother is dead?'

The maid nodded her head. 'Yes. It seems as if she was destined to die on Burmese soil. As the saying goes, where one will die is preordained. Apurbababu had left Rangoon when she boarded the ship from the other end, after having quarrelled with her eldest son, accompanied by just one servant. She developed fever on the ship itself. By the time she reached the boarding house she was seriously ill and almost in a coma. Babu returned by the next steamer, but by then his mother was dying. Soon afterwards she died. But I really don't have the time to sit and chat with you. There's so much work to be done. I'll come again in the evening.' Holding out this promise of some further gossip later in the day, the maid departed hurriedly.

The food remained untouched. At first her eyes grew moist and her vision blurred, but soon tears began to roll down in profuse streams. She had not seen Apurba's mother even once. Indeed, except for the fact that she had suffered much misery in the hands of her husband and her elder sons, there was little that Bharati knew about her. Yet, on many a sleepless night, in the loneliness of her room, her thoughts had turned towards this elderly widow. If not during happier times, in her days of sorrow then, Bharati used to wonder, how would she have reacted towards her if she alone had to look after her. Would she have rejected her just because she was a Christian? She had been curious to know if she would be able to pass that test and be accepted by her. She had been desirous of getting the matter resolved once for all. Whether religious differences would remain intractable in times of distress — she had got an opportunity to test her thesis, but unfortunately she let it slip through her fingers. The matter remained unresolved for ever!

And Apurba? Who knew better than her how helpless, how lonely he would be today. Maybe it had been his mother's blessings that had been protecting him till today, like a talisman. But today that talisman was no more; he was unprotected. Bharati told herself, perhaps she was imagining things, perhaps it had been nothing but dreams, and yet how could she deny that it had been these dreams that had given a meaning to her life, that had brought some colour to her arid life, given a purpose to her future that had been without a sense of direction so far? Who knew better than her how helpless, how friendless he would be today?

In this alien land, maybe he was without a job. Maybe he had been deserted by his relatives and detested by his friends as timid, selfish and mean. But the greatest misery of all was that his mother was no more. It now struck Bharati that possibly because he had been ashamed to approach any of his acquaintances that Apurba had rushed to her for solace and help without hesitation and without any qualms. He was inefficient, lacked determination and resourcefulness, and yet in the noise and congestion of that boarding house, amidst want and innumerable difficulties, how miserable he must have been as his mother lay dying! Thinking about all this, Bharati continued to weep uncontrollably.

As she wiped her eyes it struck her that all of Apurba's miseries had started from the day he came in contact with her. This thought had haunted her many times in the past and it struck her once again. Otherwise, why hadn't his self-interest failed to deflect him from the path of truth when he chose to support his mother against the perversity of his father and elder brothers? Could he really have been so mean? He had remained steadfast in his performance of his religious rituals — daily prayers, his daily dip in the Ganga, even sporting the customary tuft of hair — despite ridicule and derision from all sides. Was this indicative of his capriciousness? Why had he then changed so radically on arriving in Burma? What was the reason for his irresolution now? Many a time she had thought she would ask Sabyasachi to analyse this for her, but had never been able to bring herself to ask him. Not out of curiosity alone, but because it was a matter that touched her heart, she had wanted an answer. Sabyasachi knew everything that was to know; he would solve her problem for her. And yet her shyness and hesitancy prevented her from posing this question to him.

As she pondered over this, another thought occurred to her. At a time when everyone had turned against Apurba, only one man stood by his side. The only person who was sympathetic to Apurba even then was Sabyasachi. But why? Was it only out of consideration for her? Didn't Apurba have anything of his own to deserve Doctor's sympathy? How could she have loved someone so undeserving, so mean? Did he have no quality that would redeem him, nothing that had endeared him to her? Was it all futile then, this love of hers?

She did not realise how the time flew as she sat at the same place, in the same posture, for over a couple of hours, musing in this fashion. The maid returned. Her work at the hotel had prevented her from continuing with the discussion earlier. But now she had some time off. That there was something between Apurba and Bharati was known to many, including the maid. Then what had happened that Bharati did not go and stand by his side in the time of his greatest need? As a woman, Khanto would get no peace till she had ascertained the reason for this. And so at the slightest pretext she had appeared once again. Seeing the food untouched, she was surprised. 'You've not touched your food,' she remarked.

Bharati was embarrassed. 'No,' she said, and stood up.

The maid shook her head. 'I know that,' she said sympathetically. 'One doesn't feel like eating after hearing such news. If you don't believe me, come and see for yourself. I've scarcely touched my food myself.'

Bharati found the maid's unwanted sympathy greatly embarrassing. Forcing a smile on her lips, she said, 'Will you send someone to call a carriage for me?'

'You'll go then?'

'Yes. Let me go and see how things are at present.'

'Oh, the entreaties the Babu made to the master today!' gushed Khanto. 'I said to myself, if I don't come to one's aid at the time of his need, when else will I do it? Leaving my work unfinished, I rushed out with him. Luckily . . . .'

Bharati was afraid Khanto would start all over again. She interrupted her and said, 'What you've done for him is indeed praiseworthy. However, you mustn't delay anymore. Send for a carriage immediately! In the meantime, let me try to finish my household chores.'

The maid was basically a good soul. She went to

325

fetch a carriage, but before she left, she told Bharati not to bother about the household chores. She would do it for her. She would also clear away the plates which Bharati had not even touched. It would be quite all right if she changed her clothes and sprinkled some Ganga water on her body afterwards. One had to help one's neighbour in a foreign country, et cetera, et cetera.

Fifteen minutes later when the carriage arrived, Bharati picked up some money, locked the door, and left. When she arrived at the boarding house, it was still not dark. Pointing out a room on the first floor, the north Indian watchman informed her that the Bengali Babu was in. He went on to tell her that rules did not permit one to stay on for more than three days. It was six days already and if this came to the notice of the manager, he would possibly lose his job.

Bharati got the hint. She tipped him a couple of rupees. Entering the room that had been pointed out to her by the watchman, she found that the floor was still slippery with water. Things lay strewn all around and in one corner of the room lay Apurba, huddled under a blanket. His head was covered with the customary mourning cloth. It was not clear whether he was asleep or awake. Bharati had heard that a servant had accompanied his mother, but no one seemed to be around, because had he been, he would surely have objected to a stranger thus walking into the room. After remaining like this for five minutes, Bharati called out softly, 'Apurbababu!'

Apurba sat up and glanced at her. He then put his head between his knees and remained like that for a while. After some time, he again sat erect and looked at her. Though his anguish at having lost his mother was apparent from his face, he appeared to be calm and composed. The whole world seemed to have suddenly become meaningless for him. He was no longer the Apurba she knew; he seemed to have transformed overnight. Bharati was stunned; she did not know how to react. Apurba solved the problem for her. He spoke up. 'There's no place for you to sit,' he said. 'The whole place is wet. You'd better sit on that trunk.'

Bharati gave no reply but continued to stand as before, holding on to the doorframe, with her eyes downcast. Both remained silent for a long while.

The servant, who had gone out to purchase kerosene, now returned. He was surprised to see a stranger. Picking up the lantern, he left the room.

'Won't you sit down, Bharati?' asked Apurba.

'It's already late. If I sit down now, it'll be dark before I can return,' replied Bharati.

'Do you have to return immediately? Can't you sit for a little while?'

Bharati went and slowly sat down upon the trunk. After remaining quiet for a moment, she said, 'I didn't know that your mother had come here. I never got to see her, but I still feel aggrieved at her death. Don't tell me anything that might cause me further unhappiness.' As she spoke, tears rolled down her cheeks.

Apurba appeared dumbstruck. Bharati wiped her tears with the end of her *sari* and said, 'Her time had come; so she went to heaven. When I first heard about it, I felt I wouldn't be able to face you. But then I thought, how could I leave you alone like this? Could I live myself? I've got a carriage waiting. Come away with me.' Her eyes filled with tears again.

Bharati had been afraid that Apurba would break down. But he retained his composure and said calmly, 'The austerities to be observed during mourning will entail a lot of trouble. It'll be inconvenient over there. Besides, I'm returning home by the Saturday steamer.'

'Saturday is still four days away,' replied Bharati. 'And so far as austerities are concerned, I'm not unaware of them. But how could you say that it'll be convenient over here, and inconvenient over there? Let's not waste any more time. Come, let's go.'

Apurba shook his head. 'No.'

'If I had to accept that and return without you,

327

I wouldn't have come here in the first place.' She added after a while, 'Today I've nothing to hide from you, nothing to be ashamed of. I know that your mother's last rites remain to be performed and that you'll be returning home by the steamer on Saturday. I also know what'll happen after that. I'll not object to any of your decisions, but if you refuse to stay with me these few days, I swear I'll take poison on returning home. I'm sure that'll only enhance and not lessen your sorrow.'

Apurba kept quiet for a few minutes with his face downwards. But then he stood up and said, 'Then you'd better call the servant. Let him pack up the things.'

There was not much of luggage. It did not take more than half an hour to pack everything and load it on the carriage.

On the way Bharati enquired, 'Your elder brother couldn't come?'

'No. He couldn't get leave.'

'Have you left your job over here?'

'It's as good as that.'

'Do you propose to stay at home after your mother's last rites are over?'

'No. Now that mother is no more, I don't think I could stay in that house a single day more than what is necessary.'

Bharati asked no further questions and only heaved a deep sigh.

CHAPTER 30

A meeting was in progress in the same deserted, dilapidated temple in the middle of the forest, far away from human habitation where, not long ago, Apurba had been tried. The air of anger and vengeance that had filled the room that day was missing today. The plaintiff and the defendant were missing; no one came forward to accuse the other, everyone seemed overwhelmed with despair and the apprehension of danger. The atmosphere was gloomy, sad and melancholy. Bharati's eyes were moist with tears, while Sumitra sat, her head down, silent, still.

Talwarkar had been arrested. Wounded and blood-stained, he had been removed to the jail hospital. He had still not regained consciousness. After running around from door to door in great distress, his wife and daughter had at last been given refuge by a Maharashtrian Brahmin the previous night. Sumitra had sent a telegram to her father, but no reply had still been received.

'What'll happen to Talwarkar?' Bharati asked Doctor in a low voice.

'If he survives, he'll face imprisonment,' replied Doctor.

Bharati shuddered. 'But he may not survive,' she said.

'Not impossible; but if he does, he'll have to face a long spell of imprisonment.'

After a while Bharati asked, 'And what of his wife and daughter?'

Sumitra replied, 'Perhaps her father will come and take her home.'

'Perhaps? What if no one comes? What if her father is dead?'

Doctor smiled. 'Not impossible. In that case, her fate will be the same as that of any other helpless widow.'

329

He added after a while, 'We're not householders. We've no wealth; we're outcasts . . . the law doesn't permit us to live in our motherland . . . we've to hide in the jungles like wild animals . . . we've no means to relieve the distress of others.'

Bharati was pained. 'You may not have the means,' she said, 'but what of those who have? Can't they come to the help of such people?'

'But why should they?' said Doctor, with a little smile. 'They didn't ask us to indulge in such activities. We're like a thorn in their flesh. They've no sympathy for us. When the Britishers say that Indians don't want freedom, that they're quite happy under British rule, they're not absolutely wrong. But, those who've spent their lives in darkness and have become blind, what's the point in complaining against them?'

After remaining silent for a while, he added, 'If Talwarkar were to die in jail here, and after death if he were to see his wife and daughter begging in the streets, he may weep, but he'll never complain to God against his countrymen. I know him well — he'd die of shame before he did that!'

Bharati groaned indistinctly.

Krishna Iyer could not speak Bengali, but could understand bits of it. He nodded his head and said, 'That's true.'

'Yes, this is the truth,' said Doctor. 'This is the supreme lesson which every revolutionary must learn! Cry, for whom? Complain, to whom? If you ever hear that I've been hanged, know that it was our own countrymen who fastened the noose round my neck at the behest of the foreign rulers. It's but natural that they should do so. Have you seen beef being carted from the slaughter houses? It's oxen who pull those carts! Then why complain at all?'

Bharati sighed deeply. 'Is this the reward then?'

Doctor's eyes glowed for a moment. 'Isn't this enough?' he said. 'I know our people will never understand the value of our sacrifice; they may even

330

laugh at us. But one who'll reap the consequences one day . . . laughter will not come easily to him.'

Suddenly he burst out laughing. 'Being a Christian, how could you forget the basic tenets of your religion?' he asked Bharati. 'Did you think Jesus's sacrifice was in vain?'

Everyone was stupefied. Doctor continued, 'All of you know that I don't believe in senseless killings. In fact, I abhor it. I can't even kill an ant. And yet, if it becomes necessary . . . . What d'you say, Sumitra?'

'I know that,' remarked Sumitra. 'I've witnessed at least two such occasions.'

'Those who've usurped my motherland, who've deprived me of my rights, deprived me of my humanity, my dignity, the food which I eat, the water that I drink — they alone have the right to kill me and not I? Does your religion teach you this, Bharati? Pah!'

But Bharati was unconvinced. She shook her head violently and said, 'No, you can't cow me down today. These are cliches. Those who support violence always talk like this. This can never be the final solution. There are better, far better ways than this.'

'What better ways? Tell me.'

'I don't know, but you will know it,' cried Bharati. 'Hatred has blinded you. Throw off those blinkers and come back to the path of peace! You'll find that with your knowledge and brilliance there's nothing that you can't achieve. Violence against violence, hatred against hatred, and tyranny against tyranny . . . this is barbaric! Can't we think of something nobler?'

'Who'll do it?'

'You will,' replied Bharati without a moment's hesitation.

'You'll have to excuse me,' said Doctor. 'I'll find it difficult to talk of peace, throttled as I am under the boots of our British masters. It'll not escape my lips. You'd better ask Sashi to do it. He may even do it for your sake.' Doctor laughed.

331

Bharati felt hurt. 'You laugh at me! But I've discussed this with many of those English missionaries whom you detest and they've all appreciated this.'

'Naturally,' observed Doctor. 'If you stand unarmed in the forest and preach the message of peace, the bears and tigers will certainly be delighted. They're such pious creatures!'

Bharati paid no heed to this sarcasm and said, 'India may be facing bad times now, but it was not always so. Our civilization was one of the world's greatest! It was the message of love and peace, not of hatred and malice, that we had spread from country to country then. I believe those glorious times will return one day!'

For a long time Bharati's words had found an echo in Sashi's poetic heart and had filled him with reverence. He now said emotionally, 'I agree with Bharati. I too believe that we're bound to get back our ancient glory.'

Doctor looked at them and said, 'I don't know what civilization you're talking about. But even civilized behaviour has a limit to it. If you cross that limit, whether for the sake of religion, non-violence or peace, nemesis will overtake you. Nothing can save you from that, not even your Gods! Do you recall the time when India was defeated by the Huns? That's when they burnt their children and skinned their women. Indians couldn't retaliate with equal cruelty. And what was the result? Our sovereignty was lost, country usurped, our temples ransacked and desecrated. We're suffering the consequences of our weaknesses till today.'

He addressed Bharati, 'You often recite the poem — "Grieve not for the loss of freedom, learn to be men again." But what do you understand by the phrase "manhood that helps you regain your freedom?" You think the path to manhood is unobstructed? Free? Or do you think that manhood simply means to serve the poor and distribute quinine among those afflicted by malaria? No. Manhood refers to the realisation, the awareness of the dignity of having been born as a man! It refers to the freedom from the fear of death!'

After a moment's silence, he added, 'It's not really your fault, Bharati. You've been brought up in that atmosphere. So you think there can be nothing nobler than the European civilization. And yet, nothing can be further from the truth. Does civilization refer simply to the ability to build machines that kill people? The wicked find no dearth of deceptions . . . so they invent new ones to justify killing others on the grounds of self-protection. But if civilization has any significance, it is this that the weak should never be dominated by the strong. Have you ever seen them practise this principle?'

'One day I had asked you to look at the map of the world. Do you remember that? Do you remember what I had told you about the Boxer rebellion in China? The barbarism of Chengis Khan and Nadir Shah pales into insignificance when compared to the atrocities perpetrated by the European powers during this rebellion. As insignificant as a lamp before the sun. However insignificant and unjust may be the reason, they don't hesitate to declare war. The aged, the womenfolk, the infants — none are spared! They've no hesitations, no scruples! Their cruelty is limitless. No ethics, no moral scruples seem to restrain them. Anything that helps them in achieving their aim is acceptable and holy. Ethics, moral scruples — these are applicable only to us whom they treat as their slaves!'

Bharati remained silent. How could she protest against these accusations? Did she have the ability to argue with this ruthless, resolute, fearless and unforgiving revolutionary who possessed such wisdom, intelligence and erudition? She remained silent, but her woman's heart which was pure and unblemished, and full of compassion, cried out helplessly.

Sumitra had long given up taking part in such debates. She therefore remained silent with her eyes downcast. But Krishna Iyer grew impatient. He was

333

unable to follow most of what was said. He now asked, 'What's holding up the business for which this meeting has been called?'

'Nothing at all,' replied Doctor. Turning to Sumitra, he asked, 'Have you finally decided to go to Java?'

'Yes.'

'When?'

'Most probably next Wednesday. I couldn't go on Saturday.'

'You're cutting off all links with Pather Dabi?'

Sumitra. nodded her head.

Doctor gave an amused smile. Then, taking out a telegram from his pocket, he gave it to Sumitra. 'Go ahead, read it. Hira Singh delivered it last night.'

Iyer leaned forward. Bharati held up the lighted candle. It was a lengthy telegram in English, the meaning of which was quite clear. But Sumitra's face turned grave as she read it. Finally, after a couple of minutes she looked up and said, 'I don't seem to remember the code fully. Except for the fact that it has been sent by Kruger from the Jamaica Club at Shanghai, I couldn't understand anything.'

'Kruger has wired from Canton,' replied Doctor. 'The police surrounded the Jamaica Club at Shanghai in the early hours of the morning. Three policemen and Binode died in the encounter. The brothers, Mahatap and Surya Singh, have been arrested. Ayodhyay has fled to Hongkong and Durga and Suresh to Penang. The police have got a warrant for the Jamaica Club in Singapore. This, in short, is the news.'

Krishna Iyer turned pale on hearing the news. Only one word escaped his lips, 'Undone!'

'I had no information as to why and when these two brothers deserted their regiments and came to Shanghai,' said Doctor. Then, turning to Sumitra, he asked, 'By the way, d'you have any information about Brojendra's whereabouts?'

Sumitra turned to stone on hearing this question.

Doctor repeated, 'Do you know anything?'

At first she was unable to give a reply, but then she shook her head and uttered just one word, 'No.'

'I don't believe that he was behind all this,' remarked Krishna Iyer.

Doctor said nothing.

'He was under the impression that you've since left Burma,' said Sashi.

Doctor did not react to this either. He continued to sit silently as before.

Everyone seemed to have been transformed into statues. They sat rooted to their seats in silence. The telegram fluttered on the ground before them. The candle was burning out. Sashi lighted another and placed it on the floor. They sat like this for about ten minutes.

Krishna Iyer was the first to show signs of consciousness. He fished out a cigarette from his pocket and lighted it from the candle. Exhaling the smoke, he sighed deeply, 'Everything is finished.'

Doctor glanced at him. Iyer took another drag at his cigarette, but this time he exhaled only smoke.

Sashi was a habitual drunkard, but could never tolerate tobacco. But now, for some reason, he too lighted a cigar and began to puff at it, filling the room with clouds of smoke.

'Worst luck!' exclaimed Krishna Iyer. 'It seems like we must stop now.'

'I knew from the beginning that nothing would come of it,' cried Sashi. 'Simply . . . .'

Doctor cut in by asking Sumitra once again, 'When was it you said you'd be leaving? Wednesday?'

Sumitra did not look up, but simply nodded her head.

Sashi once again said, 'It's futile, sheer madness, to fight against such a world power! I've been telling you, Doctor, no one will stick to you till the end.'

It was not clear what Krishna Iyer understood, but he suddenly let out a huge cloud of smoke and nodded his head, 'True.'

Doctor sprang to his feet. 'The meeting is dissolved,' he proclaimed.

Everyone stood up. Bharati had not uttered a single word so far. She now sidled up to Doctor and, putting her hand into his, whispered, 'You mustn't go away without telling me.'

Doctor said nothing; he simply took her soft, tender hand in his iron grip, pressed it softly, and then left the room.

CHAPTER 31

The weather turned bad the following day. Since early morning the sky had been overcast with clouds; there had also been a light drizzle the previous night. But it turned really bad from midday, with a storm impending.

The previous night Sumitra had stayed back. Bharati had not let her go, she had much to talk to her about. Sumitra had decided that she would leave after lunch. But the weather turned so foul that it was impossible to venture out, not to speak of crossing the river. Sashi had come over from the Hindu hotel where he was putting up. He had come over at noon, but was held up because of the storm.

No one knew when the afternoon had turned into evening. Lamps were lighted. Bharati's room felt snug with the doors and windows tightly bolted. Everyone had gathered there. Sumitra lay on the easy chair, wrapped from head to toe in a shawl. Sashi squatted on the bed. Apurba relaxed on a blanket that had been spread out on the floor. A short distance away, Bharati sat paring fruits for Apurba with a kitchen knife. In one corner of the room the *khichri* was boiling and bubbling on a stove.

Apurba had earlier stated that he was fed up with this world and preferred to become an ascetic. Sashi could not approve of this proposal. He was adducing arguments to support his contention that there was no fun in becoming an ascetic these days and that it would be better for Apurba to accept the job of a teacher that was being offered to him in the college at Barisal.

Apurba felt hurt but did not say anything. Bharati was familiar with the whole issue. She now said, 'Can't a man have any greater aim in life other than mere enjoyment of fun? After all, one man's way of looking at things may not be the same as the other's.'

The way she spoke upset Sashi. She added, 'He's not in a proper state of mind. To discuss his future at such a time is not only futile, but also inappropriate. Rather, let's talk about ourselves . . . .'

'I'm sorry. I wasn't aware of this.'

It was natural for Sashi to be unaware of anything. In the meantime, however, another development had taken place which only Bharati was aware of. From the practical point of view its repercussions were no less serious than the death of his mother. On hearing about his mother's death, Apurba's elder brother, Binodebabu, had simply sent his condolences, but nothing more than that. On reaching Calcutta, when Apurba came to know that his mother had left for Burma in anger and ignominy, he was filled with sorrow and anguish. During the two days that he stayed in Calcutta, Apurba did not go home, either to have his meals or to sleep. And, before returning, he had a regular fight with his brother. Still he had been confident that in view of the tragedy, someone would definitely come to Rangoon to fetch him back. But no one came. It is difficult to say what would have happened if Tewari had been in Calcutta, but he too had gone home on leave.

Bengali priests were available at Rangoon also. Apurba had therefore told Bharati in the morning that he would not return to Calcutta; he would perform his mother's last rites there itself, as best as possible.

Apurba had ascertained the reason for his mother's sudden departure for Burma — her distress and disillusionment with her sons and daughters-in-law. But to what extent his intimacy with a Christian girl was responsible for this, Apurba could not get to know. His mother was seriously ill, almost in coma; so she could not speak. Binodebabu was angry and preferred not to say anything.

Suddenly Sumitra threw off her shawl and sat up. 'I hear someone opening the door downstairs and coming

338

in,' she said to Bharati.

It was impossible to hear anything due to the storm. Everyone became apprehensive. Bharati pricked her ears and listened. Then she said mildly, 'No, there's no one. It's only Apurbababu's servant moving around.' But the next moment she heard the familiar footsteps on the stairs and cried out in joy, 'It's Dada! I welcome you a thousand times, no, ten thousand, twenty, no, one hundred thousand times!'

Dropping the fruits and the knife, she ran to the landing. 'One million, ten million, twenty million, one thousand million times good evening to you! Do come in!'

Sabyasachi entered the room. As he bent to remove the huge bundle from his back, he said, 'Good evening, good evening, good evening!'

Bharati took his both hands into hers and said, 'See, I'm cooking *khichri* for you. Take off your overcoat first . . . Ugh! Your boots are completely wet! Wait, let me take them off.' She was so flustered, she could not decide which one to remove first — the boots or the overcoat!

She dragged him to a chair and made him sit down on it. 'Let me take off your boots first,' she said. 'Why did you have to come on foot in this rain? Couldn't you've taken a coach? Did you have lunch? Are you hungry? I heard they've cooked meat in the hotel today. Should I run across and fetch some for you? Will you take it? Tell me, honestly.'

Doctor laughed. 'She's going to drive me mad today!'

Bharati took off his boots and then stood up. She ran her fingers through his hair and exclaimed, 'Just what I'd thought! Completely drenched, as though you've just had a bath!' She ran to fetch a towel.

Seeing her behave like a child, Sashi burst out laughing. 'It seems as though she's seeing you after a decade,' he told Doctor.

'Worse than that.' Snatching the towel from Bharati's hand, Doctor said, 'Your affection is taking the life out

339

of me.'

'Really? I won't trouble you anymore.' Saying this Bharati stomped off in a show of pique and sat down to pare the fruits once again.

Her friend, well-wisher, companion — one dearer to her than her own relatives — had dropped in unexpectedly in this stormy night. She was filled with affection, reverence, pride and pure, selfless love. How could she check her exuberance? And, why should she?

Sumitra had been watching this scene silently all this while. Though she did not speak even now, the canker of hatred and jealousy that had blinded her so long, lifted. She realised that except for pure, unadulterated friendship, there was nothing more between these two persons. Her head hung in shame when she remembered that she had once imagined their relationship to be illicit. It was clear to her that Bharati could be so demonstrative about her affection for Doctor, extrovertly one may say, because she had nothing to hide, nothing to be shy about.

Till now Bharati had been fussing over Doctor. But now her eyes fell on his huge bundle. She became apprehensive. 'Why have you brought this thing with you in this horrible weather?' she asked anxiously. 'You aren't thinking of going away anywhere, are you? Don't try to deceive me.'

Doctor attempted to smile, but seeing the expression on Bharati's face, checked himself. Still he tried to make the situation light by saying, 'Do you want me to get arrested like Ramdas instead?'

Sashi nodded his head and said, 'Quite so.'

'Quite so?' said Bharati angrily. 'What d'you know that you're giving your comments on this matter?'

'Bah! Don't I know anything?'

'No, you don't!'

Doctor laughed. 'If you go on quarrelling like this, the *khichri* which you're cooking will get burnt.' Turning to Apurba, he said, 'If you don't catch tomorrow's ship, you'll be late in reaching Calcutta.'

'I've decided to perform my mother's last rites here itself,' replied Apurba gravely.

'Here? Why?'

Apurba remained silent; Bharati too did not say anything.

It was apparent to Doctor that something had happened in between which neither wanted to disclose. He said, 'All right. Then what's the necessity for your going back? I suppose you've still got your job over here?'

'Apurbababu has decided to become an ascetic,' piped in Sashi.

Doctor laughed. 'An ascetic? That's unusual.'

Apurba felt hurt at this. He said, 'What else can one do if he's disillusioned with his life?'

'These are difficult philosophical questions,' replied Doctor. 'Please don't drag me into this. I'd suggest you consult Sashi instead. He has some experience in this line. He had once run away with a mendicant for one year after having failed at his school examination.'

Sashi corrected him, 'For more than eighteen months . . . nearly two years!'

Both Sumitra and Bharati started laughing. But Apurba remained unmoved. He said gravely, 'I hold myself responsible for my mother's death. I've not been able to shake off this feeling ever since she died. The world has no use for me; it too has become bitter to me.'

Doctor continued to gaze at him intently for a while, as if to understand his anguish. Then, in a gentle voice full of affection, he said, 'It has never been necessary for me to ponder over one's life from this angle. Nevertheless, my common sense tells me that this may not be a right step that you're contemplating. If one renounces the world out of a sense of bitterness, he'll only find frustration and unhappiness; the peace and tranquillity that he hopes to attain will be denied to him. Unless one has compassion and joy, can one

341

. . . . But then, I really don't know . . . .'

Bharati felt as if she could see the sense in what Doctor was saying. She said excitedly, 'You know everything. Nothing that's wrong will escape your lips. That's not possible. This is the truth, the plain truth.'

'I too think that way,' replied Doctor. Turning to Apurba he said, 'Your mother died. Why had she come here, why is it that you refuse to go back . . . I don't know anything, nor do I have the curiosity to know it. But if someone's behaviour has made you bitter today, is it necessary that it should determine your entire future life for you? At the same time, why do you choose to ignore another who made your life happy and meaningful?'

'But if my elder brother . . . .'

'Well, if there are people like your elder brother, Binodebabu, in this world, aren't there also people like Bharati's elder brother, Sabyasachi? If you can no longer go back to your ancestral house at Calcutta, does that mean you've nowhere else to go in this wide world? Emotion is a very valuable thing, Apurbababu, but if you allow it to obstruct your vision, it'll prove to be your worst enemy.'

Apurba kept quiet for a long time. Then he said slowly, 'I did not propose to renounce the world out of religious fervour or for attaining salvation. If ever I do so, it'll only be to serve the common man. I know it's difficult for you to believe me — I don't blame you if you can't — but I can tell you that after my mother's death, I'm no longer the same person that you once knew.'

Doctor came up to him and patted him on his back. 'I hope for your sake that what you say is true.'

'Henceforth I shall devote myself to the service of my country and its people, especially the poor,' Apurba said in a voice choked with emotion.

After a while he added, 'I was born and brought up in Calcutta, but henceforth I shall sever all connections with city life. I shall confine my activities to the rural areas. There was a time when villages were the life-blood of the nation. But today the villages have been ruined. The gentry have deserted the villages and migrated to the towns from where they continue to lord over the villagers and exploit them. Their relationship with the villages is limited to this. On the other hand, the peasantry, who had once provided food and clothing to the gentry, are themselves starving, illiterate and helpless today. They're facing annihilation. Henceforth I shall devote myself to their welfare; Bharati too has promised to help me to the best of her ability. She'll teach the village children by opening primary schools and, if necessary, by visiting each cottage. My renunciation, Doctor, is not for my own salvation; it is for the welfare of my countrymen.'

'Very praiseworthy indeed,' remarked Doctor.

No one expected such a lukewarm response from him. Bharati remonstrated with him, 'In a way we'll be doing your work for you,' she said. 'In an agrarian country like ours, unless you improve the lot of the peasants, you can have no real development of the country.'

'I didn't contradict him,' replied Doctor.

'You didn't encourage him either.'

Doctor shook his head. 'If you want to improve the lot of the peasants,' he said, 'you have my best wishes. But don't be under the misconception that thereby you'll be doing my work. I wish the farmers happiness and prosperity, but I don't expect any help from them.'

He addressed Apurba, 'If you want to do good to someone, it doesn't necessarily mean that you should denigrate someone else. The gentry are not responsible for the miseries of the peasants; you'll have to search for its cause elsewhere.'

'But that's what everyone says,' Apurba said uncertainly.

'Let them,' said Doctor. If something is wrong, it'll not become right even if everyone were to say other-

343

wise. The truth is that there's no section of the society as misunderstood, humiliated and oppressed as the gentry. Why do you want to add to their miseries by further blaming them? Do you think what holds good for other countries will also hold good for our country? There's already an external threat to our country; why do you want to add to it by fomenting internal dissensions? There's widespread dissatisfaction . . . the bonds of friendship and respect have broken down. Do you know why? It's because of a handful of people like you . . . because of their bloody egos! Sashi, d'you remember I'd once told you to refrain from such activitiés? When one speaks ill of his own people, he gets a kick out of it. Possibly he feels proud of being able to speak out; moreover, he earns a bit of cheap popularity. But it's not only wrong; it's totally false! Do good by all means, but not by slandering others or spreading disaffection among them . . . by instigating one against the other! A time may come when this may become necessary, but this is not the right time for this!'

Everyone remained silent; only Bharati spoke out. Slowly, she said, 'Don't take it otherwise, but I've always noticed that you're least concerned with the rural folk; you're only bothered about the city dwellers. You've no sympathy for the peasants; you're only interested in the factory workers, the labourers and the artisans. That is the reason why you started Pather Dabi. And if at all you possess a heart, it cries only for the educated, bourgeois intelligentsia. They represent your only hope; they're your own people! Tell me, am I wrong?'

'Not at all,' replied Doctor. 'You're absolutely right. I've told you many times, Pather Dabi was not established to work for the betterment of the peasantry; it was to help me win freedom for the country. Peasants and factory workers don't belong to the same category, Bharati. It's because of this that whilst you'll find me in the midst of factory workers, within the factory

344

premises, you won't find me visiting the huts of the peasants in the villages. However, don't get carried away by this discussion and neglect the more important task at hand,' he said, pointing to the stove. 'The freedom of the country can wait for a while, but it'll be a shame if the *khichri* were to get burnt.'

Bharati hurried over to the stove. Knocking over the lid, she peered in. 'Don't worry,' she said smilingly, 'You won't miss your *khichri* on this rainy night.'

'But how long will it take?'

'Not much. About fifteen/twenty minutes more, that's all. But why this hurry?'

Doctor smiled. 'I came to say goodbye to all of you tonight.'

No one took him seriously. The storm continued to rage outside. Bharati opened the window a bit and peeped out. 'My God!' she exclaimed, shutting it immediately. 'It appears as if the heavens have opened up! An appropriate time to bid goodbye indeed!' She seemed to remember something and said, 'But you'll have to sleep in the smaller room tonight. I'll make a comfortable bed for you there.' Saying this, she went about happily with her cooking. She failed to notice that Doctor remained silent.

When the food was ready, Doctor shook his head and said, 'It won't do if you stay back on the pretext of having to serve us. We'll all eat together.'

Bharati did not protest. 'All right,' she said. 'We'll form a circle.'

'That's okay, excepting that Apurba shouldn't cast a greedy eye at what we're eating and give us indigestion. Warn him against doing that.'

Apurba laughed. Bharati said smilingly, 'That risk is always there, but who can give you indigestion? I'd believe it if someone were to tell me that you can digest even stones and rocks. Ugh! the kind of food I've seen you eating!' Bharati shuddered even as she recollected the food she had recently observed Doctor eating.

345

The dinner commenced. Paeans in praise of the dishes and good-humoured jokes and banter made the atmosphere of the room light. But just then Apurba introduced a topic which spoiled the mood. 'I read in the newspapers a piece of good news a couple of days back,' he began. 'If the information is correct, there won't be any need for your revolution. The government has announced that it'll reform the entire administrative machinery.'

Sashi was quick in denouncing it. 'It's a lie!' he cried. 'A hoax!'

Bharati was not entirely convinced, but nevertheless she said with genuine eagerness, 'For all you know, it may not be a hoax, Sashibabu. Our leaders have been agitating for the last half century — no, you mustn't laugh, Dada! — so won't their agitation yield any result at all? Those who rule over us are also men! It's possible that they too realise that our demands are justified.'

'Impossible! All lies! Sheer bluff!' cried Sashi unhesitatingly.

'It's true that many people think that way,' said Apurba.

'Their suspicions are unfounded,' said Bharati. 'Is there no God?' Then she added with intense fervour, 'Complete overhaul of the administratie system, redressal of the wrongs to us . . . if all these things are done, then there'll be no necessity for your revolution, Dada . . . no necessity for rebellion!'

'Definitely,' said Sashi.

'Undoubtedly,' remarked Apurba.

Bharati looked at Doctor and said earnestly, 'You'll give up your dangerous path and engage yourself in peaceful activities then, won't you?'

Doctor looked at the wall clock, made some mental calculations and said, as if to himself, 'Not much time left.' He then addressed Bharati and said gently, 'I don't know whether you'll call this my dreadful image or a peaceful one, but I know this much that there

346

can be no change in my life. As for your venerable leaders, no, don't worry . . . . I've neither the time, nor the inclination to make fun of them tonight. I know nothing either about the reforms promised by the foreign rulers, or what our leaders are demanding, how much of these reforms are genuine and how much of it fake, what would be regarded by Sashi as not being a hoax and would satisfy our revered leaders. They threaten the government by saying, "We're no longer asleep; we've woken up. You've injured our self-respect. Either accept our demands or else we swear in the name of our motherland that we shall definitely achieve self-governance within the existing political structure." Such a demand, its nature and intention, are all beyond my comprehension. I only know this much that I can have nothing to do with such a demand or its achievement.'

He added after a pause, 'Reforms signify merely repairs, not a complete change! This seeks to make the tyranny a little more tolerable. Possibly, they aim at nothing greater than an overhaul of the machinery that has become obsolete. I've never wanted such a hoax even for a day! I don't believe in requesting them to oblige me by making my prison cell a little wider. Bharati, there's no scope for self-deception in my creed, my struggle. The outcome can only be two things — either my death, or the attainment of India's independence!'

There was nothing new in what Doctor said. Yet the reiteration of his dreadful determination and the possibility of his death disturbed Bharati deeply and filled her eyes with tears. 'But what'll you do all alone?' she asked. 'One by one all have left you and gone away.'

'That was expected,' replied Doctor. 'It's because my creed doesn't permit deception.'

Bharati wanted to say, 'Everyone is not deceptive. If only you hadn't a heart of stone, you'd have realised this.' But she did not utter these words tonight.

When the dinner was over, Doctor washed his hands

and came and sat on the chair. Nobody noticed that his eyes had grown restless in anticipation of someone's arrival, and that his ears were fixed on the front door. A muffled sound was heard on the road below; no one paid any heed to it, but Doctor sat up with a start. 'Isn't Apurbababu's servant downstairs?' he asked. 'Is he awake? Hey you, open the door!'

Bharati was huddled with Sumitra, trying to decide the sleeping arrangements. She turned around in surprise and asked, 'Who has come?'

'Hira Singh,' replied Doctor. 'I'd been keeping a vigil for his arrival. Doesn't that sound rather poetic, eh poet?' He laughed.

'We're already petrified by your poetry on a terrible night like this,' said Bharati. 'But why has this *Bhagnadoot* chosen to come at this unearthly hour?'

'Don't underestimate a *Bhagnadoot*,' said Sashi. 'But for him, the great epic poem *Meghnadbadh Kavya* wouldn't have been written.'

'Let's see what poem this one composes!' Bharati peeped out of the window and saw that the person entering the house was indeed Hira Singh.

After a minute or so, he came upstairs. After wishing everyone present, he turned to Doctor and bowed to him with folded hands. He was dressed in his usual official uniform and wore his official badge and belt. The leather bag of a telegraph peon hung from his waist. Everything was wet and soggy with rain water. Water dripped from his huge beard and moustache. He tried to squeeze the water with his left hand so as to lighten it somehow, and muttered, 'Ready!'

Doctor jumped up. 'Thank you,' he said. 'Thank you, Sardarji. When?'

'Now.' He wished everyone once again and turned to go, when they cried out in a chorus, 'What's happening, Sardarji? What d'you mean by saying "Now"?'

Yet everyone knew that he would rather die than utter a single word without the permission of his leader. So nobody was really surprised when except

348

for revealing a few teeth through his jet-black beard and moustache, he gave no reply to their questions. They knew that he cared neither for praise or reproach, respect or insult, friend or foe. He had accepted Sabyasachi as his leader in the service of the motherland. He was just a disciplined soldier under him. He had no doubts to clear, no arguments to make, no discussions to carry on, no concern for time or discomfort. He had been entrusted with a difficult job; he had accomplished it, had discharged his duty. He left the room without a single word. The task of satisfying the curiosity of the others now fell upon Doctor.

He explained that it was difficult to assess the extent of damage from this distance; probably the damage was extensive. But whatever may have happened, he now had to do two things: first, he had to save the Singapore branch of the Jamaica Club, and second, he had to search out Brojendra from wherever he may be hiding. A Chinese ship lay anchored near Siriyam on the right bank of the river. The loading had been completed and it would leave for China early next morning. A berth had somehow been arranged for him on it. This was the information which Hira Singh had brought.

Sumitra turned pale on hearing this. Possibly Brojendra was at Singapore; if he was, there was no one who could save him from the man who was now out in search of him. He would then be tried for treachery. Everyone in the organisation knew the punishment for treachery; Sumitra too was not un-aware. Brojendra was none to her and if he was guilty of treachery, he deserved punishment. It was not her concern for Brojendra that made her lose colour, but her conviction that Brojendra was not weak and help-less as an insect; he knew how to protect himself. Apart from the pistol which he always carried in his pocket, he was also very cunning and shrewd, and an exceptionally cautious person. His only mistake was that he believed Doctor had already left on foot. Now if he somehow got to know about Doctor's whereabouts, he would definitely try to kill him. In fact, when it is a question of life and death for someone, that would be the only logical course of action for him to take!

Hira Singh's words continued to reverberate in their ears. Bharati recollected how on the occasion of a birthday party at their house at Moulmein their guest and family-friend, Reverend Lawrence, had suddenly died of cardiac arrest at the dinner table itself, thereby throwing a pall of gloom over the festivities. In the same way Hira Singh had entered the room like a messenger of doom and in a moment shattered their peace and happiness.

Suddenly Sashi spoke out. Heaving a deep sigh, he said, 'Everything seems to have become meaningless, Doctor.'

It was a simple statement and yet it seemed to strike a chord in everyone's heart.

Doctor laughed. Sashi immediately said, 'You may laugh for all you want, but what I say is correct. When I think that you'll no longer be with us, the world becomes blank, hazy. But I'll continue to obey all your commands.'

'Such as?'

'I shall not drink, I shall keep away from politics, I shall look after Bharati, and write poetry.'

Doctor glanced at Bharati, but she had turned her face away. He then said jocularly, 'But I hope you aren't going to write about the peasants.'

'No,' replied Sashi. 'Let them compose their own poems if they can; I won't. I've pondered deeply over this matter. I shall also never forget your statement that it's only the intelligentsia who can die for an idea, not the peasants. I shall become their poet!'

'Very well,' said Doctor. 'But remember that this is not the last word. Human progress doesn't end here; a day will come when the peasants will assert themselves. They will have the power and determine the course the country will take in future.'

'We'll see when that day comes,' replied Sashi. 'We'll abdicate then and hand over the reins of power to them peacefully, and relax ourselves. But the time is not ripe yet. They are not capable of making the supreme sacrifice as yet.'

Doctor came over. He placed his hand on Sashi's shoulder and stood silently for a while.

Apurba had been listening to this discussion so long without a single word. He felt aggrieved at Sashi's remarks about the peasants and said, 'Drinking is a bad thing; he may give it up. He may also continue to write poetry. But are the peasants of India so insignificant that they should be neglected? If they don't prosper, who'll carry out your revolutionary activities? And why should they? As regards politics, if I hadn't decided to give up all worldly ties for the sake of betterment of the peasantry, I'd have devoted myself to politics.'

Doctor looked intently at his face for a few moments. Then a pleasant smile appeared on his face and made it radiant. 'I pray that you may succeed in your mission,' he said. 'Politics is not a trifling matter. If you give up worldly ties for the sake of the country and its people, you'll be loved and respected by all. But I want to remind you that everyone is not fit for every type of work.'

Apurba concurred. 'Who knows this better than I?' he said. 'Had it not been for your kindness, I would've had to pay the supreme penalty for my mistake.' The memories of those days sent a shiver down his spine.

Sashi was not aware of this incident; no one thought it necessary to enlighten him either. He took Apurba's words to denote merely the customary humility and reverence, and nothing more. He said, 'Mistakes are made by many, but it's only our motherland which suffers. I often think, Doctor, there's none as worthy as you. Has anyone more wisdom than you? Has

351

greater experience in politics? Feels as greatly as you do for your countrymen? And yet, what use are all these things? Your experiments in China, in Penang, in Burma, have all been reduced to nothing; the same fate awaits you in Singapore too. In short, all your efforts, for all these years, have come to nought. All that remains is your life, and that too is under grave threat.'

Doctor smiled. 'You may smile,' continued Sashi, 'but I can see clearly what's going to happen.'

'Can you see anything else?' smiled Doctor.

'Yes, I can,' said Sashi. 'That's why I feel, every time I see you, how much better it'd have been if the activities of Pather Dabi could be carried on peacefully!'

Apurba blurted out, 'Bah! Two contradictory statements in the same breath!'

Sumitra turned her face away to hide her amusement. Doctor also could not resist laughing. 'The reason for this,' he said, 'is because he has two split personalities. One is Sashi; the other is the poet. That's why his statements appear inconsistent.'

He added after a while, 'Many people have split personalities. It's not easy to detect it. Hence it'd be wrong if we were to be harsh towards anyone at the slighest inconsistency between his words and his actions. Apurbababu, I had assessed you properly; Sumitra had not. Bharati, if you're ever hurt at someone's inconsistent behaviour, remember these words of mine, even if I'm no more. But I must delay no longer. The boat is waiting for me. The tide is low, so we'll have to row through the night if I'm to catch the ship at dawn.'

Bharati cried out, 'In such a stormy night as this? It's dangerous!'

Sumitra's self-control broke at Bharati's piteous cry. Her face ashen, she asked, 'Will you really be disembarking at Singapore? For God's sake, don't do such a thing! The police over there know you well. You'll never be able to . . . .'

Before she could finish, Doctor said, 'Don't they know me well over here also?'

It was useless carrying on with the discussion, futile to put forth arguments. Sumitra might not have even heard Doctor's last words. She now blurted out something that had been in her mind all this while but which she could not bring herself to express. 'Once, only once, Doctor, depend upon me just once. See whether I can take you safely to Surabaya. Then everything can be arranged with money!'

Doctor had bent down and was tying his shoelaces. He looked at her and said, 'Many things are possible with money, Sumitra. You mustn't waste it.'

It was pointless to argue with him. Utterly helpless, Sumitra turned her tearful eyes away.

'You're leaving me alone and going away,' cried Bharati. 'And you used to say how much love and affection you had for not only me, but girls of my age everywhere. Is this the way you show your love for us?'

'Believe me, Bharati, I do have great affection for girls of your age,' said Doctor. 'I didn't get the opportunity to tell them how much I value their services, how much I depend upon them. But if you can, do tell them this on my behalf.'

Bharati burst into tears. 'I'll tell them that you wanted to sacrifice us instead,' she said. 'I'll tell them that.'

Doctor looked at her for a while and then said, 'Very well, tell them that. If even one of them understands what I meant, I'll consider myself blessed.' Saying this he slung the huge bundle on to his back.

The others followed him downstairs. Bharati made a last attempt to dissuade him. 'One whose mission in his own motherland has ended in smoke, how can he expect success in a foreign country?' she said. 'Those who were close to you have all left you one by one. You're completely alone today!'

353

'Yes, quite so,' said Doctor. 'But you forget, Bharati, I had started alone. And as for foreign? God had not raised barriers and partitioned this world into thousands of prisons to suit the whims of men. His highways are open to all — from north to south, east to west. To create barriers is now beyond the powers of man. If a spark is ignited at one place, its flame is bound to spread from one place to another, irrespective of the distance and the geographical boundaries!'

Inside the room no one could even realise how furious the storm had turned in the meantime. Thunder, lightning, wind and rain, all conspired to wreck vengeance. It seemed as if the world was coming to an end.

As Doctor opened the door, a gust of wind and rain rushed in, drenching everyone. The lights went off; everything was swept off and the room itself plunged in darkness.

Doctor called out, 'Sardarji?'

'Yes, Doctor. Ready,' came the reply.

Everyone was taken aback. It was beyond their imagination that anyone could brave this torrential rain and gale and keep a silent vigil outdoors in the darkness.

Doctor said lightly, 'All right, then I take your leave.'

The moment he stepped out, Apurba cried out from inside, 'I shall always remember the day you saved my life, Doctor.'

From the darkness outside, the reply came. 'You made the most of getting back your life, but didn't remember who gave it back to you.'

'Remember it?' shouted Apurba. 'I shall never forget it. I'll remember this debt as long as I live . . . .'

From the distance, out of the darkness, came Doctor's voice, 'I hope so. I pray that you may realise to whom you actually owe your life some day. That day the debt to Sabyasachi . . . .' The last few words were drowned in the gale.

For a few minutes all of them stood rooted to the ground like statues. Then, suddenly, Bharati seemed to come to her senses. She ran upstairs. The others followed her. She entered her room, ran to the window and flung it open. She stood in front of it, peering into the dark with unblinking eyes.

A few moments later there was a clap of thunder near by. Lightning flashed and for a moment gave them a last glimpse of Doctor.

Though no policeman could be so crazy to venture out in the open in such awful weather, yet the duo had skirted the main road and were plodding slowly along the southern fringe of the field. Shrubs and thorny bushes sprouted here and there. Carefully making his way through the slush and mud, weighed down by a heavy burden, one walked ahead in pitch darkness; the other followed, shielding himself from the downpour with his huge turban.

Just for a second! The next moment everything seemed to disappear in the darkness again.

Sashi heaved a deep sigh. 'Friend in our days of adversity,' he said. 'I salute you, Sardarji.'

Apurba too folded his palms in a silent salutation. A heavy load seemed to have lifted from his mind.

Bharati continued to stand, peering into the dark, like a statue of stone. Sashi's words failed to reach her ears. She was equally oblivious of the fact that, like her, profuse tears continued to roll down the cheeks of the other woman who stood near her.

GLOSSARY AND NOTES

Chapter 1

Holy tuft of hair: The original Bengali word is *tiki* — a tuft of hair worn long and sometimes plaited, from the back of the head, by orthodox Brahmins; more specifically, priests.

Sacred thread: a few strings of cotton thread worn across the body neck to waist, by Brahmins. When a Brahmin boy attains a certain prescribed age, he has to undergo a religious ceremony for his initiation into Brahminhood. He is invested with a sacred thread, which is the insignia of his Brahminhood.

Brahmin: member of Hindu priestly caste.

The head of the family: The original Bengali word is *karta* — the male head of the household. In the absence of the father, the eldest son is usually recognised as the head of the family.

Shiva (or Siva): Hindu god of destruction; along with Brahma and Vishnu, symbolizing the Hindu Trinity.

Hindu: Hinduism is a religious and social system, with belief in reincarnation, worship of several gods, and caste as the basis of society. *Hindu:* adherent of Hinduism.

Sari (or Saree): length of cotton or silk draped around the body, worn as the main garment by women, especially in India.

Prayers: The original Bengali word is *Ahnik* (same as *Sandhya-ahnik* — an obligatory worship or prayer. A devout Hindu is required to say prayers three times a day — in the morning, at midday, and in the evening.

Took the dust from her feet: In Hindu society, younger

people do this to older people and lower castes to the upper castes, particularly Brahmins, to show submission and humility.

Swadeshi: Historical movement in India (1905) for production of home-manufactured goods, and boycott of foreign-made goods.

Chapter 2

Pressed rice: The original Bengali word is *chire.* Pressed and puffed rice are popular snacks among Hindus in rural India. Unlike freshly cooked food, preserved foodstuff such as dry pressed rice, or puffed rice, is considered not to become impure; hence useful during journeys.

Sandesh: A sweet made from cottage cheese kneaded with sugar boiled to a thick consistency; a popular Bengali delicacy.

Ghee: clarified butter. A cooking medium in India.

Mahabharata: Along with *Ramayana*, forms the two best-known epics of ancient India. It recounts the story of the struggle for power between the Kauravas and their Pandava cousins, resulting in a victory for the latter; symbolically denoting the victory of good over evil. Here the reference is to the particular episode in the epic in which the evil Kaurava prince Duryodhan builds a house of lac in which he plans to burn to death his Pandava cousins.

Khichri: Indian dish of rice, split pulse et cetera. The European dish of kedgeree has been adapted from it.

Sahib: An European or an Anglo-Indian gentleman.

Memsahib: An European or an Anglo-Indian lady.

Hindi: vernacular language of northern India.

Chapter 3

Marathi (or *Maratha*): inhabitant of Maharashtra, a province in western India, just as *Bengalis* are inhabitants of Bengal, *Oriyas* of Orissa, and *Punjabis* of Punjab.

Talwar: sword.

Chapter 5

Dharamsala: traditional Indian rest-house, usually run by charitable trusts; a boarding house.

Mantra: Vedic hymn; Hindu or Buddhist devotional incantation. *Gayatri mantra:* a specific type of religious incantation, in Sanskrit.

Dhoti: loincloth worn by male Hindus.

Chadar: wrap used by male Hindus as an upper garment.

Chapter 6

Sabyasachi: one who can wield both his hands with equal dexterity — one of the names of Arjuna, the legendary hero of the Hindu epic, *Mahabharata*.

Bidis: local cigarettes made with tobacco wrapped in tendu leaves.

Chapter 7

Hemp pipe: The original Bengali word is *kalke*. It is an earthen pipe used for smoking hashish.

Chapter 10

Board the ship and lose my caste: The orthodox Hindus believed that crossing the sea or "black waters" would entail loss of caste.

Chapter 11

Sita and *Sab(v)itri:* female characters from Hindu mythology, representing traditional feminine virtues such as chastity and fidelity.

Story of the sage's son: The reference is to a story from Hindu mythology that tells about the son of a sage who was fed powdered rice mixed with water in place of milk by his poor parents.

Armless Jagannath: an incarnation of the Hindu god, Krishna. The famous temple of Jagannath is situated at Puri, on the eastern coast of India. The idol is totemic, having stumps in place of hands.

Chapter 12

Pathans: inhabitants of Afghanistan and the north-western province of Pakistan.

Chapter 15

Didimoni (or *Didi*): Elder sister; also used as a respectful form of address for a lady. Similarly, *Dada* means elder brother, or one who is familiar enough to be addressed as such. It is not necessary that these should denote actual blood relationships. For example, Sumitra is referred to as Didi, and Doctor as Dada by Bharati, because they are both elder to her.

Goonda: muscleman or neighbourhood tough.

Manasa: Serpent goddess; worshipped as a deity by Hindus in parts of India.

Ola Bibi: not very clear, but the reference apparently is to a saint or holy person venerated by the Muslims.

Tabla: a percussion instrument, similar to the bongo, used to provide rhythm in Hindustani music.

Gulmohar: Delonix Regia — a tree having bright orange flowers.

Chapter 18

Vaishnava: worshippers of Vishnu, one of the gods in the Hindu pantheon.

Chapter 22

Anna: Before decimalization, the Indian currency, rupee, used to be divided into sixteen annas, which were sub-divided into four pice each. Each pice, again, was divided into three pies.

Lungi: a cloth worn like a sarong to cover the lower limbs; unlike a *dhoti*, which is draped round the lower limbs, the *lungi* is worn loose.

Chapter 23

Singhji: ji is an honorific, used with a name or surname, designation or vocation, as a sign of respect or honour. Examples, Master*ji*, Dubey*ji*, Ram*ji*.

Chapter 26

Sati (or *Suttee*): ancient custom of self-immolation by Hindu widows on the funeral pyre of their husbands. The word actually means a chaste and virtuous woman but has, by a curious process, been applied to the practice of burning chaste women along with the dead bodies of their husbands.

Charak: a form of penitence and self-torture wherein one hangs from iron hooks that are pierced to his back.

Sanyasis: Hindu mendicants or ascetics.

Thugs: a band of highway robbers, particularly active during the nineteenth century in India, who used to strangle unsuspecting wayfarers and then rob them. They were put down by Colonel Sleeman during 1831-1837, when Lord William Bentinck was Governor-General of India.

Bargis: Marhatta horsemen who harassed the peasants and forcibly collected a share of the produce of the land.

Khasis: members of a particular hilly tribe in north-eastern India, just like the *Garos*.

Nawabs: nomenclature used to describe the Muslim kings and noblemen in India, just as the title *Raja* was used for Hindu monarchs and noblemen.

Chapter 27

The Brahmin's fee for having eaten: Brahmins, who were invited to traditional feasts or religious and social functions, were supposed to be paid a token fee for having graced the occasion by their presence.

The three celestial nymphs: the reference here is to a tale from Hindu mythology wherein Indra, king of the gods, sent the three celestial nymphs — Urvasi, Menaka and Rambha — to break the penance of the great sage, Vishwamitra.

Pure like the waters of the river Ganga: River Ganga (or Ganges) is considered to be holy according to traditional Hindu belief; consequently its water, however polluted it may otherwise be, is considered pure and holy.

Chapter 28

Raja Man Singh: Hindu general under the Mughal Emperor, Akbar, who helped him extend the Mughal empire by annexing several Hindu kingdoms.

Rana Pratap: the ruler of Chittor, a Hindu principal ity, between 1572 and 1597, who successfully resisted the Mughal incursions led by Raja Man Singh. Rana Pratap's defiance of the Mughal empire, almost alone and unaided by other Rajput states, constitutes a glorious saga of Rajput valour and the spirit of sacrifice for cherished principles.

Brahmins, Kshatriyas, Vaishyas and Sudras: the reference is to the *Varnashram dharma*, the fourfold division that forms the basis of Hindu society. Commonly described as the caste system, it seems to have been first enunciated by the ancient Hindu sage, Manu, who propounded the concept of *Varna*. Modern historians, however, challenge the interpretation of *Varna* as caste. The fourfold division referred to by the ancient Hindu writers, it is felt, denotes the classification of the Hindu population under four *varnas* or orders with reference to their occupations, namely, (i) the learned and priestly class or the Brahmins, (ii) the fighting and ruling class or the Kshatriyas, (iii) the traders and agriculturists or the Vaishyas, and (iv) the common humble folk whose business it was to serve their superiors.

Chapter 31

Bhagnadoot: messenger of doom; a literary artifice, somewhat like the Chorus in ancient Greek drama.

Meghnadbadh Kavya: an epic poem by the Bengali poet, Michael Madhusudan Dutt (1824-1873), in the manner of the ancient Greek epics of Homer, describing the siege and fall of Lanka and the defeat of Ravana and his heroic son, Indrajit (or Meghnad), in the hands of the Hindu epic heroes, Rama and Lakshmana.

Sardarji: respectful form of address for a Sikh from Punjab.